GATHER THE BONES

England 1923 and the Great War still casts a dark shadow over the lives of ordinary people.

Grieving widow, Helen Morrow and her husband's cousin, the wounded and reclusive Paul, are haunted not only by the horrors of the trenches but ghosts from another time and another conflict.

The desperate voice of a young woman reaches out to them from the pages of a coded diary and Paul and Helen are bound together in their search for answers, not only to the old mystery but also the circumstances surrounding the death of Helen's husband at Passchendaele in 1917.

As the two stories become entwined, Paul and Helen will not find peace or happiness until the mysteries are solved.

WHAT THE CRITICS ARE SAYING ABOUT GATHER THE BONES

'Gather the Bones is breathtakingly romantic. This moving and dramatic love story will haunt you long after you turn the last page...' *Anna Campbell, best selling author.*

'...Oh, my goodness. What a wonderful read... It had everything I want in a good book. An historical setting, a paranormal theme, attractive if slightly flawed characters....' *Maria, Romance Book Haven*

'...Gather the Bones is a fast paced, thrilling and keeping me on the edge of seat historical story. It's full of intrigue, tension and danger. Alison Stuart brought this gripping historical tale of second chances, past secrets and unexpected attraction and it's highly worth reading!...' *Nas, Paranormal Romance Reviews*

'...You don't want to miss this exciting story of love, tragedy, loss and grief mixed with historical and the paranormal world. 'Gather the Bones' will have you turning pages to find the answers Paul and Helen seek.' *My Book Addiction Reviews*

Gather the Bones has received nominations in the 2012 Australian Romance Readers Awards, The Award of Excellence, the Booksellers Best Awards and an honourable mention in the RONE Awards.

GATHER
A romantic historical mystery
THE BONES
ALISON
STUART

Gather the Bones

Copyright ©2012 by Alison Stuart

ISBN (epub): 9780995434196

This edition: Oportet Publishing 2023

Cover Design: Fiona Jayde Media

Spelling and styles throughout is UK English

Discover other titles by Alison Stuart at

Author website: https://www.alisonstuart.com

DEDICATION

Dedicated to the memory of my father-in-law, CHB.
Educator, philosopher and friend.

Foreword

In a quiet war cemetery in France is the grave of a young man, a cousin of my father. An old family photograph shows a solemn little boy with fair hair and glasses who was destined to go into the church when he finished university.

Instead he went to war and died at Pozières in 1916 at the age of twenty-two with the rank of Captain and a Military Cross to his name.

Richard Conway Lowe was just one of thousands upon thousands of young men from all over the world who found themselves in this small corner of France and Belgium. They went for the adventure and in a belief that they were serving their King and Country but so many never came home.

As I sat by the simple white head stone, the mother in me wept for the boy, the soldier empathised, and the writer decided it was time to tell a story about the Great War.

PROLOGUE

3RD LONDON TERRITORIAL GENERAL HOSPITAL OCTOBER 22, 1917

Paul turned his head on the pillow and watched as Evelyn Morrow, clutching her purse to her chest like a shield, followed the nurse past the rows of beds. Her gaze did not move from the woman's starched back as if she was unable to bring herself to look around her at the carnage the war had wrought.

The breath caught in the back of his throat and a coward's voice in his mind whispered: *Not here, not now.*

He knew she had been watching and waiting for him to return to the world. Through the haze of drugs and delirium, he had been aware of her standing sentinel by his bed, clad in black from head to foot, a shadow. He knew he had to face her, but he lacked the strength to match her grief against his.

Feigning sleep, he shut his eyes.

'Now, only a few minutes, Lady Morrow. He is still very weak,' the nurse said. 'I will be at my desk if you require anything.'

Paul heard the efficient clack of the nurse's heels on the linoleum floor as she returned to her place at the end of the ward.

Through the pervading scent of carbolic, he could smell his aunt's perfume and once again he stood on the platform at Waterloo station, a small boy clutching a battered suitcase. A beautiful woman in a blue gown had bent down and taken his hand, enveloping him in a cloud of lavender.

She hadn't kissed him then and she didn't kiss him now. Lady Evelyn Morrow just stood at the foot of his bed, looking down at him.

'Paul? Can you hear me?' Her tone commanded obedience and his eyes flickered open, meeting hers, dark pools behind the black netting that covered her face.

Evelyn clutched the metal bar at the end of the bed and the feather on her hat began to quiver as her whole body shook with the force of her emotion. 'You promised.' Her voice rose on a crescendo of despair. 'You promised you would keep him safe. Where is he? Where's my son? Where's Charlie?'

Paul felt her grief as a palpable force, sending shock waves down the rows of beds that lined the ward. He wanted to say, 'I promised. I know I promised but I couldn't keep it. Charlie is gone.'

His fingers tightened on the starched sheet and his breath came in short, sharp gasps as the words formed and then stuck fast.

The chair at the nurse's station scraped on the floor and her hurried footsteps beat a rapid tattoo on the linoleum floor.

'Lady Morrow. Really, I must protest. Come away with me this instant.'

The nurse placed a firm arm around Evelyn's shoulder, leading her away. Evelyn shook off the encircling arm and turned back to look at him, the tears Paul knew she had probably not allowed herself to shed were now spilling down her face.

'Lady Morrow, please. You are overwrought. I'll fetch you a nice cup of tea.' The nurse's tone softened and with her arm around Evelyn's shoulders, she led the woman into the glassed-in office at the end of the ward.

Paul turned his head on the hard, lumpy pillow, feeling the starched linen crackle beneath his cheek. In the bed next to him, a young subaltern who had lost both his legs lay immobilised by the stiff sheets and blankets. The impeccable bedclothes, pulled up to his chin, hid the reality of his horrific injuries from his visitors, reducing the war to something neat, tidy, and manageable.

In the office, beyond the line of beds, the nurse handed a cup to

Evelyn. The door opened and the Matron of the hospital entered the little office and began to berate the errant visitor for her unseemly behaviour. Lady Evelyn Morrow sat hunched in a chair like a schoolgirl and even through the glass snatches of the scolding—inappropriate behaviour and upsetting the patients—filtered out into the ward.

The nurse returned to Paul's bedside, making a pretence of straightening his pillow.

'Really,' she tutted as she fussed over him. 'I would have expected better from a lady.'

'Outward displays of grief should be reserved for the lower classes?' he murmured.

'Pardon?' the nurse replied.

'Tell her I want to see her,' Paul said.

The nurse straightened. 'Are you sure?'

He nodded and with a sniff, the nurse bustled back to the office. She whispered in Matron's ear and the older woman stiffened, casting a quick glance in Paul's direction. Evelyn looked up as the Matron spoke. She too glanced through the window toward him and rose to her feet, tucking her handkerchief back into her purse.

Her back straight, Evelyn looked the Matron squarely in the eye and her words, audible through the glass, echoed down the long ward. 'I assure you, there will be no repeat.'

Once more the nurse, this time in the company of Matron, conducted Evelyn to his bedside. A rustle of anticipation rippled through the ward and Paul imagined the faces of the other patients turned expectantly toward his aunt. If nothing else, her outburst had provided an entertaining highlight in an otherwise dull day.

'Now, Lady Morrow,' the Matron said as Evelyn took the seat beside Paul's bed. 'I am sure I don't need to remind you, Major Morrow is easily tired. A few minutes, that's all.'

Paul looked up at the ceiling while his mind framed the words. He knew what had to be said and that the words would not bring her the comfort she sought.

'Evelyn?'

She raised her eyes and once more they looked at each other, these two strangers, bound together by ties they could not sever.

'Evelyn...I'm sorry...' he said, shocked at how weak his voice sounded.

She leaned toward him. 'No,' she said in a low voice. 'I was unfair on you, Paul. It is I who should apologise.'

'I know what you want to ask me,' he said.

Evelyn did not hesitate. 'Is he dead?'

Paul closed his eyes as he struggled with the simple word that would give her the answer she sought. He had no tears of his own to shed for Charlie. Three and a half years in the trenches had robbed him of the ability to show sorrow and his own grief for his cousin ran too deep for such an outward display.

He heard her breath catch and knew she had read the answer in his face even as he answered. 'Yes.'

Her lips tightened in a supreme effort to control herself. 'What happened, Paul? Please tell me how he died and why I cannot bury my son.'

He turned his face away from her. 'I don't know, Evelyn. God help me, I don't remember. I just know he is dead.'

Evelyn sat in silence, watching him. As she rose to leave, in a gesture that would have seemed foreign to her in the long days of his childhood, she placed a gloved hand over his good hand. Her fingers tightened on his, binding him to her.

ONE

HOLDSTON HALL, WARWICKSHIRE JULY 24, 1923

Helen Morrow took a deep breath, her hand tightening on her daughter's. She felt a corresponding squeeze, looked down into Alice's upturned face, and smiled. Why were children so much braver than adults?

She raised the knocker on the old oak door and let it fall. The sound reverberated around the quiet courtyard and she took a step back as the door opened to reveal a small, round woman wearing a spotless white apron over a flowered dress.

Before Helen could speak, the woman's face lit up with a smile.

'Mrs. Charles,' she exclaimed. 'Welcome to Holdston. I'm Sarah Pollard and you must be Miss Alice.' She turned a beaming smile on the child before standing aside to usher them both inside the cool, dark hallway and through to a grand room, smelling of beeswax and dominated by a long table and a large fireplace emblazoned with carving. 'We expected you on the later train. Sam was all set to take the car to the station to meet you.'

'We caught the bus from the station and walked. Sorry if that caused any inconvenience,' Helen said

'Oh, not at all. You're here and that's what matters. Come in, come in. Leave your suitcase. I'll take it up to your room. Lady Morrow is in the parlour. I'll show you through.'

Helen removed the pins from her hat and set it down on top of the case. She took off Alice's hat and fussed over the unmanageable fair hair that refused to stay confined in a neat plait.

'Are you ready to meet Grandmama?' she asked her daughter, with what she hoped was a confident smile. She didn't need Alice to see the nerves that turned her stomach into a churning mass of butterflies.

They followed Sarah Pollard's ample girth across the wide, stone-flagged floor. Helen looked up at the portraits of long-dead Morrows who glared down at her from the wainscoted walls. If Charlie had lived, she would have been the next Lady Morrow and her portrait would have joined theirs, a colonial interloper in their ordered society.

Sarah opened a door and announced her. A slender woman, in her late middle age, her greying hair piled on her head in a manner fashionable before the war, rose from a delicate writing table by the window.

'Helen. You're earlier than I had expected,' Lady Evelyn Morrow said. 'I would have sent the car for you but you are most welcome to Holdston at long last. And you.' She turned to the child. 'Let me look at you, Alice.'

Alice looked up at her mother, her eyes large and apprehensive. Helen gave her a reassuring smile and with a gentle hand in the girl's back, urged her forward for her grandmother's inspection.

'You're not much like your father,' Lady Morrow concluded.

Helen could have listed all the ways in which Alice was, in fact, very much like her father, the father she had never known, from the hazel eyes to the way her upper lip curled when she smiled, and her utter lack of concern for her own safety. She must never stop forgetting.

Sarah Pollard bustled in with a tea tray and Lady Morrow indicated two chairs. Alice perched awkwardly on the high-backed chair, her feet not quite touching the floor. Her eyes widened at the sight of the cake and biscuits piled high on the tea tray.

'I trust you had a good voyage?' Lady Morrow enquired as she poured the tea into delicate cups.

'Yes.' Helen smiled. 'It was a wonderful adventure. Wasn't it, Alice?

We thought about Cousin Paul as we sailed through the Suez Canal. He must have some incredible stories to tell about the archaeological digs.'

The lines around Evelyn's nose deepened. 'If Paul has incredible stories, he does not share them with me, Helen.'

'But he writes to me and tells me all about them,' Alice said. 'Every Christmas and every birthday. Last birthday he sent me a little glass bottle from...where was it, Mummy?'

'Palestine,' Helen replied. 'He said it was Roman.'

'Does he indeed?' Evelyn's eyebrows rose slightly. 'I am glad to hear he recognises his responsibility to you, Alice.'

'I'm looking forward to meeting him. They told me he was with Charlie...' Helen began.

Evelyn stiffened, the teacup halfway to her lips. She set the cup down and folded her hands in her lap. 'If you are hoping that Paul will shed any light on what happened that day, Helen, then you will be disappointed. Paul was badly injured in the same action and has, apparently, no memory of—' her thin lips quivered, '—the incident.'

Helen caught the sharp edge of an old bitterness in the older woman's voice. 'I see,' she said.

'You and I, Helen, must mourn over an empty grave,' Lady Morrow said.

She rose to her feet, walked over to the piano, and picked up one of the heavy silver-framed photographs that adorned its highly polished surface.

'Did you ever see this photograph?' She handed it to Helen. 'I had it taken before Charlie went to France in March 1915. Paul was home on leave and Charlie had just taken his commission.'

The photograph showed two young men in the uniform of infantry officers, one seated and the other standing, a photograph like thousands of others that were now the last link with the dead. Helen had a single portrait of Charlie, taken at the same photographic session, sporting an elegant, unfamiliar moustache and grinning from ear to ear, like an over-anxious school boy, keen to join the '*stoush*', kill the '*bloody Bosch*'. She felt a keen sense of pain that reverberated as strongly as it had on the day he told her he would have to return to England.

'I can't leave them to fight the Huns, Helen,' he said. 'Damn it, I have a duty to England.' The drunken words came back to her and she could see Charlie in the kitchen of Terrala with his arm across her brother Henry's shoulders, as they celebrated their mutual decision to join the war.

Henry had already enlisted in the Australian Light Horse and Charlie told her a few days later that he intended to return to England to join his cousin's regiment.

'Do you think I would leave Paul to uphold the family honour?' he said.

And he'd gone.

Even as she had stood on the dock at Port Melbourne, the cold winter wind whipping at her ankles, she had known he would not return. She wondered if his decision to go would have been any different if they had known she was carrying his child. Probably not.

She turned from her husband's smiling face to his cousin, Paul Morrow, the professional soldier, never destined to take the Morrow title until one day in a muddy field outside Ypres had turned his fortune.

The long months of war had already begun to leave their mark and, while he affected a smile, she saw no warmth in his eyes. In normal circumstances, with a strong jaw and good bone structure, it would be a handsome face but he looked tired and drained, and years older than his cousin, although he was older by little over a year.

Yes, Paul Morrow had survived, but at what cost, she wondered.

'Is Paul here?' she asked. 'When he last wrote to Alice, he said he would be in Mesopotamia for the digging season.'

'The digging season is over for the year and I expect him home in the next few days.' Evelyn stood up. 'Now, let me show you your bedroom, Helen. I've given you the green room. As the nursery wing is shut up, I thought Alice could sleep in the dressing room. It's so hard with just the two of us.' Her voice wavered and she looked past Helen to a point just beyond her shoulder before recovering her composure and continuing. 'Much of the house is shut up, but Sarah can let you have the keys and you are free to go wherever you want, except my rooms and, of course Paul's rooms. When he returns, he will also be working in the library.' Evelyn looked at Alice. 'Then it will be strictly out of bounds. Sir Paul is not to be disturbed, Alice, do you understand?'

Alice nodded.

———

Upstairs in the green room, Helen found Sarah Pollard unpacking the suitcase.

'I can do that,' Helen said.

Sarah looked at her with such appalled surprise at the suggestion, Helen took a step back.

'You've not brought much with you,' Sarah commented as she set Helen's silver-backed hairbrush and mirror on the dressing table, along with the photograph of Helen and Charlie on their wedding day.

Helen refused to display the photograph Charlie had sent her of him in his uniform, ready for war. She wanted nothing to remind her of why he had died, even if she did not know the circumstances of his death.

Sarah paused for a moment looking down at the photograph. 'He was a fine man,' she said. 'Everyone he ever met liked him.'

Helen's throat constricted and to distract herself, she looked around the room. The faded green curtains and bed coverings on the old half-tester bed gave the room its name. A small bookshelf of leather-bound books stood against one wall and the heavy mahogany dressing table dominated the other. A door led through to the room Evelyn had called the dressing room, where an iron bedstead, covered in a pink eiderdown, had been set up for Alice.

Helen stooped to look out of the low window at the view across the parkland, at the unfamiliar richness of the English countryside. Summer wrapped the world in a thick green plush, unlike home where summer bleached the land and everything living in it.

'Can we go exploring now?' Alice pleaded.

'Supper will be at six,' Sarah said. 'Her ladyship eats a main meal at lunchtime and takes only a light supper. She said to tell you there's no need to dress.'

Helen smiled. 'That's fine.' No one dressed except for the most formal meals at Terrala.

Sarah handed over a bunch of keys before leaving and Helen and

Alice started at the top of the house, opening all the doors and peering into the dark, dusty rooms. The old house was built in the shape of a letter C with a front wing facing the main entrance, the side wing dominated by the Great Hall through which they'd entered, and the back wing which housed the kitchen on the ground floor and more bedrooms above. They found the nursery and Alice gave a squeal as she rushed toward a magnificent dollhouse.

'Do you think Grandmama will let me play with it?' she asked.

'I am sure she will,' Helen said, taking the opportunity to search a bookshelf for suitable books for Alice. She was delighted to discover the complete set of books by E. Nesbit. There seemed to be books in every room in the house.

'Daddy told me there were secret hidey-holes and passages,' Helen said, caught up for a moment in a childish marvel at the antiquity of the house.

Alice's eyes shone. 'Did he say where?'

Helen shook her head.

'Perhaps Grandmama or Uncle Paul will know,' Alice said.

When Paul Morrow's birthday and Christmas letters had begun arriving for Alice, Helen had decided to accord this distant, but important, relative an avuncular title. It seemed easier for a small child to comprehend than Cousin Paul and, knowing the close bond between Charlie and his cousin, it also seemed more appropriate.

On the upper floor of the house, Helen and Alice passed the solid, oak door that Evelyn had pointed out as Paul Morrow's rooms occupying the corner between the front and the side wings. They also walked through a gallery lined with faded tapestries and paintings, a large airy parlour over the old gateway into what would have been the inner courtyard, and then into the passage leading to Lady Morrow's rooms at the end of the wing. A narrow, winding staircase at the end of the passage led them down to a locked oak door. Helen tried most of the keys on the ring until one massive iron key turned reluctantly in the lock.

When the turn of the handle still did not shift the ancient door, Helen leaned her shoulder against the wood and pushed. The door creaked reluctantly and opened onto a large room dominated by two massive bookshelves taking up the spaces on either side of an old fireplace. A long, low window looked out over the moat to the driveway. Ancient framed maps and paintings of Holdston Hall crowded the remaining wall space. Several smaller family portraits were dotted among the maps and watercolours, including two head and shoulders studies of a man and a woman painted during the Georgian era and a couple of later Victorian models with severe, frowning faces.

Helen walked over to the Georgian pair and studied them closely. She could see at once that they had been painted by different hands, probably at different times, and yet they had been framed identically and hung together as if in life they had belonged as a pair.

The man had obviously been a Morrow. Like the other portraits of the Morrow forebears, dark hair tumbled over his handsome aristocratic brow and he glared at the artist, his stiffness emphasised by the high collar of a scarlet uniform. Charlie's fair hair, inherited from his mother, made him quite a cuckoo in the family portrait gallery.

In contrast to the formality of the male portrait, the woman beside him glowed with life. A fierce intelligence burned from her light grey eyes. A tangle of chestnut curls framed her face and her mouth lifted in a half smile as if any moment she would burst into laughter. She wore a green gown that exposed a great deal of décolletage in a manner fashionable in the early part of the nineteenth century and no jewellery except a slender gold chain, with a locket hanging from it, nothing more than a blur of gold under the artist's brush.

Helen shivered and pushed the windows open, admitting a breeze that carried with it the waft of warm grass and the sounds of the country —birds and the distant hum of a steam engine driving a threshing machine.

Along with these comfortable, familiar sounds drifted another faint sound, a whispering, a woman's voice half-heard, the words indistinct and undecipherable.

Helen frowned and tilted her head to listen, turning back into the room.

'Can you hear something, Alice?' she asked.

Alice looked up from turning an old globe on the table.

'No,' she said.

Helen looked around. The whispering seemed to come from within the room, not through the open windows. She stood transfixed, staring at the two wing chairs by the fireplace. The whispering grew more insistent, more urgent. Wrapping her arms around herself, Helen gripped the sleeves of her cardigan. The back of her neck prickled, and she held her breath for a moment.

As she took a step toward the chairs, the whispering ceased and she let out her breath and straightened her shoulders before crossing to the windows and pulling them shut.

'Come on, Alice,' she said. 'We'll be late for supper and I don't want to annoy your grandmother on our first day.'

Two

In the morning, Helen induced a reluctant Alice away from the dollhouse with the promise of a visit to the village shop. Rather than follow the drive, they cut along a neglected path that led from the house to the village church. Their feet crunched on the weedy, broken gravel and the hinges of the small gate into the churchyard squealed in protest as Alice pushed it open.

Walking through the gravestones to the church, they paused at one or two to read the inscriptions and marvelled at their age. In the cool interior of the church, Helen stood still, allowing her eyes to become accustomed to the gloom. She was fascinated by old buildings. No building in Mansfield was older than fifty years, and to stand in the nave of a church where men and women had worshipped for centuries filled her with awe.

They wandered down the side aisle of the church past carved stone knights and their ladies resting on their tombs, and walls covered in memorial plaques, mostly to long-dead Morrows. Beside the choir stalls in plain view of the nave, a bright brass plaque, headed *In memory of those of this parish who died in the Great War 1914-1918,* caught Helen's eye.

Her own town had subscribed to a public fund and erected a solid memorial in the centre of the town, the plinth inscribed with the names of the fallen of the Mansfield district. She scanned the list of about twenty names. This simple plaque was no different; it could have been the same names, the same young, hopeful faces.

Captain Charles Morrow MC headed the list.

She swallowed. Seeing his name so starkly written made it all so real. The fact it did not appear on the Mansfield war memorial had been a matter of some dispute with her father who chaired the public subscription to raise funds for the Memorial. Treacherously, her brother had sided with their father pointing out that whatever their personal feelings for Charlie, he had not fought with the Australians.

'Look, Alice,' she said. 'Here's Daddy's name.'

Alice stood beside her, slipping her hand into her mother's. They stood hand in hand, looking at the plaque and allowing the silence of the old building to engulf them.

'Can I help you?'

Both Helen and Alice jumped and Helen turned to see the vicar, a middle-aged man with greying hair, in a dog collar and long dark robe, watching them from behind heavy horn-rimmed spectacles.

'I'm sorry if I disturbed you.' The vicar blinked behind his spectacles as he looked up at the memorial plaque. 'I shall leave you to your prayer.'

'It's all right, Vicar. It was just something of a shock to see my husband's name here. I'm Mrs. Morrow,' Helen said.

'Of course, I quite understand. Welcome to Holdston, Mrs. Morrow. My name's Bryant.'

Helen dutifully shook his proffered hand. 'This is my daughter, Alice,' Helen said, placing her hands on Alice's shoulders.

'You are most welcome too, Miss Morrow,' the vicar said. 'I have a daughter your age who would love to meet you. My youngest,' he added, looking up at Helen. 'The others are all away at school now and Lily gets terribly lonely.'

'That would be wonderful. It is a little quiet for Alice up at the Hall and she would be glad of a playmate.' She turned back to look at the church. 'It's a dear little church.'

The vicar beamed with pride. 'Twelfth century, if not older, I believe. Indeed, the Manor of Holdston is mentioned in the Domesday book.'

'I can't imagine what it must be like to live in the same place as my ancestors have lived for all those centuries,' Helen said. 'Where I come from, there's nothing older than sixty years.'

'Ah, you're an Australian, if I remember rightly? Young Mister Charles met you when he went out to Australia to work as a...' He searched for the word.

'A *jackeroo*?' Helen suggested.

'Good heavens, what a strange expression. He always wrote so fondly of Australia. We feared he may never come home. You know there are six centuries of Morrows in the family crypt under the church? They're all there except, of course, young Charles...' He broke off. 'I'm sorry. I'm sure you don't need to be reminded.' Turning to Alice, he changed the subject. 'There is a story that a secret tunnel runs from the house to the church.'

'Why?' Alice asked.

He shrugged. 'I believe the Morrows of the sixteenth century kept getting their religion wrong, Catholic when they should have been Protestant, Protestant when they should have been Catholic. I'm sure a secret tunnel would have been very useful in those circumstances. They say Charles II used it when he fled the battle of Worcester, but of course, every old house in this area has a Charles II story so I have my doubts as to its credibility.' He looked at Helen. 'Is Sir Paul home yet?'

Helen shook her head.

'I do enjoy my chats with him. He was in Palestine last year, you know? If he'd had the chance to get a proper university education, there's no telling what he would be doing now, but the war...' He shrugged. Helen had heard it before. The war accounted for so many things that should have happened. 'Of course, his work takes him away from Holdston and he doesn't have the time for the church and the estate. Your own dear husband...' The church clock struck eleven and he glanced at his watch. 'Is that the time? Mrs. Morrow, Miss Morrow, if you'll excuse me, I have a sermon to write. Shall I see you in church on Sunday?'

Helen smiled. 'Of course.'

Helen watched as the vicar entered the vestry, closing the door behind him. She gave the memorial plaque one last look and walked gratefully into the warmth of the summer day.

––––––

Carrying magazines and a bag of humbugs procured from the village shop, Helen and Alice strolled back to the big house. From the driveway, Helen could see the stable courtyard where a man washed a large, old-fashioned Rolls Royce. She looked at Alice and they turned down the driveway toward him. He straightened when he saw her, wiping his hands on a cloth.

'Mrs. Morrow, Miss Alice,' he said. 'Sorry we didn't meet yesterday. I would have brought old Bess here to meet you at the station. I'm Sam Pollard.'

'How do you do, Mr. Pollard,' Helen said with a smile.

'Call me Sam or Pollard,' the man said. 'Mr. Pollard just doesn't sound right.'

Alice opened the packet of sweets. 'Would you like a humbug?'

'Don't mind if I do.'

Pollard sat down on the running board of the car and selected a sweet from the bag. Helen leaned against the mounting block.

'Is Lady Morrow going out?'

Pollard shook his head and shifted the humbug to his cheek as he replied. 'No. These days, if her ladyship goes up to London or into Birmingham, she takes the bus or the train. This old girl,' he patted the Rolls affectionately, 'doesn't often get much of a run. The Major thinks we should sell her and get something smaller.'

'It's a beautiful car,' Helen said.

'I remember when Sir Gerald first bought old Bessie here. The whole village turned out to watch him drive it. He took all the village children for rides. He was a good man, Sir Gerald.' Sam's lips tightened. 'Master Charles's death broke his heart and to see the old place now—' he looked up toward the hall, '—falling down around our ears and not the money to fix it. If Master Charles were here...'

Helen looked up at the house. It seemed clear, in the opinion of some people, that the wrong Morrow had come home from the war. If Charlie had ever intended to return to Holdston, he had not shared his thoughts with her, but at the time of his death his father had still been alive and inheriting Holdston had seemed a distant problem. They had made plans for a future together in Australia.

'Mummy.' Alice's excited voice came from the stables and she peered around the door. 'Come and see the horses.'

Helen straightened and walked over to the stables, pausing in the doorway to breathe in the familiar smell of warm horse and hay that reminded her of the stables at Terrala.

'Used to have the best bloodstock in the county.' Sam Pollard had followed her to the stables. 'All gone now except for her ladyship's old hunter, the Major's grey, and a couple of trap ponies.'

Alice stood beside one of the stalls stroking the nose of an elegant chestnut with a white star. Sam rummaged in a sack by the door and handed a couple of withered carrots to her. She held them out on her palm, giggling as the horse's soft nose tickled her.

'This 'ere's Minter.' Pollard ran a loving hand down the nose of the chestnut. 'Her ladyship's hunter, only she don't ride anymore on account of her bad hip. Pity. He's getting old and lazy, aren't you?' Minter's ears swivelled, as if aware he was being talked about in disparaging tones.

Helen dipped her hand into the oat bin and offered some to Minter, who snaffled them appreciatively. She patted him on the graceful curve of his neck.

'He's beautiful,' she said. 'I miss my horses.'

'If you've a mind to it, her ladyship would probably have no objection to you taking Minter out for a ride sometime. The old boy could do with the exercise.'

'What about me?' Alice asked. 'Can I ride one of the trap ponies?'

Pollard shook his head. 'I wouldn't like you to do that, Miss Alice. Awful mean those ponies can be.'

Helen put a hand on her daughter's shoulder, seeing the child's disappointment in the droop of her mouth. 'Never mind, Alice, I am sure we will find something suitable for you.'

Pollard moved to the next stall and stroked the nose of a beautiful dappled grey with a dark mane and tail.

'And this here's Hector, the Major's horse.'

'Does the Major ride much?' Helen asked.

'When he's home,' he said. 'He'll take him out most mornings—if his leg isn't botherin' him too much. Fine rider, the Major. He should have joined the cavalry, but old Sir Gerald insisted he joined his father's regiment.'

'His leg?'

'Aye, smashed it the night...' Pollard stopped. 'He was wounded you know.'

Helen nodded. 'So I've been told.'

Pollard cleared his throat and Helen, deciding against pushing the man with any more questions, repeated the exercise with the carrots, handing a couple to Alice who fed them to Hector. Minter looked over expectantly and nickered at her.

'You've had your share,' Alice told the horse.

'And you, young lady, have some lessons to do this morning,' Helen said, steering her daughter toward the stable door.

Alice looked over her shoulder at Pollard. 'Can I come and visit the horses?'

The man smiled. 'Any time, lass.'

THREE

Every time he returned to Holdston, Paul Morrow paused for a moment to look up at the old house that he knew he should call home. The familiar weathered stone walls of the medieval house, pierced with mullioned windows, slumbered peacefully in the summer sun. It still felt no more a home to him then it had when he first saw it twenty years ago.

He straightened his shoulders, hefted his suitcase in his right hand and strode across the bridge over the moat.

Sarah Pollard waited at the door, her face wreathed in a welcoming smile.

'Hello, Sarah.'

'I heard the car,' she said. 'It's good to have you home, sir.'

A normal response would be '*It's good to be home*' but Sarah knew him too well to expect such a response. He smiled and kissed her on her forehead, a gesture that would have appalled his aunt.

'Lady Morrow's in the parlour,' Sarah said and Paul nodded in acknowledgment.

Striding across the stone flags of the Great Hall toward the living rooms of the house, the sound of his boots echoed in the silence, betraying the slight unevenness of his stride.

His aunt sat at her writing bureau, spectacles perched on the end of her nose. He knew she would be here without Sarah telling him. Lady Evelyn Morrow always wrote letters from two to three in the afternoon.

'Hello, Evelyn,' he said.

His aunt started, turning abruptly on her seat and removing her glasses as he entered the room.

'Paul.'

She rose to her feet, still as slender and elegant as she had been the day he had first met her.

They made no move to greet each other with any more intimacy than that of polite acquaintances. Although physical displays of affection were not in Evelyn's nature, a smile greeted him as she gestured to the armchair for him to sit.

'You look well, Paul,' she said taking the high-backed chair across from him. 'Palestine must agree with you.'

'Mesopotamia,' he corrected her.

She frowned and said more to herself than to him. 'Why did I think it was Palestine?'

'I was in Palestine last season,' Paul said.

'Of course. I lose track. I suppose you will be locking yourself in the library again like you did last summer?'

The question needed no answer so Evelyn continued. 'Well, I hope you are not too busy to greet our guests.'

'Guests?' Paul raised an eyebrow. Guests at Holdston had been almost unheard of since the war.

'Helen and Alice. They arrived a few days ago.'

Paul involuntarily straightened in the chair. 'Charlie's Helen?'

'Of course. Who else? I wrote and told you that I had invited her,' Evelyn said.

Paul glanced at one of the many photographs on Evelyn's bureau, his cousin Charlie grinning like the Cheshire cat, his new Australian wife beside him, her arm tucked lovingly into the crook of his elbow.

'When this bloody war is over,' Charlie had said over a cup of warm liquid that their orderly had loosely described as tea, 'I can't wait to bring Helen to England. You'll like her. She's not like any of those hothouse roses you find in Ma's drawing room. She's got real spirit, Paul.'

After Oxford, Charlie had been smitten with wanderlust and sailed for adventure in Australia. Paul couldn't remember what had thrown Charlie into Helen's path but in his letters to Paul, he had told him it had been love almost at first sight. He had married her within six months. Charlie had always acted on impulse.

Sir Gerald and Lady Morrow had been incandescent with rage. Charlie had shown him some of the letters that had passed between them at the time. Paul had been spared the family hysteria by an absence on a rather boring army posting in Wales that was interrupted by the outbreak of war.

On one of Paul's rare visits back to Holdston, it had been clear that there had been no anticipation on the part of his uncle and aunt that the marriage would have lasted. Charlie's parents expected him to return to Holdston unencumbered by inconvenient colonial wives. Whatever the long-term prospects, the marriage had outlived Charlie, and now Helen and her daughter were another of his responsibilities.

Responsibilities he would have preferred to have stayed in Australia.

Paul's fingers beat a tattoo on the arm of the chair. The thought of any strangers in the house, let alone Helen Morrow, filled with him dread.

'I hope you aren't expecting me to play at being the perfect host?'

'I long since ceased to have any such expectations of you,' Evelyn responded with a trace of acerbity in her tone.

He brought his gaze back to her and forced a smile as he rose to his feet. 'Good. Now if you'll excuse me, Evelyn, I'll leave you in peace to finish your letters.'

'Shall I tell Sarah to lay a place for you at supper tonight?'

He turned at the door and looked at her. 'No,' he said. 'I'll take supper in my room.'

Their eyes met in perfect understanding and he felt a trace of remorse as she said through tight lips, 'Paul, she is Charlie's wife.'

'I know,' he said as he shut the door behind him. 'God help me, I know,' he muttered under his breath as he climbed the familiar, worn oak stairs to his room.

———

Upstairs in the suite of rooms that should have been Charlie's, Sarah had already begun to unpack for him. Paul shook out a cigarette and wandered over to the window to smoke it while Sarah tutted over the state of his clothes.

He perched on the broad windowsill, looking out over the park as Sarah's gossip drifted over him. Beyond the fresh lily pads on the moat, lay the Holdston lands, neglected and unloved by him. Now he was home, he would have to work harder on Evelyn, to convince her that they had no choice but to sell up.

'Her ladyship's told you that Mrs. Charles is visiting?' Sarah asked.

Paul brought his attention back to the housekeeper. 'She has.'

'It's wonderful to have a child in the house again,' Sarah continued. 'Just lovely to hear a child's laugh again. This old house needs that. Miss Alice is how old? Let me think...'

'Eight,' Paul said absently.

Alice Evelyn Morrow had never known her father. Charlie had left his pregnant wife in Melbourne when he sailed off to join Paul's regiment on the Western Front. Would Charlie's daughter look at him with her father's eyes, wanting answers to questions she didn't understand?

Paul rubbed his left shoulder. The chill and damp of the house had already begun to seep into his shattered and badly healed bones. Conscious that Sarah was watching him, her gentle expression full of concern, he managed a smile.

'Thanks Sarah. Leave the rest. I'm expecting some boxes from the museum. They'll arrive either tomorrow or the day after. Please have them sent to the library.'

'Will you be dining tonight?' Sarah asked.

Paul shook his head. 'I'll take supper in here, Sarah. Hope that won't be too much of a nuisance for you?'

Sarah hesitated before she replied. 'Mrs. Morrow and the lass will be disappointed not to meet you. You can't avoid them indefinitely.'

Paul stubbed out his cigarette and looked up at the housekeeper. Only Sarah really understood him. He managed a wry smile. 'Not tonight, Sarah.'

Sarah opened her mouth to speak but he gave her a warning look and she left the room, closing the door with the faintest click.

Paul straightened, thrust his hands into the pockets of his trousers, and turned back to the window in time to see a horse and rider galloping across the nearest field toward the house.

'Good Lord,' he said out loud, recognising the horse as Minter, Evelyn's old hunter. 'They'll never take that hedge.'

The great horse took the hedge with ease, the slight figure on his back barely shifting in the saddle.

The rider, a slender woman who hardly looked strong enough to control the huge horse, drew the magnificent beast to a slower pace, allowing Paul the opportunity to study her. Her long legs were encased in khaki jodhpurs and highly polished long, brown boots. She wore an old jumper and her thick, honey-coloured hair was tied loosely at the nape of her neck.

'Helen.' he whispered her name and almost as if aware that some unseen eye watched her, she looked up at the house. Paul stepped back into the shadows as her gaze raked the old stone walls, resting for a moment on the window of his room.

She raised her hand and tucked a wayward strand of hair behind her ear and Paul leaned forward again. The young woman bore little resemblance to the sepia-tinted bride in the dog-eared photograph Charlie had kept in his field notebook. A photograph was only ever a two-dimensional representation of the real woman, and now that reality, Mrs. Helen Morrow, was at Holdston

'Mummy!'

The sound of the child's voice startled him. He looked down toward the bridge over the moat and saw a small girl in a blue dress running from the house and his breath caught in his throat.

Charlie's daughter.

There had been many times in the last few years when he had cursed Charlie for producing a girl, not a boy. A boy would take the entail and the tedious responsibility of all that went with the title. As the reluctant titular head of the family, Paul had tried to fulfil what was expected of him. Every Christmas and birthday since the war, he had dutifully sent the appropriate money order and cursory greetings and had been rewarded with a brief, polite letter of thanks that always began '*Dear Uncle Paul...*'

Paul ran his hand across his eyes, pinching the bridge of his nose, conscious of the familiar tightening sensation behind his eyes that he had been trying to ignore for the last few hours. He never thought he would ever have to face Charlie's daughter. Helen Morrow should have stayed in Melbourne. Turning away from the window, he bumped into a chair.

He swore and ran his hand over his eyes. He knew what was coming.

Migraines had afflicted him since childhood—he couldn't blame them on the war. In the trenches and on archaeological digs, he rarely suffered from them. As soon as he set foot in this house, they started again.

All the more reason to sell up and be rid of the damned place.

Paul swore under his breath and stumbled into his bedroom, throwing himself, fully clothed on the bed. As he closed his eyes he heard a whisper, like the slightest breath of wind, no more than a sigh, the words indecipherable. *They* knew he had returned.

FOUR

'Hurry, mummy!' Alice fidgeted under her mother's hand as Helen worked the wayward hair into two neat plaits.

'Ribbons?' Helen asked and Alice handed her the blue velvet ribbons, carefully chosen by her for the occasion of meeting her mysterious Uncle Paul. Helen tied them in two neat bows at the end of each plait.

'Do you think he'll like me?' Alice asked, her eyes wide with anticipation.

Helen smiled. 'I'm sure he will. Now come on, we'll be late for supper and Grandmama will be cross.'

Helen set her hairbrush back on the dressing table. Checking her own hair in the mirror, she smoothed her skirt and followed Alice down to the dining room.

Alice's shoulders slumped as she saw the dining table. Her grandmother sat alone in her customary place at the head of the table with only one other place set beside her.

'Good evening, Grandmama,' Alice said, her eyes sweeping the room as if expecting her mysterious relative to emerge from behind the curtain.

'Good evening, Alice. What brings you downstairs? I thought you would be in bed by now?'

'Alice thought she saw Sir Paul arrive home and she was anxious to meet him,' Helen said.

Evelyn stiffened, her lips pursed. 'Yes, Paul did return this afternoon. I'm sorry to disappoint you both, he'll not be joining us for supper. However, the house is only so big and I've no doubt you will meet him in his own time. Now come and kiss me goodnight, Alice.'

Alice complied with the command and after pausing to kiss her mother, left the room.

Helen took her place beside her mother-in-law, unfolding the immaculate linen napkin.

'Since he has been doing this work for the British Museum with archaeological digs, I hardly see Paul,' Evelyn said, the faintest note of complaint in her voice. 'He's gone for months on end over winter and when he returns from his digs or whatever they call them, he has a great deal of work to do—reports to write, that sort of thing. I'm sure that's not what the doctors meant when they said he needed peace and quiet.' She glanced across at Helen, her shoulders straightening. 'Anyway, don't expect too much of him, Helen.'

The warning in her eyes told Helen far more than her words. She'd seen it with her own brother when he had returned. The young men who had marched off with so much hope had returned with more than just physical scars. They carried the ghosts of their comrades in eyes that had seen horror beyond the wildest imagining. Would Charlie have been the same, she wondered?

As Evelyn dabbed the corners of her mouth with her napkin, she said, 'I meant to tell you, Helen. We have been invited to Wellmore House tomorrow afternoon. Lady Hartfield is simply dying to meet you.'

'Lady Hartfield?'

'Surely Charlie mentioned the Hartfields? The Honourable Anthony was a great friend of his at school...'

'Oh, of course, you mean Tony Scarvell,' Helen exclaimed. 'He's Alice's godfather. I would love to meet him and to see Wellmore.'

Sensing her mother-in-law's disapproval, Helen curbed her excitement. 'Will Tony ... Mr. Scarvell be at home?'

'I have no idea. Anthony prefers London to the country.' Evelyn rose to her feet, signalling they should adjourn to the drawing room.

Helen spent a quiet evening, reading a magazine while Lady Morrow worked on an elaborate needlework chair seat, one of a set, she told Helen, that had occupied her since her marriage. As the clock struck ten, Helen bid her mother-in-law good night and climbed the wide, oak stairs to the gallery that connected the three wings of the house.

Before going to bed, Helen checked on Alice who lay sound asleep, curled in a ball, her favourite stuffed rabbit tightly encircled in her arms. Helen smiled and stooped to kiss the fair hair.

She tightened the sash of her dressing gown and sat down at the elegant Georgian escritoire to write a letter to her parents. The desk had been stocked with heavy cream writing paper bearing the Morrow coat of arms. The yellowed edges indicated that it had been on the desk for some considerable time, probably long before the war.

Helen unscrewed the top of her fountain pen and drew one of the sheets of paper toward her. It almost seemed a crime to desecrate its pristine surface but she filled the creamy sheet with the details of the last few days at Holdston, signed her name and put the letter in an envelope.

Seated at the dressing table, Helen began to pull the pins from her hair. In the short months of their life together, Charlie had reserved that task for himself, running his fingers through it as it tumbled to her shoulders. He would bend and kiss her...

Letting the pins fall to the glass top, Helen looked down at the photograph of her husband taken by a Melbourne photographer just before he left for England. Charlie, as she remembered him—slightly rumpled, his fair hair drifting across his forehead, his smile wide and his eyes twinkling with life and mischief. The army officer with the moustache in Evelyn's photograph would never be her Charlie.

She picked up the frame, smiling as her fingers brushed the glass. She could no longer remember the lilt of his voice or the touch of his hands, but just sometimes the tang of a familiar shaving cream would cause her to pause in the street and turn in hope, knowing even as she did so that it would never be Charlie. Strange how smell could evoke a memory in a way sight never could.

Helen sighed and set the photograph back. Here in his home, she felt Charlie's absence more keenly than she had for years and, overwhelmed by memory, she crossed her arms on the glass top of the dressing table and lowered her head, the tears soaking the sleeves of her dressing gown.

She heard the rustle of silk petticoats and her nose twitched at the faint scent of Lily of the Valley. Something brushed her cheek, with no more force than a feather, leaving an icy trail across the skin. A slight weight, as if someone had placed a comforting hand, rested on her shoulder. Helen jerked upright, instinctively throwing back her arm to fend off whoever stood behind her. She met no resistance and she looked up expecting to see Sarah Pollard or Lady Morrow, words of apology for her action and disheveled appearance already forming on her lips. Only her own face in the mirror, wan and red-eyed, looked back at her.

She sat quite still staring at her reflection as the silence of the room closed around her. The sensation of the hand on her shoulder seemed to linger and she raised shaking fingers to touch her cheek. It had been so light but she could have sworn that it had been the touch of a woman's fingers.

Her heart thudded in her chest and she spun around on the stool to confront an empty room. Conscious she had been holding her breath, Helen let it out in a slow, shaky expiration as she fumbled for her handkerchief in her dressing gown pocket.

'Alice, is that you?' she said aloud, her words sounding thin in the cold air of the room.

She rose to her feet and went to check again on Alice. The child turned and murmured in her sleep but did not wake.

Helen took a deep breath and wiped her eyes and nose with her handkerchief. In an attempt to regain her composure, she splashed her face with cold water from the washbasin and took a sip of water before climbing into the bed. She flicked through several pages of the cheap novel she had bought for the train journey, without seeing the words.

Long after she had turned out the light, she lay awake staring at the ceiling, trying to make sense of what had occurred. She had been thinking of home and had willed herself to wish her mother was there to hold her in her arms and comfort her, nothing more. With this thought in her mind, Helen fell into a fitful sleep.

FIVE

s the car drew up before the colonnaded entrance portico to Wellmore House, Alice gasped. Helen hid a smile behind her gloved hand. Had she been Alice's age, she would have gasped too, but she had to pretend that taking tea at such an impressive house was as natural to her as taking tea and scones in her mother's country kitchen.

A footman ushered them into the marbled entrance hall, from which parallel stairs curved upwards to a dome, painted with a mural of sporting gods and goddesses.

He took their outer garments and solemnly informed them, 'Lady Hartfield is expecting you.'

Alice slipped her hand into Helen's as they followed the footman's rigid back through formal rooms rich in gilt mirrors and fine tapestries, to be shown into a spacious drawing room with long, French windows facing out onto a terrace.

Lady Hartfield rose to meet them, kissing Evelyn Morrow on both cheeks before turning her attention to Helen. She held out her hand in such a way Helen was unsure whether she was supposed to shake it or kiss it.

She duly introduced Alice and Lady Hartfield scrutinised the small girl over the top of a pince-nez.

'I can see a lot of Morrow in the child,' she said and indicated they should sit on the overstuffed, gilded, baroque settees. Alice's feet did not touch the ground and she swung them until Helen laid a gentle warning hand on her knee.

'So, Mrs. Morrow,' Lady Hartfield began, as she poured tea from a silver teapot. 'What do you think of Holdston?'

'It's just as Charlie described it,' Helen said with a smile, recalling Charlie's description of his home as, '*cold, draughty and damnably inconvenient.*'

'Dear Charlie always loved Holdston.' Lady Hartfield expanded on her theme. 'He would have made a fine baronet.' She picked up her cup. 'And what is the news of Paul?'

'Paul is home,' Evelyn said.

Lady Hartfield raised a heavily plucked eyebrow and took a delicate sip of tea before she spoke. 'And where was he this time?'

'Egypt...no, Mesopotamia or somewhere like that. Of course, he's shut himself up in his room with his papers and I've not seen hide nor hair of him since he returned.' Evelyn cast a glance at Helen and Alice. 'He has yet to meet poor Helen.'

Helen had never heard herself referred to as '*poor Helen*' before. She looked Lady Hartfield to Lady Morrow. Was that really what they thought of her? An object of pity?

'That's just so like Paul. No thought for anyone but himself.' Lady Hartfield clucked her tongue in disapproval.

'Did someone mention Paul?' A man's voice came from the doorway.

Helen turned her head to see a young man dressed in neat country tweeds advancing toward them.

Evelyn rose to her feet. 'Tony, darling, how lovely to see you.'

He kissed her proffered cheek and turned to Helen.

'You must be Helen.' He held out his hand. 'Tony Scarvell.'

Helen took his hand with genuine pleasure. 'I'm so pleased to meet you at last. Charlie talked so much about you.'

'Did he?' Tony's smile transformed his broad, plain face. 'None of it good, I presume. And this must be Miss Alice Evelyn Morrow? It's about time your godfather made your acquaintance. How do you do, Miss Morrow?'

Alice flushed as he shook her hand with great solemnity.

'Tea, dear?' his mother enquired proffering the silver teapot.

'Gasping for a cup,' Tony responded. 'Just driven up from London,' he added, taking the cup his mother held out for him. He sat in one of the overstuffed armchairs and crossed his legs.

'This is an unexpected pleasure, Tony. What brings you home?' Evelyn asked.

Tony looked across at his mother. 'Ma's organised a house party for the weekend,' he replied. 'I'm expected to charm the ladies.'

'Nothing fancy. An informal supper party on Friday night. Tennis on Saturday... you know the sort of thing,' Lady Hartfield said. 'Mrs. Morrow, you would be most welcome to join us.'

'Excellent idea,' Tony said.

'Yes, of course. Thank you.' Helen glanced at her mother-in-law. 'If that's all right?'

'And of course, Evelyn, you will come to the party on Friday night?' Lady Hartfield managed to make it sound like an order rather an invitation.

'I would be delighted,' Evelyn said.

Lady Hartfield set her teacup down and folded her hands in her lap. 'Evelyn was just saying Paul is home, Tony. Perhaps you can prevail on him to come and be sociable?'

'I'll pay him a visit tomorrow. I'm simply dying to hear about his adventures in Mesopotamia. Pity he wasn't in Egypt. Did you read about the tomb they discovered there, Mrs. Morrow? Tutankhamun or something like that, they say.'

'Yes, I did,' Helen said. 'I saw some of the photos of the tomb in the newspaper before we left and it was all the buzz in Suez. It must be extraordinary.'

Tony set down his cup. 'Ma, would you have any objection if I show Mrs. Morrow and young Alice here, about the house?'

'If Mrs. Morrow has no objection,' his mother said.

Tony rose to his feet and cocked an eyebrow at Helen. 'Allow me to be your tour guide?'

'Thank you. I'd love to see the house.'

'And you, Miss Morrow?'

Alice beamed at him and slid off the sofa.

Once away from his mother, Tony turned to Helen. 'Do you mind if I call you Helen?'

'I would prefer it,' she said.

'And call me Tony, please. Charlie hated all this stuffy formality. We'll start in the picture gallery and then we'll go for a stroll in the gardens. They're particularly fine I'm told.'

After they had been through the house and admired the Rembrandt, the Constables, the Van Dyck, and the other artistic masterpieces, Tony led them out onto the terrace, which afforded a wide vista of parklands, lakes and classical statuary.

'It's a William Kent garden,' he explained. 'The family made its fortune in the new world and came back to England in the mid-eighteenth century. The old house was destroyed during the civil war.' He looked down at Alice. 'Do you want to see the ruins?'

Alice's eyes shone as she nodded.

'Kent rather cleverly incorporated them into the garden design,' Tony explained as they rounded a corner of the house to see the ivy-covered walls of the old building, rising mysteriously from the woods.

Alice looked up at him with wide eyes. 'Are there any ghosts?' she asked.

'None that I've ever seen,' Tony said. 'Although one of our gardeners claims to have seen spectral figures walking around the outside of the old house. Personally, I think the sighting may have had more to do with a penchant for whisky than a genuine paranormal experience. If you want to know about ghosts you need to ask Sarah Pollard, she's the local expert.'

'Is she?' Helen said.

'My sister, Angela, once thought she saw civil war soldiers in the garden at Holdston. It was besieged too, you know.'

'No, I didn't,' Helen said. She sighed and looked around at the beautiful garden. 'There is so much to learn about Charlie and this place.'

Alice had skipped on ahead, disappearing among the ruined walls.

'I can see a lot of Charlie in that young Sprite,' Tony said.

'Can you?' Helen asked, trying to keep the yearning out of her voice. 'It's so strange to be with people who knew Charlie so much longer than I did. I sometimes wonder if we are talking about the same person.'

'We may have known him longer, Helen. That doesn't mean we knew him better. Have you met Paul yet?'

Helen shook her head. 'Not yet. He only got home yesterday. Lady Morrow left me with the impression that he's not terribly sociable.'

Tony shrugged. 'Paul and Lady Morrow have a particular relationship. I'm sure you already know that Paul has had a pretty rough time of it all round.'

'I knew he'd been badly wounded.'

'Oh, it's not just that,' Tony said. 'Goes back to before the war. His father was posted somewhere out in the Far East and Paul was sent to Holdston after his mother died. Paul was the poor relation and he felt it. Evelyn and Sir Gerald did their best but his father drank away any money he had before he died so there wasn't much to spare for education and the like. The only reason Paul went to Winchester with Charlie and me was because he won a scholarship. He excelled at school but there was no question of him going to Oxford. Instead, he got packed off to the Army while university was wasted on Charlie and me. I'm betting Paul would have been a professor by now if he'd had the chance.' Tony sighed. 'Little wonder he hates being shackled to Holdston now.'

'Charlie talked about him of course but he never told me any of that. They seemed very close.'

'As close as brothers. Charlie worshipped the ground Paul walked on.'

Helen smiled. 'Charlie did not consider joining any regiment except Paul's,' she said. 'I think he saw the two of them winning the war together.'

Tony cleared his throat. 'They gave it a damn good shot.'

They rounded another corner of the house and walked toward a grand building with a high arched entrance surmounted by an elegant clock tower.

'Who lives here?' Helen asked.

Tony laughed. 'These are the stables. Do you ride?'

Helen felt her face colour at her stupid mistake. 'Of course I do. I've been riding since I could walk. In fact, I've Lady Morrow's permission to take Minter out.'

'He's a grand horse but getting on in years now. Can't even remember the last time Evelyn would have ridden him. What about young Alice?' he asked, addressing Alice who had run back to them. 'Do you ride, young Sprite?'

Alice pulled a face. 'There are only the trap ponies at Holdston and Sam says they bite and Hector and Minter are too big for me.'

'We'll have to see what we can do. I've been a dashed poor godfather up to now.' He furrowed his brow and then smiled. 'Just the answer,' he exclaimed. 'Turnip.'

He summoned a groom who fetched a fat little piebald pony with bright, gentle eyes out of the stable.

'He's yours for as long as you're at Holdston, Sprite.'

Alice gaped at him. 'Really?'

Tony cocked an eye at the groom. 'I think we can spare him, can't we?'

The groom grinned. 'I think we can manage, sir.'

'Good. We'll have him sent around to Holdston tomorrow.'

'What do you say?' Helen nudged her daughter.

Alice looked up at Tony. 'Thank you, Uncle Tony.'

'Uncle Tony, is it? I rather like that.'

They stopped to admire the beagle pack, Alice exclaiming in delight over a litter of small, round puppies.

'What about hunting, Helen?' Tony asked.

Helen shook her head. 'It's an English preoccupation,' she said. 'Some damn fool decided to introduce foxes to Australia to hunt and they've become vermin. We shoot them. We don't hunt them.'

'The Wellmore hunt is in early December. If you're still at Holdston I hope you'll join us.'

Helen smiled. 'I doubt I shall still be here by then. I plan to spend some time with Evelyn and then do some touring in Europe over summer.' She glanced at her wristwatch. 'Hadn't we better get back to your mother? It's getting late and she will think I'm terribly rude.'

'Of course she will. My mother is a dreadful snob. The fact you are an Australian is sin enough and even though I have detained you over-long it will, of course, be your fault.'

He laughed when he saw her stricken face. 'I'm jesting. Mother will have been quite happy to spend the time moaning about her unsatisfactory children to Evelyn.'

'Are you unsatisfactory?' Helen asked as they walked back along the well-tended paths to the house.

'Lord, yes.' Tony said. 'Mother wants me married to some simpering debutante with money and a title and as for Angela...'

'Angela?'

'My sister. No sign of any grandchildren there either. Angela is an independent woman of our time and Mother simply can't cope with that. We are her eternal despair.'

He had been right. As they walked into the drawing-room from the terrace the two women appeared immersed in earnest conversation

Evelyn looked up as Alice, forgetting all manners, ran the length of the room toward her exclaiming, 'Grandmama, Uncle Tony is going to lend me a pony. He's the dearest thing. I can't wait to ride him.'

Evelyn turned to Tony. 'Is that correct?'

'I've promised her an indefinite loan of Turnip.'

'That's very generous of you, Tony,' Evelyn said as she rose to her feet. 'I hope you thanked your godfather, Alice.'

'She did indeed,' Tony said.

Evelyn pulled on her gloves. 'Thank you, Maude. It was delightful to catch up with you. We will look forward to joining you on Friday night.'

Lady Hartfield turned to Helen. 'There will be a number of young people coming.'

'Young ladies?' Evelyn suggested, with a meaningful glance at Tony.

Lady Hartfield smiled. 'Of course. I am determined to have at least one of my children married by next spring.'

SIX

'Good ride, sir?' Sam Pollard enquired, stepping forward to hold Hector's head while Paul dismounted.

'Thank you, Pollard,' Paul said, wincing as he took the weight on his bad leg.

The doctors had said he'd never ride again. In fact, the doctors had said a great many things and he'd proved them wrong but his stubborn perseverance came at a price.

'Want me to see to 'im?' Pollard asked.

Paul shook his head, taking the horse's reins from the man. 'No, leave him to me. It's the least I can do for him after making him work.'

Hector snorted, as if in agreement and Paul smiled, turning to rub the horse's ears. 'You've got lazy while I've been away. That's your problem.'

Paul settled the horse in his stall with a well-earned feed, and picking up the grooming brush, fell into the customary, almost hypnotic pattern of the brush strokes, the horse warm and familiar beneath his hand. Hector grunted his appreciation.

A change in the light as someone passed through the door and the sound of light footsteps on the cobbled floor alerted him to another presence in the stable. Without turning around, Paul knew who stood at the door to the stall watching him,

'Good morning, Mrs. Morrow,' he said without missing a stroke of the brush.

'Good morning, Sir Paul,' Helen Morrow replied, stumbling a little on the *Sir*.

His mouth quirked with bitter amusement. The title had never sounded right, not like Sir Charles Morrow would have done. Most people got around it by referring to him by his military rank, the Major.

'If you're going to address me as anything it may as well be Paul,' he said.

'I didn't wish to appear rude. I wasn't expecting to see you here. Have you been for a ride already?'

She had an interesting accent. He'd met Australians in the war and generally found their almost cockney accent strident and grating. She had a softer inflection, the vowels were more rounded, but not, definitely not, an English accent.

He straightened and Hector gave a snort and turned to him his ears pricked in enquiry.

'I always get up at seven just to groom my horse,' he said, conscious of the heavy sarcasm in his voice.

'Oh,' she sounded crushed and he instantly regretted his words. 'I thought perhaps, if you hadn't been out yet, you may have been able to show me around the estate?'

Paul ducked under Hector's head, putting the horse between himself and Charlie's widow. For the first time he looked at her. A pair of startling light grey eyes met his gaze without flinching. Helen Morrow, Charlie's beloved Helen, stood leaning on the stall gate, resting her chin on her folded arms.

'You seem quite capable of finding your own way around without my assistance,' he said. He applied himself to Hector's grooming again, breaking the eye contact with the woman.

'It's not the same as going with someone who knows the country.'

'I've seen you riding Minter. You ride well, although I'm not sure Evelyn approves of young ladies riding astride.'

Helen smiled. 'We did have that discussion,' she said. 'It's good of her to allow me the use of Minter.' Helen turned her head to indicate Hector's stable companion.

'Evelyn hasn't ridden for years,' Paul said. 'However, the fact she's never been able to bring herself to sell Minter betrays something of her sentimental side.'

Helen smiled. 'Just as you can't part with Hector?'

Paul stopped in his task and straightened. He could have said that the unconditional affection of this animal gave him a greater reason to return to Holdston than his other responsibilities, but he held his tongue.

'We went to Wellmore House yesterday,' Helen said.

'I know,' Paul said brusquely. 'Evelyn suggested I should accompany you. I had work to do.'

'Tony Scarvell sends his regards.'

At the mention of Tony's name, Paul looked up. 'Tony's at Wellmore?'

She nodded. 'He's lending Alice a pony. She's terribly excited.'

Paul felt a stab of guilt. It should be his responsibility to provide a suitable mount for the child but he could offer her nothing except two ill-tempered trap ponies.

He opened the door to the stall and Hector turned his attention back to the oats. Only a few feet of floor now stood between him and Helen. His eyes rested on her oval face. She had the fresh healthy glow to her skin that came from a life lived in the high country of Victoria, which Charlie had loved so much, and even through the horsey odours of the stable, she smelled clean and fresh.

'Charlie talked about you so much...' she began.

'Then you must have had some dull conversations,' he cut her off, pushing past her to restore the brushes to a shelf outside the stall. 'Good morning, Mrs. Morrow. I hope you have a pleasant ride.' He strode off down the line of empty stalls without a backward glance.

SEVEN

'Sam says you and Mrs. Morrow met this morning,' Sarah placed the tray with tea and biscuits on the library table.

'Couldn't avoid her,' Paul replied, looking up from unpacking the first of six neat wooden boxes. He knew Leonard Woolley would not have sent him the most interesting pieces but the fact he trusted him with any of the precious finds, said much for the great archaeologist's respect for Paul's talents.

'What's that?' Sarah indicated the artefact in his hand. 'Looks like a lump of dried mud.'

'It is, Sarah,' Paul set the clay tablet down on the table. 'And it is my task to translate what is written on it.'

Sarah peered at the cuneiform inscription. 'That's writing? You can read that?'

He picked up the unedifying object and smiled at the pattern of what looked like little arrows that had been pressed into the still-damp mud two thousand years ago. 'Most of the time.'

Sarah sniffed. 'You always were the clever one,' she said. 'I'll leave you in peace. What time do you want lunch?'

'One will be fine,' Paul said, already absorbed in the little tale of domestic life revealed on the 'lump of dried mud'.

As it always did when he became lost in a task, the morning drifted away and his tea went cold. The clock on the mantelpiece struck eleven and he frowned in annoyance at the sound of some sort of commotion going on above him. Beyond the heavy oak door leading to the narrow, wooden stairs, he could hear a child's voice raised in what sounded like protestation. What had Sarah said about the joy of a child's laughter?

Paul leaned back, tipping his chair on to its back legs, and stretched his stiff limbs. He gave the library door a glance as he heard the clatter of small feet on the stairs. The door crashed open with such ferocity that Paul nearly lost his balance.

A small girl, her fair hair done in two plaits stood with her hand on the door latch, staring at him. The child appeared to be frozen in fear, her eyes large orbs in her thin brown face.

He regained his balance and his composure.

'I take it you're Alice?' he asked.

The girl nodded and her eyes widened even further. 'I'm going to get into terrible trouble, aren't I?'

'Why?'

'Grandmama said I was not on any account to make any noise and disturb you or come to the library.'

'Grandmama said that, did she?'

The plaits bobbed on her shoulders as the child nodded.

'Then we'd better not tell her,' he said.

Alice let go of the door latch and took a few steps into the room, looking around as if searching for something.

'I was trying to catch the dog,' she said. 'Have you seen it?'

Paul frowned. 'What dog?'

'A cocker spaniel. I know he's a cocker spaniel because Aunt Chloe has one. He ran in here. I saw him.'

Paul closed his eyes and pinched the bridge of his nose. Now it was dogs?

'Alice, there are no dogs in here,' he said. 'We haven't had a dog since...'

Since your father's old spaniel, Reuben, died.

'But I saw him,' Alice persisted. 'He ran right in here.'

'Through a closed door?'

'But the door was open...' She looked back at the door and frowned. 'Are you sure you don't have a dog in here?'

'Quite sure, but I'm glad to make your acquaintance, Alice.'

She smiled and Paul's fingers tightened on the arm of the chair. She had her father's bright, disarming smile.

'You're not scary at all,' she said.

'Did you think I would be?'

'Mummy thinks you're scary. She makes me tiptoe every time we go past your door.'

'And where is your mother?'

'She's gone to Birmingham with Grandmama.'

Alice had advanced all the way into the room and stood beside the table, looking down at the clay tablets he had unpacked.

'What are these?'

'Each tablet has writing on it, called Babylonian cuneiform. It's the oldest writing ever known,' Paul picked up one of the tablets and held it out to her. 'That is thousands of years old.'

She lifted her hands to take the object but at the last minute pulled back, looking up at him. 'Can I hold it?'

He nodded and Alice took the tablet with a reverence that impressed him. She turned it over, her eyes wide and curious.

'If it's writing, do you know what it says?'

'Yes. It's a list of all the grains that this man has in his store house.'

Alice pulled a face. 'That sounds very boring.'

'It can be but sometimes you come across little stories, like this one about the boy who wouldn't go to school.'

He retrieved the tablet from her and tapped another one on the table with the end of his pencil.

'What is the story about?'

He rifled through the notes he had already made that morning and read the rough translation out to her. She rewarded him with a bright beaming smile.

'That's a funny story,' she said. 'It sounds like my cousin, Alf. He doesn't like to go to school much.'

'People are still the same aren't they, even though this story is thousands of years old,' Paul said.

'Oh, is that a typewriter?' Alice stood in front of the old Remington Paul had retrieved from the estate office. 'Do you know how to type?'

'Not well,' Paul admitted with a rueful smile.

Alice ran her fingers over the keys of the old machine.

'You should ask Mummy. She's really good. She even showed me how to do it.'

Unbidden, Alice knelt up on the chair facing the typewriter, fed some paper in and began to thrash away at the keys.

'There.' She looked at him. 'That's how you type.'

'Very good,' Paul said. 'Maybe I should ask you to do my typing?'

Alice looked down at the papers on the table. 'I can't read your writing,' she said pragmatically. She looked up at the window. 'You've got a lovely horse.' 'Sam lets me feed him carrots. Uncle Tony is going to lend me a pony to ride. His name is Turnip and he's a piebald.'

'That's nice of Uncle Tony,' Paul commented with the same flash of guilt he had felt that morning.

'Mummy's been riding Minter,' Alice said.

'I know. I've seen her. Your mother is a good rider,' he observed.

'She is.' Alice said with evident pride. 'Grandad says she's better than some of the men on Terrala.'

The child wandered over to the bookshelves and pulled a large folio book from the bottom shelf. She opened the book on the carpet and lay down on her stomach, turning the heavy pages.

Paul glanced at the clock. 'Alice, I do have work to do.'

She turned an earnest little face to look up at him. 'Can I stay here with you? I won't make any noise.'

Just for a moment, he saw her father and heard himself saying without conscious thought, 'Of course you can.' He glanced at the tray of untouched tea things on the table. 'On the condition you go and ask Sarah to bring us some fresh tea and biscuits.'

EIGHT

After lunch, Paul sought out the room in the house that had always been known as the estate office. He opened the safe and took out the books, settling himself at the desk to make some sense of the finances.

As he ran his eye down the columns of figures, he could not miss the change in handwriting from Prynne, the former estate manager, to his own interspersed with Evelyn's familiar spidery hand. One by one the staff, both in the house and on the land, had gone. Now only the Pollards, and he and Evelyn remained.

'What are you doing in here?'

Paul looked up. His aunt stood at the door, her hand resting on the handle and an incredulous look on her face.

'Doing what I always do when I get home, Evelyn. I'm going through the estate books and wondering how we can keep going.'

He saw a flush of colour rise to her pale cheeks as Evelyn stepped into the room. 'I've been looking for you,' she said. 'I've had a telegram from Edith. She's unwell so I thought I should go up to London to see her.'

Paul considered his aunt and bit his tongue against the scathing comment that rose to his lips. Her older sister enjoyed a state of perpetual ill-health, usually exacerbated when her husband had business that took him away from her constant demands.

'I think it would be good for you to have a few days in London. See some friends, go to the theatre. Enjoy yourself.'

She visibly relaxed as if she had been expecting him to argue with her.

'When do you leave?'

'I thought I would catch the six o'clock train this evening,' Evelyn took a step into the room, thrusting her hands deep into the pockets of her cardigan. 'Since you're taking an interest in estate matters, I need to talk to you about the church restoration appeal.'

Paul shut the account book with a thump intended to punctuate his next comment. 'No, you don't need to talk to me about the church. I have no interest in the church, its restoration or its lack of appeal. I have at least two farms that have leaking roofs which, in my opinion, take precedence over the church.'

Evelyn opened her mouth to say something then clamped it shut again, viewing her nephew with evident displeasure.

'You really don't understand your position, do you?' she said at last. 'You have obligations and responsibilities.'

'None of which I asked for,' Paul snapped back. 'I am only too well aware of my obligations and responsibilities and it is a matter of priorities, Evelyn. The church is not one of them.'

'You are the last of the Morrows.'

'You know damn well I am long beyond caring about what happens to the Morrows, or to this bloody estate.'

'Don't swear, Paul,' Evelyn said.

'Sorry.' Paul ran his hand through his hair and softened his tone. 'Evelyn, I never wanted it to be like this and you're wrong, I do understand my responsibilities. That is my dilemma.' He tapped the account book. 'We can't go on trying to pretend that everything is just as it always was. There is simply no money.'

'We can sell the library—' Evelyn began but he cut her short.

'Then what will we sell? Will we go on selling everything until we're left with nothing but packing cases in large empty rooms?'

'There are five centuries of your family history in this house. You can't just walk away.'

Paul sighed. He had heard it all before from Evelyn, a circular argument he would never win. 'The world has changed, Evelyn. We have to do things differently now.'

'No, we don't.' Evelyn exclaimed. 'If it had been—' she broke off, cutting off the words that should have followed.

If it had been Charlie instead of you sitting there, we wouldn't even be having this conversation.

The unsaid words lay between them, an unbridgeable gulf. Paul took a breath and closed his eyes. He swivelled the chair around to look out of the window as he said, 'Go to London, Evelyn. Enjoy yourself for a couple of days.'

'How can I possibly enjoy myself,' she snapped. 'You've just told me, there's no money.'

Paul turned back to face her. 'You've held everything together for so long. Who am I to begrudge you a new hat and an evening at the theatre? Please go and forget our troubles.'

She met his eyes and he could see the defiance in them. 'Yes,' she said. 'I think a few days away will do me good. I will be back on Friday morning in time for Maude's party. Will you be coming?'

When he didn't reply she said, 'It would do you good to have some people around you.'

'I've just returned from three months on an archaeological dig, Evelyn. No shortage of people, trust me.'

'That's not what I mean and you know it. You're away for months on end and then you shut yourself in here. Little wonder people talk...' she broke off.

'And what do they talk about, Evelyn?' Paul kept his tone even. 'I thought the doctors told you I needed peace and quiet, not the meaningless chatter of your friends.'

Her lips tightened. 'You've never understood,' she said, pulling her cardigan tight around her slender frame as she turned on her heel leaving him alone in the silent room.

NINE

Helen set down her novel and rose to her feet, glancing at her little clock that stood on the bedside table. It showed ten thirty. With Evelyn gone, the house seemed empty. To make life a little easier for Sarah, she and Alice had eaten their evening meal in the kitchen and played cards for a little while before Alice went to bed.

Sitting down at the dressing table she reached for her hairbrush, uttering an unladylike curse when she found it was missing from its usual place. Annie, the girl from the village who helped Sarah, seemed to be always moving the contents of her dressing table. Just this morning she had found the photographs face down and the hand mirror on the bed. Now it was the turn of her hairbrush which she located on the mantelpiece behind a vase. She stood in the middle of the room with the hairbrush in her hand and decided that before settling down she would make herself some cocoa and bring it back to bed while she finished reading her novel.

As she opened the door into the corridor, the utter silence of the house closed in on her. She pulled her dressing gown tighter and walked briskly toward the main staircase, her way lit only by the thin moonlight shining in through the old, diamond-paned windows.

At the top of the stairs, she stopped, resting her hand on the newel post. In the overwhelming silence of the old house, she could hear the distant, but unmistakable sound of someone crying. For a moment she held her breath, every nerve in her body taut, as the pathetic sobbing of a woman drifted through the house.

She looked back toward her room but the sound didn't come from that direction. The only inhabitant of that part of the house, Alice, had been fast asleep, curled up with her arms wrapped around her rabbit. Frowning with concentration, she decided that the crying came from the front of the house. Her curiosity piqued, Helen walked along the gallery toward Paul Morrow's rooms, the ancient floorboards creaking at every step.

A faint light came from beneath his door but the house had fallen silent again. It crossed her mind to knock on his door and check everything was all right but the crying had been a woman. What if he had company? That could account for the sound, or perhaps the noise came from an animal outside the house? Either way Paul would not thank her if she disturbed him.

Helen took a breath and but as she turned back toward the stairs the sobbing came again louder and more insistent. Spinning on her heel she looked at Paul Morrow's door. It did not come from his room but from the direction of Evelyn's room at the end of the gallery, above the library. She followed the sound and approaching the end of the corridor, she took a startled breath. A yellow light emanated from the staircase leading down to the library. It appeared that the lights were on and the library door left open.

She shook her head. This wasn't unusual. Paul Morrow kept his own hours and had work to do in the library. But even as the thought crossed her mind, the heart wrenching sobs rose to a crescendo. Helen crept forward along the corridor. As she reached the stairs to the library, she hesitated. If Paul Morrow had a woman in the library, it was none of her business and neither of them would welcome her intrusion.

She thought about the man she had met in the stable that morning, the man Charlie had spoken of so often. Paul Morrow, as distant and apparently reclusive as he appeared to be, did not seem the type to reduce women to such heartbroken sobs. Whatever was going on in the library was none of her business.

Helen turned to make her way back to the kitchen. As she passed the door to Lady Morrow's room, it swung open and a draft of cold air enveloped her. She shivered, her breath frosting in the chilly atmosphere, and reached out her left hand to close the door. As she grasped the doorknob and started to pull the door shut, cold fingers closed around her wrist and an unseen hand grasped her with such force she could feel each finger and the pressure of a thumb. Where the phantom fingers touched her skin, it felt like ice had been pressed against her.

She tried to scream but could only manage a strangled gurgle as the invisible force on her wrist tugged at her, pulling her toward the staircase. The more she resisted the tighter the grip became resembling the 'Chinese burns' her brother, Henry, used to give her as a child.

Behind her a floorboard creaked and as suddenly as it had appeared the apparition vanished, leaving Helen motionless, staring at her outstretched hand. Her heart thudded in her chest and her breath came in short gasps.

She turned blindly, screaming as a shadow loomed up behind her, blocking the light from the windows.

TEN

In the shadowy corridor, Paul could see the slight figure in a blue robe of some kind standing at the door to Evelyn's room. She stood quite still her arm outstretched as if pointing to the library stairs.

As he reached her, Helen turned and screamed. Her knees appeared to buckle and he caught her and held her by the forearms, turning her to face him.

'Steady,' he said. 'Just take a deep breath and tell me what's going on.'

She sank in his grip, and for a moment he thought she had fainted. In the watery moonlight that filtered in through the windows her face looked ashen.

'Paul?'

His name came out in a whispered rush as she hung limp in his grasp. Instinctively he put his arms around her, drawing her in toward him like he would a small child. Helen leaned against his chest and he could smell the sweet, floral scent of soap in her hair.

'Helen?' She looked up at him and frowned, stiffening in his embrace. He released her, taking a step back as she ran a shaking hand through her hair that fell loose around her face.

'You look like you need a drink,' he said.

'Cocoa. I was going to make cocoa,' Helen said in an uncertain voice.

'I think you need something stronger than cocoa,' Paul observed. 'I've brandy in my room.'

She straightened her shoulders and pulling at the belt of her dressing gown, tipped her face and looked up at him with a shaky smile on her lips.

'Brandy would be good.'

With some hesitation, he put an arm around her shoulders, expecting her to baulk at his touch but she leaned in against him. Underneath the thin fabric of her dressing gown he could feel her shivering. Beneath his hand, her slight figure seemed to have no more substance than a bird.

Paul guided her to one of the shabby armchairs beside the fire and fetched a blanket from his bedroom. Helen pulled it around herself as he crouched awkwardly and stoked the embers of the fire into life.

He poured them both a brandy and as he handed her the glass the sleeve of her dressing gown fell back revealing a livid welt around her left wrist.

'What caused that?' he asked.

She pulled the sleeve back with a shaking hand.

'Silly accident,' she said.

Paul sat down in his usual chair and sipped his brandy, watching as Helen cradled the glass in both hands and took a hefty gulp, almost draining the contents.

She had her own reasons for not telling him the truth, probably assuming he would think her a fool. Despite himself, he smiled.

'I never met an Australian, who didn't know how to drink. Did it do the trick?' he asked.

Helen took another, more ladylike sip. 'Thank you. Much better than cocoa.' For the first time, she met his eyes and gave him a watery smile. 'I'm sorry. I'm not normally given to the female vapours. I didn't mean to disturb you.'

Paul shook his head. 'You didn't disturb me. As you may have guessed, I don't keep regular hours.' He jerked his head at an upturned book on the side table beside his chair. 'I heard you walk past my door. If you were going to the kitchen, there are no kitchen stairs at this end of the corridor.'

'I know. I... I heard a noise.'

'A noise?'

'It was stupid. I must have imagined it,' she said with a self-deprecating laugh. She did not, he was certain, imagine the red mark on her wrist and he saw her right hand move to rub it.

'It's an old house, full of creaks and groans,' Paul said. 'Easy to imagine you hear things.'

'That must have been it, but it seemed so real.'

'What sort of noise?'

'You'll think I'm a fool,' She ran her hand through her hair again. It fell through her slender fingers like rivulets of gold in the light from the fire. The photographs he had seen of her did not do her justice. Helen did not possess the classic English beauty of Tony's debutantes, rather she had a life and light in her face that drew the eye like a magnet. Paul drained his glass.

'Try me,' he said.

'It sounded like a woman crying.'

'Ah...' Paul heard the note in her voice. She craved a logical explanation and he had to provide it. 'Most likely an owl. They can sound uncannily like a human being at times.'

Paul wondered for a moment how he had managed to say that with a straight face. He knew whatever she had heard had not been an owl.

'I thought it came from the library and then I saw the light and thought you must be working late.'

He held up a hand. '*Mea culpa*. I must have forgotten to switch the light off when I finished work this evening. I assure you, Helen, there's nothing to worry about. As I said, it's just a creaky, old house.'

Helen finished the brandy and set the glass down on the side table. 'I should leave you in peace,' she said, standing and neatly folding the blanket.

'Are you sure you're all right?'

She smiled. 'I'm fine, thank you.' At the door, she paused, her hand on the handle. 'Thank you for the brandy.'

'Helen.'

She looked back at him.

'If you are riding in the morning, be at the stable at seven,' he said. 'There is something Charlie would have wanted you to see.'

At the mention of Charlie's name, her face brightened, as if a light had come on in her life. A shard of pain caught Paul's breath. She still loved Charlie.

'Thank you. I would like that. Goodnight, Paul.'

The door closed behind her and he heard her footsteps on the crooked floorboards fading away down the gallery.

'Goodnight, Helen,' he murmured.

ELEVEN

Helen woke early and left Alice still asleep in the big bed, where, craving company, she had put the sleeping child on her return to her bedroom the previous night. A gentle mist swirled up from the hollows to a clear, bright sky presaging a beautiful day. She had begun to get a sense of the rhythm of this country, so different from the blue mountains of her own beloved Terrala.

As she rounded the corner of the stable block, Helen saw Paul already sitting on the mounting block, holding the reins of the two horses. His utter stillness caused her to pause. The early morning light leeched the colour from the world and he could have been one of the statues of his ancestors in the church. She had never met anyone who seemed so solitary and she wondered if he had always been so self-contained or if the war had turned him inward as it had done to so many young men.

Helen touched her left wrist. There had been no sign of the mark when she had woken this morning but the terror of the moment still burned in her memory. She had turned and Paul had been there, stilling her fright by his mere presence. For all his outward reserve, when Paul had taken her in his arms last night, she had been conscious of a depth of warmth and humanity. He had taken all the fear from her, and absorbed it into himself.

It had been so long since a man had held her as Paul had, even for a few fleeting seconds. As she looked at Paul Morrow, his still figure reminded her for the first time in a long time of her own loneliness. In a world where a generation of young men had died, she knew there was little chance of finding someone to fill that empty space in her life. Yes, she had Alice, but the company of the child did not fill the aching void in her heart left by Charlie's death.

The horses sensed her presence and turned their heads toward her, their ears pricked. Paul looked around and seeing her, jumped down from the mounting block. He winced as he landed.

'Are you all right?' she asked as she joined him.

'I must stop doing that. I forget...' he said, wincing as he rubbed his right thigh. He caught the question in her face and added, 'Broken femur.'

'I'm surprised you can still ride,' Helen said.

'So I've been told, but I couldn't envisage a life without it. Want a hand?'

'I can manage. Horses are a way of life at home,' Helen said as she took the reins from him, springing easily into the saddle.

'Charlie told me about an annual cattle muster? It sounded like hard riding,' he replied as he mounted Hector.

'We graze our cattle in the high country during summer and every autumn we have to bring them down. It's rough and dangerous riding, but Charlie took to the muster as if he had been born to it.'

'He would,' Paul replied with a smile. 'Never had any respect for his own neck.'

The birds greeted them with their morning chorus as they turned the horses out onto the narrow road. Helen turned to look at the man riding beside her. Like his cousin, Paul rode with ease and grace, at one with the horse.

'Where are we going?' she asked.

'I thought I'd show you one of Charlie's favourite places,' he said. 'Stoneman's Hill.' He cast her a sideways glance. 'Unless, of course, you've already been up to the Standing Stones?'

'No. I've tried to find them. Sam even gave me directions, but I just became hopelessly lost.'

He smiled. 'They'll let you find them when they're ready.'

'That sounds like local superstition,' she said. 'You don't seem to be the type to pay heed to folk stories.'

His gaze held hers. 'I spent my early childhood in a country that thrived on spirits and had a mother who believed in the fairy folk. I don't take anything in this world for granted.'

Paul turned Hector's head off the road, up a narrow hacking path Helen had never seen before, despite her morning excursions. Helen's horse automatically fell into step behind Paul as he urged Hector up the overgrown path that wound up through the thick trees on Stoneman's Hill. Helen had ample opportunity to contemplate his straight back and broad shoulders beneath the old sweater he wore. She noticed he carried his left shoulder slightly higher than his right and she wondered if that was another legacy of the night Charlie had died.

The path flattened out and the trees cleared to reveal five granite monoliths silhouetted against the early morning sun, the Celtic warriors turned to stone by a druid's curse of Charlie's stories.

Helen slid from the saddle and tied Minter's reins to a tree. Almost afraid to breathe, she walked toward the ancient stones. Two had fallen on their sides and two leaned haphazardly as if they would fall if she touched them, but the last one still stood tall and straight within the circle.

She placed her hand on the lichened and weathered surface, half-expecting to feel the beat of a living heart within the granite.

'You're the archaeologist,' she said at last, turning back to Paul. 'How old are they?'

He stood on the edge of the circle watching her, his hands thrust into the pockets of his trousers.

'No one knows,' he said. 'I would say a couple of thousand years at least. If not older.'

'Are they on your land?'

He nodded. 'They were here before the Morrows and will be here long after we've gone. Tony will tell you that on the Wellmore land, they have seven standing stones, but they're nothing more than an eighteenth-century folly. These,' as he spoke, he walked into the circle and sat down on one of the fallen stones, 'are real.' He straightened his right leg and rubbed it.

Helen sat down next to him. A flight of birds rose from the trees above their heads, spiralling into the soft grey morning light. Charlie had loved Australia but this had been his home long before he met her, this was where he truly belonged. More than at any time since she had come to England the question nagged at her mind, the need to know how he had died, the need to lay his memory to rest and turn her face to the future.

'Paul...' Her fingers twisted the wedding band on her left hand.

'You're going to ask me about Charlie?' he interrupted.

She looked down at the toe of her riding boot. 'Am I that transparent?'

'No, but it's the question you want answered, just as Evelyn does. That is why you came to England, isn't it?'

Helen opened her mouth, the denial forming on her lips. 'Partly,' she admitted.

Paul crossed his ankles and looked up at her. 'I can't give you the answer you want, Helen, because I don't know. My memory of what happened between a mortar shell blowing up in front of me and waking up in the field hospital is a complete blank.'

'I'm sorry, I didn't mean...'

He rose to his feet. 'You have every right to ask, Helen, but you will just have to accept that you may never know the answer.' He started to walk away and then turned back to look at her. 'And if you do find the answer, it may not be the one you want to hear. I had to write letters.' Paul took a heavy breath and looked up at the trees. 'Every time one of my men was killed. The grieving mothers and widows would not have thanked me for honesty. We all take refuge in platitudes as a defence against the horror of reality. Let him go, Helen.'

He looped the reins over Hector's head and swung into the saddle. Man and horse had already been swallowed up by the undergrowth before Helen had time to follow him.

As she emerged from the path, she found him waiting for her. He raised a questioning eyebrow and put his heels to Hector. Accepting the unspoken challenge, Helen urged the old horse into a gallop. Neck and neck the two horses pounded down the quiet country lane.

They arrived back at the stables, flushed and exultant. Sam came out to meet them. He gave the panting horses a glance and shook his head.

'Leave the horses,' he said. 'I'll see to 'em. Sarah's got your breakfast going and will be wonderin' where you both are.'

———

'You two look like you could do with a cup of tea,' Sarah said as Paul and Helen walked into the kitchen.

Alice sat at the kitchen table with a glass of milk in her hand.

'Now you're here, I'll put on the eggs.' Sarah bustled over to the large kitchen range. 'Good ride?'

'Paul took me up to Stoneman's Hill,' Helen said. She kissed the top of her daughter's head. 'When that pony arrives from Wellmore, I'll take you there.'

'If you go through, I'll bring you breakfast in the parlour,' Sarah said.

'Don't be silly,' Helen responded. 'I don't see any point in setting up in the parlour. I'm quite happy to eat breakfast here. Paul, can you pour the tea?'

Paul looked at Helen and then at the large, brown teapot Sarah had set on the table. A smile quirked the corner of his mouth. 'Of course. Pass those tea cups, Alice.'

Sarah Pollard put her hands on her hips and glanced at Helen as the man took a chair at the end of the table and dutifully poured four large cups of tea.

'We always eat breakfast in the kitchen at home,' Alice said as the adults arranged themselves around the table.

'Just don't tell Grandmama,' Helen said.

Paul regarded Alice over his teacup. 'Definitely don't tell Grandmama. Anyone else want that last piece of toast?'

Helen pushed the platter across to him. Sitting at the kitchen table with his sleeves pushed up, his dark hair falling across his eyes as he buttered a piece of toast, he seemed more relaxed then he did in the world beyond the green baize door.

The outside door opened and Annie, the girl from the village walked into the kitchen.

'Good morning, Mrs. Pol...' she stopped mid-sentence, her hand still on the door latch, staring at the breakfast crowd. She bobbed a curt-sey. 'Good morning, sir... madam.'

'It's all right, Annie,' Paul rose to his feet. 'I've finished. I'll leave you all in peace. Thanks for breakfast, Sarah.'

'You go and make a start on the dining room, Annie,' Sarah said as the kitchen door swung shut behind Paul. Humming to herself the girl picked up her basket of cleaning rags and followed Paul out of the kitchen.

Helen set down her empty cup. 'I should go too. I'm holding you up,' she said, pushing her chair back from the table. 'Have you finished that toast yet, Alice?'

Alice set the crust she had been eating around, back on the plate and looked up.

'If you're not in a hurry, I've something to show the two of you.' Sarah rose to her feet and fetched a large parcel, loosely wrapped in brown paper from the sideboard. She set it down in front of Alice. The child knelt up on the chair and pulled back the wrapping to reveal a heavy old-fashioned scrapbook.

'It's just something I've kept all these years,' Sarah said, collecting the breakfast plates and carrying them over to the sink.

Helen pulled her chair up beside Alice and they began to turn the pages. The scrapbook contained a history of the Morrow's lives, chroni-cled in newspaper cuttings, yellowed invitation cards, and photographs, beginning with the wedding of Sir Gerald Morrow and the Honourable Evelyn Vaughan. There followed birth announcements for Charlie, clipped from *The Times,* items from the social pages of the county news-paper recounting Charlie's prowess at cricket and rugby, and a photo-graph of Charlie playing Dick Dauntless in a school Gilbert and Sullivan production. There were newspaper photographs of Sir Gerald's funeral, including one of the villagers turning out to line the route of the coffin to the church.

A couple of small articles mentioned the success of the Winchester First Eight, stroked by P.N. Morrow, at the Head of the River and Paul as captain of the First Eleven in their win against Harrow in the cricket.

Then the war, a brief item recounting that Captain Charles Morrow would be awarded a posthumous MC for gallantry in the face of the enemy and a couple of newspaper epitaphs, none of which Helen had seen before. She looked at the neatly printed words recounting Charlie's bravery and the nation's collective sorrow at his death. They meant nothing to her, it was almost as though they talked about a total stranger.

Helen closed the book. 'Thank you for showing that to us.'

'I want you to have it,' Sarah said. 'I thought Alice may like to keep it.'

'May I?' Alice's eyes shone and she turned the pages slowly, revisiting each one as Helen helped Sarah with the washing up.

Alice swivelled on the chair and looked across at the two women by the sink. 'Mrs. Pollard, Uncle Tony said you know all about the Holdston ghosts,' she said.

Helen started and nearly dropped the cup she was drying. 'Alice, we've talked about this before. There is no such thing as ghosts.'

'Have you ever seen any, Mrs. Pollard?' Alice persisted, ignoring Helen's protest.

Sarah cast Helen a quick glance. 'I have to disagree with you, Mrs. Morrow. There's ghosts at Holdston right enough.'

Helen glared at Sarah. She did not need Sarah filling Alice's head with such nonsense.

Alice's eyes widened. 'So they're real?'

Sarah frowned. 'They're not real in the sense you and I understand, Alice. There's old Ben. You never see him but you know he's around because you can smell his tobacco. Then there's some civil war soldiers. There was a battle near here and they reckon they was brought here and died of their wounds.'

'Are they scary?' Alice's eyes resembled saucers.

'No,' said Sarah. 'They're in their own place in time, love. If I know one of them is around, I say good morning. They like to be acknowledged but they're not scary and they won't hurt you.'

Helen rubbed her wrist and shuddered inwardly at the memory of that icy touch. If she allowed herself to believe that what happened to her in the dark corridor the previous night was indeed paranormal, then she had to disagree with the last assertion. There had been malice and an intention to hurt in that grip.

'I think that's enough talk of ghosts,' she said firmly.

Sarah smoothed down her apron. 'Mrs. Morrow, if you don't mind, I've choir practice tonight. If I leave some soup for you and Miss Alice, will you be able to manage without me? There's fresh bread and cheese in the larder.'

'Of course, Mrs. Pollard. What about the Major?'

'The Major'll fend for himself if he wants to eat.'

Helen caught the older woman's wry smile. 'You do worry about him, don't you?' she observed.

'Someone has to. He hasn't got anyone else. My boy, Fred, was in his regiment and there weren't a man who served under the Major who wouldn't have put their trust in him.'

It was the first Helen had heard about Sarah's son and she sensed the answer even before she asked, 'And your son? Where is he now?'

Sarah stiffened. 'He was killed ten days before Armistice,' she replied. 'If the Major'd still been with the regiment he'd have seen Fred through to the end.'

'Oh Sarah,' Helen's voice broke. 'I'm so sorry.'

Sarah shook herself. 'We're just two of many women in this country, Mrs. Morrow. Mothers, wives, daughters, sisters. We've all got someone to mourn but the Major came home, lost and silent just like he was when he first came to this house when he was eight years old.'

'Eight?'

'Aye, motherless and fatherless, for all his father was still alive. I don't think there'd been much room in his folks' lives for him even before his mother died.' Sarah heaved a theatrical sigh. 'Her ladyship tried her best but he wasn't an easy child to love. Some children aren't, but here in the kitchen with me and the staff he was a different boy. So yes, I worry about the Major.'

Helen looked at the door as if she expected Paul Morrow to reappear through it. She rose to her feet and tapped her daughter on the shoulder. Alice, still absorbed in the scrapbook didn't move.

'Would Miss Alice like to help me with the baking this morning?' Sarah asked.

Alice brightened and looked from Sarah to her mother. Helen relented. It suited her to have Alice gainfully employed. She had other plans.

TWELVE

Paul ran his hand through his hair and contemplated the paper-strewn table, his gaze coming to rest on the Remington. He needed to start typing up the report, but the thought of tying himself to the ancient machine with his laborious two-fingered typing did not thrill him. He turned his head at a knock on the library door. Helen stepped into the room, her hands thrust into the pockets of her cardigan.

'I thought if you didn't mind, that perhaps I could help you?' she said.

'Help me?'

She looked past him at the disorganised mess on the table. 'I will die of boredom if I don't find something useful to do. Is there any typing or filing I can do?'

'I won't say no to the offer of help with the typing,' Paul admitted. 'As your daughter has already observed, I'm no typist.'

Helen walked over to the table and picked up the pile of photographs of the recent dig. 'This is extraordinary. Who is that man?' She pointed to a figure in one of the photographs.

Paul stood up and joined her at the table. 'Woolley, Leonard Woolley. He believes he has found the ancient Sumerian city of Ur.'

Helen looked up at him, the wonder shining from her face. 'The Ur that is mentioned in the Bible?'

'The same.'

She drew an awed breath and replaced the photographs back on the table. 'What is your role on these digs?' she asked.

'Officially, I do what the army trained me to do. I organise things. An archaeological dig is no different from a military operation. People have to be fed, watered, housed, moved around, so that's what I do. But I have some aptitude with ancient language and I do help out with this sort of thing.' He swept a hand at the tablets in their padded boxes. 'I leave the digging work to the others.'

He made a pretence of shuffling some of the papers on the table to avoid her eyes. While part of him yearned to join the dig, he could not bring himself to descend into the diggings. Woolley had tried to persuade him to join in but he had stood on the edge of the trenches and broken out in a sweat.

'As interesting as Woolley's work is, I have no particular passion for ancient Babylonian history.'

'What is your passion?' She cocked her head and looked at him with a smile.

'Ancient Greek,' he said without hesitation and without really knowing why he said it, he added, 'In my spare moments in the trenches, I worked on a translation of Homer's *Iliad*.'

As soon as he said it, he regretted the confidence. She looked at him with large grey eyes that invited his trust in a way no one else had for a long time.

'Tony said you never went to university?'

Paul felt the old grievance shift on his shoulders. 'I'd won a scholarship to Magdalen in Oxford but my uncle insisted that it was my father's dying wish that I follow him into the regiment. So off to Sandhurst, I went.' He wondered if she could hear the bitterness in his voice.

Helen's gaze lingered on his face for a few moments before she squared her shoulders and picked up some papers with his scrawled notes. She squinted at the papers in her hand. 'Your writing is atrocious but I am used to my father's scrawl so it shouldn't take me too long to decipher this.'

'Your father?'

'Yes, I work for my father,' she said. 'When I'm not doing the paper-work for Terrala, I type out his speeches for parliament. The boys went to university, I went to secretarial college. Father deemed that a far more useful skill for a woman.'

He heard the irony in her voice and smiled. 'And you would have rather done something else?'

'I don't see why I couldn't have gone to university. They're taking women now. I could have studied medicine.' He raised his eyebrows and she smiled. 'Although it is far more probable I would have ended up a school teacher so maybe secretarial college wasn't such a bad idea.'

'This is the administrative report for the season,' he said. 'Very boring and unromantic but if Woolley wants the money to continue digging, it must be done. To keep myself amused, I also do some of the more tedious translation work which is why I have these tablets.' He picked up one of the tablets from its box and handed it to her.

She turned it over, her eyes widening. 'How old is this?'

He shrugged. 'Probably older than the stones on the hill.'

She handed it back to him. 'I'd hate to drop it,' she said. 'What does that one say?'

He smiled. 'It's a household inventory.'

She pulled a face. 'How dull.'

'I suppose it is, but at the same time it is like a photograph of their way of life.'

Helen looked at the Remington. 'Well, then let's get to work,' she said.

He passed her a stack of handwritten pages and she rifled through them, pulling a face. Paul gave her a rueful smile. 'I'm sorry. Just tell me if there is something you can't read.'

Helen sat down at the Remington, took two pieces of plain paper and carbon, and began to type with a speed and dexterity that left him staring at her in amazement. At this rate the report would be finished in no time.

With a few stops to decipher his atrocious handwriting, after typing for an hour Helen pushed back her chair and stood up, stretching her arms above her head. She walked over to the enormous mahogany bookcases that flanked the old fireplace and surveyed the books for a moment before pulling one out.

'Whose crest is this?' she asked pointing to a regal coat of arms on the bookplate.

Paul shook his head. 'No idea. It's not the Morrow crest. I suspect you'll find that most of the books have the same bookplate. One of my illustrious ancestors would have purchased the library as a job lot.'

Helen replaced the book and pulled out another one. 'The pages on this one haven't even been cut,' she exclaimed.

'Evelyn's brother has looked over the books. He seems to think as a collection it's worth quite a sum these days,' Paul said, sitting back in his chair and tapping his nose with the end of his pencil.

'Will you sell it?'

Paul shrugged. 'Evelyn has suggested that and I have no great affection for it. It will buy us some time.'

'Time for what?'

He sighed. 'I suppose you should know, Helen. The estate barely makes ends meet. This house alone,' he looked up at the ceiling, 'costs us a fortune. Did you wonder why we live only in a few rooms with two staff? As well as the house, we have eight farms to run and maintain. We need to improve the way we farm but there is no money for new equipment and hardly enough to make running repairs to the farm buildings.' He gave a rueful smile. 'Sorry. None of this is your concern.'

'But it is, isn't it? I'm a Morrow too and I'm only too aware of the difficulties of running a large estate. Is there anything I can do to help?'

He looked at her. She was involved in the affairs of her father's property so, yes, she would understand his difficulties but he wouldn't ask her for help. The trust Charlie had left was for her and the child and he knew little of Helen's family situation. Holdston was his problem. His alone.

'The rents haven't been raised in twenty years and I can't do so now, not while the buildings are in such poor condition so that's why I work. The museum pays me quite well. Enough to keep body and soul and this house together, but we can't go on this way.'

'What will you do?'

He met her gaze. 'I want to sell Holdston.'

Her eyes rested on him for a moment. 'Would Charlie have come back and saved Holdston?' she asked.

Paul shook his head. 'No. He told me he had every intention of settling in Australia after the war, and even if he'd wanted to, Holdston is beyond saving. My aunt and uncle lived in another world.'

'Charlie and I bought some land in the King Valley but I was afraid that once he went home, he'd change his mind.'

'Evelyn is convinced Charlie would have returned to Holdston but his mind was made up. He would have gone back to Australia. Sorry, I didn't mean to bore you with tedious family business.'

'But I am family, Paul.' She echoed her earlier words. 'For better or worse, I'm a Morrow. Generations of your family have lived in this house. Your blood, Charlie's blood, Alice too. There must have been hard times before, but they still managed to get through them.'

'You're quite right, Helen. There have been hard times before. A couple of civil wars and several kings intent on taxing the lifeblood from their subjects, but I doubt any of my ancestors would recognise the world we live in now.'

Paul rose to his feet and looked out of the window while he fumbled in his pocket for his cigarettes. An odd procession was making its way up the drive toward the house. Tony, mounted on his black hunter headed the cavalcade followed by a groom on horseback leading a piebald pony.

'Good lord,' he exclaimed. 'Is that rotund little beast the one Tony is lending Alice?'

Helen joined him at the window. 'Oh, it is. I must get Alice. Excuse me, Paul.'

Paul followed her out of the courtyard door, crossing the bridge over the moat to meet the Wellmore party.

'Morrow. I heard you were back.' Tony dismounted, greeting Paul with an outstretched hand and a clap on his good shoulder.

Paul gave the pony a quick appraising glance. 'Using me as an agistment stable, I hear?'

'I didn't think one more new resident would make much of a difference,' Tony replied.

Paul glanced back at the house. 'Holdston is becoming quite used to new residents,' he observed. 'What brings you to the country?'

'Ma is on the matchmaking path again. She's intent on filling the house with dismal debutantes for me to make my selection.' Tony gave a mock shudder. 'Suitable young women, Anthony. It's about time you settled down.'

Paul smiled at the fair impersonation of Tony's mother.

'There's a soiree planned for Friday night. Angela's coming down for the weekend to lend me support.' Tony continued.

'Angela?'

'I thought that would interest you,' Tony said. 'Enough to inveigle you to Ma's party?'

Paul shook his head. 'I can't imagine anything I would like less.'

'Be a sport. There's some pretty girls in the herd and if it's time for me to 'settle down', it must be time for you as well.'

'Uncle Tony.' Alice called out as she ran across the bridge.

'True to my promise, Sprite. One Turnip for you to ride,' Tony said with a mock bow.

Alice giggled at the joke, and at the sight of the child's delighted face, a rush of regret surged through Paul at his own failure to be the child's benefactor.

Obviously brought up around horses, the child did not rush to the piebald pony, but walked over slowly, approaching him from the front. The pony eyed her with his ears pricked. Alice had come prepared. From her pocket, she produced two crumbled and lint-impregnated sugar lumps.

'So, Sprite. Shall we take this lazy beast for a ride?'

'Please can we, Mummy?' Alice addressed her mother who had joined the group, standing beside Paul with her arms crossed.

'Of course,' she said. 'I just need to change and get Minter saddled. You will stay for lunch, Tony?'

Tony shook his head. 'Expected back at Wellmore, I'll ride with you as far as the crossroads, Sprite. What about you, Morrow?' Tony turned to Paul.

'Please, Uncle Paul?' Alice pleaded.

Paul shook his head. 'I have work to do,' he said, not willing to admit that the ache in his leg made another ride an unattractive prospect, 'but you're welcome to take Hector, Helen. I think you'll find him easier than Minter.'

The men watched as Alice scampered back toward the house with her mother following. Tony produced a silver cigarette case and offered it to Paul.

'I have a message from Angela. She said if you didn't come and relieve the tedium of the party, she would personally ride over and haul you out.'

Paul laughed. 'That's an invitation I can't resist,' he said tapping the ash off his cigarette. 'She knows how I loathe those sorts of occasions.'

'We all do,' Tony admitted.

'Liar,' Paul responded. 'All those girls fawning over you, Scarvell?'

'A title and a large estate do compensate for my lack of good looks,' Tony said with a wry grin. 'So, what do you think of Charlie's widow?'

Paul coughed on the smoke. 'Does it matter what I think?'

'Charlie did rather paint her as a paragon,' Tony said, 'so I thought the reality would be disappointing but I have to say, old man, she's a beauty.'

Paul contemplated the exterior of the old house and drew thoughtfully on his cigarette. He'd met many beautiful women but Helen had more than just striking good looks. Even in their short acquaintance, she shone like a beacon in his bleak life.

Mistaking Paul's silence, Tony continued. 'She's the most interesting woman I've met in years, Morrow.'

Paul brought his attention back to his friend. 'Don't go falling in love with her. You know your mother would never approve.'

'Love? What makes you say that?'

'Because despite all your talk, Scarvell, you fall in love with any woman who looks twice at you.'

'Unlike you. When was the last time you were ever in love, Morrow?'

Paul shook his head. 'A state of bliss I have avoided,' he said with a smile. *Except, perhaps, for Angela. He had loved her once.*

'Here come the girls.' Tony drew a deep breath. 'My God, look at those legs. Are all Australian girls such stunners?' He straightened. 'See you on Friday night, Morrow.'

Paul stubbed the cigarette out on the wall. 'Tell Ange I'll think about it,' he replied.

THIRTEEN

Helen put Alice to bed and read her a chapter of *The Railway Children*. The weather had changed and the beautiful day had ended in dark clouds and growls of thunder so she pulled the window shut and drew the curtain tight, pretending not to notice the corner of the scrapbook sticking out from beneath the child's pillow.

As she straightened, Helen laid a finger on Alice's cheek, 'The holiday is over, Miss Morrow. I have decided you are going to school.'

Alice's eyes widened. 'Where?'

'Just to the village school. I've spoken to the vicar and I've got an appointment to speak to the headmistress tomorrow afternoon. His daughter, Lily, goes there so you will know someone.'

Alice screwed up her face. 'School,' she said with no real resentment in her tone. Helen kissed her daughter's forehead. It must have been lonely for Alice with just adults for company.

'You can read until half past seven. I'm going down to the kitchen for supper if you need me.'

To her surprise, she found Paul Morrow standing at the kitchen table slicing a loaf of bread. He looked up at her.

'Would you mind my company for supper? I think it's soup.'

'I'd be glad of it,' Helen said, 'As long as you have no objection to eating in the kitchen again.'

'None at all. Bread?'

'Thank you. I'll make some tea, is that all right for you?'

'Fine.' Paul set the bread in the middle of the table.

Helen put the soup on to reheat and Paul found the kitchen crockery and cutlery.

'My aunt is still trying to live in the last century,' he said, pulling up a chair at the table. 'Back in the days when we had a dozen staff.'

'I don't think any of her generation will find it easy to change,' Helen responded, conscious that he watched her as she stirred the thick vegetable soup waiting for the steam to rise from it. 'She'll be even more shocked when I tell her that I'm going to send Alice to the village school. She needs to be with children her own age.'

'A Morrow? At the village school?' Paul's voice held a fair imitation of Evelyn.

Helen's lips twitched and she turned to glance at him over her shoulder. 'You do that well.'

Paul shook his head. 'I've lived with Evelyn for a long time.'

'When did you come here?' Helen enquired, knowing the answer but curious to find out more about Paul Morrow from the man himself.

'I was eight,' he said. 'Same age as Alice. My father sent me back to England after my mother died.'

'Where did you live?'

'Malaya. Father had command of a regiment based in Ipoh. When my mother died he didn't know what to do with an eight-year-old boy so he sent me home.'

Although Helen had her back to him, she could hear the anger in his voice, even after all these years.

'And your father?'

'I never saw him again. He died when I was ten.'

This time she turned to look at him. He met her gaze. 'That's the way these things go, Helen. It was a hard life in the Far East and I was fortunate that I had family and a home to go to in England. Even if my parents had lived, sooner or later I would have been sent to boarding school either in England or some other corner of the Empire.'

'Do you remember your mother?' she asked.

'My mother? Not well.' His mouth twisted in a bitter smile. 'She was Irish, the daughter of the regimental sergeant major. My father married beneath himself, for which Evelyn and Gerald never quite forgave him. She used to tell me stories of banshees, *cluricauns* and the *lianhan shee* and I can remember her dark hair and her Irish lilt. My only memory of her now is a photograph. How's the soup?'

Helen turned back to the stove. 'Just a few more minutes.'

They lapsed back into a companionable silence broken only by the tick of the old clock on the wall, the crackle of the coal in the oven, and lashing rain on the windows and the water of the moat.

As the soup started to bubble, a sharp crack sounded from the furthest reaches of the house. Helen started, the wooden spoon falling into the pot. She spun on her heel to look at Paul. 'What was that?'

He met her eyes and frowned. 'What was what?'

'That noise. It sounded like a shot.' She stared at him. 'You didn't hear it?'

He shook his head.

'It was a shot. A pistol or something with a small caliber and it came from inside the house.' She moved toward the door. 'Alice. Oh, my God, Alice...'

Paul jumped to his feet and caught her arm as she ran toward the door. 'It's just lightning, Helen.'

She turned to confront him. 'That wasn't lightning, Paul. I know a gunshot when I hear one.'

She shook off his hand and began running. At the door to Alice's room, she slowed, panting from her sudden exertion, but the night-light revealed a peaceful, sleeping child under the pink and green quilt.

Relieved, Helen turned to go back to the kitchen. Paul waited for her in the gallery, looking down into the dark, rain-lashed courtyard.

'Is she all right?'

'She's fine,' Helen gave a small dismissive laugh, 'You were right, just my own stupid imagination.'

As she spoke a high-pitched and terrified scream came from the far end of the gallery; a woman's scream followed by the sound of breaking crockery.

Helen glanced at Paul. 'Don't tell me you didn't hear that!' she said. 'It came from the library.'

At the top of the library stairs, she hesitated, letting her breath steady. A soft yellow light spilled from under the ill-fitting door at the bottom of the stairs. Helen stopped for a moment before descending, her heart thudding in her chest.

Slowly she descended the stairs and put her hand to the half-open door. It swung open at her touch and she took a step back. The light she had seen came not from the electric lights but from two candlesticks on the table and the fire burning in the hearth. In all other respects, the library looked as it always did, but for a man sitting in one of the chairs at the table. Only he wasn't sitting. He had fallen forward, sprawled across the table, a small pistol in his outstretched right hand, his head turned toward the door and his eyes wide and staring. Blood from the gaping wound at the side of his head ran in a steadily increasing pool across the papers on the desk and dripped onto the carpet beneath the table.

Helen's foot crunched on something that snapped beneath her weight. She looked down at a wooden tray and a mess of broken crockery and glass. A scream caught in her throat but no sound came from her mouth.

'Come away, Helen,' Paul's voice intruded into the nightmare and his hand was on her arm, dragging her back up the stairs. The door slammed shut.

'There's ... a ... dead man in the library,' she stuttered, looking up into Paul's face.

Paul grasped her by her upper arms, bringing his head down to her level. 'There is no one in the library,' he said firmly.

'There's a man. His head ... there's blood over the papers. I saw him.'

Still holding her by one arm, Paul opened the door revealing a room in darkness. No candles, no fire. Paul pulled the cord of the electric light, its incandescent glow flooding the room with startling clarity. No corpse lay sprawled across the table only the old Remington typewriter perched at the far end of a table littered with papers.

'I saw him,' she insisted.

'Helen, there is nothing here. It is just as I left it this evening.'

She looked up into his face, seeing the hard eyes and the rigid set of his mouth as if he willed her to believe him. Only a momentary flash of something uncertain behind the green eyes belied his words.

She shook off his hand and straightened.

'No,' she exclaimed. 'You saw him too. You had to have seen him. I'm not going mad, Paul.'

When he didn't answer, she looked around the room and then back at his implacable face. She rubbed at her arm where he had gripped her.

'What's happening in this house?' she said. 'I don't understand.'

His face relaxed. 'I'm sorry, I didn't mean to hurt you. Come back to the kitchen and let's have supper.'

Back in the kitchen, Helen slumped into one of the kitchen chairs while Paul retrieved the saucepan from the stove and served the soup. He produced a half-full, opened bottle of wine from the pantry and poured them both a glass.

Helen drained her glass and set it down on the table, watching as Paul refilled it.

'I'm sorry, but I'm not a hysterical person, Paul,' she said. 'I'm not imagining things.'

'I didn't say you were.'

'It's just—' Helen began to shake again and hot shameful tears welled in her eyes. 'It's just that ever since I came to this house, things have been happening to me. Things that have no logical explanation.'

Paul sat back in the kitchen chair, holding the wine glass and staring beyond her at the rain-lashed windows. 'What sort of things?'

She told him about the photographs and personal belongings being moved in her room, the crying she had heard, and the hand on her wrist.

Paul glanced at her wrist. 'That mark I saw?'

She nodded and shivered. 'It was terrifying, Paul, but when I say it all out loud, it sounds so senseless. You must think I'm such a fool.'

He shook his head. 'I don't think that, Helen.'

'Sarah says the house is haunted. Is that true?'

He shrugged. 'This is an old house. A great many people have died in it, not all of them peacefully in their beds. It's no different from any old house in this country.'

'Have you ever seen them?' Helen persisted.

He remained quite still for a moment before he spoke, 'I have more things in my life to haunt me than the Holdston ghosts.'

Helen set her glass down, and taking comfort in the routine of the meal, finished the soup he had set in front of her. As Paul sat at the table twisting the soup spoon in his fingers, she set the pot in the sink to soak and found the cheese. She sliced off enough for both of them, boiled the kettle and made a pot of tea and they finished their meal in silence.

Paul stood up, placing his plate in the sink. 'If you'll excuse me I have work to do.'

Helen rose to her feet as he headed for the door. 'I...' she began. She wanted to say that she didn't want to be left alone, that she craved company tonight, anyone's company. Instead she said, 'Goodnight, Paul.'

He turned to look at her. 'I hope you're not bothered by any more disturbances tonight.'

He closed the kitchen door behind him, leaving Helen alone in the silence, a dark, oppressive silence. She leaned her elbows on the table and thought about Paul Morrow. Just when she thought she could see glimpses of the real man beneath the reserved exterior he presented to the world he pulled away. She wondered if he had ever learned to trust anyone. His mother had died when he was eight, his drunken father had sent him away, his aunt and uncle treated him like a poor relation. Perhaps the only person in his whole life who had got past the wall Paul had built up around himself was Charlie and Charlie had died.

Helen washed the dishes and scoured the pan before climbing the stairs to her silent bedroom. When she opened the door, she gasped in horror. Every book had been turned out of the little bookcase, the drawers to her dressing table opened, the contents strewn across the room, her hairbrushes were on her bed and the photographs turned face down on the dressing table.

Stepping over the mess, she checked on Alice, but the child slumbered peacefully just as she had last seen her, the dressing room undisturbed.

Helen turned back to her own room and she stood in the doorway contemplating the chaos. Despite the fire in the hearth, tentacles of cold wrapped around her body and her breath misted the air. She knew the signs now. She wrapped her arms around herself as her dread mounted. She considered running to Paul Morrow again, but then she recalled Sarah's words. '*They're in their own place in time, love. If I know one of them is around I say good morning. They like to be acknowledged...*'

'Who are you?' she addressed the cold, silent room. 'What do you want of me?'

No answer came except the rattle of the rain on the windowpanes and a slight dimming of the electric light. The fire roared into life sending a warm blast of air through the room. Helen drew a deep breath. Tomorrow she would talk to Sarah about moving rooms. There had to be other bedrooms in the house that did not have a resident ghost.

She started picking up the books and replacing them on the shelf. To judge by the dust, the shelf had been undisturbed for a long time. A dusty leather-bound volume lay apart from the others. Helen picked it up and sat back on her heels. '*A Commentary on the Gospel of Saint Matthew.*' It fell open to the title page and she carefully turned back the first two pages. To her surprise the rest of the book had been vandalised, the pages glued together and a large section cut from them to form a cavity. A green, leather-bound book, smaller than the Commentary, had been tucked into the cavity.

As Helen stared at it, a frisson of cold air brushed the back of her neck. She shivered and looked around. She pried the little book from its hiding place and as she turned it over in her hand, the whispering started, just as it had in the library on her first day at Holdston.

The book fell to the floor as she jumped up, casting wildly around the room for the source of the sound. The voices were quite distinct—a man and a woman—but the words were indecipherable.

She swallowed, steadying herself with Sarah's mantra—*They're in their own place in time. They are not here.*

Picking up the book with shaking fingers, she turned the little green volume over in her hands, not daring to open it.

The whispering became more urgent.

Helen looked up and turned a slow circle, seeking out the source of the whispering. 'I'm not afraid,' she said aloud and held up the book. 'Is this what you wanted me to find?'

The whispering stopped and Helen sat heavily on the edge of her bed and opened the cover of the book.

To my dearest Suzanna. I hope that this small trifle may be of some use to you. Yr loving husband Robt. was neatly inscribed on the front page in immaculate copperplate.

Flicking through a couple of pages, she could see this was a journal written in a spidery, hasty scrawl. Apart from the first few entries, the remaining entries appeared to be written in ancient Greek.

She changed into her nightdress and climbed into bed, opening the book to the first page.

The first entry was dated December 26, 1811:

Robert has sent me this little book as a token Christmas present. He tells me in his letter how hard it is to find food and shelter for his men, let alone to spend time in searching out trifles for his family. It is Christmas when I miss him the most and I am reminded more painfully than ever I can recall that in our four years of marriage we have spent so little time together. How fervently I prayed in church yesterday that this war would end and he will come home to us.

January 1, 1812: What a wonderful evening we enjoyed at Wellmore last night. I am quite exhausted. Adrian Scarvell, Robert's dearest friend, was home on leave, recovering from a wound to his shoulder which he describes as an inconvenience. He says he saw Robert a few months ago and that he was fit and well and talked of me often. How tedious that must be for his audience!

To my surprise, Lady Morrow was most complimentary about my new green gown and has suggested that we send for an artist from London to paint my likeness as a birthday present for Robert. It will complement the delightful portrait I have of him, looking so dashing in his scarlet jacket.

Adrian had brought with him some friends, fellow officers of the 6th and they were the life of the party. They insisted on dancing every dance and would not rest until every lady had been obliged. I was conscious that it was not proper for me to dance when my husband was absent but

Lady Morrow said she did not disapprove and that I was young and should be allowed to enjoy myself on such an occasion. Modesty aside as none will see these entries but myself, I was by far the most popular dance partner of the evening. Barbara Scarvell was not amused. She was wearing an unbecoming gown of yellow muslin which bared quite a sufficiency of her chest which was not a pretty sight, being somewhat pale and freckly.

'Really, Suzanna!' Helen said aloud.

One of Adrian's friends was most attentive. He was different from others in ways I cannot find the words for. Although an officer, he is on the naval staff in London where he works on matters of great secrecy or so he told me. I have no reason to disbelieve him.

Tired by the strain of the evening and the difficulty of deciphering the irregular handwriting, Helen set the book down beside the bed and switched off the light. As she began to drift off to sleep, she thought she sensed the rustle of fabric and a faint smell of Lily of the Valley as a woman's voice whispered in her ear.

'Take it to him. He'll know.'

FOURTEEN

Helen stood in her bedroom looking down at the little green book in her hand. She should show it to Paul but it meant braving the library and the gruesome tableau of the night before still burned fresh in her memory. The woman who haunted this room no longer scared her, and in the morning sun, she dismissed her notion of changing rooms. She had a strong sense that a message had been sent to her and it was now her responsibility to resolve it. The answer lay in the diary and Paul Morrow with his background in classics was the person to decipher the code.

Thrusting the book into her cardigan pocket, Helen went down to the kitchen and made tea, setting a tray for two. She carried the tray up through the house to the library but, on seeing Paul standing by the table apparently lost in thought, she pulled back before entering the room.

As she watched, he ran his fingers along the uneven, burnished oak surface and looked at his fingertips as if he expected to see dust—or blood. Her heart skipped a beat. Paul *had* seen what she had experienced. He must have.

Shaking his head, he crossed to the fireplace, crouched down, and lit a match to the coals. The flame flickered and then died.

He swore and turned his head to look at one of the wing chairs saying aloud, 'You've had your fun. At least let me light this bloody fire.'

Making a show of rattling the tray in her hands, Helen pushed open the door and walked into the room.

'Who are you talking to?'

At the sound of her voice, Paul started and turned awkwardly. Grimacing in pain, he fell back into the wing chair, rubbing his leg. He glanced up at her and the wariness in his eyes dared her not to make some solicitous remark. She'd done some work with the Red Cross in Melbourne in the years after the war and knew the last thing he wanted or needed was her pity.

'You seem determined to damage that leg again,' she remarked, setting the tea tray down on the table.

He gave her a wry smile. 'It's just a reminder I'm not unbreakable. If Evelyn and the doctors had their way, I would be tucked up in a bath chair with a rug over my knees.'

Helen considered that picture. Charlie would have been thirty in July. Paul could only be thirty-two years old and he had overcome what could have been crippling injuries to another man. The Morrows were a stubborn lot, she thought.

'Where's Alice this morning?' Paul asked.

Helen crouched to light the fire, which caught and burned at the first strike of the match. 'She's gone to play with Lily at the vicarage. This weather is foul. I can't believe how cold it is. People warned me about English summers.'

She sat down at the table and studied the first page of Paul's notes for a moment before beginning to type. Paul sat down across from her, pushed his sleeves up, and contemplated one of the tablets that lay in several pieces in its box before he started scribbling notes in a notebook.

The regular tapping of the typewriter provided a comforting sound in the otherwise quiet room and they worked in companionable silence for an hour until the growl of the engine of the old car broke the peace of the room.

Paul looked across at Helen. 'Evelyn's home.'

Helen sat back from the typewriter as Evelyn entered the library, pulling off her gloves.

'Helen, what on earth are you doing?' she exclaimed with a disapproving glance at the Remington.

'Helen has volunteered to help me with typing my report,' Paul answered before Helen could speak.

'Oh? How fortunate that you can manage one of those machines.' Evelyn waved at the typewriter with a look of distaste.

'How was London?' Helen asked, deflecting her mother-in-law away from what she feared Evelyn saw as another black mark against her.

'Marvellous,' Evelyn said. 'We took in a show and did a little shopping. I found a lovely dress for Alice.'

'That's very kind,' Helen said.

'And your dear sister?' Paul enquired.

A slight flush stained Evelyn's cheeks. 'Better for my company,' she said. 'Now I must get changed. I have letters to write.'

'Before you go,' Helen said, rising to her feet. 'I wondered if you could tell me about Suzanna Morrow?'

Evelyn stopped with her hand on the door to the stairs and turned. 'Suzanna? The scandalous Suzanna?' She indicated the two regency-era portraits on the wall. 'That's her portrait and, of course, her husband, Robert Morrow.'

Even as Helen turned to look at the now familiar likenesses, a cold breath blew lightly on the back of her neck and the whispering started. Her fingers closed on the slender volume hidden in the pocket of her cardigan

'Why was she called scandalous Suzanna?' Helen asked

'Ran off with another man, they say,' Evelyn said. 'Oh dear, it was quite a family disgrace. Her name was not to be mentioned in the hearing of my parents-in-law. Her husband, Robert,' Evelyn cocked her head and looked at the painting of Robert, 'was badly wounded in the Peninsula campaign. He never recovered from Suzanna's desertion and died a few years later. If you're really interested, there is a brief family history in here somewhere.' Evelyn shivered. 'I don't know why you work in here, Paul, it's always cold. You really should light a fire.'

Helen glanced at the fire that had been burning cheerfully only a few minutes previously. Now the coals showed no glimmer of ember.

With an impatient sigh, Evelyn crossed to the bookcase and scanned the shelves, pulling out a dusty leather-bound folio with the family crest on the cover. She carried it over to the table and ignored Paul's frown of disapproval as she moved several of his clay tablets to make room for it.

She opened the folio, spreading out a detailed family tree written in neat copper plate with the coat of arms carefully drawn and coloured in the right-hand corner.

Helen traced her finger over the family crest, a silver chevron cut across a turquoise shield with three black birds emblazoned on it.

'What does *Nec Cuplas Nec Metuas* mean?' she asked.

'Neither covet nor fear,' Paul replied.

'And the blackbirds?'

'Heraldic martlets,' Evelyn said with the faintest curl of her lip.

Helen refrained from showing any further ignorance by asking what sort of bird a martlet was and turned to the details of the formidable family tree. It began, as far as she could see, in the thirteenth century and ended with the birth of Evelyn's husband, George, and Paul's father, Edward.

Evelyn looked up at the portraits and then back to the family tree. 'Here they are, Robert married Suzanna Thompson in 1807.' She frowned. 'He died in 1814. Of course, there is no date of death noted for Suzanna. She was reputed to have fled to the colonies and had no further contact with the family. There's a brief history here as well.' Evelyn closed the family tree and flicked through the book.

She read aloud:

As the second Baronet's health began to fade, it was thought necessary to find a suitable bride for his eldest son, Robert. On leave from service in the 27th Regiment of Foot, serving in Spain, he was introduced and proposed to Suzanna Thompson. Lady Cecilia Morrow wrote to her sister, 'On first appearance Miss Thompson gives the impression of being a biddable girl of good breeding and well-versed in household skills but I detect in her a spirit of rebelliousness brought on no doubt, by the absurd notion of her father's that she should be, in his words, properly educated. Too much education does not become a woman. However, Robert seems enamoured of her and she of him and the wedding date is set.

The couple were permitted only a few weeks together before Robert returned to his regiment in Spain. Happily, in that time Suzanna conceived a child and their son, George, was born the following spring to much rejoicing in the family. Robert returned on leave at Christmas and this time the couple enjoyed a few months in each other's company before duty once more called Robert back to Spain. Their daughter Adele was born later that year.

Robert sustained a serious wound at the siege of Badajoz in April 1812 and was sent home to recuperate. Some months later, his wife, after nursing him through his illness, left the family home and was not seen or heard from again. It was generally believed that she had absconded with another man and that she and her paramour removed themselves from respectable society to some far-flung corner of the empire to start up life anew under assumed names and in the unhappy knowledge of the perfidy that they had committed. Her husband was inconsolable at her loss and some fourteen months after his wife's disappearance he died in a tragic shooting accident.

Helen held her breath. 'A tragic shooting accident?' she asked through stiff lips.

'I believe it was in this room,' Evelyn said, with obvious relish. 'Cleaning a gun. There are those who say he took his own life, but of course that would be too much of a disgrace and he would not have been buried in consecrated ground.'

The scene in the library came back to Helen with a frightening clarity. She saw the blood dripping off the table and the wide staring eyes of the man turned toward the door. She looked up at Robert's portrait, knowing now, without a shadow of a doubt, that the dead man had been Robert Morrow. She had seen, or been shown, his death at his own hand.

She glanced across at Paul, but he had turned away while Evelyn read the story and stood at the window with his back to them, lighting a cigarette.

Evelyn closed the folio and straightened. 'That's enough of the family scandal. Do you have any more questions, Helen?'

Helen, her eyes still on Paul's straight back, shook her head.

Evelyn smiled. 'I've treated myself to a new dress for the party at

Wellmore tonight. It will do us all good to get away from this dreary room. Will you be coming, Paul?'

Paul gave a non-committal grunt.

Evelyn considered her nephew and her lips compressed before she turned to Helen. 'Is there anything you need, Helen?'

'If it's all right with you, Lady Morrow, I will catch the bus into Birmingham this afternoon. I am in desperate need of some new stockings and I would love to see a hairdresser.'

'A hairdresser?' Evelyn looked perplexed. 'Whatever for?'

Helen tucked a lock of hair behind her ear. 'I thought I would do something a little different with my hair for the party.'

Evelyn sighed. 'I used to have the most wonderful French maid,' she said. 'Michelle could work miracles with my hair.'

Paul turned and walked to the door, opening it.

'If you'll excuse me, ladies, I have work to do. If you two want to discuss parties and hairstyles, please do so elsewhere.'

'Helen, if you want to catch Sam before he puts the car away you could ask him to drive you into town,' Evelyn said.

Helen glanced at Paul.

He waved a hand at the door. 'Go. Thank you for your help this morning.'

Helen felt the weight of the little book in her pocket. Suzanna's diary would have to wait.

FIFTEEN

In the late afternoon, Paul abandoned the library and adjourned to his own rooms. He sat at a table by the window, a pencil in his mouth and his right hand curled around a glass of whisky, looking at a sheet of paper on which he had scribbled some notes for his translation of *The Iliad*.

'I knocked but you didn't answer.'

At the sound of Helen's voice, Paul started, nearly knocking over the whisky. Helen stood with her hand on the door handle.

'Come in,' he said. 'Sorry, I was a bit preoccupied. When did you get back?'

'About half an hour ago. I brought the cigarettes you asked Sam to get,' she said.

'Thanks, leave them on that table.' He waved a hand in the direction of the small table. Helen set the packet down and crossed over to the window to join him.

'What are you working on?' she asked.

Paul set his glass down and removed the pencil from his mouth.

'Homer. It makes a diverting change from storehouse inventories.'

He looked up at her and for a moment, he wondered if this was the same woman he had seen in the library that morning. Her hair—Helen had cut her hair.

'Good grief, what have you done to yourself?'

'I had my hair cut. What do you think?'

'What do I think?' Paul stared at her bemused. It had been a long, long time since a woman had asked for his opinion on her appearance. A dangerous minefield.

He felt a brief twinge of regret as he remembered the night he had encountered Helen, the slight figure in a blue silk dressing gown with her long, honey-blonde hair cascading down her back. Trapped in a sliver of moonlight, she had looked like a goddess of old.

He brought himself up with a start.

'For whatever my opinion is worth, it suits you,' he said, hoping that was the right answer. It did give her face a sort of elfin charm. 'Toss me the cigarettes, will you?'

He saw a flash of disappointment in her eyes at his non-committal answer, but she threw him the packet and he caught it in his right hand with the practiced skill of a cricketer. To distract himself, he opened the pack, tapped out a cigarette, and offered it to her.

'Do you?' he asked.

She shook her head. 'I don't smoke. You wouldn't—' Helen still hovered by the door, '—you wouldn't reconsider coming tonight?'

Paul studied her face for a moment. The short hair made her grey eyes larger, her face more vulnerable. He thought of the gathering awaiting her at Wellmore. Letting her go alone would be like throwing a Christian to the lions.

He turned back to the table without answering and reached for the glass. As he looked up, he felt the familiar cold rush of air. *Not now*, he willed the spectre at the window.

He glanced at Helen who stood with her hand on the door catch, apparently transfixed. Their eyes met.

'You can see him' she cried. 'You know I'm not mad.'

As she spoke, the apparition faded.

Paul took a moment to gather his composure before answering. 'No,' he said at last. 'I don't think you're mad. I never thought you were mad.'

He picked up the cigarette from the ashtray and turned to look at her. He gestured at the window as if the spectre still stood there.

'Allow me to introduce you to...'

'Robert Morrow,' she said. 'When I saw his portrait this morning I knew who he was. How long have you been seeing him?'

Paul shook his head. 'He has been my almost constant companion since the day I came back to Holdston after the war.'

He'd learned to live with his ancestor's shadow just as he'd learned to live with his injuries.

'Does Evelyn know you see him?'

He stared at her and gave a snort of derisive laughter. 'Do you think I'm going to tell Evelyn I'm seeing ghosts? She already thinks I'm—' he frowned as he grappled for the right word, '—unstable. I know she tells her friends in hushed tones that she thinks I suffer from shell shock.' His mouth tightened at the bitter words and he looked away.

'I know men with shell shock,' Helen said. 'You're nothing like them.'

He turned back to look at her, surprised at the vehemence in her voice.

'Thank you,' he acknowledged, 'but it would seem that I still see things that aren't there. That could be viewed a number of different ways, not least of which is my tainted Irish blood.'

'But they are there,' Helen insisted. 'The other night. In the library. You saw him?'

Paul picked up his glass of whisky. Slowly he looked up at her.

'Yes,' he admitted with a quirk of his lips. 'That was a charming little scene.'

'I think ... I think Suzanna is here too.'

That revelation surprised him. 'Suzanna?'

'I haven't seen her but I know when she's around. She has a scent, like Lily of the Valley. It's as if she has been trying to attract my attention, moving things and whispering.' Helen frowned. 'She doesn't frighten me, except for that night outside Evelyn's door. She grabbed my hand. There was real viciousness in that grasp.'

'Helen, they're shadows of the past. Don't try and read anything into their appearances.'

Helen gave a self-conscious laugh. 'Sarah Pollard said I should acknowledge them.'

'You can try striking up conversations if you wish but don't expect me to.'

'But you do. I heard you this morning when I came into the library. You were talking to someone. Was it Robert?'

'I don't make it my habit to hold conversations with my ancestors,' Paul said.

'There's another thing,' she continued. 'I found Suzanna's journal.'

She pulled a small green, leather book from her cardigan pocket. 'It was hidden in a book in my bedroom.'

He held out his hand and she handed him the book.

'Take a seat, Helen, and let's see what Suzanna has to say.'

They sat down and Paul turned the book over in his hands before opening it and reading the dedication on the front flyleaf.

'No doubt it belonged to Suzanna,' he said, looking up at her. 'How much have you read?'

'I've only read halfway through the second entry.'

He handed it back to her, 'Then read on.'

Helen reread the part she had already read and continued the second entry.

As it turned out he, I shall call him 'S', was my partner for supper and we talked about books and poetry. Oh how I miss my books. The library here at Holdston is deadly dull. S was enchanted to discover that I am proficient in the classics and we enjoyed a witty riposte in Latin that drew admiring applause from our audience, only a few of whom would have had the slightest idea what we talked about. Lady Morrow told me off in the coach on our return to Holdston. She said I had been acting in a forward manner and it was not considered ladylike to show off like that. I often wish Robert was more enamoured of learning and less of horses. Still, Robert has other virtues. I have so many things to tell Robert. I must put aside this book and recount last evening for him. Maybe I should be a bit more circumspect about S and my dancing. Being so far away Robert may not understand...

'Damned right, he wouldn't,' Paul growled. 'Go on.'
Helen raised an eyebrow and smiled at him.

Adrian came to call this morning. While it is always such a treat to see Adrian, the delight was compounded by the company of S. Lady Morrow being indisposed with a headache, it fell to me to entertain the two gentlemen. Adrian complained that we were the dullest dogs he had ever kept company and he proved it by falling asleep. He later excused his rudeness by saying he still tired easily from his wound. S joins me as a great admirer of Henry Fielding and Dr. Johnson and the new poets Byron and Shelley. I showed him the library, which he agreed, while impressive, is not of any particular interest. I must say he is a fine looking man, a few years older than Robert and not as tall but with a good bearing. He would look fetching in a military uniform. I must close, I can hear Lady Morrow's bell which means her headache must be better and she wishes to see the children.

Helen raised her head. 'The next couple of entries are about household matters, mainly concerning the children.'
'Skip those,' Paul said.
Helen flicked through the next few pages and began to read.

January 19, 1812. I received a letter and a package in the mail this morning. When I opened it, I found it was a small volume of poems by Lord Byron. Lady Morrow was most anxious to know who would have sent me such a pretty thing. You can imagine my horror when I opened the letter to find it was from S. He wrote that he had thought of me continuously since his return to London and when he had seen these poems, he felt compelled to send them to me. He was fully aware of my situation but hoped I would look favourably on the gift as that of a friend. Lady Morrow was most insistent I read the letter so I was forced into an untruth and said it was from my brother. I thank God that I have always been blessed with a quick wit and so was able to invent a missive that would have purported to come from my brother. Lady Morrow seemed quite satisfied with my brother's accounting of the doings of his parish and I was able to escape to my bedchamber where I read S's letter until I had it committed to memory. Then I burned it and concealed the book behind the others on my shelf. Oh, I am in torment. How could a simple piece of paper bring me so much happiness and so much fear? I long to meet with S again and yet I dare not lest I reveal feelings quite inappropriate to my station in life. I am a married woman, the mother of two wonderful children. What am I to do? No, I know what is right. I shall write at once to him and thank him for his gift and request that he communicate no further with me.

January 24, 1812. A boy from Wellmore delivered a message to me this morning. S bade me meet him in the woods behind the church. I was in a foment of indecision. My head told me I should not go but return a proper message to him repeating what I had told him in my letter but my heart bade me go and tell him to his face. My heart has ever been my mistress and I followed its dictates. He was there as he said he would be. When I saw him, I knew I could not send him away. All my well-rehearsed lines vanished from my lips and I smiled in welcome. Oh, I am lost, lost. What am I to do? Who do I turn to? There is no one, save this book on which to unload my torment. If it were to be found I shall be truly undone so I must devise a way to keep its contents from prying eyes.

Helen stopped reading and looked up at Paul. 'I can't read any more. It looks like she's writing in ancient Greek.' She passed the book over to him. 'I thought you might be able to help with the translation?'

Paul scanned the page and frowned. 'It's certainly Greek but she is using some sort of code of her own devising. I can't read it as it's written.'

'How would a woman of that time know ancient Greek?'

'You heard the family history. My great-grandmother was a woman ahead of her time, intelligent and educated.' He tapped the book. 'Leave it with me. I'm sure I can decipher it but it may take a little while. Now what time are you expected at Wellmore House tonight?' he asked.

'Seven-thirty.'

Paul glanced at his watch. 'You had better get a move on.'

Helen hesitated. 'Do you suppose I will be all right?'

'You're not Cinderella, Helen. You're Charlie Morrow's widow. Just be yourself. Anyway, Tony's a gentleman. He'll take care of you.'

Tony had every intention of taking very good care of her. Paul had recognised the look in his friend's eyes.

Helen smiled in response and Paul remembered Charlie's words in a letter his cousin had written, like a brush stroke across his memory.

'I have asked her to marry me and she has consented. I can't imagine ever finding a girl in England who could fill my heart the way Helen does when she smiles.'

The door closed behind Helen, and Paul picked up his whisky glass. In the distance, he heard a dog barking. He rose to his feet and took Robert Morrow's place at the window. Below him, Alice played with a black and white cocker spaniel.

SIXTEEN

'You look lovely, Mummy,' Alice said wistfully.

She lay on her stomach on Helen's bed, her head propped up in her hands, as she watched her mother dress for the supper party at Wellmore.

Helen peered at her reflection in the inadequate mirror. The couturier in Melbourne had assured her that this dress was the latest fashion. She twisted to have a better look at the plain, straight, midnight blue satin dress, the skirt gathered and fastened at her hip with a gold clasp, and wondered if the latest fashion in Melbourne would still be fashionable in London.

'I'll just have to do. Now, let's see if Grandmama is ready.'

Evelyn was already waiting for them in the hall. Dressed in a black velvet evening dress of the latest style, her iron-grey hair was dressed loosely at the nape of her neck and held in place with diamond clips. For the first time, Helen saw a glimpse of the youthful beauty last seen in the stiff wedding photographs Evelyn had scattered around the house.

'Very nice, Helen,' Evelyn said as Helen descended the stairs toward her. At the compliment, Helen felt the colour rising in her cheeks.

'I wish I was coming,' Alice said from her perch halfway up the staircase.

Both women turned to look up at the child.

'Your time will come, Alice,' her grandmother said, her expression changing to one of surprise. 'Paul!'

'Going without me?'

Alice swivelled to look up at the sound of the uneven tread on the steps above her. 'Hello, Uncle Paul.'

'Hello, Alice. Don't wait up for us.' Paul ruffled the child's hair as he passed her.

'Sarah's taking her to the vicarage to stay the night,' Helen said.

'I didn't think you were coming?' Evelyn straightened her already perfect gloves. as Paul reached the bottom of the steps.

'Tony twisted my arm,' he said. 'I'm afraid the suit needs taking in but I think I pass muster otherwise.'

Despite his assertion that the suit needed taking in, the jacket sat well across his broad shoulders. The stiff evening collar was still undone, the bow tie hanging loosely around his neck.

The tall, elegant man in the dinner suit bore little resemblance to the slightly shabby archaeologist Helen had come to know over the last few days. The formality of his evening wear had transformed plain Paul Morrow into Sir Paul Morrow Baronet and winner of the Military Cross.

'You look fine,' Evelyn said. 'Let me do the tie for you.'

He bent toward his aunt and with practiced fingers, Evelyn buttoned his collar and executed the complicated knot.

Paul straightened and smiled at the two women.

'You both look charming,' he said.

'And you scrub up well,' Helen replied with a smile.

'I 'scrub up well' do I?' Paul said in passing mimicry of her Australian accent. 'Glad to hear it.' Paul looked from one to the other. 'Let's get this tedious function over with.'

———

From the number of motor vehicles parked on the front lawns of Wellmore, it appeared to be a sizeable party, hardly the simple gathering of a few close friends Lady Hartfield had described.

Evelyn took Paul's arm and he turned to Helen proffering his other arm.

'Helen?'

She slipped her hand into the crook of his elbow, feeling the warmth of his body through the suit and glad of the reassurance of his presence as they crossed the marble hall to be shown through to the reception rooms.

'Sir Paul Morrow, Lady Morrow, and Mrs. Charles Morrow,' A footman announced them in a solemn voice.

Lady Hartfield came forward to meet them.

'Evelyn, darling.' The two women kissed and their hostess turned to Paul. She took his hand. 'Paul. I'm so delighted you could come. You're looking well. Egypt must suit you.'

'Mesopotamia,' Paul said with a slight tightening of his lips.

'Were you there when that Carter person found that tomb?' Lady Hartfield continued.

'No,' Paul said with barely contained irritation. 'That was in Egypt. I've been in Mesopotamia.'

'All the same to me.' Lady Hartfield laughed. 'And Mrs. Morrow, looking charming. That's a courageous decision you've made.' She indicated Helen's hair. 'Not many girls can get away with it. The Porters are here and Paul, I just know everyone will be simply dying to see you and hear all about your adventures in the desert. Mrs. Morrow, the young people are in the withdrawing room, dear.'

Lady Hartfield took Evelyn by one arm and Paul by the other, leaving Helen standing by the door with the eyes of a dozen strange men and women watching her. As she shifted uncomfortably, not quite knowing what to do, they turned back to their groups, talking in low voices.

'Oh God, has Mother left you stranded here?' Tony hurried across the room toward her. 'Mrs. Morrow, may I say how splendid you look tonight.'

Helen's spirits lifted at the sight of Tony's pleasant, smiling face. At least one person seemed genuinely pleased to see her.

'Thank you, Tony.'

'What did you do to persuade Paul to come tonight?'

Helen shook her head. 'Nothing to do with me. I thought you twisted his arm?'

'I had a small word but I didn't think he'd come. You know, the doctors kept saying he needed peace and quiet. Quite frankly, I think that's the last thing he needs. Diversion and noise, in my opinion, are to be infinitely preferred.'

He steered her into a room where a dozen young women dressed in expensive, elaborate gowns, engaged in animated conversation with each other or equally well-dressed young men, some of Tony's age and some a little younger. In this bright gathering, Helen felt dowdy and old-fashioned. The conversation dropped away as she entered the room and the immaculately coiffured heads turned to look at her.

A dark-haired woman of Helen's age holding a cigarette in a short holder came up to them.

'You must be Helen,' she said, holding out her gloved hand, 'I'm Angela Lambton, Tony's sister.'

Helen shook the proffered hand.

'I'm pleased to meet you.'

'Ange, Paul's here,' Tony said. 'Be a dear, and go and rescue him from Mother or we will have him beating a retreat to Holdston.'

'Paul?' Angela glanced into the next room. 'Oh God, she's got him cornered with those ghastly Porters. I'll be right back.'

Helen watched over her shoulder as Angela sashayed into the main reception room, cutting a swathe through the older guests.

Tony laughed. 'Ange on a mission can't be resisted. Mrs. Morrow, come and meet the others. Champagne?'

She took a glass from a passing footman and Tony propelled her into a circle of his guests, his hand resting gently in the small of her back. He introduced her to a series of titled young people. The young women looked Helen up and down in much the same way as they would a horse they were considering purchasing. From the curl of their lips, they found her wanting. Helen decided, compared to their fine breeding pedigrees, she would be considered little more than a stock horse.

On the other hand, the gentlemen did not seem to have quite the same reservations and Helen found herself in the centre of a circle of young men who all appeared to have known Charlie and were keen to talk about him, reminiscing about the happier times of their shared youth. It was strange and disorienting to hear her husband talked about with such familiarity.

'I say is that Morrow?' one of the men drawled.

Her companions fell silent and turned to the door, where Angela and Paul stood. Angela had her hand tucked into Paul's arm. Both were tall and carried themselves with a natural elegance, enhanced by the good cut of their evening dress. With their dark hair and finely chiseled faces, they made a stunning couple, Helen thought with a twinge of envy. They were both born to this life; she would always be an outsider.

Angela relinquished Paul, took a glass of champagne and joined Helen. Taking her arm, she steered her over to a window seat.

'God, these parties of Mother's are such a bore. Tell me how did you get Paul to come?'

'I didn't. He appears to have come of his own volition.'

Angela gave her a skeptical glance before lighting another cigarette. 'Darling, I haven't seen Paul Morrow at a society event since before the war.' She blew out the smoke, watching the haze as it climbed to the ceiling. 'So you're the girl Charlie Morrow broke all these hearts for?' She gestured to the young women across the room

'Surely not? They're all too young.'

'It doesn't matter if it were these girls or the matrons in there, Charlie would have stolen their hearts the moment he stepped through the door.' Before Helen could reply, Angela continued, 'I can't think what Mother is thinking. Do you suppose for a moment Tony, or any of these men, want to marry vapid women like this?'

'What do you mean?'

'I was a VAD ambulance driver in the war.' She laughed. 'You look shocked. Can't imagine me out there in the mud and the filth? I know what these men went through. Not just Paul but the others, like Tony, who came through without an injury. Believe me, none of them came through untouched. When you've looked death in the face every day for four years, a man needs more than just a comfortable home with a well-bred wife. They might not know it, but they're looking for something different, something that will provide them with a bit more excitement.' She leaned in toward Helen. 'Look at these girls, Helen, they hate you.

You can see it in their eyes. You're exotic, a colonial. You've already snared one of their own. I think they're frightened of you.'

Helen shivered. 'What a dreadful thought. Should I leave?'

Angela's eyes widened. 'Leave, darling? Not for a minute. You're a breath of fresh air. You stay and charm the men and have a wonderful night. God knows, I fully intend to enjoy Father's best wine and have a marvellous time.' Her eyes moved to Paul who leaned against a wall, a glass of champagne in his hand, his head bent to one side, listening to the conversation around him.

As if aware of being observed, he looked up and his gaze met Angela's. A quick conspiratorial smile flashed across his face.

The dinner gong announced supper and Tony crossed the floor toward Helen, a dozen women watching his progress.

He crooked his elbow at her. 'Helen?'

'I think you should ask one of the other girls.'

'You're my guest, Helen, and this is my party. I'm damned if I'm going to be caught all night making polite conversation with a debutante whose only interest is dresses and parties. I want to know all about Australia and the place where you live. Tralee?'

'Terrala,' Helen replied with a laugh.

———

Across the room, Angela took Paul's arm. 'Are you taking me into supper?' she asked.

'Do I have a choice?' he enquired.

Angela smiled up at him. 'None. I want you all to myself for a few moments. I must say you look well, Paul,' she said as they walked into the dining room.

'Thank you,' he said. 'I am.'

'The dust of the desert must agree with you.'

'It is preferable to the cold and damp of an English winter.'

He held out her chair for her and they sat, passing the appropriate pleasantries with their neighbours before allowing the conversation to turn to themselves.

'Tony said you weren't coming,' Angela said. 'What made you change your mind?'

'I thought I'd better wave the Morrow flag. I didn't think Charlie would thank me if I left Helen to the vultures.'

'Oh, she seems to be managing,' Angela observed.

Paul glanced down the table. Every male within Helen's circle appeared to be watching her as she talked.

'You know, I think Tony is more than a little in love with her already?' Angela said.

Paul turned sharply to look at Angela. 'He hardly knows her.'

Angela shrugged. 'Don't you believe in love at first sight, Paul?'

Paul evaded the question. 'What does your mother think?'

'What do you suppose she thinks? Look at her face, Paul.'

Lady Hartfield, while giving every impression of paying animated attention to her neighbour, had her attention firmly fixed on Helen. If those eyes could have shot blue sparks, they would have done.

'I was right,' Paul said, 'They'll eat her alive.'

'There's nothing you can do, Paul. She's an adult. She'll manage and at the end of the day she'll go back to Australia and her coming will just have been a diversion in an otherwise dull world.'

Paul picked up his wine glass and looked at the contents, golden in the beautiful crystal and the candlelight.

'What about you, Ange?'

'Me?'

'I hear your paintings are selling well.'

Angela shrugged. 'I can't complain.'

'And your current lover?'

She gave him a sideways glance from underneath her long lashes. 'That would be telling.'

'Ah, so he's married?'

'Darling, it would be no fun if I told you.'

He leaned his head toward her. 'You and I have no secrets, remember, Ange?'

She put a long nailed finger to her lips. 'Yes, we do, Paul.'

———

Dinner was served at the longest table Helen had ever seen in her life. It easily accommodated the fifty guests. Lady Hartfield sat at one end and her husband, a bald man with a luxuriant moustache, sat at the other.

Helen glanced up the table and saw Angela Lambton's dark head bent close to Paul's in a close and private conversation. Paul smiled in response to something she said to him. The two had an air of familiarity that went deeper than mere long friendship. A strange sensation of envy, or maybe even jealousy tugged at Helen's heart. She had no right or claim to Paul Morrow. He and Angela had known each other since they were children, and of course, they had a whole shared life to which she did not belong.

Helen turned to look in the other direction, seeking out Evelyn who was seated at the far end near the Viscountess. Even as she watched, Evelyn's gaze turned to her nephew as if drawn by some magnet.

Helen turned her attention back to her immediate companions. A retired general had been seated on her right and after several abortive attempts at conversation, she concluded he was deaf. Abandoning the frustrating one-sided conversation, she turned back to Tony on her left.

'Do you know much about your ancestors?' she asked.

'This lot?' Tony waved a hand at the walls from which generations of Scarvells glowered down on the party. 'Why do you ask?'

'I've been amusing myself with some research into the Morrow family. In some of the family papers, I came across the mention of an Adrian Scarvell. He was an officer in the 6th Regiment of Foot during the Peninsula War.'

Tony shook his head. 'Can't say I've heard mention of him. That family group over there dates from about then.'

He indicated a massive family portrait that took up a whole wall. The Viscount, resplendent in an immaculate powdered wig, stood behind his wife and a brood of eight children and assorted dogs.

Tony contemplated the painting for a moment. 'It's quite likely he was a younger son. You know how it goes. The eldest son inherits, the second goes into the army and the third into the church.'

'What happened to four and five?'

'Oh, they went out to the colonies. If you really want to know about the family, I shall have to introduce you to Great Aunt Philomena. She's the family historian.'

'Where does she live?'

'In the village. Pa offered her rooms here but she prefers her cottage.'

Helen glanced down the table as Angela threw her head back, laughing at something Paul had said. Angela bent toward him, whispering in his ear. He shook his head, raised his wine glass, and smiled. He leaned toward her responding to his companion with an animation she had never seen in her short acquaintance with him.

Tony followed her gaze. 'What do you think of Angela?'

'She's not what I expected,' Helen said.

Tony laughed. 'Somewhat unconventional you mean? Strong-minded, Mother calls her, when she's feeling generous. Did Ange tell you she drove ambulances on the western front?'

Helen nodded. 'That must have taken considerable courage.'

'She can tell you the story, but her husband was killed at Pozières, so that was how she coped with it.'

'Her husband?' Helen asked, reaching for her wine glass.

'Harry Lambton.' He leaned closer to her. 'Frankly, I always thought Ange had her heart set on Paul but after he got engaged, she snared Harry. Poor blighter must have wondered what hit him.'

Helen's hand stayed frozen to the stem of the glass. 'Paul? Engaged?'

'You didn't know about that?'

Helen shook her head. 'Charlie never mentioned it.'

'It was one of those 'early in the war' romances. More on her side than his, I suspect. It was considered romantic to have a fiancé at the front but in 1917 the reality of a badly wounded fiancé who may have been crippled for life was too much for Fi and so she broke off the engagement and six months later married Freddy Adamson.'

'What was she like?'

'Fi?' Tony looked up and down the table and tapped his wine glass thoughtfully. 'Pretty but dull, just like this bunch. Paul was better off without her.'

'Did he mind?'

'Don't think he even noticed and by the time he did, he was past caring and she was married.'

'Does your sister live here?' Helen asked, returning her gaze to Angela.

'God no. She and Mother couldn't live in the same house together.'

Helen thought about the size of Wellmore House and smiled. They could live in different wings and never see each other.

'She has a flat in Chelsea,' Tony continued. 'Not sure that you would know, but she's a bit of an artist, is our Angela. Actually, she's bloody good. Did some pretty graphic stuff of the trenches and showed them in London. Critics raved and the authorities tried to shut it down. They only like the stuff the official war artists did, let alone anything done by a woman.'

Helen looked at Angela with new eyes.

'Have Angela and Paul, ever...' she began to ask, but at the quizzical look on Tony's face, picked up her napkin. 'Never mind.'

'Ange and Paul?' Tony picked up her train of thought and blinked in surprise as if the idea had never occurred to him. 'No. Not that I know of. They've known each other since we were all children. Just like Charlie.'

———

As dinner concluded, the Viscountess rose to her feet and the ladies left the dining room, adjourning to the reception room.

'Oh God,' Angela Lambton whispered in Helen's ear. 'Let's skip this, shall we? I can't bear it. I can see they're dying to gossip about you. Better you and I go for a stroll on the terrace and leave them to their tattling.'

She seized Helen's arm and propelled her out of the French windows onto the terrace. Beneath a high moon, the lovely gardens stretched away below the terrace toward the ornamental lake, which shimmered with the silver light.

'It's so beautiful,' Helen leaned on the wall and breathed in the fresh, cool air.

'Did a painting of this once. About the only one of my paintings Mother ever liked. It hangs in her bedroom.'

'Tony said you were an artist.'

'I dabble.' Angela lit another cigarette.

She took Helen's arm again and they promenaded the length of the terrace.

'He said your war paintings were held in high regard.'

'Did he say that?' Angela spoke without taking the cigarette out of her mouth. 'Never heard him say anything about my work before. How sweet of him.'

'He also told me about your husband.'

'Ah, I see you got the whole family history,' Angela said 'Yes, Harry, poor sod. I miss him. He was damned good fun.'

'There's been no one else?'

'Men? Oh God yes, hundreds but nothing serious. To be quite honest, when you've seen men like I have, they sort of lose their mystique. Fun to have around but I wouldn't want to have one on a permanent basis.'

'Not even Paul Morrow?' Helen ventured.

'Paul?' Angela stopped and removed the cigarette from her mouth. She crossed her arms, holding her cigarette between her fingers. 'Way too much history there. Did Tony tell you, I was the one who brought him in? Can't tell you what a fright it gave me when I got to the clearing station. You don't expect to have to bring in someone you know, let alone someone you...' She drew on her cigarette and blew out the smoke, watching it disperse into the night air.

Helen tried to read the other woman's face. Had she loved Paul Morrow or was it just the affection of a shared childhood?

'No, he didn't mention that,' she said.

Angela's mouth tightened. 'I really didn't think he would live. Terrible mess. I'd given up believing in God by then, but I prayed for Paul...' She looked down at the cigarette, before stubbing out the butt on the wall and taking Helen's arm. 'When that bloody Fiona ditched him, I could have clawed the little cat's eyes out but it was probably for the best. She'd only have made Paul miserable.' Angela screwed up her face at some unspoken sentiment. 'It's getting cold, let's go in. Good. I can hear the men, let's get some music going and have some fun.'

The gramophone had been wound by the time the two women stepped into the room. Helen found her hand grabbed and Tony whirled her away in a lively and not always rhythmic foxtrot. After Tony, came a succession of partners until she collapsed exhausted onto a sofa next to Paul Morrow.

'You seem to be having a good time,' he remarked.

She smiled without looking at him. 'Oh yes. I haven't danced so much in years.'

'You dance well. I do believe you made Scarvell look like a flash dancer.'

Helen gave him a sideways glance. 'Are you glad you came?'

He took a drag on the cigarette. 'I suppose so,' he said. 'It's been a diverting evening. Good to see some old faces.'

His eyes followed Angela who was dancing with an older man. Something about the way the man held her and the way their gazes locked indicated that more than mere acquaintance lay between them.

'Do you want to dance?' Helen blurted out and then at the look on his face, she flushed scarlet. 'Oh God, how forward. Sorry, Paul.'

To her surprise, he laughed. 'I don't dance, Helen.' He tapped his right leg.

'No, but I do,' Helen rose to her feet. 'I promise not to have any expectations.'

Before Paul could respond, she felt a hand on her arm and turned to see a fair-haired man standing at her elbow. He held out his hand, with a quick glance at Paul.

'Morrow, you don't mind if I steal your companion?'

'Helen, this is an old school friend of Charlie's, James Massey,' Paul said. 'Massey, the decision is entirely Mrs. Morrow's. I have no claim on her.'

Helen looked from one man to the other sensing a tension between them.

'Mrs. Morrow, you will break my heart if you don't dance with me,' Massey said, and taking her hand, he swept her into his arms for a two-step.

He proved to be the best partner of the evening. As he held her close, she smelled the tang of expensive cologne and his grip on her was sure and confident.

'Coming to the tennis tomorrow?' Massey asked.

Helen nodded. 'Yes, although it's been a while since I've played, so I'll probably be hopeless.'

'I hope you'll partner me at some point in the day. Ah, a fox trot. Up for another dance, Mrs. Morrow?'

Helen saw Paul rise to his feet and look at his watch. She excused herself from her partner and joined Paul.

'It's getting late, Helen, and I've got to get that report finished for Woolley by Monday. Do you mind if we decamp?'

She shook her head. 'Not at all.'

'What, not leaving?' Tony exclaimed as Paul bade him goodnight. 'What about Helen? You can't take her away?'

Paul looked down at Helen and shrugged. 'Helen's free to stay if she wishes.'

'No,' Helen said, shaking her head. 'If I'm going to play any sort of tennis tomorrow, I'd better go now. Thank you, Tony. It's been a lovely evening.' She held out her hand to shake his and to her surprise, he seized it and lifted it to his lips.

'Good night, Helen. What about you, Morrow? Joining us for tennis.'

Paul shook his head. 'My tennis, like my dancing days, are over. I'll leave it to Helen to uphold the Morrow pride.'

'Helen, I'll send the car over for you at nine,' Tony said. 'Goodnight.'

————

'Did you enjoy the evening?' Evelyn asked Helen as the car pulled away.

'I met some charming and interesting people,' Helen said.

In the dark, Paul could not see Helen's face but he sensed a slight tension in her voice and wondered if, despite being the centre of attention, she had really enjoyed herself.

'What about you, Paul?' Evelyn drew him into the conversation.

'Tony and Charlie's crowd, Evelyn,' he replied. 'I never had much in common with them, even at school.'

'I found Angela Lambton quite a surprising person,' Helen said.

'She is the despair of her mother,' Evelyn responded.

'I'd like to see some of her paintings,' Helen continued.

'Those ghastly war paintings?' Evelyn said. 'Should never have been shown. The girl thrives on controversy.'

'What was her husband like?'

Evelyn did not reply, so Paul answered. 'He was all right, but Harry had too much of an eye for other women and the drink. Now, of course, he rests in hallowed memory, like so many others, sanctified by their violent deaths. People forgive sins easily.'

'Really, Paul. That's no way to speak of the dead,' Evelyn chided from her corner of the car.

'She told me you were engaged,' Helen said.

Paul smiled, wondering if Helen could read his face in the dark of the car's interior. 'Oh, did she? Another disaster in the making. I'm just grateful to Fiona for having the sense to break it off. We'd have hated each other within a year.'

'Dreadful girl,' Evelyn said. 'Treated you shamefully.'

Paul shook his head. 'Too harsh, Evelyn. She was just like those girls at the party tonight. Pretty, spoiled, and entirely without a thought of their own. She belonged to a time before the war.'

Evelyn sniffed. 'According to you, Paul, everything belongs to a time before the war. Why can't we have that time back again?'

He looked across at his aunt and shook his head. Evelyn would forever pine the passing of the golden ages of Victoria and Edward.

Alone in his room, later that night, Paul poured himself a whisky and stood at the window, looking out over the dark countryside thinking for the first time in years about Angela and the night she had first come to his bed.

SEVENTEEN

The Wellmore Rolls Royce. carrying Helen and Evelyn to the tennis, had departed and Paul sat at the library table contemplating a small clay tablet with scant attention. His great-grandmother's journal peeked out from underneath a pile of papers he had brought down from his rooms, and he pulled it out, tapping the green leather cover with his pencil before opening it up to the first of the coded passages.

He glanced up at Suzanna's portrait and silently cursed her. She had not written the entry in ancient Greek but rather used the ancient alphabet in a simple substitution code. Simple it may be, but it would take a little effort to translate. Still, it made an interesting alternative to the finances of the Ur dig, he thought, as he pulled a blank piece of paper toward himself and picked up a pencil.

'What are you doing, Uncle Paul?'

He started at Alice's voice and looked up to see her standing in the doorway watching him. He smiled at her.

'Good morning to you too, Alice,' he observed. 'I didn't hear you knock?'

She ignored his dry tone and unbidden, walked up to the table and started to spin the globe.

'Mummy wouldn't take me with her,' she said in a sulky tone.

'It's not a day for children,' Paul said.

Alice pulled a pack of cards from her pocket and held them out to him.

'Do you want to play cards?' she asked.

He considered her for a moment. 'Why not? What do you play?'

'Snap?' she suggested and then added with a cheeky grin, 'Really fast.'

They cleared a space on the table and she knelt up on a chair and began dealing the cards.

'Tell me about your home.' Paul asked. 'Terrala, is that what it's called?'

A grin spread across Alice's face and she nodded. 'We live with Granny and Grandpa in the big house. We used to live in the cottage down by the dam but Uncle Henry lives there now.'

'Uncle Henry?'

'Mummy's brother. He went to the war and when he came back he married Aunty Violet and Mummy said it wasn't fair for us to live in the cottage since Daddy was dead and Uncle Henry and Aunty Violet needed it.'

'And who else lives at Terrala?'

'Well there's Uncle Ben and Uncle Frank and Uncle Fred but they were all too young to go the war. Uncle Fred's still at school. He wants to be a doctor.'

'Your mother doesn't have any sisters?'

Alice shook her head. 'She's the eldest. The others think she's bossy. Are we going to play?'

They played three games, all of which Paul lost. Halfway through the fourth game, which Paul was winning, a voice came from the door to the courtyard.

'That looks fun, can I play too?'

'Angela. Doesn't anyone in this house knock on doors?' Paul rose to his feet, as Angela Lambton, dressed in jodhpurs and riding boots strolled into the room. 'What brings you here?'

Angela looked around the room. 'Had to get out from under Mother's feet and that beastly tennis party. So I thought I'd ride over here and see what you were doing to amuse yourself on this glorious day. Hello,' she addressed Alice. 'I'm Angela, who are you?'

'Miss Alice Morrow,' Paul replied for Alice who seemed to have been struck dumb by Angela's entrance. 'Alice, this is Mrs. Lambton.'

'Charlie's daughter?' Angela raised an eyebrow at Paul. 'I'm pleased to meet you, Alice.'

'Mrs. Lambton is Mr. Scarvell's sister,' Paul explained.

The suspicion on Alice's face dissolved and she smiled.

'So, are you going to deal me in?' Angela said. 'I warn you, I'm a mean Snap player.'

Paul looked across at Alice and gave her a rueful smile. 'So is this young lady,' he said.

After two games, Sarah appeared at the door with a tray of tea and biscuits. 'Miss Alice, Lily's here to play with you.'

Alice jumped to her feet. 'Thank you for the games, Uncle Paul, Mrs. Lambton.'

'Have fun,' Angela said. 'Have you found the dollhouse?'

Alice stopped at the door. 'I love the dollhouse.'

Angela poured two cups of tea as the door shut behind Alice and Mrs. Pollard. 'Nice child. I like her mother too. I can see why Charlie fell head over heels for her.'

'He shouldn't have left her,' Paul said.

Angela sat back in one of the winged chairs by the hearth, one leg hooked over the arm. Paul offered her a cigarette, which she took, inhaling with a deep sigh.

'Mother has Tony bailed up with those ghastly women for the whole weekend,' she said. 'I don't know how he puts up with it.'

'*Noblesse oblige.*' Paul sat in the chair opposite Angela. 'Mercifully we don't have the money for Evelyn to even consider a similar tactic on me.'

'She wouldn't dare anyway,' Angela smiled. 'As for those poor cows Mother is trotting out for Tony, I don't think any of them compare to your Helen.'

'They don't,' Paul agreed. 'And what do you mean 'my Helen'?'

Angela gave him a sidelong glance and blew out a cloud of smoke. 'She's a Morrow, that makes her your responsibility doesn't it?'

Paul rubbed a hand across his eyes. 'I'm not sure she would agree with you.'

Angela regarded him thoughtfully for a moment. 'Mother doesn't approve of her.'

'That's hardly surprising. Your mother is the greatest snob I've ever met.' Paul changed the subject. 'How long are you staying down?'

'I have to be back in London by Tuesday,' she said. 'I've an exhibition opening on Wednesday night. All very respectable and saleable paintings, darling. I should do well.'

'One day a Scarvell will be worth as much as a Rembrandt,' Paul remarked.

Angela threw back her head and laughed. 'Only in my dreams.' She looked at her wristwatch. 'How about we ride over to Wellmore and join the luncheon party?'

Paul looked across at his table where the small, green journal sat on top of a pile of papers.

'All right,' he said. 'I've nothing here that won't wait.'

EIGHTEEN

Only England could turn on such a glorious summer day, Helen thought, as she sat in a deck chair, watching the match in progress. Out of deference to the Lady Scarvell's disapproving frown, she had accepted James Massey as her tennis partner before Tony had a chance to ask her. He had been partnered with one of the debutantes who had a high-pitched giggle that echoed around the tennis court every time her racquet connected with the ball.

Massey proved to be an elegant and competent player and they had advanced to the quarter-finals that would be played after lunch.

The last ball spun off the court to a smattering of applause, and Lady Hartfield stood and announced luncheon would be served by the lake.

Those who had not joined the tennis party were already gathered by the picnic tables, the women dressed in pretty summer dresses and wide-brimmed hats and the men in flannels and blazers providing contrast to the tennis players in their white uniforms.

'Join me, Helen,' Tony whispered. 'If I have to sit next to that giggling Gertie, I will be forced to slay her with my tennis racquet.'

Ignoring Lady Hartfield's moue of approbation, Helen took her place beside Tony.

'I say, we've got visitors,' Tony indicated two horses coming up the drive. 'It looks like Angela and Paul Morrow. Room for two more, Ma?'

Helen watched the riders, crouched low over the necks of their beautiful horses, hardly moving in the saddles as they raced each other toward the luncheon party. Angela Lambton drew her mount to a halt just a nose in front of Paul and slipped down from the saddle. Breathless and flushed from the hard ride, they tethered the horses and strolled toward the party.

'How's the tennis?' Angela enquired.

Tony clapped Helen on the shoulder. 'I'm predicting Mrs. Morrow here will take the prize this afternoon. Are you joining us for lunch?'

Paul cast an eye over the assembled party. 'Thank you for the invitation but I must be getting back. I just came over for the ride. Good afternoon, all.'

Paul turned and Helen watched him walk back toward Hector, measuring the ground in a long easy pace, his limp barely discernible to those who did not know him.

'You're an admirable partner, Mrs. Morrow.'

Helen turned to James Massey who took the other chair next to her.

'I've played a bit of tennis,' Helen said. 'We have our own court at Terrala.'

The man's mouth quirked. 'Terrala? What a peculiar name. Is it a large estate?'

'Twenty thousand acres,' Helen said and watched the man's face as he comprehended the size of the property. She changed the subject. 'Were you a particular friend of my husband's?' she asked. Leaving the words *Strange, he never mentioned you* unspoken.

'I went to school with both the Morrows and Scarvell of course,' Massey replied. 'Good chap your husband, but then we lost a lot of good chaps in the war.'

'Are you local?'

'I have a little place in Hampshire.' Massey named the estate, in such a nonchalant manner that Helen suspected she should be impressed.

They made desultory conversation about the weather and the morning's tennis and after lunch the party dispersed in groups to 'allow lunch to settle' before the tournament recommenced. Helen took advantage of

Tony's momentary distraction and slipped away by herself to find a quiet part of the lake to sit by herself and absorb her surroundings.

If the designer of the garden had envisaged how his design would look in two hundred years, then he had been visionary. Statuary of Greek gods and little temples could be glimpsed through the wooded glades, which edged the lake. A picture of peace and tranquility, far removed from the cares of the working classes.

Helen followed a well-trodden path to a boat shed. The old building appeared abandoned, the green paint faded and peeling from its wooden boards. When she glimpsed inside she saw it still contained a rowing boat and a flat-bottomed punt. She entered the building, carefully picking her way along the staging until she reached the end and stood looking out over the peaceful lake.

From the path behind the boathouse, she heard voices and recognising James Massey's voice, drew back inside out of sight. Peeping around the corner, Helen saw Massey and a party of five including a couple of the young women walking along the bank of the lake. She could not leave the boathouse now without being seen and having no particular wish to spend any more time in James Massey's company, she leaned against the wall to wait until they moved on. The tournament would start again in ten minutes so the wait wouldn't be long.

'I'll say one thing for the Morrow woman, she's a damn good tennis player,' Massey said, his voice carrying clearly into the boathouse. Helen stifled a gasp. Her mother would be appalled. *'Eavesdroppers hear no good of themselves,'* was one of her mother's favourite adages.

'Of course, there's only one reason Morrow married her,' Massey continued.

'What's that?' one of the girls asked.

'In the family way,' Massey continued without lowering his voice. 'I've heard Charlie Morrow couldn't get out of the country fast enough. Damned cheek on her part to come over here and play at being lady of the manor.'

The others laughed and Helen balled her hands, appalled at the cruel supposition. She felt sick.

'She's setting her cap for Paul Morrow now if I'm any judge,' another girl said.

'Paul Morrow? Have you seen how she's flirting with Tony Scarvell,' the first girl said. 'Outrageous.'

'You know there were stories about Morrow,' Massey said and Helen heard a plop as if he had flicked a stone into the lake. Two startled ducks rose into the air with a flutter of water and indignant honks.

'What stories?' the girl asked.

'Just some rumours about how Charlie Morrow really died.' Massey's voice remained neutral.

'Now steady on, Massey,' the second man said. 'It doesn't do to spread gossip.'

'They say,' Massey ignored the last speaker and launched into full flight, 'and I've had this story from someone who was close to the trenches, that Charlie Morrow didn't die at the hands of the Germans.'

'Oh, do tell?' the second girl egged him on.

'What better way to secure your inheritance than popping off your cousin under cover of an attack.'

Appalled, Helen pressed her eye to a gap in the rotting boards. Massey's party sat on the grass by the lake, their tennis racquets lying beside them.

'That's enough, Massey.' One of the men, Helen had been introduced to as John Albright, jumped to his feet, glaring down at Massey. 'Paul Morrow's a friend of mine. There's no truth to those stories whatsoever.'

Massey raised his hands. 'And how do you know, were you there? I'm just repeating what I heard, Albright.'

'From what I know of the affair,' Albright said in a stiff, cold voice, 'which is a damn sight more than a staff *wallah* such as yourself, Massey, Charlie Morrow was done for when Paul pulled him out of the German trench. I'll not hear any more slurs on his good name. Time we were getting back. Are you coming, Sissy?'

'Now then Albright, no need to take on,' Massey said, rising to his feet in a languid movement. 'I was just telling you what I heard. I suppose I'd better find the girl. If she plays as well as she did this morning, the trophy's in the bag and if I play my cards right she will be too. These Australian girls are easy. Anyone up for a wager I bed her before the weekend's over?'

Everyone except Albright laughed.

'You're a damned cad, Massey,' Albright's tone was heavy with disgust.

Their voices began to fade as they walked away. Helen crouched down on the dusty slats, her hand over her mouth as she attempted to stifle the sob that rose in her throat.

She had been married three months before Alice had been conceived. Did they really think Charlie had married her for that reason? Did they only see her as a jumped-up colonial gold digger, hell-bent on obtaining the title Charlie's death had denied her?

And as for what they had said about Paul. Did that explain why he hated these gatherings? The rumours he could not deny, growing faster than a game of Chinese whispers?

A sudden desperate urge to go home overcame Helen; home to Terrala. Why did she think she could just come over to England and play at being the widow of a man it seemed she had hardly known? Of course, people would talk.

Splashing water from the lake on her face, Helen rose to her feet, took a deep breath, dried her eyes, and blew her nose on her handkerchief. She had to go back and face them, knowing what they thought of her.

'I am a Morrow. I'm not a coward.' The words said aloud gave her a measure of courage.

She heard Tony calling her name. Stuffing her handkerchief into her pocket she hurried out of the boathouse and met him on the path.

'There you are!' he said, a grin breaking across his face. 'I was about to send out a search party. I say, are you all right?'

The look of genuine concern on his face almost sent her off into tears again. 'Sorry, Tony. I've got the most awful headache. I think I should go home now.'

Tony tucked her hand into the crook of his arm. 'Of course, old thing. I'll walk you up to the house and have the car sent around. I'll send Lady M. home later.'

His kindness was more than she could bear. Taking a deep breath she fought back the rising emotion. She wouldn't give any of the cats the satisfaction of seeing her in tears. Making her apologies first to Lady

Hartfield she sought out the odious James Massey. He did not look pleased as his plans for both the tennis trophy and bedding her disappeared. He disgusted her and she hoped their paths would not cross again.

'I hope you had a nice day,' Tony said, handing her into the car.

'It was lovely,' Helen lied. 'Thank you for the invitation.'

'My pleasure,' Tony beamed.

Once the car had rounded the bend away from the house, Helen sank back against the leather seats and let the silent tears roll down her face.

NINETEEN

Paul dismounted and led Hector into the stable courtyard. After leaving Wellmore, he had visited one of the Holdston tenants and spent two long and frustrating hours discussing the work that needed to be done on the farm.

The conversation with the farmer still occupied his thoughts as he settled Hector into his stall and began to unsaddle him. As he hauled the sweaty saddle and cloth off the horse's back, an unfamiliar sound in the quiet stable made him pause. Four years of pounding shells had dulled his hearing and for a moment, he thought he had imagined it.

Picking up the brush to give the horse a quick rubdown before returning to the house, he paused again as he heard stifled weeping. He set the brush down and walked down the line of stalls, now mostly empty.

A flash of white in Minter's stall caught his eye and he leaned over the gate.

'Helen?'

The woman sat huddled in a corner of the stall, her knees drawn up to her chin and her arms wrapped around her legs. She raised her head and he could see the tracks of tears on her cheeks

'I'm all right. Just leave me alone,' she said in a thick voice.

He lifted the latch and walked into the stall and sat down next to her.

'Please, Paul. Leave me.' She dabbed ineffectually at her eyes with a sodden handkerchief.

'No. Not until you tell me what's wrong.' He pulled out his own large, clean handkerchief.

Helen took it and blew her nose. 'Nothing,' she mumbled into the handkerchief.

Paul sighed. A woman like Helen did not strike him as the sort to dissolve into tears at the slightest provocation, let alone such obvious misery. Something had happened at the tennis party.

'When I saw you at lunchtime you were winning a tennis tournament, happy and smiling,' he said. 'What happened at Wellmore? Did the old cats get their claws into you?'

'I don't belong here, Paul,' she replied with a crooked smile

'Hmm. Do you mean you don't belong *here* or you don't belong at Wellmore?'

She shook her head. 'Just a bad case of homesickness.'

He didn't push her. If she wanted to tell him what had happened at Wellmore she would in her own time.

'Well, for what it's worth, Helen, I'm glad you came to Holdston.'

He pushed himself upright and held out his hand to help her to her feet.

Helen looked down at the once white tennis dress and gave a rueful laugh. 'Oh dear, look at what I've done to myself. I can't let Alice see me like this.'

Paul couldn't help but smile. No woman of his acquaintance ever looked lovely after tears and Helen with her puffy eyes, blotchy face and crumpled, dirty tennis dress was no exception.

He had never wanted to kiss a woman so much in his life.

The sudden thought caught him by surprise and he took a step back and made a pretence of reaching for the gate to the stall.

'Sam and Sarah are off duty; Alice is at the vicarage and Evelyn's still at Wellmore. There's just us, so how about I make a pot of tea and I'll be in the library if you feel like some company.'

She nodded. 'I think company would be good.'

———

After she had washed and changed, Helen studied her wan face in the mirror. She was embarrassed that Paul had found her in the stables. Being thought of as weak mortified her. She should not have allowed James Massey's cruel words to affect her the way they did.

Her mother had been right about eavesdroppers, but it hadn't just been Massey's spiteful words about her. The allegation against Paul hurt. That sort of gossip could prove to be malicious and dangerous.

Taking a deep breath, she picked up the *Woman's Weekly* magazine she had picked up in Birmingham the previous day and ventured down to the library. A note had been pinned to the door.

'*Bring a hat. We will take tea in the garden.*'

The sound of an operatic aria sung by a tenor rose to meet her as she crossed the garden bridge over the moat. Sarah had told her before the war, there had been two full-time gardeners and two labourers. Now one boy from the village maintained the once lovely gardens.

Helen followed the music down the weedy gravel paths and overgrown rose beds.

'How wonderful. Thank you,' she said when she found the source of the music, a wind-up gramophone. In the time she had taken to restore herself to normality, Paul had set up a rough picnic in an old pergola at the bottom of the garden and now lounged on a folding deckchair of dubious age with his feet crossed at the ankles and a straw hat over his face.

'It was too beautiful to spend the afternoon indoors,' he said removing his hat and sitting up. 'I think we both deserve an hour off. There's tea in the flask and I found some cake in the pantry. Help yourself.'

Helen poured milky tea from the flask into a battered, enamel mug and picked up an inelegant hunk of cake from the chipped enamel plate. She smiled. Paul's idea of tea in the garden, while practical, lacked finesse.

'Where did you find the gramophone?'

'It was Charlie's so I suppose strictly speaking it's yours now. Charlie's taste, as I'm sure you know, ran more to Gilbert and Sullivan. On the other hand, Edmond Clement is my choice.' Paul leaned back in the deckchair and closed his eyes. He held up his hand. 'Just listen to this. His rendition of the 'Dream Aria' from Massenet's *Manon* is sublime.'

Helen sat down gingerly in the other deck chair, quite sure the aged fabric would give under her weight but it held. Closing her eyes, the music drifted over her.

'There you are.' Evelyn's voice jerked them both out of reverie as she strode across the lawn toward them.

'Good afternoon, Evelyn. Have you had a pleasant day?' Paul rose to his feet as she reached them.

Evelyn ignored him, fixing her eyes on Helen. 'I thought you had a headache. Instead, I find you lounging around the garden without a care in the world. How dare you walk out on Lady Hartfield this afternoon, leaving your tennis partner completely in the lurch.'

Helen's stomach churned at the ferocity of her mother-in-law's anger.

'I genuinely wasn't feeling well,' she said. 'I made my apologies to Lady Hartfield.'

'Helen, I don't think you understand your position at all. This is extremely difficult for me to say. I am very fond of you and you are Charlie's widow, but you have a certain informality in your manner that is easily misinterpreted.'

'Evelyn.' Paul growled a warning but Evelyn was in full flight now. In the background the gramophone ground to a crackling halt.

'What do you mean?' Helen bristled.

'To speak frankly,' Evelyn continued, 'you have an unfortunate way of leading men on.'

'What men?' Helen felt the heat rushing to her cheeks.

'Tony Scarvell for instance. You flirted outrageously with him last night and today. Everyone noticed.'

'I wasn't flirting!' Helen protested, mortified as tears of shame pricked her eyes. 'I don't have designs on Tony Scarvell, or any man for that matter. He is just a friend.'

'And James Massey was furious to be left in the lurch like that. Scandalous behaviour, Helen.'

'James Massey...' Helen began and could not continue. James

Massey's anger had been directed at his failure to seduce her and win whatever wager he had laid.

'Massey is a fool,' Paul said. 'Evelyn, you've gone too far. You owe Helen an apology.'

'Lady Morrow.' A band of iron tightened around Helen's chest and she had to force the words through a dry mouth. 'I assure you I did not come to England in the hope of snaring a husband, and I am shocked you should think so little of me.'

'It's not me, Helen. It's others who talk.' Evelyn looked away.

'It's not like you to listen to gossip, let alone relay it in this way,' Paul interceded. 'You're no better than Maude and that bunch of cats who start the whispers in the first place.'

'It had to be said, Paul. I'm sorry, Helen, but I only have your best interests at heart. All I am asking is that you please be a little more circumspect in your behaviour.'

Stricken, Helen stared at her mother-in-law. The tears surfaced again, spilling down her cheeks.

'Excuse me,' she mumbled and walked away without looking at either Evelyn or Paul.

As the humiliating tears spilled over she broke into a run.

Evelyn called after her, but she was in no mood to face another barrage of vitriol. Upstairs in her bedroom, she curled up on the green silk bedspread, the unwelcome tears soaking the faded silk. The curtains billowed in the soft breeze and a sigh whispered through the room, every bit as heavy as her heart felt.

'Not now, Suzanna,' she whispered. 'Not now.'

TWENTY

Every Sunday, Lady Morrow attended the service at the church and had made it clear that Helen and Alice would join her. Sitting in the Morrow family pew within a few feet of the gleaming brass of the war memorial, Helen bowed her head to her hymnbook and tried not to look at Charlie's name.

Evelyn had made no mention of the previous day's exchange over breakfast but Helen, still bruised and hurt by the events at Wellmore and Evelyn's reaction, could barely bring herself to respond to Evelyn's attempt at conversation.

The familiar words of the Morning Prayer service provided the balm she sought and by the end of the service, she felt that she had a better perspective on what had occurred, how it had been perceived, and how circumspect she needed to be in the future.

Evelyn had a meeting about the church fete after the service and Helen took Alice's hand and walked along the ill-kept path toward the hall. As she put her hand on the rusty gate between the church and the Holdston lands she heard Angela Lambton call her name and looked up to see Angela and Paul walking down the path toward her.

'How was God this morning?' Angela said as they joined her at the gate. 'I hope you put in a good word for me. I need someone on my side. Where's Evelyn?'

'Church fete meeting,' Helen said. 'Angela, have you met my daughter, Alice?'

'Yes, I have. She owes me a rematch over Snap,' Angela smiled at Alice. Glancing up at Paul, she said, 'We've just been for a walk. This weather is glorious. Almost makes one like the countryside.' She looked up at the church. 'You know, I haven't been into this church for years. When I was a little girl, I always thought it would be the church I would like to get married in. Let's go inside shall we?'

Before Helen could reply, Angela took her arm and propelled her back toward the church. The parishioners had dispersed and the massive oak door stood open. Angela led them back inside and they walked slowly down the chancel, the women's heels and Paul's uneven step echoing in the empty building.

'Have you seen the Morrow family vault, Helen?' Angela said with a mischievous smile. 'They're all there, right up to Sir Gerald.' Her face sobered. 'God, that was a dismal funeral. You were—' she glanced at Paul, '—fortunate to miss it.'

Helen recalled Sir Gerald had died not long after Charlie's death, at a time when Paul would still have been hospitalised. For Evelyn to have lost her son and then her husband in rapid succession must have been heartbreaking.

'Do you have the key to the vault, Paul?' Angela asked.

'Why would I carry a key to the vault?' Paul responded tersely. 'You don't really want to go down there, do you?'

'Of course I do. It's so deliciously creepy. Alice will love it, won't you?' She addressed the child who was tracing the carved face of the first Morrow at Holdston, Sir Albury, with her finger. 'The Scarvell family vault is positively antiseptic in comparison.'

Paul sighed. 'The verger's outside. Alice, can you go and ask if we can borrow the keys?'

Alice skipped off in search of the verger and returned with a heavy iron key which she presented to Paul. He tossed it to Angela.

'There you go, be my guest.'

Angela caught the key and slid it into the lock. It turned stiffly and she swung the grating open. Beyond the gate was a wooden door with a heavy latch but no padlock. Angela lifted it and the door swung back on creaking hinges.

She looked back. 'Anyone else coming?'

'Not me.' Paul leaned against the nearest pew.

'Helen?'

Helen looked at Paul, but his attention was fixed on the beams of the ceiling.

'See if you can find a candle, Helen,' Angela said. 'It's as black as pitch in here.'

Curiosity overcame natural revulsion and Helen had no difficulty finding a box of half-burned candles near the prayer books at the back of the church. Angela lit two with her cigarette lighter and they stepped into the vault. Alice looked up at her, her eyes wide with excitement.

'May I come too?'

'Certainly not,' Helen said. 'You may wait here with Uncle Paul.'

Alice's face fell and she sank into a sulky heap on the nearest pew.

The air in the vault smelled close and musty and Helen's nose twitched. Death, even old death, had a particular scent. Angela held up her candle. The stone-flagged room was lined on two sides with stone shelves on which rested a large number of coffins. From what Helen could see, the older coffins were pushed to one side to make room for the newer ones. The overall effect was one of careless neglect as if the more recent occupants had been shoved in where they would fit.

The oppressive atmosphere closed in on her and her candle went out as a breath of icy air touched the back of her neck.

Helen shivered. 'That's enough for me,' she said.

'Don't you want to find the secret tunnel?' Angela said.

'No thank you,' Helen said. 'I'm going back up.'

Compared to the gloom of the crypt, the church seemed filled with warmth and light. Helen ran a hand through her hair as she rejoined Paul. 'I would hate to be buried down there.' Paul nodded. 'I agree with you.'

'I'm glad Charlie isn't in there,' Helen said.

He looked down at her but his eyes were in shadow and unreadable.

'So am I.'

'What are you two talking about?' Angela emerged from the vault, blowing out her candle. She shut the door, locked the grate, and gave the key back to Alice. 'Take that back to Mr. Potter, Alice.'

'If you've seen enough, I would like to breathe some of that fresh air now.' Paul strode from the church. In the churchyard, he took a deep breath and leaned against the wall.

'Do you believe there is a tunnel from the house to the church?' Helen asked as they strolled back along the path to the house.

Paul shrugged. 'An old house, an old church. It's possible. Charlie and I looked for it when we were boys but we never found it.'

Alice, trailing behind the adults, piped up. 'Mummy? Where's Daddy?'

All three adults stopped quite still. Helen and Angela turned to look at the child. Paul didn't move. Helen glanced at him and saw the colour had drained from his face.

Alice looked up at her mother with large, serious eyes. 'I mean,' she continued, oblivious to the adults' discomfiture. 'I know he's dead, but I was just wondering if we could go and visit him?'

Helen swallowed. 'Daddy doesn't have a grave like these,' she said, sweeping a hand over the tombstones. 'He ... he's somewhere in Belgium where the war was fought. I don't know where.'

'Oh,' Alice said. 'Never mind.'

Angela looked up at the church clock. 'Oh, good lord, is that time? I'm expected back at Wellmore for lunch. With any luck, those dreary debutantes will have dispersed. Paul, be a dear and walk me to the stables.'

When Paul didn't respond, Helen touched his elbow. He seemed lost, his eyes fixed on nothing in particular. 'Paul?

Paul looked down at her, the green eyes refocusing on her face.

'Sorry,' he said. 'Something about stables, Ange?'

Angela tucked her arm into his and they walked together in the direction of the stables.

Alice, bored with the company of adults, ran on ahead. She turned and looked back.

'Coming, Mummy?'

'I left my riding gloves in the stable this morning, Alice. I'll just fetch them,' Helen said and followed the path others had taken.

She stopped at the entrance to the stable yard, drawing back into the shadows as she saw Paul and Angela beside the mounting block. Angela had the reins of her horse looped over her arm and unaware of Helen's presence, they turned to face each other. Angela lifted her hand and touched Paul's cheek in a gesture that was at once tender and solicitous.

Paul bent his head and kissed the woman, a light kiss on the mouth that Angela responded to by placing her hands on his shoulder. As Angela climbed into the saddle she bent down and said something to Paul. He laughed in response and slapped the horse on the rump.

Helen turned and hurried back toward the house. In the courtyard she stopped and leaned against the wall, gathering her breath and her thoughts. Angela had intimated that there had been something more than friendship between herself and Paul. Did she want to revive the relationship? Helen took a steadying breath. She should be glad if they had rediscovered each other. They both deserved happiness in their lives. Anyway, she told herself fiercely, as she walked back into the house, it was none of her business.

What she didn't understand was the unfamiliar ache that the thought left in her heart.

Twenty-One

Paul stood at the stable yard gate long after Angela had ridden away. He thrust his hands deep into his pockets, his thoughts not of Angela but of a simple, obvious, innocent question from a child. A question he couldn't answer: '*Where's Daddy?*'

He braced himself, dismissing the dark memories. It would be a good half hour until lunch. That gave him time to sort through some notes. He found Helen in the library standing at the window, her arms folded in front of her in a curiously defensive posture. He could not see her face, only her straight back and the long graceful neck, revealed now by her short haircut.

'Helen?'

Her shoulders rose and fell but she did not turn to face him. 'Do you know where he is, Paul?'

Paul took a deep breath but said nothing.

Helen turned to face him. He expected to see signs of tears again but her face, while pale and strained, showed no sign of obvious distress.

Paul looked up at the ceiling, trying to find the right response, all the platitudes he had worked so hard at developing deserting him when he needed them most. When he brought his gaze back to Helen's, he said, 'What do you want me to tell you, Helen?'

'As much as you do remember.'

He looked away, the confused visions of his nightmares crowding in on him. He closed his eyes, knowing as he did so, that the bursts of light and the tightening band around his temples presaged a migraine.

'Did you kill him?'

Her words took his breath and he knew the shock registered in his face. It was not the first time he had heard the whisper but to hear it come from Helen appalled him. 'Why do you say that?'

'I heard some of the others gossiping yesterday. They said there were stories that you —'

'Helen,' he cut in sharply. 'Is that what upset you yesterday?'

She lowered her eyes. 'Mostly. There were other things to do with Charlie and me.'

'James Massey,' Paul said in disgust. 'He is one of those malicious people with nothing better to do with their time except cause trouble. Helen, Charlie was as close to me as any brother could have been and there is not a day goes by when I don't feel his loss as keenly as you must, but I can't tell you what happened.'

'Will you ever, Paul?'

He met her eyes wanting to say, '*Perhaps one day. One day I will, but not now, not here.*'

'You heard Alice?' she continued. 'It's the first time she has ever asked about her father. What do I say? How do I explain it to her?'

'You can't, Helen.'

She turned back to the window, bowing her head.

He knew he hadn't answered her question, hadn't denied the accusation. He longed to touch her, reassure her, tell her what she so desperately wanted to know—instead, he turned away, closing the door behind him, intent only on reaching the sanctuary of his bedroom before the black beast of the migraine felled him completely.

———

Passchendaele, Belgium September 16, 1917 2200 hours.

It seemed almost impossible that in the middle of a war there could be such complete and utter silence. Paul twisted the matchbox in his fingers, conscious of the three taut faces turned toward him. Brent, only just twenty, a Lieutenant commanding a company, chewed his lip and glanced nervously at Collins, Captain and Commander of B Company. Collins had been at the front too long. His nerves had gone and he had trouble hiding the fact that his hand shook as he brought the stub of his cigarette to his mouth.

They all knew the answer and they all knew why Paul hesitated.

He set the matchbox down on the table and turned to the third person seated at the table.

'Charlie,' he said, forcing himself to meet his cousin's eyes.

Charlie neither blinked nor looked away and in that brief moment his eyes said more than words ever would. They had discussed it often enough over the past few weeks.

'Captain Morrow, your objective is the pill box,' Paul said, spreading his hand over the map on the table before him. They all knew the layout of the German lines. They had been staring at them for months.

'How?' Brent exclaimed

'The pillboxes are designed for mutual support,' Paul said. 'The slits are on the diagonal.' He drew a rough sketch on a corner of the map. 'Their front is blind'.

'Their front may be blind, but there are plenty of other eyes,' Collins put in.

Paul nodded. 'H hour is zero six hundred. Charlie will take two men armed with grenades out into no man's land while it is still dark.'

'The brass'll skin you alive!' Collins said.

'The brass won't care,' Paul said bitterly. 'It's merely a heavily armed patrol.'

'The Huns'll see them coming.'

'Charlie knows to keep low and use the shell holes as cover and if we have a feint at the far end of the line, that will keep them busy until Charlie can reach the pill box.'

'What sort of feint?' Brent asked.

'A bit of obvious movement.'

Brent creased his brow. 'But, won't that give the whole game away?'

'It won't matter. We're going over at H hour and the game will be on for one and all,' Paul said.

'What about the artillery barrage?' Collins put in. 'Those idiots can't hit anything,' Charlie said.

'You've spent too long in Australia. You're starting to sound like them.' Paul said with a half smile. 'Brent, you'll provide the diversion and then act as the reserve once we go over the top. Collins, you'll take your company and Charlie's as the main attack force.'

Collins raised his shaking hand and wiped his mouth. 'And you, sir?' he asked.

'I'll be with you in the main charge,' Paul said. 'Our objective is to take these trenches.' He indicated the map. 'And if we can push through the objective, then we damn well will.'

'Is that in your orders, sir?' Collins asked with a suspicious frown.

Paul just looked at him.

After the others had gone, Paul and Charlie sat back against the cold earth of the dugout and smoked in silence.

'I've no choice, Charlie.'

Charlie blew out the smoke. 'I know that. We've discussed it often enough. Time to see if it works.'

Paul closed his eyes. 'I can refuse—'

'Don't be a bloody fool, Paul. If you refuse it won't change anything. You'll be shot as a coward and we'll all still be going over the top into certain death. It's better for us all if you're with us.'

Paul shot his cousin a rueful look. 'Well, you better damn well make sure it works, Captain Morrow.'

TWENTY-TWO

Helen knocked on Paul's door and sighed with relief when she heard his voice. He sat in his chair by the fire, a book in his hand. Looking up at her, he set the book aside. Sarah had told her at breakfast that a migraine had laid him out and his face was still ashen with dark circles under his eyes.

'Sarah said you wanted to see me,' Helen said. 'Are you better?'

He shrugged.

'I'm so sorry about what I said yesterday,' she said, filled with remorse and a nagging fear that it had been their confrontation that had brought on the migraine.

'What for? You didn't give me a migraine,' he said. 'It had been threatening all morning.'

'I've not been idle while you've been out of action.' Helen smiled. 'I finished your report.'

She handed him the papers and he flicked through the report, before laying it to one side.

'Thank you. That's saved me days of work. Now, I have something for you.'

He pulled himself to his feet in a manner that suggested every bone in his body ached. When he saw her face, he gave a rueful smile.

'I feel a hundred years old tonight.'

He limped over to the table by the window and gathered some sheets of paper together. He turned back to face her and gestured at the spare chair.

'If you're in no hurry, sit down.'

He handed her the papers and resumed his own chair.

'The diary. You broke the code.' Helen looked up at him.

'It wasn't that hard but I have to give the credit to my great-grandmother, it was clever.'

Helen scanned the pages, trying to make sense of Paul's now familiar scrawl that was completely at odds with Suzanne Morrow's feminine hand in the diary itself.

'January 30, 1812,' she read aloud.

For the last two days I have been employed in the compilation of this simple yet effective code. I am sure a man of no great intelligence could see through it at once but for a simple woman, it will serve my purpose well enough.

Paul smiled ruefully. 'It is good to think of myself as a man of no great intelligence. It's taken me hours.'

...A letter came from Robert this morning. A brief epistle which I dutifully read to Lady Morrow. Another recounting of a battle, of the cold and the shortage of food. Robert is so far away. S is here in England and I do not know when I will see him again. At night before I sleep, I imagine his face. Why is it that when I close my eyes, I can see this man so clearly and not the face of my husband?

Lady Morrow remarked on my high colour and asked me if I ailed. Indeed she insisted I retire to my bedchamber for the morning. She is of the opinion that I am far too excitable.

'She seems to be a woman ruled by her heart, not her head,' Helen commented. 'Surely she knew the consequences of conducting an affair of this nature. If she was to be found out, she would be ruined.'

'February 5,' she continued.

A letter from S. He will put no identifying mark on the letter and if asked by Lady Morrow I shall say the letters are from an old friend or my dear brother and of a personal nature. My heart trembles at such deceit. I feel at every step I am being drawn into a net from which there is no escape but I cannot prevent it.

I have burned the letter but every word is committed to my memory. 'February 12: Last night Viscount Hartfield held a farewell party at Wellmore House for Adrian who must return to his regiment. You cannot imagine my joy on beholding S among the guests. I could not meet his eyes or pretend any knowledge of his presence beyond the formal presentation by Lady Hartfield.

"Of course, we met at New Year,' he said, taking my hand. His touch sent a thrill from my fingers to my heart. His fingers, so firm, so sure, held mine, only so long as propriety required. 'Lady Morrow,' he said. 'You look enchanting tonight.' We continued with the pretence of genteel acquaintance throughout the evening. After supper, Lady Hartfield declared that I should entertain the company with a song. Oh, how I hate such occasions. My good father in his earnest desire to educate me, neglected instruction in the most basic of female arts and left me quite unskilled in matters of needlework, painting and piano forte. Lady Morrow was so scandalised by my upbringing that she insisted I should have lessons and Signor Montefiore has attended Holdston on a weekly basis to correct my shortcomings but despite his best efforts, I fear I will always be but a mediocre artiste.

Nonetheless I acquiesced to the request with a smile on my face and to my great delight S offered to turn the pages of the music for me. To have him so close to me that I could breathe in the very scent of him was a distraction I could well have done without. As he leaned over my shoulder, I felt the hairs on my neck rise in anticipation of his proximity. I sang for him alone. When I was done, the company applauded politely and S took my hand and kissed it. The touch of his lips was no more than gossamer but his eyes spoke more words then I cared to hear.

Paul shook his head. 'I feel like I am reading some penny dreadful romance novel.'

Helen looked up at him and smiled, before continuing,

February 13: I cannot contain myself. I have devised a way that we can meet in perfect secrecy and I am beside myself to impart the information to him. When will he come? Adele is teething and fretful. I held her in my arms and wept from fear of what the future may hold. My children have been my life. What am I doing?

'*February 15: Lady Hartfield called yesterday afternoon accompanied by Barbara and S. I suspect that Lady Hartfield has some designs on S for Barbara and why indeed not? He has ten thousand a year, if Lady H is to be believed, and she comes with a sizeable dowry. I smiled to see the pathetic girl simpering over her cup of tea, trying to interpose on our conversation with some inanity of her own. I had to bide my time until the party came to leave at which point I slipped a note into his hand.*

'There is a certain arrogance about her, isn't there?' Helen remarked. 'I feel quite sorry for Barbara.'

'Jealousy?' Paul suggested.

'Undoubtedly,' Helen agreed. 'Barbara was untrammelled by an inconvenient husband. Shall I go on?'

Paul nodded.

...What I propose is audacious beyond belief and certainly not to the taste of god-fearing folk but I must see him and talk with him in complete privacy.

It came to me only the other day that there is a tunnel that runs from the house to the family crypt in the Church. Robert showed me the entrance and told me how he and his brothers would play royalists and roundheads in it and that at time the tunnel was quite clear. He did not venture into it as he said he is now quite afeared of such a confined space and neither would he let me past the entrance, saying that it was not a place for a woman.

'*A couple of nights past when the household was all abed I dressed in an old gown and taking a candle, ventured down to the library. The entrance was as I remembered it, although a little stiff to open and my heart leaped to my mouth for fearing of waking Lady Morrow who sleeps in the chamber above the library. With great trep-*

idation I descended into the dark bowels of the tunnel. It smelt of damp and indeed where it passed under the moat, as needs it must, it was quite wet underfoot. I was able to follow it, although at some points I was almost doubled up. It was, as Robert had said, quite clear. The entrance to the crypt was also a little stiff but I had prudently brought oil with me and was able to oil the hinges so they gave quite easily.

Helen looked up at Paul. 'So, there is a tunnel! But where's the entrance? I can see nothing obvious in the library.'

'It's not supposed to be obvious,' Paul observed drily.

It is a silent place. Not the place for lovers, dare I say that word? Just writing it brings a tremor of fear to my heart. Yet that is where my lover will be waiting for me. This will be our assignation where we can meet away from the curious eyes. I have left the gate to the crypt unlocked for I doubted that the verger would routinely check it. For what cause would he do so? Today I crept to the library while Lady Morrow was abroad visiting one of the tenants who was ailing. The servants would think nothing of seeing me enter the library for I am often in there and they know to leave me in peace.

'My hands shook as I slipped through the entrance to the tunnel. Would he be there? You cannot imagine my fear and pleasure when I beheld him sitting on the steps, his hat in his hand, tapping his boot with his stick. I think my entrance must have startled him for he leaped to his feet, his face quite white. We stood still and just stared at each other and then, oh how can I relate this, we were in each other's arms. He covered my hair and my face with his kisses and I returned them tenfold. We spent but a half hour together lost in each other. Talking of such follies and fancies as took our mind.

'I know now I am a lost woman, my marriage vows forsaken for a few stolen moments with this man. He is like a drug that I crave. I cannot live without him. Every moment away from him tears my heart and yet I must remain circumspect. There is too much at stake, too much to fear to allow rein to such foolishness...

'There's just one last entry and that's as much as I've done,' Paul said.

February 18: He is gone, returned to London and my heart is breaking. I have met him every day since our first venture into the crypt. You cannot imagine what liberty it is to know that you are unseen and unregarded. We can talk freely without recourse to polite convention. Surely this is how man and woman should be, not bound to the politeness of discourse as dictated by society? I have been reading, in secret, the writings of Mary Wollstonecraft. How I admire her that she could speak her mind so freely on such issues. To my surprise, S has read her too and is in full agreement with her sentiments. Robert would not give a jot for them and Lady Morrow would burn the book. Oh, just the mention of his name is like a knife in my heart. What am I doing? What madness am I infected by?

Helen set the paper down. 'What do you know of her family?' Helen asked.

'Suzanna? Only what Evelyn read the other day.'

Helen frowned. 'Surely her family would have been concerned over her disappearance, even if the Morrows weren't? Perhaps they made their own enquiries?'

Paul's fingers beat a tattoo on the arm of his chair. 'We know her father appeared to be some sort of eccentric who believed in educating girls and she had a brother, John with a parish so we can assume he was in Holy Orders. It would not be too hard to trace him through the church records.'

'Where would we find those?'

'They would be kept at Lambeth Palace in London,' Paul said. He picked up the report of the archaeological dig. 'Helen, would you consider a trip to London for me? This has to be given to Woolley at the British Museum and—'

'I could check the records at Lambeth Palace? Why can't you go?'

'I just thought you might like a break from Holdston,' Paul said. 'You can stay with Angela. I know she would like that.'

'What about Alice? I've arranged for her to go start at the local village school on Wednesday.'

Paul raised his eyes. 'Have you told Evelyn about the school?'

'Not yet,' Helen replied.

A knock at the door, made them both jump. Sarah Pollard entered carrying a tea tray and behind, her Evelyn Morrow.

Evelyn's gaze flicked to Helen and then to her nephew. 'Sarah said you were feeling better.'

'Thank you, Evelyn,' Paul said as Sarah set the tea tray down on the table.

Evelyn pulled up a chair and poured the tea into the two cups that had been set out on it. Paul declined the cup she proffered and she handed it to Helen instead.

'Paul, I need to talk to you about your plans for Willow Farm,' she said.

A shadow crossed Paul's face. 'Evelyn, we've had this discussion. I've given you my decision.'

Evelyn's mouth set in a tight line. 'Paul.' She broke off and glanced sharply at Helen. 'Paul wants to spend the money we need to repair the roof of the Hall on some new-fangled machinery for Willow Farm.'

Helen looked from Evelyn's face to Paul. Both as stubborn as each other, she thought.

'Surely it is more important to improve the efficiency of the farm?' Helen ventured.

'My argument exactly,' Paul said. 'I'm going into Birmingham tomorrow to talk to the bank. In fact, I was just asking Helen if she would be willing to go up to London for me and deliver my report to Woolley at the British Museum.'

'I can stay with Angela,' Mindful of her confrontation with Evelyn on Saturday, Helen added, 'If that would be appropriate?'

Evelyn waved her hand. 'Angela? Of course. But why do you need to go? Can't you post the report, Paul?'

'I could, but it's already late and I thought it might be pleasant for Helen to have a couple of nights in London with Angela instead of stuck here with you and me,' Paul snapped.

Evelyn sniffed.

'I would only go if you don't mind me leaving Alice with you here? She is starting school on Wednesday,' Helen said

'School?' Evelyn looked bemused.

'Yes, the village school. I've been trying to do school work with her but I think she's better in a classroom so I've spoken to the headmistress and it's all arranged.'

'A Morrow at the village school?' Evelyn said. 'It's unheard of.'

She caught the smile that passed between Paul and Helen. 'What do you find so amusing?'

'Nothing,' Paul replied, his face all innocence. 'I think it's an excellent idea.'

'Well I'm sure I can give you a recommendation to a good school. The one Angela attended—'

Helen set her cup down. 'I'm not sending Alice away to a boarding school for the sake of a couple of months. She has made friends with some of the children from the village and I think it will be good for her, and for the Morrows, if she is seen to be part of the village life.'

Evelyn stood up. 'I don't claim to understand you, Helen. And you, Paul, I thought you would know better. Next thing you will be eating in the kitchen!'

With that, she stalked out of the room.

Helen bit her lip and glanced at Paul. To her relief, he smiled.

'Eating in the kitchen will be the end of civilisation as we know it,' he said.

'I can't seem to do anything right in her eyes.' Helen's hands began to shake as the tears that seemed to be lurking under the surface ever since Saturday threatened to engulf her again.

Paul leaned forward in his chair and removed the teacup from her hand. He set it down on the table and took her hands in his.

'Evelyn has her faults but she is not normally so callous, Helen. Something must have been said to her over the weekend that prompted the outburst.'

Helen felt the hot tears begin to drop from her eyes onto her hands. 'Things were said and it's not just Evelyn. I can't get what was said about me out of my head.'

'It's just the idle talk of people with nothing better to do with their lives. The fact is people like you and I, Helen, will always be outsiders.'

She looked up at him. 'But you're not an outsider?'

'Of course I am. The poor relation who ended up with the title? Good lord, I work for a living.' He sighed. 'I've never fitted neatly into their pigeonholes. Here...'

He released her hands and produced another large, clean handkerchief. She seemed to be accumulating quite a collection.

Paul sat back in his chair as Helen dried the scalding tears. She looked across at him.

'I'm sorry,' she said, noting how drawn he looked. 'You didn't need this today of all days. I don't know what's wrong with me. I'm not normally such a misery.'

He shrugged. 'I think you need to get away from Holdston. A few days in London would do you good. Alice will be fine here.'

Helen stuffed Paul's handkerchief into her pocket and rose to her feet. She packed up the tea things and picked up the tray, leaving Paul Morrow sitting back in his armchair, his green eyes lost in thoughts she could never share.

TWENTY-THREE

Helen set her bag down and looked around the large living room of Angela's flat in Chelsea. The room also appeared to serve as her studio. Stacks of unframed canvases leaned against any spare space and the room smelled, not unpleasantly, of linseed oil and paint. It was as far removed from the grand halls of Wellmore House as Holdston was from Terrala.

'Like it?' Angela waved a hand around the room.

'It's not ...'

'Not Wellmore? That's why I love it!'

Helen picked up the nearest painting, a painting of a shelled church.

'Is this one of your war paintings?'

'It is. The village of Ville Neuf.'

Helen walked around the room looking at the paintings, picking up the smaller ones, standing back from the large canvases, and allowing herself to take in the representations of water-filled trenches and ragged stumps that had once been forests.

'I can't even begin to imagine what it was like,' she murmured. Charlie's letters had given no hint of what he endured and the official reports and photographs were those approved by the censors. What

Angela had seen and what Charlie had lived through were starkly portrayed here in Angela's vivid style.

Helen paused in front of a series of three portraits. The first was of a young officer in a crisp, starched uniform, the second the same officer but his uniform all but obscured by mud, his unshaven face ravaged by exhaustion, and the third depicted the same man on a stretcher, one of many stretchers, in what looked like a half-ruined church. The man had his face turned toward the artist, his eyes closed, his unshaven face a mask of blood and mud. He should have been unrecognisable, but Angela had caught the fall of the dark hair across his face and the long fingers that clenched the blanket, leaving Helen in no doubt that this young man had been the subject of the other two portraits.

Her hand flew to her mouth in recognition. 'Oh my God, that's...'

'Paul,' Angela said.

Helen tore her eyes away from the third painting and turned to look at the artist. 'Does he know?'

'He knows about one and two because I had him pose for them.' Angela took the third from Helen and looked at it critically. 'This one, no. I told you I brought him in from the clearing station after the push. You can imagine the field hospital was overrun with wounded. If a man survived the night, then they would see him. If he didn't—'

'And Paul?'

'They didn't think he'd live so they left him there with the others but I wasn't going to let him die alone. I sat with him all that night and kicked up a god-almighty row in the morning.'

'He was lucky he had you,' Helen remarked.

Angela shrugged and took a drag on her cigarette. 'I suppose he was.'

'How do you think he'd feel about the painting?'

'I don't know. I've never shown it in public. Too personal.'

'What do you call it?'

'The whole series is intended to be a triptych. Like the old religious paintings. The beginning and the end. Alpha and Omega.'

Helen gave the picture one last look, trying to reconcile the badly wounded soldier with the man she knew. She felt like a voyeur; that she had been shown something she had no right to see.

'Where am I to sleep?' she asked.

Angela gestured to a door. 'Through there. You should find whatever you need. Don't mind me if I'm working.'

In contrast to the rest of the flat, the guest room was a neat, tidy room with a single bed covered in a floral eiderdown. Helen set her bag down on the luggage rack and removed her hat and coat. When she returned to the main room, Angela was back at work on her canvas. Not a war picture this time, but a huge canvas of Waterloo Bridge.

'Be a dear,' Angela said. 'My daily has left some supper for us. It just needs warming. Can you manage? The kitchen's through there. We'll have a sherry while we're waiting.'

Helen found a shepherd's pie on the table and placed it in the small, gas oven. She cleared a space on the kitchen table, laid out knives and forks, and poured sherry into two unmatched sherry glasses. She handed one to Angela who continued with her work. Helen cleared some papers from an armchair, sat, and watched Angela at work until the smell of the pie filled the flat.

'I think supper might be ready, shall I serve?' Helen volunteered.

'Would you? I'll be right with you. The light's gone now.'

Helen served two helpings onto a pair of cracked dinner plates and summoned Angela.

Angela washed her hands in the kitchen sink and pulled up a chair at the table. She picked at the food on her plate.

'God, Mavis knows I hate shepherd's pie. It reminds me of nursery dinners when I was a child.'

Helen made no comment although it occurred to her that Mavis obviously knew her employer well and that shepherd's pie was at least one way of getting nutritious food down her employer's skinny frame. Angela ate half of what was on her plate and pushed the rest to one side. She lit another cigarette and sat back and watched Helen finish her meal.

'What has darling Paul got you doing?'

'I have to deliver his report to the British Museum and then I have a little research on the family to do.'

'Sounds deadly. Since when has Paul been interested in genealogy?'

Helen shook her head. 'Just a puzzle that has intrigued us.'

Angela's mouth quirked and she stubbed the cigarette out on her dinner plate.

'That picture shocked you didn't it?'

Helen nodded. 'It was...unexpected.'

'I aim to shock people. I want them to see past the propaganda to the truth. Of course, my agent doesn't like me showing the pictures.'

'What made you want to do it? Go to the Front I mean?'

Angela looked up at the ceiling. 'When Harry died I went to stay with his mother and sister in their pretty little manor in Hampshire. Knock at the door one morning about six weeks after the telegram and it's a dispatch rider with a parcel. Harry's kit and personal effects. I couldn't face it so I went outside for a cigarette. I heard his sister Delia scream.' Angela's face twisted at the memory. 'God damn those insensitive bastards to hell. They'd packed his tunic, the tunic he'd been wearing when he was killed— bloodstains, bullet holes, and the lot. Those two lovely, innocent women stood holding this obscene object with tears running down their faces. It was then I decided to do something so I joined the VAD.'

Helen sat quite still in appalled silence, trying to imagine how she would have felt if she had received such a parcel.

'I would have volunteered as a nurse but I was pregnant when Charlie left,' Helen said, 'and with so many of the young men away, I was needed on the farm.' She pushed the last of the pie around her plate with her fork. 'They used to send the telegrams to the vicar to deliver. Our poor vicar, such a kindly man, found people would start to avoid him in the street.'

'Did he bring the news about Charlie?' Angela asked, blowing a cloud of smoke into the air as she spoke.

Helen shook her head. 'Because Charlie served with an English regiment, I had to wait until the telegram came from Evelyn.'

Tears pricked her eyes and Angela laid a hand on her arm. She let the tears fall knowing that Angela was probably one of the few people in the world who truly understood. Both women gave way to their own, individual grief and cried in each other's arms before Angela straightened and sniffed, dabbing at her face with a sodden handkerchief. She stood up and poured them both a glass of whisky.

'Hang it,' she said. 'I've made them large.'

Helen looked across at Alpha and Omega. Angela followed her gaze as she lit a cigarette.

'I'm an artist, Helen, and Paul was a subject. I'd done the portrait of him before he went off, more out of affection than anything else. While I was out there, I came across him in the trenches and as things were quiet he sat for me again. The third painting seemed a natural successor to the previous two. The cream of England's young men on his deathbed. It's immaterial that he actually didn't die. It made the triptych—completed the circle.' Angela inhaled and blew out the smoke.

'Do you love him?' Helen asked remembering the way she had seen Angela touch Paul's face.

Angela took another drag on her cigarette and stubbed it out on her plate before lighting another. She caught Helen's eye. 'Are you always so direct, Helen?'

Helen shrugged. 'I don't have the English reticence, Angela. I like to know where people stand, not tiptoe around, wondering whose toes I am treading on.'

'And that's what I like about you,' Angela replied. 'So, to answer your question. Do I love him? I loved him once and, yes, if I'm honest, I still do.' She swirled the whisky in her glass. 'Paul and I...Paul and I had an affair if you can call it that.'

Helen kept her tone measured as she responded, 'An affair?'

'He was in London on leave in the autumn of 1916, a few months after Harry died. The deadly dull Fiona was in Scotland with her family so he had no obligations. It lasted all of the week he was home and it was the most intense, passionate week of my life. But that's all it was. Two lonely people finding solace in each other.'

'And now?'

Angela's mouth curled into a sad smile. 'Now? There's too much between us and we're different people. Quite frankly, Helen, I've no interest in having a husband or children and Paul's friendship means more to me than his love.' She smiled and drained her glass. 'Anyway, I have lovers of my own choosing. Preferably older men with tedious wives and plenty of money. So much more fun. My painting is my passion and it is a jealous lover.'

'Why do you think married women take lovers?'

'What sort of question is that?'

'I've been reading about a young woman of the last century, happily married who falls in love with another man.'

'A grand passion?'

'Yes, I suppose so.'

'Boredom mostly. Amiable husband but no challenge? Intelligent, passionate woman looking for something more to her life than husband and hearth?'

'Passion, excitement, adventure?'

'Of course. Here, darling, do you want a ciggie?' Angela pushed the tin over to Helen.

Helen shook her head.

'I've no doubt at all that if Harry hadn't died tragically on the Somme, we would have been bored with each other before too long. More pie?' Angela looked dubiously at the dish of congealing mince and vegetables.

Helen shook her head.

'Throw it in the bin for me, be a dear.'

'Do you mind me asking but does painting provide you with a living?'

Angela threw back her head and laughed. 'Good God, no. Harry left me with a comfortable income to allow me to indulge my interests. Oh God, is that time?'

Helen looked at her watch. It was late. She stood up and dealt with the remains of the meal and excused herself, leaving Angela sitting at her table doing a rough drawing on a sketch pad

Tucked up in the narrow single bed, Helen undid the envelope Paul had left for her that morning. It contained several more pages of the diary with a rough note attached.

'*Couldn't sleep so amused myself with some more of Great Grandma-ma's adulterous ramblings. P*'

Helen unfolded the pages and began to read.

February 29: Lady Morrow has announced that we shall go to London for the Season. Her niece, Anthea, is to make her debut and Lady

Morrow sees it as incumbent upon her to make sure the girl is engaged by the end of the Season. She thinks the change will do me good. If she but suspected how my heart leaped at the thought of London. London means S.

March 29 Easter Day: We have been here nearly four days and no word yet from S, although I sent him notice that I should be arriving. I thought I saw him at Church this morning but there was such a press of people that he was gone before I could ascertain whether it was him. I have to endure the endless round of visits, knowing that he could call in my absence or send a message that must wait for my return. I smile and nod and make polite conversation. The first great occasion will be on Wednesday night at the Duchess of N.'s ball where Anthea will be coming out. Anthea is a thin, pale girl who seems incapable of holding any form of conversation so I despair of Lady Morrow's hopes to have her wed by the end of the year. Lady Morrow has engaged a painter to paint my likeness for Robert's birthday. He is a most fashionable painter at the moment and we were fortunate to secure his services. My first sitting is on Tuesday and I shall wear my green dress, although it is only to be head and shoulders so I don't suppose much of it will show.

March 31: A message, at long last, a message brought to me by my faithful servant Annie in whom I have confided some of the story. I care not whether Annie approves or disapproves, I know only that she is loyal to me and will not breathe a word to another living person. Joy! He will be at the Duchess' ball. I can hardly breathe for knowing he will be so close.

April 2: Oh cruel, cruel world that I live in. To be so close to S and yet propriety would allow us no more than a casual conversation about, of all things, the weather. At such a grand occasion it would not do for me to dance so I had to sit with the other matrons watching as Barbara danced with S, not once but four times. How I hate her. How I wish I was dead. Even Anthea, pathetic creature that she is, danced with him. Around me, the women cackled and gossiped like old farm hens. Oh S, Lady Y, was heard to exclaim. I hear he has quite a reputation among the ladies. He is not the settling kind despite his handsome income. What reputation? I enquired. Oh, my dear, haven't you heard? There was a fearful scandal two years ago with the wife of Mr. W. The poor woman was quite ruined. Her husband had to send her to the country and she has not been heard of since. He has an eye for married ladies, they do say. Do they indeed? I replied, snapping my fan shut. They do not know him, cannot know him as I do.

Helen put the papers back in the envelope and switched off the bedside light.

TWENTY-FOUR

The opening of Angela's exhibition attracted a large audience and the fashionable art gallery on the Strand bustled with elegant society matrons and gentlemen in dinner suits. Waiters moved among the crowd with trays of champagne. Angela, dressed in a simple grey silk sheath dress, drifted anonymously among her admirers, only occasionally stopping to accept the plaudits due her.

The paintings, mostly still life or landscapes, were what Angela described as 'safe and saleable' and exhibited under her own name. However, scattered among the safe and saleable were small vignettes of the underbelly of London life, a woman standing by the door of a slum house in the docks, with a grubby child on her hip, her eyes dull and hopeless; a legless ex-serviceman, begging on a street corner. These snap-shots from a different reality seemed to be overlooked by the throng who exclaimed appreciatively over the landscapes and the vases of wilting lilies.

Helen, dressed formally in her blue satin dress, watched from a safe corner, clutching a glass of champagne that dripped damply on to her gloves.

'Helen, you took some finding!' At the sound of Tony's voice,

Helen started, slopping her champagne. She looked around and smiled as Tony joined her.

Angela waved and pushed through the crowd to greet her brother. They kissed on both cheeks. 'So pleased you came,' she said

'Mother threatened me with debutantes again.' Tony pulled a face. 'And look who came along for the ride.'

Both women turned to look at the tall, elegant figure of Paul Morrow, in evening dress, standing just inside the door, looking around the room. He saw them and raised a hand.

As he joined them, Angela put her hands on his shoulders in the gesture Helen had noticed at the stables and kissed him on the cheek.

'Paul, darling. How wonderful. I hoped you would come.'

A conspiratorial smile passed between them. Helen, now knowing their history, understood and, not for the first time, wondered if their relationship was quite as dead and buried as Angela proclaimed it.

'Tony told me you were the talk of London and I thought I should see for myself,' Paul replied. 'It would seem he was right. What a crowd.'

Tony turned to Helen. 'Helen, what do you think of my sister's daubings?'

Helen, her eyes on Paul's face, saw only 'Alpha and Omega' and wondered at the power of Angela's painting.

She turned to Tony with a smile. 'They are quite extraordinary,' she said.

'There's no doubt my talented sister is a success.' Tony looked around the crowded gallery. 'I've booked a table at the Savoy for four. I think this calls for a celebration.'

'Oh, darling boy,' Angela said. 'That will be marvellous. Let's flee, shall we? I've done my bit. They're selling like hot chestnuts. The man with the huge grin is my agent.'

Tony offered Helen his arm. 'You don't mind a bit of a walk, do you? It's not far.'

Helen accepted and they stepped out into the cool, night air.

TWENTY-FIVE

Tony did not relinquish Helen's arm as they walked into the Savoy. Helen looked around at the grand entrance hall with its black and white marble tiles and he grinned. 'Have you ever been here?'

Helen refrained from saying the 'Hardly!' that sprang to her lips. 'No,' she said simply.

'I think a slap-up feed and a couple of bottles of champers does the soul good,' Tony said as they sat at the table.

'I haven't been here since for years,' Paul remarked. 'Fiona and I came here for our last dinner before I shipped out to Belgium. Cost me two week's pay.'

Tony refilled it and stood up. 'A toast. To my clever sister,'

'To Angela!' The other three lifted their glasses.

A band struck up a foxtrot. Tony took Helen's hand. 'A dance, Mrs. Morrow?'

As she had at Wellmore Helen found herself swept along with Tony's lively but unaccomplished dancing.

'If you're wondering how I persuaded Paul to come to London, it was his idea,' Tony said.

'Oh dear, Lady Morrow seems to think that I'm the bad influence on him.'

'She's quite right,' Tony said.

'What do you mean?'

'You're a terribly bad influence. You've made Paul Morrow behave like a normal human being instead of some sort of madman in the attic.'

Helen cast a glance at the table where Paul and Angela sat in apparently rapt conversation.

'Is that how people think of him?'

'Of course they do. He comes back from the war, badly wounded, reputedly shell-shocked, and decidedly anti-social. Disappears for long seasons on archaeological digs. What do you expect people to think?'

'Is that why people talk?'

Tony frowned. 'Talk?'

'Stories about Paul ... about Paul and Charlie ...'

'Ah,' Tony said. 'You've heard the rumours? There's no truth to them, you know. For people who don't fit, of course there'll be stories. And there's probably an element of jealousy. Paul did a good job in a bad war. There were two, no three types of officers in the war.'

'Three?'

'Those, like Paul, who were the true leaders. He never endangered his men unnecessarily and he had their complete trust. That's why I know the decision to take the machine-gun post would have been Charlie's idea, not Paul's. Paul knew it meant certain death and Charlie had a complete disregard for his life.'

'What about the other types of officers?'

Tony scowled. 'Then there were idiots like ... James Massey for example.'

Helen stiffened in Tony's arms. 'Massey?'

'An absolute fool and a coward,' Tony's mouth twisted in disgust. 'Unfortunately, there were too many like him. Then there were those like me.'

'Like you?'

'Angela did a perfectly ghastly painting called 'The General Staff.' Get her to show it to you. Then you'll see what I did during the war!'

Tony laughed, but his eyes didn't echo the apparent humour on the subject. 'Looks like dinner is on the table and I'm famished.'

Keeping hold of Helen's hand, Tony led her back to the table. 'What have you two been talking about?'

Angela and Paul looked at each other. 'We were just remarking on how well you two dance together,' Angela said.

Tony pulled a face. 'Now, now, Ange. No need to insult poor Helen.'

'Where are you staying?' Helen asked Paul as the waiter served their supper.

'Tony's flat,' Paul replied. 'My club memberships lapsed years ago. Did you make the appointment with the bishop?'

'An appointment with a bishop? How intriguing?' Angela said. 'Are you thinking of taking holy orders, darling?'

'Stranger things could happen.' Paul smiled. 'No, just some rather tedious family business.'

'I didn't think your family ran to bishops,' Angela remarked. 'Oh, a waltz. Come on, Paul, you should be up for that! You've finished your soup.'

'Angela...' Paul protested but she had him by the hand, leading him onto the dance floor.

Helen picked up her glass of champagne and sat back, watching them. Any casual observer would think they were indeed a couple as Angela rested her head against Paul's shoulder. Contrary to Paul's protestations about his leg at the Wellmore evening, he moved well to the gentle music of the waltz.

'Penny for your thoughts?' Tony broke her reverie.

Helen flashed him a quick smile. 'I was just thinking that Paul and Angela do look good together.'

Tony raised his glass. 'You know, I think Paul and Ange may have had a bit of thing once but it's long over.'

Angela whispered in Paul's ear and he laughed in response. Once more Helen felt the nagging doubt that for Angela at least the affair was far from over.

They returned to the table and Tony insisted on taking his sister for a turn around the floor. Paul sat down and stretched his right leg out, rubbing his thigh.

'That was an error of judgment,' he said. 'Helen, I'd like to ask you for a dance, but my leg…'

She smiled. 'That's fine. I delivered your report. I even met Mr. Woolley. He speaks highly of you.'

Paul made a dissembling gesture with his hand. 'And the other matter?'

'I paid a call on Mr. Bryant's contact at Lambeth Palace and he was most helpful. Suzanna's brother, the Reverend John Thompson lived to a ripe old age and left a large flock of children, several of whom went into the church. There is one grandson, a retired Bishop, living at Godalming in Surrey so I rang and made an appointment to meet him tomorrow. Now you're here you can come as well.'

'What time?'

'Eleven. The bishop was curious to know what it was about so I told him I was researching the Morrow family history.'

'At least you didn't have to lie,' Paul remarked drily.

'There's a train at 9:30 tomorrow morning from Waterloo.'

Paul looked at her and gave her the benefit of one of his rare smiles. She wished he smiled more often. It transformed his face.

'You did well.' He stubbed out the cigarette he had been smoking and looked at his watch as Tony and Angela returned to the table. 'Tony, if you don't mind, I'd like to call it a night. I've a busy day tomorrow.'

'What are you up to?'

Paul smiled. 'I'm going to visit a bishop.'

Tony rolled his eyes. 'You can tell me about it later. Come on, girls. We've had our marching orders. I'll get us a cab.'

Paul touched Helen's arm and pulled her back. 'I'll meet you at Waterloo at 9:15,' he said.

'You still want me to come?'

He looked at her with surprise. 'Of course. It's your story too. Tomorrow morning, Helen?'

'Yes, sir.' she replied softly, responding to the sudden authority in his tone.

TWENTY-SIX

'You're very quiet,' Paul remarked.

Since they had boarded the train back to London from their visit to the bishop, Helen had been staring out of the window, her chin resting on her hand. Her simple grey felt hat put her face into shadow but the line of her neck and the tension in her shoulders gave him a sense that something bothered her.

Helen brought her attention back to the train carriage and patted the thin folder on her lap. The bishop had found among his family papers, a collection of contemporaneous correspondence addressed to Suzanna's brother, which he had given to them. The letters now posed more questions than they answered.

'I've been thinking about Suzanna,' she said.

'Go on.'

They had the carriage to themselves and it would be a good hour before they reached Waterloo. It seemed an ideal opportunity to discuss what they had discovered.

Helen opened the folder and took out the first sheet, a letter from Suzanna herself dated only a few weeks before her disappearance. She read aloud.

Oh, my dearest, dearest brother I cannot begin to tell you how utterly wretched my life has become. I wish you were here so I could talk with you and indeed, confess to you in the fullest sense of the word, the woes that have been laid on my heart. I am heartsick and long for your wise counsel and caring heart. Can you conceive some excuse to come to me soon? I know only that I cannot go on living in this fashion and I fear despair will drive me to a reckless act. Yr. Loving sister, Suzie.

Helen flicked through the other letters, the first from Lady Cecilia Morrow advising of Suzanna's disappearance. She read:

Holdston, September 16, 1812. My dear Reverend Thompson, Your letter of the 10th inst addressed to my daughter-in-law arrived this morning and I fear that it falls to me to be the bearer of bad news. Three nights hence your sister left Holdston taking with her a valise and a small amount of money. I am ashamed to say it, but it has been strongly rumoured for some time now that she has been carrying on a secret liaison with a man of good birth but dubious reputation and we are left with no other conclusion. She has absconded with this man. I cannot describe to you the effect her wanton abandonment has had on her children who cry piteously for her and as for my son, in his already weakened state, we fear again for his life. I have caused enquiries to be made and to date have received no information on the whereabouts of this wicked woman and her paramour. The shame that she has brought to this family, and indeed to your own good name once her desertion becomes common knowledge, cannot be measured. I do not see how, should she somehow be retrieved, she can ever be admitted back into decent society, let alone the good graces of this family. I shall, of course, keep you fully informed of any developments in this matter as of course, I would expect of you, should she endeavour to make contact with you. Yrs. Respectfully, Lady Cecilia Morrow.

'You know I really don't like Lady Morrow,' Helen looked up at Paul. 'Why doesn't she name the man involved?'

'We know that S was a man of respectable family and, sadly, if she did indeed run away with him, she would be considered the guilty party,' Paul replied.

The good reverend must have written to Lady Morrow, suggesting his sister's mind may have been suicidal. Lady Morrow's terse response followed. Helen read it aloud.

Holdston, September 20, 1812. My dear Reverend Thompson, I am in receipt of your letter of the 18th inst and I am afraid I cannot agree with your conclusions. At no time did your sister appear so distressed that I would have thought her capable of taking her own life. Such a notion is preposterous. The fact she took a valise and money with her is, to my mind, and that of the Chief Constable, proof positive that she did not intend to return. However, at your insistence he has caused the moat and the nearby river to be dragged to no avail. I fear we must accept the fact that your sister has proved herself a woman of the basest moral fibre and as far as this family is concerned, we are well rid of her. I will entertain no further correspondence from you on this matter, unless either you or I have news of mutual interest. Yrs respectfully, Lady Morrow

'But he was right to have drawn that conclusion. In her letter she sounded so desperately unhappy,' Helen said. 'Do you suppose she could have taken her life?'

'A suicide would not generally pack a valise or take money with her,' Paul pointed out.

Helen closed the folder.

'But if she was still alive, why no other communication at all? I can understand her not dealing directly with the Morrows, but she was close to her brother. Surely she would have written to him? Put his mind at rest? Sent messages for her children?'

Paul shrugged. 'Shame can render people silent. Wherever she was, mail may have been erratic. She could have written letters that never reached him.'

'But why did she never try to contact her children? I can't imagine walking away from Alice without a word,' Helen persisted.

Paul looked out of the window at the passing fields and thought of the jungles of his childhood. 'I told you my mother died when I was eight? That's not strictly true. I was told she died but in fact, she had run off with the manager of one of the tea plantations. It was only after I was commissioned that a friend of my father's, from the regiment, told me the truth. I wrote to my mother, but it was too late, she had died three years earlier. The man she had been living with wrote to me, telling me that she had written to me every year on my birthday, trying to explain what she did and why she did it. I never received those letters. Evelyn had intercepted them and destroyed them.'

'Evelyn?'

'Yes, my dear aunt. I confronted her with it and she told me that she judged it better that I consider my mother dead than to live with the scandal of having a mother who was a bolter.' He brought his gaze back to Helen, seeing the shock in her eyes. 'So, you see it is quite possible that Suzanna tried to contact her children but someone, maybe her mother-in-law, destroyed the letters.'

She stared at him, her brow furrowing as she struggled to master her emotions. 'Oh, Paul, I'm so sorry. I can't believe Evelyn could be so heartless.'

He shrugged. 'It was a long time ago and I've no doubt Evelyn's motives were pure.' But he could still feel the stab of pain as he thought of those missives consigned to the flames, the words of love and comfort from his mother that he had craved, disappearing in an instant. He changed the subject. 'Is there anything else you need to do in London?'

Helen shook her head. 'I just need to collect my suitcase from Angela's flat.'

'If you don't mind the company, we'll catch the five PM train.'

———

Angela sat on a stool, chewing the end of a brush, regarding her canvas of Waterloo Bridge as Helen and Paul entered the flat. It appeared to take her a moment to comprehend Paul's presence. When she did, her eyes widened and she jumped off her stool like a startled rabbit.

'Paul!'

'Hello, Ange. You don't look particularly pleased to see me.'

'Of course I am,' she said. 'I just wish I'd known to expect you.'

As she spoke, her eyes flicked across the room to the paintings of Alpha and Omega, still on prominent display. Paul stood quite still in the doorway, the color draining from his face. Slowly, as if drawn to the paintings, he crossed the room and picked up the third canvas.

He turned to Angela, his eyes blazing. 'Why...?' he started to say but seemed unable to find the words to express himself.

'I'm an artist, Paul.' Angela said.

Paul set the painting down and turned for the door. 'I'll go and hail a cab, Helen. Be quick or we will miss the train.'

Angela cast a despairing look at the door as it slammed behind him and sat back on her stool, fumbling for a cigarette.

'Sod it,' she said as the match she broke against the flint. 'Sod it! Sod it! Sod it!' She flung the matches at the painting. 'Why did you have to bring him back here?'

'I didn't even think about the paintings,' Helen said. 'I'm sorry, Angela.'

Angela's shoulders sagged. 'I suppose he had to know about it some time.'

Helen collected her case from the spare room.

'I don't know what to say to him,' Angela said. 'Tell him...' She lit another cigarette. 'Tell him I love him too much to hurt him.'

Helen stood in the doorway. 'Do you really want me to tell him that?'

Angela shrugged. 'No...yes...tell him what you like.'

Paul waited on the corner, his hands thrust into his trouser pockets. When he saw Helen approaching, he flagged down a cab and they proceeded in silence to Euston station.

Twenty-Seven

The taking of tea in times of stress was a peculiar preoccupation, Paul thought, staring at the cup of brown liquid that Helen had ordered for him. He had no taste for it. A whisky would have been preferable.

He lit a cigarette and looked out of the window of the café at the passing throng on the station, drawing slowly on his cigarette.

'She's never shown it,' Helen said at last.

He brought his gaze around to her and frowned. 'What?'

'The painting. She's never shown it.'

How could he explain that it wasn't the painting itself? He didn't care one way or another what Angela painted. He admired her talent for bringing the visceral reality of war to a two-dimensional canvas. The stark representation of the ruined church that had served as a field hospital had torn a jagged hole in his memory. Over the smell of coal smoke from the trains, he could once again smell that strange mixture of blood, excrement, and antiseptic.

'What does she call it?' he asked to divert his thoughts.

'It forms a triptych. She calls it Alpha and Omega.'

Paul gave a snort of laughter. 'The beginning and the end?'

Helen nodded.

'It was not personal, Paul. She's an artist. She saw only a representation of an idea.'

Paul stubbed his cigarette out.

Helen continued, trying to fill the silence between them. 'I can see how you would feel it was an—' she struggled for the right words, '—an invasion of privacy.'

'It's not that.'

Paul's eyes moved away from her, staring back at a place he didn't want to remember but remembrance had jerked itself up through the blackness like the rotting flesh of a long-dead corpse had done in the trenches.

He took a swig of his nearly cold tea.

'We have a train to catch.' He knew he sounded brusque but the memories tugged at him and he had no time for social niceties.

Picking up Helen's suitcase, he strode off, leaving her running to keep pace with him. They found an empty carriage and he stowed the case on the luggage rack. Helen sat down opposite him and unfolded a magazine she had bought at the station.

As the train pulled out, Paul looked at her, seeing the concern on her face. He wanted to share his thoughts with her but the words and the pictures in his mind couldn't bring themselves into a cohesive whole.

'Helen...' She looked up, fixing him with her steady gaze.

As he wondered where to begin, the door slid open and a young couple pushed into the carriage with nodded apologies and the moment passed.

Paul looked away, conscious that Helen still watched him with hurt and confusion in her eyes. He stared out into the peaceful, lush, English countryside but saw only the mud, filth, and death of a battlefield in Flanders.

———

British Field Hospital, Furnes Belgium, September 22 1917

Somewhere above him, a single light bulb swayed, casting shadows across a ceiling painted with a mural of some biblical scene. Bits of the ceiling had collapsed leaving several of the wandering Israelites armless or legless.

A shadow loomed over him.

'Well, sorr, 'tis good to see you.'

Devlin. He tried to speak but the words only circled in his head.

'Walker packed your trunk so I found some excuse to visit headquarters and brought it in for you. Don't think you'll be coming back to us for a while, sorr.'

He could hear footsteps, a woman's heels clacking on the stone floor.

'Sergeant Major Devlin.' Angela's voice.

'Mrs. Lambton, sure it's good to be seein' your pretty face.'

'Enough of your Irish charm, Devlin. How are things at the front?'

He shook his head. 'Battalion's been broken up, scattered through the Brigade, no officers and hardly any men.'

Angela frowned. 'No officers at all?'

'Well as ye know, the Colonel's back in old blighty with a broken arm, the Major...' Devlin looked at the bed. 'And with Cap'n Collins and Cap'n Morrow both dead...' He stopped and Paul heard a stifled gasp from Angela. 'You didn't know?'

Angela's voice sounded strangled. 'No. How?'

Devlin shrugged. 'As near as we can say, he was caught in the same shell blast as the Major. Only the Major came back. We don't know what happened out there and we've no body to bury that we could see so we just suppose that he's dead. Missin' in action they'll call it officially and that'll be what they tells the family.'

Back and forth the light bulb swayed.

Charlie... Charlie is dead.

The words echoed in time to the swaying light as Devlin continued, 'I'm sorry to be the one to tell you.'

'No, it's all right. Thank you, Devlin.'

It seemed a long silence before Devlin spoke again. 'How is he?'

Were they talking about him now?

'They're waiting for his condition to stabilise and then they'll ship him back to England.'

'Ah well, his war's over, I'm thinking. It's poor sods like me that's got to go back to the lines. I brought his things. Figured he wasn't coming back.'

'Thank you, Devlin.'

'Well, Mrs. Lambton, I'll be biddin' you good day.'

As the sound Devlin's boots faded, someone picked up his hand. Angela. Angela had been here before. Angela...he felt her lips brush his fingers.

'Well this looks cosy!'

Another shadow blocked the light bulb. A staff officer, his uniform crisp and immaculate came into his line of sight.

'Tony. What are you doing here?' Angela said.

'Same thing as you, Ange.'

'I've just learned about Charlie,' she said. 'Oh, Tony, he's dead.'

Her voice sounded muffled as if she had buried her face in her brother's pristine tunic. Charlie is dead, Paul thought.

Angela is crying because Charlie is dead.

'There, there, old thing,' Tony said as Angela's sobs subsided to choking gulps.

'How's Paul?' Tony asked.

Angela sniffed and blew her nose. 'Not good. They'll put him on the boat train as soon as they can and get him out of here,' she said. 'Does Evelyn know about Charlie?'

'She got the telegram advising he was missing in action. I managed to ring Ma and she told me that Evelyn is carrying on stoically. Sir Gerald is the one they are worried about.'

'Does Evelyn care that Paul is still alive?'

'Of course, she cares, Ange. He's all she has left. She will see it as her duty.'

————

'Duty, duty must be done, the rules apply to everyone and painful though that duty be to shirk the task of fiddle-de-dee...'

The words of the Gilbert and Sullivan song that Charlie used to sing whenever some particularly unpleasant task came his way, clanged through Paul's head. He hated Gilbert and Sullivan.

'Pardon?' Helen looked up from her magazine.

'*Duty, duty, must be done...*' Such a catchy tune. He wasn't even aware he had been humming it.

Paul swung his gaze to her puzzled face.

'Nothing,' he said.

TWENTY-EIGHT

P aul poured himself a whisky and walked over to the window. He propped himself on the wide windowsill. In the glorious summer evening, the view across the village and the church was mesmeric and he wondered if his silent, ghostly companion had sought this view as a solace to his own troubled soul.

Paul looked up half-expecting to see Robert standing sentinel beside him but he was quite alone.

He hadn't told Helen that the spirit of Robert Morrow had begun to haunt him when his uncle had given him Robert Morrow's copy of Homer's *Iliad* in the original Greek for a twelfth birthday present. From that day, he had seen glimpses of a man in the library but it was only when he had returned to Holdston after the war and taken over the main apartment that Robert had become an almost permanent fixture at the window. Watching and waiting.

Now he knew why Robert kept his vigil. He waited for his Suzanna to come home. There had been times on his own long road to recovery when it had seemed easier just to let it all go, close his eyes, and never come back, but at those times he had begun to sense a silent, watching, presence. A shared pain between two men that reached out beyond the restrictions of time. Robert Morrow had become his companion on the journey.

He reached across the table and picked up his copy of the *Iliad*. Opening the battered cover, he read the inscription. '*To my darling husband, Christmas 1805, SJM.*' Suzanna's gift to her soldier husband.

He had carried the battered leather volume with him through the blood and mud of the trenches, using the long, idle hours to translate it, a soldier's translation of that other bloody conflict. From the penciled marks in the margins, Robert had undertaken a similar exercise, one hundred years earlier. He had also recorded the dates and details of his own campaign on the Spanish Peninsula in the back pages. Paul had added his own war to Robert's and the connection that reached out through blood and battle had been forged.

He frowned and drained his whisky. Robert hadn't survived the dreadful battle of Badajoz. Robert had taken his own life, as much a victim of that war as if he had died on the battlefield. A quick, familiar rap on the door brought him back to the present and he turned as Evelyn entered. He slid off the windowsill and greeted his aunt.

'You look tired, Paul,' Evelyn remarked. 'I thought the trip to London may be too much for you. Is your leg bothering you?'

He gave her an exasperated glare. 'For God's sake, Evelyn, I'm not an invalid.'

Evelyn met his angry eyes with hurt in her own and he felt a stab of guilt at snapping at her. 'I'm fine, but thank you for your concern,' he added.

'How was Angela's exhibition?' she asked.

'A triumph,' Paul replied, unable to disguise the brittleness in his tone as he remembered the paintings she had not shown.

'I thought we might commission her to paint Holdston.'

Paul walked over to the whisky decanter and poured himself another glass, offering Evelyn a sherry, which she declined.

He took a swig from the glass and turned to face his aunt. 'It might be good to have something to remember it by.' He took a breath. 'Evelyn, I'm going to sell Holdston. I spoke to the lawyer in London. I will give the tenants the first offer and then it's going on the market.'

He saw the look of horror cross her face. 'Paul, we can manage. We've discussed this—'

'No, we haven't discussed it. You've told me what needs to be done. I have merely agreed with you. Now I think we should look at other alternatives for you. I thought we could have The Gatehouse done up for you—'

'A cottage? You want me to live in a cottage?'

'It has five bedrooms. It is hardly a cottage.'

'And what about you?'

'I'll get a flat in London, near the Museum. I'm sorry, Evelyn, but we can't go on like this.'

'No, Paul. I refuse to talk about it now,' Evelyn said, raising her chin in defiance. 'I only came to give you this.' She pulled a crumpled letter from her pocket. Smoothing out the creases, she handed it to him. 'It came in the morning mail.'

Paul opened the envelope and read the letter.

'Bad news?' Evelyn enquired.

He nodded. 'One of my men is dying,' he said quietly. 'It's from his wife, asking for my help.'

'One of your men?'

He looked up at his aunt. 'My Company Sergeant Major, Pat Devlin. He's the one who saved my life, dragged me back to the lines—' Paul folded the paper. 'I'll leave for Belfast in the morning.'

'Paul, you can't keep running off every time one of your men needs help. The war is over.'

'The war's not over, Evelyn. Devlin is dying from the effects of gassing. I owe him my life and I will do whatever is in my power to help.'

'Belfast? How long will you be gone?'

Paul shrugged. 'However long it takes. I'll telegram when I get there.'

TWENTY-NINE

Helen found a note slipped under her door when she got back from her morning ride. She recognised Paul Morrow's dark ink and strong hand.

Been called away on urgent business. Will be gone at least a week. Not much diary left. Did some last night and will finish it on my return. You'll find the papers in the library. PM.'

The neatly stacked pages had been left on the table in the library with a broken Sumerian clay tablet holding them down. Helen picked up the scrawled pages and sat down in one of the winged armchairs to read them.

A breath of cold air blew gently on the back of Helen's neck making the hairs stand up. Catching the scent of Lily of the Valley she looked up and the breath caught in her throat. A woman stood on the hearth before her, her hand resting on the corbel of the mantel, her gaze fixed on Helen.

Helen stared, taking in every detail of the woman's empire line dress, the upswept hair, and the generous mouth. She looked so real and yet at the same time Helen could see the details of the mantelpiece through her. For a long moment, she held her breath, her gaze transfixed by the ethereal figure.

'Suzanna!' she whispered the name.

As she spoke, the image turned and faded into the bookcase to the left of the fireplace.

For a long moment Helen didn't move, every nerve in her body stretched taut. She had seen Robert but never Suzanna. Did Suzanna's appearance mean she was closing in on the mystery that bound them both to this house?

She let out a sigh and turned back to the papers, wishing Paul were here to share her thoughts.

April 4: At last a few stolen moments together as we accidentally encountered one another in St. James' Park. With my maid keeping a respectful distance, we walked together as two acquaintances should. I confess that I was still feeling vexed and asked spitefully about the wife of Mr. W. Ah, he replied, his face growing grim, that poor lady. Her husband was wont to beat her and she turned to him as a friend, no more. On discovering their friendship, her husband beat her most cruelly and locked her away in their country house. S expressed his deepest sadness that their relationship should have been so misconstrued. I am not a complete fool. I have no doubt that for a man like S, a lonely married woman is easy prey without the attendant expectations of a single girl.

April 16: Oh calamity! My life is shattered. I received a letter today from Robert's Colonel advising that Robert has been badly wounded. It would appear his regiment was engaged in a siege of a town called Badajoz which they took by storm on 16 March. Many good men were lost and Robert fell in the first charge. His life was despaired of for many days and Colonel Muir says he is far from out of danger and will be unfit for service for many months, if not ever. Lady Morrow fell into a fit of weeping and has dispatched her brother and personal physician to Spain to bring Robert home. We are to return to Holdston and await news. My mind is numb, what should I feel for this man who is my husband and has given me no cause to doubt him? Undoubtedly my place is by his side as our marriage vows commanded but then I have already broken those vows. Perhaps this is a judgment from God to recall to me to my wifely duties.

April 19: We are returned to Holdston and to the arms of my two precious, precious children. I am now convinced more than ever that Robert's return is a godsend. How close I came to straying from the path and throwing myself into an abyss from which there is no return. I sent S a short note to the effect that my husband was returning from the war in a state of convalescence and my duty was to him. I wished him well and bade him never to attempt communication with me again. Oh, how my heart ached as I wrote those words but I know I am right.

May 22: Robert is returned. I had not understood the gravity of his wounds and the man who is returned to me is but a shadow of the husband I recall. As it is he barely clings to life. Adele, on seeing her father carried upstairs, began screaming hysterically. Poor child. She is too young to understand this shattered man is her father. The doctor tells me that he is grievous hurt. It would seem his company came under heavy fire from the French musketry and he was hit in right leg and a ball has grazed his face leaving him with a livid scar he will carry for the rest of his life. We placed him in our bedchamber and it is decided that I shall move my possessions to the green bedchamber during his convalescence. Lady Morrow has employed the services of a nurse and I fear that I am quite useless. He was too fatigued from the journey to talk so all I can do is sit with him and pray.

Helen re-read the passages, seeing the pattern of her experiences at Holdston beginning to emerge. When Robert had come home, Suzanna had moved to the green bedroom, the room Helen now occupied— the room where she had found the diary.

She looked around the quiet library, at the bookshelves and the paintings, her gaze resting on the portraits of Suzanna and Robert. The common thread with both of them was this room.

As she looked into their painted eyes, she recalled her conversation with Tony Scarvell the night of the Wellmore soiree. Maybe Tony's Aunt Philomena might be able to cast some light on the identity of the mysterious 'S'?

THIRTY

Tony rang her the following morning to say he had come up to Wellmore for a couple of days and would she care to meet for a ride? Helen asked him to arrange a meeting with Aunt Philomena and, although he seemed a little surprised, he promised to make the arrangements. He rang back later in the morning and they arranged to meet that afternoon and ride over and take tea with Aunt Philomena.

They met at the gates to Wellmore. With Paul away, Helen rode Hector. In his absence riding his horse made her feel closer to him.

Tony, riding his magnificent hunter, smiled in welcome. 'I gather Paul's gone off on some mission of mercy?'

'Evelyn said that he's gone to visit one of his men in Ireland,' Helen replied.

'That would be Devlin. Good man, Devlin. Paul always swore he was the backbone of the company. You know he pulled Paul out of no man's land?'

When Helen shook her head, Tony continued, 'Got mentioned in dispatches for what he did. I personally recommended him for a medal but the brass didn't follow up on it. By all accounts, he went back out into no man's land, threw Paul over his shoulder, and quite literally hauled him back to the trenches under fire the whole time. That's bravery.'

Helen glanced at him, seeing regret in Tony's face. He had no reason to be ashamed of his part in the war, yet for all his bluff words, he gave her the impression that he felt he had somehow let the side down, had not shared the horror of the trenches. Survival came at a cost.

Tony must have felt her eyes on him. He straightened his shoulders and the face he presented to her had returned to one of genial good nature. 'Now what's all this about wanting to meet Aunt Phil?'

'It's to do with the family research Paul and I are doing. You told me she knew more about the Scarvell family history than anyone else. I have a few questions she may be able to answer.'

Tony glanced at his watch. 'Well let's get going, Aunt Phil will be waiting for us with tea and cake.'

'She won't mind if we arrive looking like this?'

'Not at all. Aunt Phil is happiest surrounded by dogs and horses and people who like dogs and horses.'

Aunt Philomena lived in a long, low, rambling house in a village on the Wellmore Estate. The garden gave the appearance of rampant neglect but on closer inspection, the riot of flowers and vegetation had a magnificent order to it.

They released the horses into a small paddock behind the house and walked around to the front door. The face of the elderly maid who answered the door lit up when she saw Tony.

'Master Anthony. It is good to see you,' she said, 'She's in the living room.'

The house, like the garden, was a picture of planned disorder. Paintings jostled for room on the walls and valuable ornaments and leather-bound books seemed to occupy every spare inch of table and shelf space.

Aunt Philomena rose from her chair by a wide picture window to greet them, disturbing three slumbering dogs. She came forward to embrace her great-nephew. Her hair and clothes were of a style fashionable twenty or more years earlier and, to judge from the frayed hems and discreet mends, probably dated from that time as well. Long strands of grey hair escaped from the disorderly chignon, which meant that every couple of minutes, Philomena would stop to refasten the wayward strands.

'Oh my,' she exclaimed on being introduced to Helen. 'Charlie said he'd married a beauty. He wasn't wrong.'

Helen felt herself flushing but before she could respond, Philomena busied herself clearing books off chairs, plying them with tea, cakes, and questions about the Scarvell family. She wanted to know every detail of Angela's exhibition and seemed thrilled when Tony told her that nearly all the paintings had sold.

'I told you that girl had talent,' she declared. 'Who would have thought she could make a living from it?'

'Aunt Philomena credits herself with Angela's artistic abilities,' Tony said with a smile.

Philomena pulled a face. 'In my day it was unthinkable that a young woman would be so vulgar as to paint professionally. You young women today are so fortunate.' She sighed deeply.

Tony set his cup down. 'Aunt Phil was a suffragette. Chained herself to the railings of the House of Commons.'

Helen stared at the woman, trying to reconcile this pleasant, elderly woman with the newspaper photographs of the suffragettes that caused her father to hide the newspaper from her.

'That was a long time ago,' Aunt Phil said. 'Now, I am not so foolish as to think your visit is purely altruistic, Tony. What are you after?'

'Aunt Phil,' Tony declaimed in mock offence.

The old woman fixed him with a twinkling eye.

'It's my request,' Helen said. 'Paul and I are doing some research on the family.'

'Oh, Paul. How is he? Poor man was so ill after the war, you know, Helen. We quite despaired of his recovery and now look at him, gallivanting all over the Middle East, opening tombs and things. Such an exciting life. I would have loved to be an archaeologist. Did you read about that tomb in Egypt that man Carter opened last year?'

Helen glanced at Tony who replied for her, 'Oh, Paul's in fine form at the moment. He came up to London to see Ange's exhibition.'

'Oh, I'm so pleased. I always liked Paul. I always thought he and Angela...not to be. Anyway, my dear, what is the question?'

'We are looking at the history of his great grandfather, Sir Robert Morrow and—'

'—and the 'great scandal'?' Philomena finished the sentence. 'That was still talked about in hushed tones when I was a girl.'

'What 'great scandal'?' Tony asked. 'I can't imagine the Morrows being involved in a scandal?'

'Every family has its secrets, Anthony. If I recall rightly Robert Morrow's wife, Susan...'

'Suzanna,' Helen corrected.

'Ah yes, the 'scandalous Suzanna' ran off with another man. You can quite imagine what a shock that was. Her poor husband was quite distraught. They say he took his own life a couple of years later.'

'We think he did, but you are the first one to say that,' Helen said. 'It is generally described as an 'unfortunate accident'.'

'Oh well, I abhor calling something by another name. I suppose they preferred 'an accident' because it meant it wasn't suicide with all the attendant legal difficulties that presented. There was no doubt in anyone's mind that it was suicide. What is that you want to know about the Scandalous Suzanna?'

'We've found a diary written by her.'

'My dear, how exciting.' Philomena clapped her hands.

'And there is no doubt that she had an attachment to another man but she only identifies him as 'S',' Helen continued.

Philomena's eyes glittered. 'I'd love to see it, dear. Did you bring it with you?'

'No, I didn't. Unfortunately, she wrote in code. Paul has been working on it but he hasn't finished the translation yet and he's been called away so we will have to wait.'

Philomena looked disappointed. 'So why do you think I might be able to help?'

'She met 'S' at a ball at Wellmore where he is described as being a friend of Adrian Scarvell. She mentions he was a naval officer, attached to the Admiralty in London where he worked on 'matters of great secrecy'.'

'Oh, how very dashing and romantic. And you have no idea who he is?'

Helen shook her head. 'We ... I ... wondered if there were records of the time that may have recorded who stayed at Wellmore?'

Philomena bit her lip. 'Of course there are but I don't have them here. They're kept in the offices at Wellmore. The staff has always been scrupulous in their record keeping. I tell you what, I could go to the house tomorrow and see what I can find. What date are we talking about?'

'The ball where they met was held on New Year's Eve 1811. Suzanna absconded in September of 1812. It seems S was a frequent visitor to the house during that period.'

'I do so love a mystery,' Philomena said. 'I shall have the greatest pleasure in pursuing this matter for you.' She glanced at Tony. 'Unless of course, you would like to take on the task?'

Tony raised his hands. 'Not me. Sounds like just the sort of thing you enjoy, Aunt Phil.'

Philomena cuffed his arm but looked pleased. 'It may take a day or so. Is that all right?'

'Paul is away at present so there's no hurry.' Helen glanced at her watch. 'I am afraid we must take our leave, Miss Scarvell.'

Philomena stood up, straightening her crumpled and faded skirts.

'It has been a great pleasure to make your acquaintance, Mrs. Morrow. I shall report in a day or so.'

Tony and Helen rode slowly back to Holdston, dismounting in the front courtyard.

Tony looked up at the old house, bathed golden in the fading autumn sunshine. 'You know I've always loved Holdston. Wellmore is a house you can admire but you can never love it. Holdston is a—'

'Home?' Helen ventured.

'Perhaps that's it,' Tony said.

He moved closer to her and Helen felt his arm around her waist drawing her toward him.

'Helen...' he began but didn't finish.

She looked up at his face and saw the pain of desire in his eyes as he bent his head to kiss her. His lips found hers in a clumsy kiss.

For a moment, Helen was too startled to react. She put her hands on his chest and pushed him away. She took a step backward, staring at him, appalled that he had misinterpreted their relationship.

'I must go,' she mumbled. Turning on her heel, she looped Hector's reins around her arm and started to walk toward the stable.

'Helen,' Tony put a restraining hand on her arm. 'I'm sorry. I didn't mean ... I shouldn't ...'

Helen recoiled. 'No. You shouldn't have ... but it didn't happen,' she said, conscious that her face burned with embarrassment. 'Forget it.'

She reached the stable yard with her heart pounding. Without daring to look back to see if Tony had gone, she left Hector with Sam and ran up the stairs to her bedroom. Still dressed in her riding clothes she flung herself full length on the bed and buried her face in her pillows. As she sobbed into the feathers, she felt the touch of a hand on her shoulder.

Her heart stopped, feeling the cold fingers even through the thickness of her jacket and shirt.

'*The wrong man*,' a woman's voice whispered in her ear.

Helen gave a yelp, muffled by the pillow, and rolled off the bed, looking around the room with wild eyes. She was alone, quite alone.

THIRTY-ONE

On Monday, a letter came from Aunt Philomena. Helen took the papers upstairs to her room to read.

Dear Mrs. Morrow, Aunt Philomena began.

I had a most enjoyable day delving into the household records of Well-more. Oh, my dear, the parties! What a wonderful world to have lived in. As I predicted, the household records of the period 1810 - 1815 are quite complete and include the guest registers of the time. A ball was held to celebrate the New Year on Dec 31, 1811. Among the guests recorded staying at the house are several Naval officers, including a Captain Stephenson. I feel strongly that Captain Stephenson is your man as his name appears quite frequently in the guest registers over the next few months. The last entry recording his name is September 12. The date tallies with the disappearance of the scandalous Suzanna. My thought was confirmed when I came across a letter to then Viscountess written by Lady Morrow. I enclose a transcript. I do hope that is of some help with your investigations. Hon. Ph. Scar.

Helen turned to the transcript of the letter from Lady Cecilia Morrow.

Holdston September 20, 1812 My dear Lady Hartfield, your letter of 19 inst is to my hand and I thank you for your sympathy in this our darkest hour. Robert has suffered a serious relapse and we fear greatly for his health. The children of course are quite distracted and the baby bawls continually for her mother. However, I cannot, in all justice, absolve of you of blame in this matter. If it were not for you, my lamented daughter in law would not have fallen into the company of such a scoundrel as Captain James Stephenson. His reputation is notorious and I am appalled that you have allowed him your hospitality and the freedom to seduce my son's wife, even as her husband lay close to death. The blackguard, when confronted by my man of business had the audacity to deny any knowledge of Suzanna's whereabouts. He admits to having indeed plotted with her to abscond from Holdston but denies the plot was ever carried through. He says he waited in the churchyard for three hours but she never came. He has the audacity to claim to be brokenhearted at what he perceives as her desertion and is to quit England for the colony of Port Jackson. England is well rid of him and indeed of her, if she is, as I am certain, with him. I need not tell you how deeply this will affect us and my grandchildren will forever bear the stain of their mother's disgrace. As far as I am concerned, her name will never be mentioned in our presence again. I remain yrs Cecilia, Lady Morrow.

Helen felt the breath stop in her throat as she read Cecilia's bitter, angry words. 'S' had a name. James Stephenson.

She carefully folded the letters and put them in the folder where she kept the transcripts of the diary that Paul gave her. A knock on her bedroom door made her jump and without bidding, Evelyn Morrow entered the room.

Helen managed a smile. 'Good morning. I was just considering a walk.'

The smile on her lips died as she saw the anger in Evelyn's eyes. 'Helen, I must talk to you on a serious matter,' she said.

Helen stared blankly at her mother-in-law.

'I have been wrestling with my conscience for the last two days and I cannot let the matter pass without saying something.'

'What have I done?' Helen asked.

Evelyn's hands twisted together. 'I thought I had myself quite clear on the subject of your unfortunate habit of flirting—'

'What do you mean?'

'I have just returned from taking tea with Lady Hartfield and she is appalled by your behaviour. She tells me Tony is quite besotted by you and is talking of asking you to marry him.'

Helen's mouth fell open. 'I assure you, I have not given him any—'

Evelyn's head came up and she fixed Helen with hard, cold eyes. 'I saw you kissing him on Saturday so don't pretend ignorance of the subject.'

'Kissing him? He kissed me. I assure you, I gave him no encouragement—'

But Evelyn was in full flight now. 'I said to Gerald when Charlie married you that you would turn out to be a common little piece, after money and a title. And I was right. Charlie would have made you the wife of a baronet, but you want more. You want to be a Viscountess.'

Helen felt the white heat of anger in her face. 'How dare you accuse me of things of which you know nothing! I loved Charlie for who he was, not what he was. I didn't even know about the baronetcy until our wedding. To me, he was plain Charlie Morrow. Unlike you, I do not judge people by how they speak or where they stand in the social order.' She paused, her breath coming in short, tight gasps. 'I came to England at your invitation, Lady Morrow but, as I am now unwelcome in this house, Alice and I will be gone in the morning.'

Evelyn stared at her, her jaw set in a rigid line. Even as Helen watched the woman's mouth began to tremble.

'Helen, I—'

'No, you have said your piece, Lady Morrow. I am an embarrassment to you so I think it is better I leave.'

Evelyn looked away.

'I am deeply hurt that you should think so little of me,' Helen continued. 'I can only give you my word that I have done nothing to encourage Tony's feelings for me. I regard him as a friend, nothing more. Please do me the courtesy of assuring Lady Hartfield of that fact. Now if you'll excuse me I had better see to my packing.'

Turning on her heel, Evelyn left the room without another word, shutting the door behind her.

Helen sat down on the edge of the bed and closed her eyes against the tears that welled up inside her. The humiliation of being labeled a flirt and a 'common piece' mingled with her own conflicted emotions about the men in her life. She did love Tony but not in the way Tony would have liked. He brought light and laughter back into her world but Paul ... enigmatic and withdrawn. She had felt a connection to him she had not sensed in a long time. It went deeper than their mutual love of Charlie. She felt safe around him and his absence from the house left her feeling cold and empty.

'I can't go,' she whispered.

An unearthly moan filled the room. Helen froze, her breath stopping in her throat as the whispering started. Helen put her hands over ears.

'Stop it!' she said to the insubstantial presence. 'I know—we were so close. I'm sorry, I've failed you.'

The room fell silent. Helen fell back on the bed and stared up at the crooked beams of the ceiling, too shocked to even weep.

THIRTY-TWO

D ressed in her hat and coat, her suitcase at her feet, Helen sat at the desk in her bedroom and penned a last note to Paul Morrow.

Dear Paul, I regret circumstances have required me to leave Holdston. The enclosed came from Philomena Scarvell this morning. I am now utterly convinced that Suzanna never left Holdston but met with an accident or foul play. That is the mystery she wants answered. I hope you are able to resolve it. There seems little point in my further involvement. Best wishes, Helen.

She bit her lip and reread the stiff, formal little note. There was so much she wanted to say but there seemed little point. Paul had enough information now to solve the mystery, if indeed there was one, on his own. Beyond that, there were no words to say what was in her heart.

Picking up her suitcase she walked out of the green bedroom for the last time and finding Paul's door unlocked, slipped inside. She looked around the empty sitting room, missing his presence with a palpable sense of regret.

Leaving the folder with her research on Suzanna under Paul's copy of the *Iliad*, she stood holding the note in her hand. If she left it in an obvious place, she had no doubt Evelyn could find it and may destroy it as she had destroyed his mother's letters. In Paul's bedroom, she slipped the envelope under the pillows of the bed, restoring the covers to pristine order.

There was no sign of Evelyn in the hall but Sarah Pollard stood by the door with a doleful Alice beside her.

'You go and tell Pollard that your ma is ready to go,' Sarah said to Alice. The girl hefted a tragic sigh and obeyed.

'I just wanted to say that I'm so sorry, Helen.' Sarah twisted her handkerchief in her hand.

'Sorry for what?'

Sarah looked around the Great Hall. 'She doesn't understand what's been happening in this house.'

Helen looked at the woman. 'What do you mean, Sarah?'

Sarah nodded. 'You and the Major have stirred the spirits. There's been two I've not noticed before.'

Helen forced herself to speak. 'Paul and I... we've both seen them. We think we know who they are. Suzanna and Robert Morrow.'

Sarah nodded. 'Ah, I thought you had seen something when we talked about the Holdston ghosts, but it's not just them, there's another one just come lately, like it's been roused from somewhere bad. There's evil in the house where there weren't none before.'

Helen swallowed. 'Evil?' She touched her wrist where the hand had grasped her. She could still recall the icy touch of those invisible fingers and the overwhelming terror that had accompanied the sensation. She had not experienced the same sense of fear when Suzanna communicated with her. Maybe it hadn't been Suzanna?

Sarah nodded. 'There's anger here, Helen, old, unresolved anger and I fear only you and he together can stop it.'

Helen forced a smile and put a hand on the older woman's shoulder. 'You're being melodramatic, Sarah. I'm sure once I am gone everything will return to normal.'

Sarah shook her head. 'No. It'll never be what it was before.'

'Mummy.' Alice appeared at the door. 'Sam's waiting for us. Do we have to go?'

'Yes we do, Alice, and we have a train to catch. We're going to visit my mother's cousin, Ann, in Cumbria and then we are going explore Paris and Rome together.'

'But I don't want to go,' Alice whined. 'When are we coming back?'

Helen looked down at her daughter. She hated lying to her daughter but the affairs of adults were not a matter for the child.

'One day,' she snapped.

'Where do I send any mail?' Sarah asked.

'For the moment, forward any mail care of the Post office in Haymere, Cumbria,' Helen replied. 'I'll give Ann any other forwarding addresses after we leave.'

'And what do I tell him?'

Helen caught Sarah's eye and smiled. 'Tell Paul I'll send a postcard.'

Sarah forced a smile. 'Well, God bless and a safe journey, Mrs. Morrow and you, young Alice.'

She gave Alice a hug and Helen a quick peck on the cheek and strode away toward the kitchen.

Helen walked out of Holdston without a backward glance.

THIRTY-THREE

In the drab Belfast hotel room Paul lay awake finishing a cigarette and staring up at the ceiling.

Devlin's wife had been expecting him and had wasted no time showing Paul upstairs to the little room where Devlin lay dying. The man lying propped up high on the pillows had the familiar waxen pallor of a man facing death, his face a skull's head over which the skin stretched like parchment. Only his bright eyes, fixed on Paul's face still danced with life.

He tried to raise himself but the effort caused him to cough. His wife wiped the blood from his lips and resettled him on the pillows.

'I'll leave you. Don't keep him talking too long, Major Morrow,' she said and slipped from the room.

Paul pulled up a chair close to the bed. 'Devlin' he said. 'I'm sorry to see you like this.'

'They got me in the end, sorr. But it does my heart good to see you hale again.'

'A little battered but I'll do,' Paul said.

They made polite conversation, exchanging news of their lives since the war. As Devlin's breathing grew more ragged, Paul put a hand over the other man's, clasping the fingers lightly in his own.

'You're tired, Pat. I should go.'

The other man shook his head. 'Bide a while longer, sir. I never got a chance to tell you that I was sorry about the Captain.'

'So am I. There's not a day goes by when I don't think of him,' Paul said with a frankness he would not normally display. 'Pat, perhaps you can do something for me?'

Pat Devlin's mouth twisted in a parody of a smile. 'Whatever's in me power.'

'That night ... I can only remember bits and pieces. Can you tell me what you saw and heard?'

'You went back for him, sorr.'

'I remember that. It's what happened out there in no man's land—' He shrugged helplessly. 'We were lagging behind the rest of the men and I remember an explosion and then, nothing.'

'All I can tell you is that those of us that could, got back to the trenches under heavy fire. I looked back and saw you with the Captain and then a bloody mortar lobbed in front of ye and that was the last I saw.' His thin chest heaved as he struggled for breath. 'They made us pay, sorr—kept up the bombardment all day and night. Nothin' we could do but keep our heads down. They let up in the morning and that's when young Evans saw you crawlin' in through the mud. Couldn't believe our eyes. Trouble was the Huns seen you too and thought you'd make some fine target practice. Tha's when I thought it best to go and bring ye in meself.'

The selfless act of going out into no-man's land went beyond words. Paul's fingers tightened on Devlin's and he hoped the simple gesture conveyed his understanding of what the man had done for him.

Devlin fought his breath and said so softly that Paul had to bend to hear him.

'There were whispers, sorr. After... that you may have 'elped him, if you know what I mean... but no truth to that... Brewer said he thought the Capn' was on his way out even before you went back for him.'

Paul's mouth tightened. 'He wasn't dead, Pat, and I wasn't going to leave him. I owed it to him to bring him back. I allowed him to go out there to take the pillbox out with the grenades before the attack.' He drew a heavy, shuddering breath.

'If you hadn't let him go? How many others would've died that day?' Devlin frowned. 'It weren't the attack that killed 'im, it were the retreat. Nearly killed you too, so are ye going to spend your whole life blaming yourself, sorr?'

Paul slowly shook his head. 'No. I've learned to live with my decision, Devlin, but it can be an uncomfortable companion at times.'

'Aye, it would.'

Devlin nodded and began to cough again. Paul saw to him with the tenderness of a father for a child and laid the wasted body back on the pillow.

The war had taken another casualty. Pat Devlin died in the dark hours of the night with his family, six children of varying ages, their eyes large and fearful in pale faces, his wife and her mother and Paul Morrow by his bedside.

Slowly the fragments of his memory were coming together. Devlin had saved his life and Devlin had given him a few more pieces of the jigsaw puzzle. Paul stubbed out the cigarette and closed his eyes. Remembrance came at a cost.

———

Passchendaele September 17, 1917.

Paul's first thought as he felt the rain on his face, was one of despair. The cold, unrelenting wetness meant only one thing. He wasn't dead. He opened his eyes and looked up into the dark sky and wondered what time it was. Midnight? Past midnight? He parted his lips and let the wetness relieve his raging thirst. It tasted of blood, everything tasted or smelt of blood and worse.

He dared not move. Any movement would attract the unwanted attention of the snipers in the German trenches and, he thought grimly, start his wounds bleeding again. He would die here in this shell hole, already up to his knees in the fetid water beneath him. It would take days to die, a long, slow agonising death. God knew in the last few years he had seen such deaths often enough.

He tentatively moved his right hand, just enough to seek out his holster. Finding it empty, he closed his eyes and grimaced in impotent despair as the memory flooded back. He raised his aching head to look down into the dark, evil water below him. Nothing disturbed its surface except the spattering raindrops. It was as if the earth itself had swallowed Charlie and now tried to suck him down too.

The persistent rain sent icy splinters of cold through his soaked tunic into his bones. If the wounds didn't kill him, exposure might speed up the process. He lay for a long time in the cold and the dark summoning up the courage to move.

A shell burst close by, spattering him with mud and filthy water. Paul shut his eyes, his body responding instinctively, despite his protesting injuries, by curling up protectively. When the ground stopped vibrating, he wiped the mud from his eyes with his good hand and lay quite still, gathering his strength and mentally plotting the one hundred yards that stood between him and the British lines.

Another shell burst and taking advantage of the confusion in the air, Paul rolled onto his right side, crying aloud at the pain. It would be a long, slow crawl back to safety.

The movement had caused the wounds to reopen and he felt warm, fresh blood against his skin, a strange contrast to his cold, sodden clothing. The effort required just to haul himself up over the edge of the shell crater took all his strength and he lay still for a long time expecting a sniper's bullet in his back.

An agonising inch at a time, he dragged himself through the thick, black mud, propelling himself with his right hand and his left leg. As the first grey fingers of the new day lightened the sky, a bullet zinged past his ear, another slapping into the mud just short of his left leg. He raised his head and a wave of despair washed over him at the insurmountable distance between himself and the safety of the British lines.

Exhausted, he laid his head on his arm, unable to go any further, and prepared to die. The next bullet or a trench mortar would finish him. He no longer cared.

He sensed rather than heard the presence of another human being. Opening his eyes, he looked into the dirty, unshaven face of his Company Sergeant Major who lay on his stomach directly in front of him.

'Well, sorr, are ye going to lie here all day?'

He could have wept at the sound of the familiar Irish lilt.

'Devlin! Oh God, Devlin, you fool.'

'We all thought you were done for until Corporal Evans spots you moving. Now we couldn't be leavin' ye out here all by yerself, now could we?'

He felt Devlin's hand on his uninjured shoulder. The touch of another human being overwhelmed him and he lowered his head.

'Sorr, what about the Captain...?'

Paul swallowed and looked up at Devlin again.

'He's dead, Devlin.'

'Ah.' The sergeant let out a deep sigh. 'I'm sorry to hear that.'

A grenade whistled overhead, exploding twenty yards from them, splattering them both with mud, followed by a fusillade of rifle bullets.

'Well, pleasant as it is to be passin' the time o' day with ye, I've a mind to a strong cup of tea and me own bivouac,' Devlin observed. 'As I sees it, there's only one way to get back to the lines and tha's to make a run for it and you, me lad, are in no state for a quick sprint.'

Paul met his Sergeant's eyes. 'Do what you have to.'

'I'm not goin' to be gentle about this, sorr...'

Those were the last words Paul remembered for a long time. They told him later that Devlin had thrown him across his shoulders like a sack of potatoes and sprinted as best he could through the mud back to the lines with the enemy bullets whistling around his head.

THIRTY-FOUR

Paul arrived back at Holdston in a heavy storm. It had been a rough crossing and he had missed the train connection at Liverpool. He felt drained and exhausted with both his bad leg and his shoulder giving him, what Sam referred to as 'curry.'

Evelyn met him in the hall.

'Hello, Paul,' she said with a tight smile that instantly aroused his suspicion.

'Evelyn,' he acknowledged his aunt.

'You need to get out of those wet clothes, sir,' Sarah said, tutting as she took his hat and coat.

'Not until I've had a drink,' he said.

In the drawing-room, he crossed to the decanters and poured himself a large, neat brandy. Clutching the glass as if it were a life preserver, he subsided into his uncle's armchair and ran a hand through his dark, wet hair.

'How did it go?' Evelyn asked seeing to a glass of sherry for herself.

'It was a mess. Devlin hasn't been able to work since the war so the family's been subsisting on charity, the earnings of a seventeen-year-old boy, and the pathetic pension the Government sees fit to reward its soldiers.'

He recounted the plight of the Devlin family. Evelyn listened in silence and when he had finished she said, 'You didn't commit your own money? Paul, you're the one who keeps telling me we don't have the money to keep ourselves let alone bail out every one of your soldiers.'

'I owe it to Devlin to see to his family, Evelyn. They are as much my responsibility as you are.'

Even as he spoke, Paul closed his eyes, trying to ignore the familiar tightening band around his eyes. Through the gathering mist, he sensed something wrong in his aunt's demeanour.

Trying to focus his eyes, he asked, 'Where's Helen? Is she in bed already?'

The long pause before Evelyn gave a nervous cough, confirmed his suspicions.

'She's gone.'

'Gone?' Paul straightened in the chair and stared at his aunt in disbelief. 'Why?'

'She's on some sort of tour of the continent,' Evelyn replied, looking down at her glass of sherry.

'That's a sudden decision.' Paul knew his aunt well enough to recognise obfuscation. He narrowed his eyes and fixed his aunt with a questioning glare. 'What did you say to her?'

'We ... we had a bit of a row,' Evelyn raised her chin defiantly.

'A bit of a row? It would have taken more than a bit of a row to upset Helen so much that she felt compelled to leave the house,' Paul said.

Evelyn sniffed and looked away. 'I was quite wrong about Helen. She is nothing more than a conniving little colonial gold digger who was only here to find some poor fool with a title just as she married Charlie.'

Paul stared at his aunt. 'And what made you arrive at that conclusion?'

'It was obvious, Paul. Anyone who met her said the same thing.'

'No, most people who met her found her beautiful and charming. You mean Maude and a bunch of old bitches with nothing better to do than gossip?'

'Oh, Paul. Don't be so blind. She set her cap for Tony Scarvell the moment she met him,' Evelyn said stiffly. 'She has flirted quite outrageously with him.'

The lights had started to dance in front of Paul's eyes. He ran a hand over them, forcing himself to focus. He didn't have time to listen to Evelyn's malicious tittle-tattle. Any moment now, he would be on the floor.

'Where has she gone, Evelyn? When did she leave?'

'She left on Wednesday. I'm not sure where she's gone but Sarah said something about a cousin in the north. The way she was so familiar with the servants ...'

Paul stared at his aunt, speechless with anger.

He rose to his feet pulling himself up to his full height, towering over his aunt.

'Evelyn, I can't believe what I'm hearing. This is not you talking. Where has this small-mindedness come from? It has to be Maude Scarvell.'

'I saw her kissing Tony. I saw her, Paul. I am quite convinced if she couldn't get Tony she would have made a play for you.' Evelyn fumbled in her cardigan pocket producing her handkerchief.

Paul tried to focus, to comprehend what Evelyn had just said.

'She kissed Tony?' he repeated slowly.

'Yes.' Evelyn wiped her eyes and added in a spiteful tone, 'She is a disgrace to Charlie's memory.'

The temperature in the room plummeted and the whispering began. Paul felt the blood drain from his face.

He closed his eyes. 'You've no idea what you have done, Evelyn,' he said softly.

'I know exactly what I have done,' she defended herself. 'I rid this house of a scheming interloper.'

With infinite weariness, he shook his head. 'You have started something you will regret, Evelyn.'

'Paul, I did it for you.'

'No, you did it for you,' he looked up and gave her a pitying glance. 'And you have driven away your only grandchild. Fine work, Evelyn.'

'You're wrong,' Evelyn subsided into the chair, the tears coursing down her face.

'No I'm not, Evelyn, and you know it.' Paul ran a weary hand over his eyes. 'From the day Helen arrived, you have resented her youth, her beauty, and her spirit. She represented everything you had lost. Charlie loved her and you couldn't accept that.'

'How dare you,' Evelyn screeched. 'If Charlie hadn't died, he would never have gone back to her.'

'Of course he would. He had every intention of going back to Australia after the war. He loved Australia in a way he never loved Holdston.'

'He would never have left Holdston. It's you who should have died, not Charlie.'

The words that he knew had festered in her heart for the last six years had finally been said.

Trembling like a leaf, she rose to her feet staring at him, wide-eyed with horror. 'Paul, I ...'

Paul's mouth lifted in a dry, humourless smile. 'I can't tell you what a relief it is to hear you say those words, Evelyn.'

He set his glass down and ran a hand over his eyes as the bright lights zigzagged and danced across his vision. At the door, he stopped and looked back at her, sitting as straight as an arrow in her high-backed chair.

'Now perhaps we can stop pretending an affection for each other that neither of us feels and begin to live our own lives,' he said.

He shut the door behind him and stumbled upstairs. He made it to his bathroom and sank to his knees on the floor closing his eyes against the crushing pain in his head. He heard voices and sensed Sarah Pollard at his side, but if she was talking to him, he couldn't hear her.

Sam's boots reverberated on the floor beneath him and his strong hands gathered him up and helped him to the bed. Sarah laid cold compresses across his eyes and pulled the curtains closed.

Alone again, he rolled over, hunching up against the blinding, nauseating pain. His hand slid beneath the pillows and his fingers closed over a piece of paper. He held it scrunched tight in his hand as he gave in to the twin demons of migraine and memories.

Somewhere in his nightmares, he heard a voice, Evelyn's voice. Her hand on his shoulder, shaking him.

'Paul! Wake up. Please wake up. I've had a telegram.'
He groaned and shook off her hand.
'They found him, Paul. They've found Charlie.'

Thirty-Five

'Tony?' Helen paused in removing her gloves as a man rose from the comfortable chair by the fireplace where he had apparently been plied with tea and cake by Cousin Ann, who sat beaming across from him. She waved at the door. 'I saw the car. I can't believe it's you.' She moved toward him and caught his hand, smiling with genuine warmth into his genial face. 'What brings you all the way up here?'

'I have to say, old girl, you were not easy to find,' he said. 'The only address I had was the post office, but fortunately, these hills don't seem to be overrun with stray Australians so the good lady there was able to direct me.'

Helen detected a change in tone and a sudden serious cast on his face.

'Is everything all right?'

'Uncle Tony.' Alice, who had just entered the parlour behind her mother, saw him and leaped toward him in delight.

He caught her and returned her enthusiastic hug. 'Hello, Sprite! Can you excuse me? I need to talk to your mother for a few minutes.'

Alice released her arms and looked from Tony's face to her mother's. Her brow furrowed with concern.

'Come and help me find some eggs for our supper, Alice.' Cousin Ann rose stiffly to her feet and held out her hand.

Helen gave her daughter a reassuring smile. 'And then get ready for luncheon.' She looked at Tony. 'You will join us?'

Tony smiled. 'Of course.'

They both waited until Alice and Ann had left the room, Ann closing the door behind her, leaving them alone together in the quiet parlour. The sonorous tick of the clock on the mantelpiece seemed to fill the room and Helen turned to Tony, her chest tight with anxiety.

'What's the matter? What's happened? Is it Paul? Evelyn?' Her fear grew with every word.

'No, they're both fine,' Tony said. 'It's...' He paused. 'It's Charlie.'

Helen's eyes widened. 'Charlie?'

'They've found him, or at least they think it's him. A telegram arrived at Holdston a few days ago.'

She felt her breath catch in her throat and she sank into the nearest chair.

'Are they sure?' she said at last.

'No, but the details fit. An officer of the Warwicks, captain rank found at the site of that last action. Paul's left for Belgium to do the formal identification. I have to let him know I have found you.'

'Paul sent you to look for me?'

Tony nodded. 'He thought you should be there, when they...inter him.'

Helen nodded her head. 'Yes, yes, of course...' Her hands twisted in her lap. 'How's Paul?'

Tony shrugged. 'Hard to tell.'

Helen balled her hand into her fist and pressed it to her mouth.

'When you get a telegram that says, 'missing in action,' you always wonder,' Helen said. 'You wonder if there's any chance that one day...'

A tidal wave of emotion overwhelmed her and the tears she had never been able to properly shed for a husband she knew in her heart was dead, welled up. Tony took her in his arms, holding her, stroking her hair as if she were a small child.

As the tears subsided, she dabbed ineffectually at her swollen, reddened eyes with Tony's pristine white monogrammed handkerchief and leaned against his shoulder as they sat looking into the empty grate of the fireplace.

'What do I have to do?' she croaked.

'I'll telegram Paul to say I have found you and then if you can pack a few things, I can take you to meet up with him and Evelyn in Belgium.'

'You'll come too?'

He nodded. 'Of course. Charlie was my friend as well, don't forget, Helen.'

She swallowed. 'Alice will be wondering where we are.'

'How will you tell her?'

Helen sighed. 'I don't know how much grief she will feel for a father she never knew. I suppose I shall just tell her as it is. She can stay here with Ann. I don't think it would be right to take her. Maybe later...when...'

Alice received the news with silence. For a long time, she sat still, looking beyond both adults to the high, wild mountains beyond the windows. She rose to her feet, crossed to her mother, and threw her arms around her neck. The maturity of her action, indicating that her mother needed comfort, not her, started the floodgates afresh and after a lunch she barely touched, Helen, wrung out like a dishrag, curled up in a ball on her bed and slept, leaving Tony to make the arrangements for their journey.

Thirty-Six

'They won't let me bring him home!' Evelyn wailed as Helen entered Evelyn's suite at the Hotel Metropole in Brussels. The woman, who had all but driven her daughter-in-law from her home, now fell weeping into her arms.

Tony heaved a sigh. 'Evelyn, I'm sure Paul has explained this to you. Under the charter of the War Graves Commission, he must be buried where he fell.'

'I want him in the family vault where he belongs.'

'Even if it were permitted to bring him home, I think he belongs here,' Helen said, trying to maintain a hold on her own emotions.

Evelyn looked up at her and opened her mouth but Helen preempted her. 'I am his wife, Evelyn. It is my decision.'

Evelyn subsided on to a chair, her chest heaving with the effort of controlling her emotion.

Helen knelt down beside her and took her hand. There was so much she wanted to say to the mother of the man she had loved but their last, angry confrontation still lay between them like a yawning gulf.

'Where's Paul?' she asked gently

Evelyn snuffled into her handkerchief. 'He went to Ypres to make the formal identification. He said he'd be back by tonight.'

Paul did not return until after supper. He walked out of the rain into the hotel foyer where the little party sat waiting for him. Helen and Tony rose as one to meet him. Evelyn didn't move.

His appearance shocked Helen. The dark circles under his eyes, and heavy lines of strain written on his face, made her wonder if he had slept at all since the news had reached him.

'Helen, I didn't expect you here so soon.'

'Is it him?' Helen asked between stiff lips.

He nodded and took her hands in his. He looked into her eyes and she read the question there.

'It's all right,' she said. 'I'm not going to make a scene. I've shed all the tears I can for the moment.'

Evelyn gave a strangled cry. Paul released Helen and caught his aunt as she fell into his arms, her sobs muffled against his sodden coat.

Helen pried Evelyn away and put her arms around her shoulders.

'Let me take you to your room,' she said.

Evelyn nodded and leaning heavily against Helen allowed her to lead her into the lift and upstairs to the bedroom. As Helen ran a bath, Evelyn just sat on the edge of the bed, as if incapable of moving. Helen paused in the doorway to the bathroom and looked at the broken woman. She wondered how she could penetrate the wall Evelyn had built around herself.

Kneeling down in front of her mother-in-law, she undid her shoes.

'You'll feel so much better after a bath.'

'Don't treat me like a child, Helen,' Evelyn said with a trace of her old spirit.

Helen rose to her feet, holding Evelyn's shoes. 'I didn't mean to patronise you.' She set the shoes down on the ground. 'I'll leave you to it. Would you like me to have some hot chocolate sent up?'

Evelyn caught her hand and looking up at Helen, her face softened. 'Helen,' she said. 'I know you loved Charlie and he loved you. The things I said before ...'

'... are forgotten,' Helen said. 'Do you want me to stay?'

Evelyn shook her head. 'I want to be alone.'

When Helen returned to the men, she found they had ordered

brandy. A third glass stood on the table. Helen picked it up and took a sip.

'How is she?' Tony asked.

Helen shrugged and glanced at Paul. The look that passed between them said more than words. Evelyn would not be all right.

Paul fumbled in the pocket of his jacket and pulled out an envelope. He emptied the contents onto the table. Tunic buttons, badges of rank, a regimental symbol and, blackened and almost unrecognisable, a gold locket. With trembling fingers, Helen picked the last object up and felt the tears rising again.

With a monumental effort, she choked them back. 'I gave this to him when he left,' she said.

She had bought the piece at an expensive jeweller in Collins Street in Melbourne and had her photograph taken especially for it. If she could open it, she knew the inscription would read, *Always loved, H.*

'I know,' Paul said. 'He never took it off. It left me in no doubt.'

Helen clasped the locket so tightly she could feel it digging into the palm of her hand. She looked up at Paul.

'What happens now?'

'The funeral will be the day after tomorrow at the Tyne Cot Cemetery. Tony, can I leave you to hire a car?'

'Whatever you want me to do,' Tony said. 'Look, you two have things to talk over. I'll see you in the morning.'

They watched him go and Paul picked up the glass of brandy. 'What do we have to talk about, Helen?'

She looked at him. 'I want you to tell me how you are.'

His face gave nothing away as he said, 'I never intended to ever come back, least of all to do what I have to do. What I should have done six years ago.'

'What do you mean?'

'I never forgave myself for leaving him there. I should have brought him back.'

'He was dead, Paul, and you were in no condition to bring him back to the lines. You know that.'

Paul raked his fingers through his hair. 'It's not something I can intellectualise. I survived, he didn't. That's what I live with.'

'Nothing I can say can change that, Paul.'

'No.'

'But for what it is worth, I'm certain had it been Charlie sitting there, not you, he would say exactly the same thing.'

He rose to his feet. 'For what it's worth, Helen, thank you.' She heard the bitterness in his voice. 'I'll see you in the morning.'

She watched him walk away, his shoulders square, his back straight, despite the awful burden that he seemed to carry.

THIRTY-SEVEN

The next day Helen procured a shapeless black dress, coat and hat. Just wearing the awful clothes brought her soul down.

She looked at herself in the mirror one last time and then straightened, lifting her chin. She was Helen Morrow and she owed it to Charlie to behave with the dignity he would have expected of her.

Tony and Paul waited in the foyer of the hotel, so unfamiliar in their stiff, immaculate uniforms that it took her a moment to recognise them. Evelyn sat in one of the chairs, in full mourning, her face obscured by a heavy crepe veil that made her look like a bedraggled crow. Helen took her arm and led the shattered woman out of the hotel to the waiting car.

The weather continued bleak and damp and Helen stared out of the foggy car window as the countryside changed from pleasant fields and hamlets to a desolate landscape of ruined villages, barely passable roads, devastated forests of tree stumps, and churned fields. If she could have imagined the end of the world this is what it would have been like.

Many of the villages through which they passed had been completely destroyed leaving nothing more than piles of rubble where there had once been a bustling little town with bakers, butchers, churches, and homes. Some new buildings had begun to rise from the ruins, but the deeper they drove into the Ypres Salient, the more dismal the landscape became. What had once been fields were now nothing more than wild earthworks from a painting of hell, dotted with small cemeteries of rows of white crosses, like a grim harvest of death.

She stole a glance at the two men, but their faces told her nothing. Evelyn's face concealed behind the heavy veil was also unreadable. The woman sat straight as a ramrod, her black-gloved hands folded over a small black handbag.

The car halted at one of the larger cemeteries. In a far corner of the field, a knot of men in khaki waited for them beside a fresh mound of sodden dirt.

'The regiment sent a contingent,' Paul said, as he helped Evelyn out of the car. 'They're all men who served with us.'

He took Evelyn's arm in his and led her across the field. Tony took Helen's arm and they followed.

The regiment had also sent a bugler and the chaplain. The soldiers snapped to attention as the mourners, led by Paul and Evelyn, crossed through the maze of white crosses to the freshly dug grave that awaited Charlie.

For the first time, Helen had a sense of Paul as the man he had been in the trenches. Charlie had described him as an officer the men would have followed to hell and back. Looking at the respectful faces of the men who waited for them, she could see for herself now that all these men had been to hell and back and owed their survival to their commanding officer.

The sight of the coffin, not so much a coffin but a slender box covered in the Union Jack, brought the reality home to her. She gave a strangled gasp and at once felt a hand under her elbow. She knew without turning that it was Tony.

The internment was short but poignant. The men formed a funeral party with their firearms reversed and carried the coffin at a slow march to the grave where they laid it with reverence in the dark, damp earth of Flanders, the earth that held Charlie these long six years. The men saluted their fallen comrade and the words of the internment were intoned, Helen removed her glove, stepped forward, and picked up a handful of the clay. The dirt fell on the lid of the coffin with a hollow thunk.

As the bugler played the Last Post, Helen stood looking down into the dark hole, not seeing the coffin, but Charlie, bare-headed, his fair hair bright in the autumn sun, whooping with delight as they brought the cattle down from the high country. That would be how she remembered him, not here, not in this bleak field.

When it was over she stood with Evelyn and waited while Paul talked to the men. She watched the way they stood, the way they laughed, easy in his company and yet deferential. Tony leaned against the car smoking a cigarette, deep in his own thoughts.

Paul strode through the cemetery, no trace of his limp. The uniform he wore had sent him back to the time before his injuries. He reached the car.

'It's going to rain again,' he said. 'I suggest we stop in Ghent for lunch and then back to Brussels.'

'Paul.' Evelyn spoke for the first time, throwing back her veil. Helen was shocked to see how old she looked as if the events of the day had aged her twenty years. 'I want to see where he died.'

Paul's face tightened. 'No, Evelyn. Don't ask that.'

Her lip trembled. 'Please, Paul. I want to understand ...'

'Seeing won't help you understand,' Paul said.

He broke her pleading gaze and looked away, into the watery sky with the heavy storm clouds closing in on them before giving a cursory nod of his head.

Helen looked away. She didn't share Evelyn's desire to see, to understand. When Charlie had left her standing on Station Pier in 1915, he had walked out of her life into a world she could never share, even in his death. Her Charlie would always belong to the mountains in that far-off country he had come to love so much.

As if he could hear her thoughts, Paul turned to her and their eyes met in perfect understanding. Evelyn's wish would take them both to a place neither wanted to go.

THIRTY-EIGHT

'Is this it?' Evelyn asked, peering out of the window of the car.

'The road's impassable,' Paul said. 'We're going to have to walk.'

He opened the car door, his polished boots sinking into the black mud. He looked down and shuddered. It felt as if the very ground once more tried to drag him back into the place from which he had escaped.

Helen put a foot on the running board of the car and hesitated, looking down at the muddy track. 'Is it far?'

Paul glanced at her and shook his head. 'Helen, you don't have to—'

Helen met his eyes and he saw no fear in her clear gaze. Where he went, she would follow. They would see this through together.

Tony took Evelyn's arm and half-carried her as they picked the driest way through the mud. Evelyn's complaints about the state of the road fell on Paul's shoulders. This was summer. Winter had been so much worse.

What he remembered as a black, featureless landscape from the imagination of the darkest painter had softened in the intervening years. Brambles and hedgerows struggled back into life and he could hear bird-song. There had been no birds on the Western Front.

What had been the British lines were still clearly visible, although there had been obvious attempts by the local farmers to attempt to restore some order to their land. Like the earthworks of giant moles, the abandoned trenches still snaked their way across a landscape pocked with crater shells filled with fetid water and tangles of rusty barbed wire.

'I can't believe it still looks like this,' Tony spoke first. 'It's been five years.'

Paul hunched into his great coat as the rain began again and addressed Evelyn. 'Are you sure you want to go on?'

She held out a gloved hand to him and he took it, leading her over the line of trenches until they stood on the brink of no man's land.

Several hundred yards of mud, barbed wire, and shell craters still clearly marked the battleground. Freshly dug earth indicated where the search parties had passed, scouring the field for the lost, like Charlie.

'That line of stumps,' Paul said indicating the distant line of severed remains of what had once been trees, 'is all that is left of Polygon Wood. The Germans had held it from the beginning and were well dug in.' He paused and took a deep, shuddering breath. 'At the end of July 1917, we tried to take Polygon Wood. It was a disaster. We lost nearly half the battalion, certainly half the officers. The colonel took one in the arm and was shipped out. It left me in command of the battalion and all I had left in the way of officers were Charlie, a man called Collins, and a few young lieutenants.'

Evelyn leaned against him, her grip tightening on his arm as he continued. 'What took us out was that bunker. From it they had inter-secting arcs of fire with the other bunkers.' He pointed across the waste-land to a cement structure lying low in the ground like a malevolent toad. 'The order came through that we would be going over again. We all knew we would be cut to pieces before we even got halfway.' He stopped. 'It looks such a little distance now...' He ran a hand over his eyes, struggling to maintain his composure.

'Paul ...' Helen's voice sounded choked. 'It's all right, you don't have to go on.'

He couldn't look at her. If he did, he would break.

'You know what happened. You've heard it often enough,' Paul continued, fixing his gaze on the bunker. 'Charlie led a party out before the attack and took that bunker with knapsacks of grenades. As a result,

we took the German lines with the loss of only a handful of men, but,'
anger replaced despair in his voice, 'we were the only ones along the line
who achieved our objective and within an hour we had to pull back or
face being cut off. All that effort, for nothing...again.'

'What about Charlie?' Evelyn's voice, ragged with emotion, cut
across the silence.

Paul turned to face her. 'Charlie was wounded in the sortie. When I
realised he wasn't with us, I went back for him. We were halfway across
when a mortar shell caught us.' He swallowed. 'The rest you know—
Charlie died and I survived.'

'I don't know what happened,' Evelyn pleaded. 'How did he die?
Tell me, Paul?'

He shook his head, barely able to speak. In his head, the guns
pounded again, the smoke, the mud, the confusion...

'I'm sorry Evelyn, I can't.'

'Was he still alive after the mortar?' Evelyn asked, her voice tight and
breathless.

'Evelyn, please.' Tony's voice cut across her.

'He died, Evelyn. That's it, that's all I can tell you. He died.' Paul
thrust his hands deep into the pockets of his coat and lowered his head.

He heard Tony say, 'Let's go back to the car, Evelyn. You'll catch
cold standing out here. Helen?'

He heard Tony moving away but he could still sense Helen standing
behind him.

'Go back to the car, Helen.' He forced the words out through stiff
lips.

'You remember. I can see it in your face,' she said, her voice shaky
with emotion.

He looked away, narrowing his eyes at the distant German trenches.

He shook his head. 'No, just fragments,' he said softly. He turned to
look at her and saw the pain in her face. 'I held him in my arms and he
died.' He took a shuddering breath. 'I remember the crater was full of
water, like these ones. I must have lost consciousness some time during
the night. When I came to, he had gone. It was as if the earth had
reached up and claimed him—' his voice broke and he closed his eyes,
forcing back the emotion.

'Paul, don't go on.' Her voice sounded broken and he felt her arms around him and her head pressed against his chest. She had responded with the instinctive need of one suffering human being to comfort another and for a long moment he didn't move, just stood within the circle of her embrace with his eyes still closed, letting her humanity and vitality seep through the cracks in his façade, breathing life back into him.

'Helen,' he whispered, his own arms encircling her, drawing her in toward him. 'I'm sorry.'

She did not respond but her arms tightened around him.

He had no sense of how long they stood there in the middle of the muddy, ugly landscape that still smelled of death and despair before he sighed and released her, drawing away from her.

They walked back toward the car in silence, once more two strangers in this barren landscape, isolated by their individual grief.

Thirty-Nine

Knowing he would not sleep, Paul had tried to read but he couldn't focus on the words. He rose from the chair to fetch a glass of water and went to stand by the window of his hotel room looking with unseeing eyes down into the quiet, rain-sodden Brussels street.

Passchendaele September 18, 1917.

Paul dreamed a cold, wet pillow was being held over his mouth and nose and the more he struggled, the tighter the grip became. With one last supreme effort, he fought the smothering pillow away and lay still, taking in deep breaths of air that smelled of cordite and death. His ears still rang with the percussion of the shell and the silence added to the eerie sense that he inhabited the world of the half-dead, neither alive nor dead but not permitted to cross the River Styx.

The lowering, rain-soaked sky told him that it was late afternoon and that he had been unconscious for several hours. He tried to move and the limbo world he had returned to gave way to indescribable agony. Through the ringing in his ears, he heard himself cry out in pain. A bullet zinged into the ground just beside his right hand and the damp mud spattered across his flesh, bringing him fully to his senses.

Wounds or not, he had to move and move now. He took a deep breath and tried to assess how badly he had been hurt. His right hand and arm seemed to be uninjured but it hurt when he moved his head, and a tentative exploration with his right hand confirmed his helmet had gone and he had a gash over his left ear that bled profusely. His left shoulder had a piece of shrapnel protruding from the wound, rendering his left arm useless and his right leg—he had never experienced anything like the pain of what must be a broken femur.

With a supreme effort, he rolled onto his right shoulder. Charlie lay beside him on his back and he knew what had been smothering him. It had been Charlie's weight on top of him. Charlie had taken the brunt of the shell burst. Charlie had saved him.

Paul seized a handful of his cousin's tunic in his hand and used it as leverage to haul himself toward him. Hardly daring to breathe, he reached out and touched Charlie's shoulder.

'Charlie!'

If Charlie responded, Paul could not hear him above the roaring in his ears. His head spinning, he raised himself up on his right elbow and saw with a sinking heart what he had not seen before. The torn tunic, Charlie's abdomen, sodden with dark blood and worse. Even as he lowered his head, grief threatening to overwhelm him, Charlie groaned and his eyes flickered open. He turned his head slightly and seeing Paul, something like a smile touched the corners of his mouth as the blood bubbled from his lips.

Paul felt utter despair wash over him. The fact Charlie still lived made it worse. He couldn't stay here and he couldn't leave Charlie out here to die.

Paul raised his head looking for shelter in the desolate landscape. Another bullet whistled past his ear as he saw just a few yards away, a shell hole, a massive crater in the lunar landscape, an old hole already half filled with water.

Paul swallowed. Knotting his hand around Charlie's collar and with the pain of his own wounds suddenly nothing against the basic instinct to live, he started to pull the dead weight of his cousin toward the shell hole. Charlie screamed but Paul had been a soldier long enough to know that whatever he did, however gentle he could be, it would make little difference to Charlie in the end.

The Germans now had a good sight of the two men and began the sport of trying to pick them off. Paul felt a bullet graze his already injured right leg but there was no time for pain.

He had reached the edge of the shell hole and with one last supreme effort, Paul sent them both tumbling into the water-filled crater.

FORTY

A knock on the door caused Paul's hand to jerk, sloshing water from the glass onto the thick carpet at his feet. For a moment, he thought he had been mistaken but the sound came again. A soft rap on the door.

He glanced at his watch. It was long past midnight. He crossed to the door and opened it. Helen stood in the dimly lit corridor, still fully dressed, her arms wrapped around her slender frame. When she turned her face up to him, he could see she had been crying.

They stood for a moment without speaking, both understanding in each other the need for company but not for talk.

'Get your coat,' he whispered. 'Let's go for a walk.'

The rain had stopped, leaving the cobbled streets glistening under the streetlights. The residents of Brussels kept sober hours and the old medieval houses were shut up tight and dark. Their footsteps echoed in the narrow streets as they walked in silence.

When they reached the bank of the canal, they stopped and leaned on the railing above the water looking out over the dark, still water to the far bank.

'What will you do now?' Paul broke the silence between them.

Helen's shoulders heaved as she sighed. 'When I get back to

England, I'll fetch Alice and we will come over to the continent for a couple of months. Then I'm going home.'

'You won't come back to Holdston?'

She shook her head. 'No.'

'You sound very sure.'

She tilted her head to look up at him. The light of the gas lamp cast the planes of her face in strange shadows, her eyes lost in dark pools. He thought of that moment on the battlefield when she had taken him in her arms and held him. No one had ever done that before, except perhaps his mother and Sarah Pollard when he'd been a small boy.

He had not led a monastic life but the women he had bedded had been there for one purpose only. Only in those fleeting few days with Angela had he felt a real connection with another human on a plane that went beyond the physical. Until today. As he looked down into Helen's face, he yearned for her touch again.

He put out his hand and touched her cheek and when she didn't move, he lowered his head, his lips brushing hers in a brief exploratory touch. She took a deep shuddering breath and her body turned toward him. He slipped his arms around her, drawing her close and she responded, her own arms winding around his neck, drawing him down toward her.

The moment their lips touched, the embers that had been smouldering between them burst into flame. A hunger born of the long, lonely years flared. The canal, the cobblestones, the gas lamp above them, and the memories of their grim day on the battlefields of Passchendaele faded into a world that just became Paul and Helen.

With shuddering breaths, they broke apart and stood for a long time enfolded in each other's arms. Paul closed his eyes. He wanted to hold her like this forever but he had nothing to offer her, nothing she would want. She would always look at him and think of Charlie and he could never replace his golden-haired, laughing cousin. They were the flip sides of the same coin, for Charlie there would always be Paul—as dark and closed as his cousin had been fair and open.

He gently disengaged her arms.

'We must get back to the hotel,' he said.

'Paul ...' she began but he laid a finger over her lips, shaking his head.

He saw her frown and despite himself, he reached out and brushed a lock of hair that had fallen across her eyes.

'Helen, tomorrow we will return to England and to our own lives. What happened tonight was just a moment. Take Alice on her adventure and go home to Terrala.'

The gaslight reflected unshed tears in her eyes. He knew she wanted him to say those three words that would bind her to him but to tell her that he loved her would be a mistake.

'And you?' she asked, the tremor in her voice evident.

He shook his head. 'I will do what has to be done. That is my duty.'

She laid her hand on his chest. 'Duty? What about the man in here? What do you want, Paul Morrow?' She pressed her hand hard against his breastbone.

He removed her hand and let it drop.

Turning, he walked away from her. Behind him, her quickened steps rang on the cobblestones as she hurried to catch him. Her fingers caught at his, sending sparks through him. He felt the cold metal of Charlie's wedding ring and released her clasp, stuffing his hands into the pockets of his coat and he hunched his shoulders against a flurry of rain.

As they crossed the Grand Place, the first of the flower sellers wheeled their barrows onto the cobblestones, but they didn't slow their step and parted at the door to his room without a word.

FORTY-ONE

Pollard had left the battered tin trunk in the middle of the faded and threadbare rug. Paul hadn't seen this trunk since the day he had taken his men over the top and never returned. It contained nothing he had wanted or needed since the day he had been wounded. The only thing of value to him, *The Iliad* and his notebook, had been tucked into a pocket of his tunic and had survived the day, slightly bloodstained but relatively unscathed.

He swept the dust from the top, revealing his name and regimental number stencilled in black letters. Taking a breath, he hefted the trunk onto the table and threw back the lid. For a moment, time stood still. The smell of the trenches still lingered in the trunk, as if captured in a time warp. Mud, mould, smoke, cordite, latrines and boiled cabbage wafted up at him and he took a step back.

An empty pistol holster sat on the top of a pile of neatly folded shirts and other clothing. He picked the object up and his breath constricted in his throat. On that last day, the pistol would have been on a cord around his neck. Officers only carried pistols. Rifles were considered ungentlemanly.

With a shudder, he removed the clothes, consigning them to a pile on the floor for the next bonfire.

At the bottom of the trunk, he found the leather writing case, the reason for his search, wrapped in a hand-knitted grey wool jumper. He couldn't recall who had sent the jumper. He couldn't imagine any woman of his acquaintance producing such a thing, with the possible exception of Sarah Pollard who had sent him gloves and a woollen scarf which he found tucked in a corner of the trunk. The jumper probably came from a Red Cross parcel, knitted by an unknown hand for 'one of the boys' at the Front.

He unwrapped the writing case and was surprised to find it in good condition. He traced his father's initials stamped in the corner and reflected that this one object was the only possession of his father's he possessed. It contained only a few small bundles of letters. A collection from Fi, tied up with a frayed string. He smiled at the girlish hand on the lavender coloured envelopes and consigned them to the fire without further consideration.

Besides Fi, there had been few people to write to him in those long, difficult years. Evelyn had written duty letters every month. These he had never kept. There were a few from Sarah with the Holdston gossip. He glanced through them and added them to the fire. Hastily scrawled notes from school friends, also serving on the front and now long dead, followed into the flames. It left one solitary sealed envelope.

He picked up the mud-stained envelope and turned it over. It had one word scrawled on it, in Charlie's impetuous hand.

Helen.

'Come at a bad time?'

Paul looked up, thrusting the letter back into the case.

'Tony. Always pleased to see you.' Paul looked at the trunk and ran a hand through his hair. 'Just thought it was time to clean out the cobwebs.'

Tony gave him a quick knowing glance, and crossing to the table where the decanters stood, poured whisky for them both.

The men sat in Paul's battered armchairs in silence for a long few moments before Tony spoke.

'How's Evelyn?'

Paul shrugged. 'Busy with her plans to hold a memorial service for Charlie next week. Do you know where Helen is at the moment?'

They had parted as virtual strangers at the hotel in Brussels on the morning he had kissed her. Helen had been adamant that she had to return to Alice and he did not try to prevent her. Evelyn had been prostrate with grief and he had felt unable to leave until she was fit to travel. So he had let Helen go.

He assumed she had stayed in Cumbria since her return and he envied her the peace and healing tranquility of the Lake District.

'London,' Tony replied. 'I inveigled her back down south with the promise of London treats for the Sprite. Paul...'

The sudden, unfamiliar seriousness in his friend's tone made Paul look up.

'Paul, I'm going to ask Helen to marry me.'

Paul looked down at his glass and when he didn't answer, Tony continued. 'Is that...? I mean...do you have any problems with that? Is there anything between you and Helen I should know about? You know I would never...'

Paul heard the yearning in Tony's voice and understood that he needed to be given permission to do as he intended.

Paul made a dismissive gesture with his hand. 'Good God, no. She's a terrific girl and she deserves to be happy. You have my blessing, for what it's worth.' Even as he said the words, a knife twisted in his gut.

Relief flooded Tony's face.

'What are you going to do about your mother?' Paul continued. 'She seems to have formed an unfavourable view of Helen.'

Tony set his glass down and rose to his feet, his chin set in an unfamiliar defiance. 'We will just have to show her she's wrong.'

Paul swilled the last of the whisky in the bottom of his glass before he looked up at Tony. 'Tony, I can see how you feel about her but what does she feel about you? Does she love you?'

The defiance fled from Tony's face and his mouth drooped. 'Truth? I don't think so, not like I feel about her, but love can come, don't you think?'

Paul shrugged. 'I'm the last person to ask. I've never had the luxury of being in love.'

After the door shut behind Tony, Paul set his glass down on the table and stared at the flickering flames of the fire. The fire died down and a chill descended on the room.

'You know something,' he said to the silent watcher at the window. 'I've never been in love before I met Helen Morrow and now I'm letting her go. Am I doing the right thing?'

FORTY-TWO

Helen took the seat Tony held out for her and looked around the Savoy Grill.

'Tony, this is too generous,' she said. 'A suite at the hotel and now dinner?'

'Only the best for my goddaughter and her mother.' Tony smiled. 'I haven't had much of a chance to spoil Alice and if you're intent on disappearing off to Paris, I must make the most of my time with you both.'

Helen smiled in response. 'You are a good godfather. Alice adores you.'

Tony flushed with pleasure. 'I'm glad to hear that. Everyone needs to be adored by someone.' He looked at her with serious eyes. 'I haven't had a chance to ask how you are?'

'Oh, I'm fine. At peace with myself, if that's possible. How are things at Holdston?' she asked, trying to keep the tone of her voice casual.

Tony shrugged. 'Much the same. Evelyn is soldiering on as she does, but she seems to have lost her fight.'

'I'm sorry. And what about Paul?'

'Tied up with getting the estate into something saleable. Now you remind me I'm actually on an errand from Evelyn. She asked me to give you this.' He handed over an envelope.

'Do you mind if I open it?' Helen asked.

Tony shook his head.

Helen scanned the contents of the short, sharp note.

My dear Helen, you left before I had a chance to tell you of my plans for Charlie's memorial service. It will be held on Wednesday next in the church here at Holdston. As Charlie's widow and the mother of his child, I expect you would both wish to attend. For your information, I intend to dedicate a scholarship at the local school to his memory. I thought that might please you. Lady E. Morrow.

Helen handed the note to Tony and said, as he scanned it, 'I left Brussels because I had a train to catch and she was in no state for visitors. She has such a knack of making everything I do sound like it's my fault. Of course, I will go to the service. Are you invited?'

'We all are. I'll drive you and Alice to Warwickshire.'

'Thank you. I'll arrange a hotel in Warwick. That might be easier than staying at Holdston.'

'Oh, I'm sure ... that is...'

Helen cast Tony a curious glance. He seemed discomposed. A fine sweat had broken out across the bridge of his nose and he downed his wine like cordial.

'Is something bothering you, Tony?'

He looked up and gave her a rueful smile.

'You're going to think me the most frightful ass!' Tony's mouth quirked. 'Ever since I first saw you in the drawing room at Wellmore, you've been all I've thought about.'

Helen stared at him, willing him not to say the words she knew would follow. He held up his hand, cutting short any protestation from her.

'Let me finish. I know you don't love me, Helen, but do you think you could come to love me?'

'What sort of question is that?' Helen's heart thudded against her ribs.

'I'm asking you to marry me,' Tony swallowed, staring at her.

'Tony—' Helen's hands twisted the fine linen napkin on her lap as she struggled to find the right words.

'You don't have to answer straight away,' Tony said hurriedly.

'I ... I don't know what to answer,' Helen said. 'Can I think about it?'

Tony's hand shook as he picked up the glass.

'Take all the time you need.' He added with a smile, 'As long as the answer is yes. You must have known how I felt about you?'

She shook her head, remembering the day he had kissed her. Of course, she had known but she had thought it nothing more than a passing fancy.

He picked up her hand and pressed her fingers to his lips. 'I think you are the most beautiful, enchanting, delightful, intelligent woman I have ever met.'

'Your parents will most certainly not approve.'

Tony smiled. 'Oh, Father thinks you're wonderful. Mother, on the other hand, may take some convincing. Charlie's memorial service is in two days. Let me spoil you for a couple of days and then come back to Wellmore with me. You can stay there and work your charm on her?'

'Tony you're making an assumption—' Helen began.

'Yes, I am. Come down to Wellmore, as my fiancée, Helen.'

'You said I could take all the time I needed.'

'I lied. Helen, face it, I'm charming, moderately handsome, incredibly wealthy, possessed of one of the most beautiful houses in England and a title and I am completely, utterly, in love with you. How could you refuse me?'

Helen looked at him. She could think of no logical reason to say no, except that she was, quite possibly, in love with another man.

No.

She knew without any doubt that she loved Paul Morrow. The memory of their kiss on the bank of the canal in Brussels came back with such force that she touched her lips as if she could still feel the trace of that instant in time. She had replayed that scene over and over in her mind and convinced herself that what had passed between them was nothing more than two lonely people thrown together in an unreal situation. Just for a heartbeat, it had seemed possible that her feelings had been reciprocated but then he had pulled away and the moment had gone.

Helen looked away. The band had begun to tune up and it gave her a distraction. She could forget any thought of a future with Paul Morrow. He had chosen his solitary path.

She looked back at Tony, at the boyish eagerness in his face and the love in his eyes. She liked Tony and that in itself was probably as good a start to any marriage. What was the alternative? To live out her life on Terrala as cook, cleaner, and occasional secretary to her father and brothers? Just another war widow?

A bleak and lonely future lay before her and as Tony had said, love could come in time. Friendship seemed a good start. She closed her eyes for a moment.

'Very well,' she said. 'On one condition, Tony.'

'Anything.'

'I don't want any public announcement until after the memorial service. It just wouldn't be right.'

Tony's face sobered and he nodded. 'No, of course not. I quite understand. But for tonight, Helen, let's have some fun.'

Tony's eyes lit up and he sent the waiter scurrying for the best champagne. The band struck up a tune and Helen mustered a smile.

'Let's dance,' she said.

FORTY-THREE

Tony's Riley came to a halt in front of the impressive portico of Wellmore House. Helen looked up at the haughty exterior of the house and gave a Tony a nervous smile.

He took her hand and squeezed it encouragingly. 'It'll be fine. You'll see.'

Lady Hartfield received them in her private parlour on the first floor. She stood up to greet her son, her fingers playing with a long string of pearls.

'Hello, Ma.' Tony dropped an affectionate kiss on her powdered cheek.

'Darling,' she responded but her eyes remained fixed on Helen. 'Mrs. Morrow, what an unexpected pleasure.' Her tone dripped with ice but she extended a hand, which Helen took and shook firmly.

'Lady Hartfield. It's very kind of you to have me to stay.'

Maude tightened her lips in a manner that indicated that she was not sure she had extended the invitation.

'Is your daughter with you?' she enquired.

'She's staying up in London with Angela. Ange is taking her to a show tonight and will bring her down for the memorial service tomorrow,' Tony said. Where's Pa?'

'In the library, I think.'

Tony turned to the maid who hovered in the doorway. 'Please ask his Lordship to join us.'

'Tony?' Her ladyship's gaze rested on Helen.

Tony's hand closed over Helen's and he drew her to his side as Lord Hartfield came stumping into the room.

'Anthony, my boy.' He slapped his son on the shoulder. 'What is that you have to say that necessitates disturbing my afternoon nap?'

'Helen Morrow has consented to marry me,' Tony said without preamble.

For a moment time stood still. Lady Hartfield's horrified look remained frozen on her face. Lord Hartfield just blinked.

'Good God!' he said. 'What d'ya think of that, my dear.'

The horror on Lady Hartfield's face had been replaced by an expression of refined good manners. 'Something of a surprise, I must say,' she managed with a stiff smile not reflected in her eyes.

'I would have thought it would be something of a relief, Ma,' Tony remarked drily. 'No more debutantes to entertain.'

Lady Hartfield gave a nervous laugh. 'Quite. I think some sort of celebratory dinner is called for. I shall go and speak to Cook. Why don't you show Helen to the yellow bedroom and we can discuss this more fully over dinner.'

———

Helen dressed carefully in the new green silk gown Tony had insisted on buying for her. For the hundredth time, she checked her reflection in the mirror. She had never been so nervous in her entire life.

With her heart thudding, she walked downstairs toward the withdrawing room. The door was slightly ajar and she could hear Lady Hartfield's voice cutting through the room.

'We know nothing about her, Tony.' She spoke in a harsh, uncompromising tone that chilled Helen's blood

'You're being ridiculous, Ma. I know as much as I need to know about her.'

'She could be descended from convicts for all we know.' Lady Hart-field was in full flight now.

Helen took a breath to steady her jangling nerves. She opened the door and stood there, confronting her foe, her fingers playing with her necklace. Tony and his mother turned to face her. Lady Hartfield paled as she realised Helen had probably overheard her last outburst.

'My family are respectable and respected free settlers, Lady Hart-field. We own a substantial cattle property in central Victoria. My father is a member of the Victorian Parliament. Is there anything else you wish to know about me?'

Lady Hartfield swallowed. 'My dear, you must understand. Our family—'

'Our family,' Tony interjected, 'needs an infusion of fresh blood. Helen is the best thing to happen to us in years.'

'It's all right, Tony,' Helen said. 'I would rather that everything that needs to be said is said now, upfront. I don't want to spend the rest of my life tiptoeing on eggshells.'

'Well said, young lady!' Lord Hartfield rose from his chair. 'I for one, Maude, endorse everything the lad has to say. We bloody well need some spirit in this family. All those damned ninnies you've been parading past the boy are enough to make a man puke. I like this gal.'

'Cedric.' Outnumbered, Lady Hartfield turned on her husband.

'Lady Hartfield,' Helen kept a quiet, deferential tone to her voice despite the raging anger inside her. 'I hope that as we come to know each other better, we can be friends.'

'My dear, don't misunderstand me,' Lady Hartfield said stiffly, 'My concern is only that Tony makes the right choice, and if he feels that you are that person then who am I to stand in his way.'

Lord Hartfield got to his feet. 'Good, air cleared. Now let's have some champagne and you can start planning the wedding, Maude. You'll enjoy that.'

'Do you have a date?' Lady Hartfield's hand closed over the stem of the champagne glass offered to her by the butler.

Tony opened his mouth to speak but Helen interposed. 'We've not made any plans. In fact, we think it best that any official announcements wait for a little. My husband's memorial service is tomorrow and it would be quite inappropriate to be planning weddings until a decent interval has passed.'

She glanced at Tony hoping he could read the mute appeal in her eyes.

Tony cleared his throat. 'Helen is quite right. We'll hold off on any official engagement announcement for a few weeks and then we can start making plans.' He raised his glass. 'Let's drink to future happiness.'

FORTY-FOUR

A dismal summer drizzle wreathed the little church at Holdston. Helen pulled the collar of her new coat up around her face as she followed the Hartfields into the churchyard. Tony took her arm and patted her hand. Once more dressed in uniform, he bore little resemblance to his normal, cheery self. It was as if the uniform, like the rain, shrouded him, hiding the real Tony from view.

The men, who had served with Charlie, gathered at the entrance to the church, talking in low, reverential voices. Beneath the brass memorial plaque that already bore Charlie's name, numerous wreaths and flowers had been placed and a soldier stood, head bowed over his reversed weapon. The vicar, his plump cheeks pink with importance bustled about organising the choir, the organist and the seating arrangements.

Soldiers, officers and the whole of the Holdston tenantry had gathered to pay their last respects to Charles Morrow, packing the church to standing room only. It seemed a long way from the lonely grave in Flanders where they had stood less than two weeks earlier.

Helen tightened her hand on Alice's and holding her head high, walked down the aisle to the Morrow family pew, which stood empty. For the time being, she was still a Morrow, Charlie's wife, even if it would be for the last time in her life. As she knelt in prayer, the fingers of her right hand touched her gloved left hand, feeling the presence of her wedding ring beneath the fine kid. She couldn't bring herself to remove Charlie's ring. Not yet. Tony slipped into the pew behind her with his mother and Angela.

The church fell silent, Helen turned to watch as Evelyn and Paul entered the Church. For a brief moment, she tried to reconcile her first meeting with Paul Morrow with the tall, straight officer in an impeccable uniform. Evelyn, veiled in heavy mourning as she had been on the day they'd buried Charlie, clung to his arm like a drowning woman.

Evelyn inclined her head to acknowledge Helen and sat down beside Alice, grasping the child's hand, and giving it a squeeze. Over Evelyn's veiled head, Helen glanced at Paul. He inclined his head, acknowledging her with a flicker in his eyes, and mouthed a greeting at Alice.

The eulogy, given by the present Commanding Officer of the regiment, gave few clues as to who Charlie was or why he had died. It seemed unlikely the man had known him and the generalisations and platitudes would have fitted the description of any officer who had died in the Great War. When he had finished, Paul rose to his feet. His boots rang on the cold flagstones as he took his place behind the great spread bronze-winged eagle that served as a lectern.

With deliberate care, he set his cap down and took a moment to look around the crowded church.

'You are here today,' he said, 'to remember my cousin, Charles Morrow. In your memories, he will always hold a place of significance either as a son,' he looked at Evelyn, 'or a husband,' his gaze moved to Helen, 'or a friend, a comrade or the squire's son. All of us here were touched in some way by Charlie's life. But there is one person here among us today whose right to know Charlie was denied her. His daughter, Alice.' He looked directly at the child. 'Alice, all you will ever know of the man who was your father are the stories you will be told or the photographs you will see. Your right to know him as his daughter, with that special place in his life, was taken away from you. I wish it was in my power to bring it back for you, but I can't. All I can give you is an assurance of two things that I want you to remember for the rest of your life. The first is that your father was one of the bravest men I ever met.

You have heard Colonel Pearson tell us your father showed exceptional courage in adversity. Courage is a strange thing, Alice. Courage to me means an acknowledgment of fear. Yes, your father showed extraordinary courage on the day he died, but he didn't do what he did without being afraid. We were all afraid but if it hadn't been for your father many, many more men would have died.

'The other thing I want you to know is that he loved you. He carried two photographs with him, always, and they were with him when he died, one of your mother and one of you, Alice. Carry those memories of him with you, always and they will be a part of you that will be forever that special relationship between a father and his daughter.'

As he spoke, his eyes did not leave Alice. The child sat up straight in the pew beside Helen, apparently mesmerised by him. Behind her veil, Evelyn's attempts to stifle her sobs only made them more audible. Helen sat with her hand in her daughter's, dry-eyed and oblivious to the snuffling from the others in the pews behind her.

Paul's eyes swept the congregation again and with a nod to the bugler, he turned to face the bronze plaque. The congregation rose for the playing of the Last Post by the regimental bugler. Still standing at the lectern, Paul replaced his cap and stood ramrod straight, his face expressionless as he saluted the memorial.

As the last note died away, he returned to his seat beside Evelyn. Helen glanced at him as he ran a hand through his dark, well-cut hair. He took a deep breath, the only outward sign of his own state of mind. Beside him, Evelyn raised a mangled, sodden handkerchief to her veiled face. Paul looked down at her and took her arm, folding it in his. She leaned her head against him.

———

Tea and sandwiches were provided at the house. The Great Hall, familiar to Helen as an echoing void, was filled with chattering voices and constrained laughter. Tony had been drawn away from her and had become the centre of a group of young men, all in uniform, including the odious James Massey, who beyond a few expected platitudes ignored her.

Angela appeared to be charming the regiment's commanding officer and Evelyn sat straight backed on an oak settle. Alice, dressed in a neat black dress with a spotless white collar and cuffs sat beside her grandmother, holding her hand. Evelyn had removed her hat and veil and as Tony had said, she looked as if the fight had gone from her. If Paul still intended to sell Holdston, Helen doubted Evelyn would object.

'Helen?'

At Paul's voice she started. 'Sorry, I was miles away.'

'I think you're allowed to be,' he said. 'I'm sorry Evelyn put you through this.'

She shook her head. 'No need for apologies. It was a wonderful service. Thank you for what you said to Alice. She will carry it with her always.'

He nodded and leaned back against the windowsill beside her.

'You seem so different in uniform,' she said.

Paul looked down at the toe of his polished boot. 'I never thought I'd ever wear it again. Now I've worn it twice in as many weeks. Strange isn't it?'

'No, it looks like you belong in it.'

He shuddered. 'God forbid.' He looked at her. 'And you Helen, I see you have adopted a new uniform too?'

Helen smoothed the skirts of her exquisitely tailored black skirt. 'Lady Hartfield insisted. She did not approve of my homemade wardrobe,' she said. 'I have been well and truly gentrified.'

'Tony tells me you're engaged. Congratulations.'

Helen forced a smile and glanced at Tony. 'Tony shouldn't have said anything. It's not official. I wanted to wait for this to be over but thank you.'

'You should know Tony is incapable of keeping a secret. He's a good man,' Paul said.

For a moment, their eyes met and the breath stopped in her throat. *The wrong man*, Suzanna had whispered in her ear. Helen searched Paul's face for a spark, something to convince her that she had chosen to marry the right man for the right reasons. Paul Morrow had too many years of hiding his emotions and if he felt anything, she could not read it in his eyes.

'I'm a sore disappointment to Lady Hartfield. I think she hoped for the daughter of a Duke.'

Paul smiled and dropped his voice. 'Let me tell you something about Maude Scarvell. Have you heard of the Smallwood department stores?'

Helen nodded.

'Maude was born Maude Smallwood. Her father started in a corner shop in Manchester and built a chain of very successful stores. Tony's father married the blushing young debutante for one reason only —money.'

Helen stared at him. 'Maude is ...?'

'A shopkeeper's daughter,' Paul said. 'Don't let her pretensions get to you, Helen. Nobody is ever quite what they seem.'

'And Evelyn?' Helen's eyes moved to her mother-in-law.

'Oh, Evelyn is the real thing. The youngest daughter of an Earl.'

As Helen watched, the commanding officer of the regiment approached Evelyn. She held out a hand to him and he bowed over it with old-fashioned courtesy.

'Evelyn's stopped arguing with me about selling Holdston.'

'So, you are still going to sell?'

'When I can find a buyer.'

She smiled. 'And the Holdston ghosts?'

'They can torment whoever they like.' He returned her smile. He paused and then added. 'Helen, I have something for you. Do you still ride in the mornings? Could you meet me tomorrow?'

'Yes. Where?'

'In the woods behind the church, seven in the morning?'

She nodded.

Paul straightened. 'Good. I'll see you then. I'd better rescue the colonel from Angela.'

As he turned to walk away from her, she said, 'Paul...'

He turned back to look at her the question in his eyes. She shook her head. 'Is it the diary?'

'That and something else,' he said. 'It can wait till tomorrow.'

FORTY-FIVE

After the last guest had left, Paul stood at the foot of the steps and watched as Evelyn, drawn and pale, climbed the stairs to her room. She had refused his offer of assistance and took the stairs slowly, like a person with all the cares of the world on her back.

As he watched Evelyn, he thought of Helen. It had seemed strange to see her walk out of Holdston on Tony's arm. He felt a sense of loss and grief far greater than he had expected.

Only Angela, who had driven herself across from Wellmore, remained. He shook himself out of his reverie and found her helping Sarah and Annie carry dirty glasses into the kitchen. He caught her arm as she passed him.

'Enough of that, Ange,' Paul said. 'I've got a fire lit in the library, join me for a drink.'

In the familiar room, Angela sank into one of the wing chairs while Paul removed his Sam Brown belt, undid the buttons of his jacket and poured them both a substantial glass of whisky.

'Thanks for staying on,' he said. 'I could do with some cheerful company.'

'Darling, always happy to oblige,' Angela said. 'I suppose you know about Tony and Helen?'

'Yes. Good news. I'm happy for them. How's your mother taking it?'

'Oh, badly. Poor Helen is in for a rough ride with Ma.'

'Is there nothing your mother doesn't feel compelled to interfere with? I'm sorry, Ange, but I've had enough of your mother. She is a malicious gossip.'

'Of course she is. Poor dear hasn't much else to amuse her.'

'She takes delight in destroying other people's lives.' Paul could barely disguise the bitterness in his tone.

Angela frowned. 'What do you mean?'

'Don't tell me your mother wasn't behind the reason Helen left Holdston?'

'Mother told me it was a row with Evelyn.' Angela sighed. 'But it was probably Mother's fault. She was convinced Helen was after Tony. Turns out she was right.'

'In fairness, the boot was on the other foot, Ange.'

Angela shrugged. 'Tony did rather take a shine to her on their first meeting. Anyway, Ma is of the view that no girl is good enough for Tony. Tony jibbed at all her selections and is plainly besotted with Helen so it became Helen's fault.' She took a cigarette out of her small, silver cigarette case and lit it. 'Enough talk about Helen. Let's talk about something different.'

'I'm not wonderful company at the moment.'

Angela smiled. 'Oh, I'm sure I can tolerate you for a little while.' She inhaled, blowing the smoke into the air. 'I hate this room. Don't know how you can stand working in it.'

'It's convenient. Are you going to offer me one of your cigarettes?'

Angela glanced at the cigarette in her hand and threw him the cigarette case and her lighter. She took a slow draught of her cigarette. 'Actually, Paul, I wanted to apologise.'

'What for?'

'The painting. I should have told you about it.'

He frowned. 'The painting? I'd forgotten about that.'

'Oh, had you? You mean I've been agonising for weeks over what to say to you for nothing?' Angela said. 'Paul, I'd like to show it. Just a small show in a private gallery, and you won't be identified.'

'For God's sake, Angela. You can do what you like with the bloody thing. You don't need my permission.'

She studied him for a few moments. 'Thanks. I thought seeing it had upset you?'

'It did, but not for the reason you think, Ange,' he said. 'You're a brilliant artist and it's a powerful piece of work. Good luck with it.'

Angela frowned. 'What do you mean it upset you but not for the reason I think?'

He shook his head. How could he explain the flashes of memory that left him wide awake in a cold sweat in the middle of the night? The dread feeling that the whispers and rumours about Charlie's death were closer to the truth than he dared believe.

Angela smiled. 'You're a strange man, Paul Morrow.' She gestured at the table. 'What are you working on?'

Paul looked at the jumble of papers on his desk and noticed the corner of the green leather diary poking out from beneath a quote for repairs to one of the farms.

'The things that need to be put in place to sell Holdston,' he said. 'It's not as simple as I thought.'

Angela rose to her feet and wandered over to the bookcase, running her fingers along the spines of the books. 'I must say Holdston seems empty without Helen and the child. They seem a bit lost at Wellmore.' She turned back to look at him. 'I like them enormously. I had great fun with Alice on our own in London.'

Paul agreed. It was not just the house that felt empty. Helen had taken something out of his life too. Something he wanted back. He rose to his feet and crossed to the table to pour another whisky.

Angela's perambulations brought her around the table until she stood next to him.

She laid her hands on his shoulders, slipping her arms around his neck, forcing him to look into her eyes.

'Ange...' he began.

She smiled up at him. 'I've been thinking about that week ... our week.'

Paul closed his eyes for a moment. That week in 1916 when, for the first and only time in his life, he had felt free, untrammelled by the burden of responsibility or society. His arms circled her slender waist and he closed his eyes, his lips brushing her short, dark hair. She smelled of linseed oil and felt warm and familiar in his arms.

'We were good together, you and I,' she murmured.

Paul sighed. 'We can't go back, Angela.'

'Why not?' She tightened her grip forcing him to look down into her face. 'I've always loved you, Paul. What happened in Flanders doesn't change that.'

'But I've changed, Angela.'

Angela leaned her head against him. 'Remember the Waterloo hotel, Paul? We didn't get out of bed for two days ...'

Paul gently disengaged her arms and stood holding her hands. 'Angela, they're memories. Good memories, but we can't get that time back again. It's gone.'

Angela stiffened and broke away from him. 'Is it Helen? Paul, she's not for you. Tony's a far better catch than you'll ever be.'

Paul looked away. 'I wish them both the best of luck,' he said. 'There's nothing between Helen and me except what could have been a good friendship without the interference of your darling mama and my aunt. She'll marry Tony in a couple of months.' He cupped her chin and looked into her eyes. 'When I've sold Holdston it will be time for me to move on.'

'What will you do?'

'I might go back to the Far East. Manage a tea plantation or go on working on the archaeological digs. I haven't made any decisions, except that England won't be a part of the future.'

'Paul, with my art, we could work together. You employ artists on the digs, don't you?'

He shook his head. 'No, Angela. Whatever I feel for you—felt for you—you're not part of my future.'

Angela leaned against the table and looked away. 'It is Helen. You don't even realise it yourself, but there's something between the two of you.'

'What lies between Helen and I is not what you think,' Paul said.

How could he explain the ghosts and the secret diary? Then there were those snatched moments in Belgium. He shook his head ridding himself of those memories.

'I know I owe you my life,' he continued, 'but I value you as a friend far more than as a lover and I don't want to lose that.'

Angela pulled a face and sniffed. 'Just 'good' friends? Oh, God, Paul! Please don't say that to me.'

'I'm sorry, I didn't mean it like that, but we're too different, and what happened between us, was a matter of circumstance. Two lonely people who needed each other at a time in our lives. We can never have that back again and we wouldn't want it. You'll find someone else. Someone who has more to offer you than I.'

'This bloody room is always so cold.' Angela straightened and shivered, hunching her shoulders. 'I should get back to Wellmore.'

Paul didn't move as he said, 'Goodbye, Angela.'

She crossed to the door that led out to the courtyard and tried the handle. 'It's locked,' she said.

'Try again,' Paul suggested.

Angela wriggled the door handle and pushed. The door flew open and Angela fell through, sprawling across the narrow hallway.

Paul lifted her up and she looked up at him, her eyes wide. 'Someone pushed me,' she said, rubbing her arm. 'I distinctly felt a hand in my back.'

'Don't be ridiculous. Just an uneven flagstone.' Paul forced a smile.

The whiff of Lily of the Valley caused him to pause and look around at the quiet room.

Angela brushed the dust from her skirt. 'I never trip just like that and I can't see an uneven flagstone.' She looked over his shoulder at the library. 'I always knew this place was haunted.'

Paul smiled. 'It's just an old house. Come on, I'll walk you to your car.'

FORTY-SIX

Angela stood at the window of the drawing room overlooking the gardens at Wellmore, the ubiquitous cigarette in her hand. She glanced around as Helen entered the room and resumed her study of the sodden terrace.

Helen joined her at the window looking out over the view. She wondered if one ever grew tired of it.

'I haven't thanked you for looking after Alice,' Helen said.

Angela smiled. 'I enjoyed it. She's a terrific child. Reminds me of her father in so many ways.'

Helen smiled. 'I couldn't have inflicted the confrontation with your mother on her.'

Angela raised an eyebrow. 'You seem to have managed. Pa thinks the sun shines out of you and even Ma seems to have defrosted a little.' She wrapped her arms tighter around herself. 'Beastly weather. English summer at its best.'

'I've told Tony that I will take him home for a proper Australian summer,' Helen said.

'He may not want to come back.' Angela paused. 'Like Charlie.'

'The siren song of the southern land?' Helen cast Angela a sideways glance.

'I'm right about Charlie though. He told me he had no intention of staying in England after the war.'

'We bought a property. Dad's managing it now but Charlie had such plans for it. When did you get back from Holdston?'

'About an hour ago.' Angela shook her head. 'There's something unhappy about that house. I don't want to set foot in it again unless I have to.'

'What do you mean?'

Angela gave a snort of laughter. 'I swear something tripped me in the library. You must think me a frightful idiot, but misery...or something...is hanging over Holdston like a pall.'

Helen bit her lip. 'Angela,' she ventured, 'have I said something to upset you?'

Angela turned her head to look at Helen. 'Upset me?'

'It's just you seem a little distant.'

Angela's mouth tightened. 'Do I? Just a small matter of the heart, Helen. Nothing to do with you.'

Helen looked at her. 'I'm sorry, Angela.'

Angela gave a dismissive shrug of her shoulders. 'It's a bloody thing to realise you're in love with someone when it's too late. I'll get over it, I always do.'

Angela clutched Helen's forearm, her face twisted in anguish. 'Oh, God, Helen, I made a complete fool of myself. I can pretend I'm a free spirit but I knew when I saw him in my flat that day in London that there was nobody else. There never had been.'

Helen closed her eyes. Paul. Angela was still in love with Paul.

'It's not too late,' Helen heard herself say, knowing that they were the words she would be expected to say.

Angela shook her head. 'It is too late. He made it quite clear.'

Helen looked away, angry with Paul. He seemed incapable of allowing himself to get close to anyone.

'He's a fool,' she said.

'I thought I'd convinced myself what we had was just another fling, but it wasn't,' Angela dashed impatiently at the tears that rolled down her hollow cheek. She gave Helen a rueful smile. 'I accused him of having a bit of a thing for you, but obviously I was wrong about that too.' She shook herself. 'This is bloody ridiculous. I'm behaving like a stupid deb.' Glancing at her wristwatch, she said, 'Is that the time? I suppose I'd better go and drag something suitable out of my wardrobe for dinner. Mother will expect us to dress.'

Angela turned on her heel and ran from the room.

FORTY-SEVEN

Helen stood on the edge of the clearing, her horse's reins looped over her arm, knowing that she should not have come. Like Suzanna, all those years before, she had passed the night in '*a foment of indecision*', her head telling her one thing and her heart another. But as Suzanna would have observed, ruled by her heart, she had risen early and on the pretence of taking a ride before breakfast, had stepped onto the precipice.

Paul rose to his feet and they stood facing each other for a long moment without speaking.

'You came,' he said at last.

'I came,' she agreed, as she tied the reins of the Wellmore hunter to a tree.

'I owe you an apology,' he said. 'As you know my memory of that day in '17 is ... has been ... a little sketchy. I only remembered recently that before the attack, Charlie gave me this.'

He handed her an envelope. She gave an involuntary gasp as she recognised Charlie's handwriting. She looked up at Paul.

'What does it say?'

He shook his head. 'I've no idea. It's not addressed to me. He gave it to me before he left on the sortie and it got packed away with the rest of my gear.'

Helen turned it over in her hand.

'I expect you would prefer to read it alone.' Paul gathered Hector's reins.

She put a hand on his arm.

'No, I would like you to stay.'

He looked down at her hand and didn't move.

Helen picked up a small twig and cut the envelope open, pulling out the single folded sheet.

The words of the short note, blurred on the page. She took a breath and forced herself to focus

My darling Helen. If you are reading this then I did not return from this sortie. If I had, I would have reclaimed this missive from Paul—that is if he were here to reclaim it from. I am so tired of this, Helen—tired of writing letters to grieving mothers and wives, tired of death. The only thing that sustains me is the memory of you, my beautiful girl, standing on the pier waving as the ship pulled away. How could I have left you? My last thought before I sleep is of you and the smell of the gums on the slopes of Mt. Buller and our plans to run cattle in the high country, but they are only dreams. I love you my darling girl, always, and whatever is in my power to keep you and the baby safe and well, I will do. Love always, Charlie.

Helen folded the paper. 'Thank you, Paul,' she said. 'Did you want to know what it says?'

He shook his head. 'It is between you and Charlie.'

He regarded her for a long moment with those extraordinary green eyes. They made her feel as if he looked into her soul.

'I should get back,' she said, turning her face away from the intensity of his gaze.

'Before you go, Helen—' Paul drew a crumpled sheaf of papers from his pocket and handed them to her, '—I do have some more of the diary. That is, if you're still interested?'

She took the papers. 'I would like to know how the story ends. Have you finished it?'

He shook his head. 'No, and I doubt I will. I did these some time ago. I'm not sure they give you the answer you want but have a look over them anyway.'

Helen thanked him, put the folded papers into her jacket pocket, and turned to go.

'Why are you marrying Tony?'

She stopped but did not turn to face him. 'What business is it of yours?'

'None,' he agreed. 'I have no claim on you, beyond that of friendship but I know why he wants to marry you. I am just curious as to why you said yes. I don't think you love him.'

She turned back to look at him and gave a wry smile. 'Because he's a kind man and he asked me.'

'That's it?' Paul's gaze was fixed intently on her and she could feel the green eyes burning into her soul, seeing her for the fraud she had become. 'He's kind and he asked you?'

'I'm not sure I even said yes.' She managed a faint smile. 'I don't expect you to understand but I'm twenty-eight years old, a widow with a child. Charlie left me eight years ago and—' she looked up at the over-arching boughs of the trees, '—I'm lonely.' She broke off and turned away. 'Forget it. I'm not explaining this very well.'

'I'm sorry, Helen,' he said. 'I have no right to pry.'

She breathed in the tang of his shaving cream as he moved closer. She willed him to touch her, to kiss her, hold her and never let her go. Her body ached for his touch but as she turned back to face him he took a step back.

Helen wanted to rail at him, beat her fists against his chest. All it would take would be a word and he could have her forever, but once again, he had pulled away from her. She turned her face up to the arch of the trees above. Lonely souls, that's all they had been to each other. Now she had the love of a good man in Tony Scarvell. If it couldn't be her, maybe someone else could find happiness with Paul Morrow? She thought about Angela's tears and brought her gaze down to meet his. 'Paul, about Angela...'

He narrowed his eyes. 'What about Angela?'

'She's in love with you.'

He shook his head. 'No, she's in love with a memory.'

'You're wrong. She's no different from me, Paul.'

'Don't tell me Angela is spinning you a 'lonely widow' story, Helen?' Paul stiffened. 'Trust me, I know Angela better than you. She can have any man she wants but she prefers them to be unobtainable. She would be bored with me in a matter of months.'

He turned his back on her, gathered up Hector's reins and swung himself into the saddle. 'Go back to Tony with my blessing. He is one of the few honourable men I know. He will be good to you.'

Helen began untying the reins of her horse. 'But will I be good to him?' she whispered, but she was talking only to the horse. Paul had gone.

Helen leaned her head against the warm neck of the animal and fought back the tears.

———

Paul crouched down low over the horse's neck, galloping blindly with no destination in mind. He took several difficult fences and only when the horse, lathered and blowing, reached the foot of Stoneman's Hill did he ease back.

He straightened and patted Hector's neck. 'Sorry, old chap. I forget you're not as young as you used to be.'

Hector snorted his disgust and Paul turned the horse up the narrow path to the standing stones. At this hour of the day, the clearing was deserted, although rubbish left by picnickers indicated that it had been a popular spot over the summer months.

He slid from the saddle and collected the papers and ginger beer bottles, stuffing the rubbish into a saddlebag and making a mental note that he either had to close off the walking track or put up some signs about removing rubbish. The curatorial task stopped him from thinking about Helen and only when he stood in the centre of the circle did the pain come back.

Physical pain he could bear—had borne. This crushing agony was new. He felt as if he had a band around his chest that drew tighter and tighter and he subsided onto the fallen giant with a groan.

'It shouldn't be like this,' he said aloud. 'I've done the right thing. I know I've done the right thing.'

Above him, the wind picked up, rustling the leaves of the alders and sycamores. Nearby, a dog barked and Hector's ears pricked. He stamped his hoof, pulling on the reins Paul had tied to a tree. Paul looked up and for a fleeting second, he thought he caught a glimpse of a black and white coat in the dappled shadows of the trees.

FORTY-EIGHT

I n the privacy of the sumptuous yellow bedchamber of Wellmore House that had, according to Lady Hartfield, sheltered royalty and persons of great note, Helen unfolded the wad of paper Paul had given her.

Her fingers traced the now familiar scrawl of his handwriting. Just when she thought she had a clear future, that everything had been settled, his shadow crossed the corner of her soul, like Suzanna's wraith, present but insubstantial, leaving her confused.

She forced herself to concentrate on the diary. The first two entries were written in early June 1812, and recorded the early, difficult days of Robert's return to Holdston. Suzanna found her husband silent and uncommunicative and with orders from Lady Morrow not to talk of his time in Spain, she struggled with how to communicate with him.

June 20: Adrian is home on leave and rode over this afternoon to visit Robert. To my despair S accompanied him. I saw in his eyes that he has not forgotten me and it was all I could do not to throw myself into his arms for the want of human touch and companionship. When no one was watching he slipped a note to me, begging me to meet him in the usual place. How can I comply? What sort of wife would I be if I were to go slipping away from her husband who needs her to lose herself in the arms of another man?

Helen set the paper down, her breath catching in her throat as the immediacy of Suzanna's predicament found its echo in her own life.

June 21: I met with S in our usual trysting place. My intention was to reiterate my conviction that our affaire de coeur must end but on seeing his eyes, so full of love for me, all resolve slipped away and I fell, weeping into his arms. I recounted every day of the last month, every lonely, tense moment, not knowing whether my husband would live or die and worse, not knowing if I cared if he did. S said nothing. He just stroked my hair and kissed my forehead as I would Adele's. When my passion was spent, he remained holding me. I leaned my head against his chest and all I could think was how much I belonged there in his embrace. What are we to do?

As June passed into July, Robert grew a little stronger but with his recovery, Suzanna recorded another, more worrying change in him.

July 18: Every day Robert takes a few more steps and this afternoon walked a little in the garden. For all that we rejoice at his successes, his temper grows shorter by the day. I know not where the anger is directed, only that somewhere within him there is enormous fury. Whether it arises from his injuries and his frustration with his disabilities or from some other experiences of which his mother and I have no knowledge, we cannot say. However, for the first time Lady Morrow and myself are united on this. Robert is to be avoided when he gets in one of his tempers. I fear also that he is turning to brandy to assuage the pain and frustration he is feeling. The combination is not to be recommended.

S writes to me once a week and how I long for his letters, his words of love and assurance. I am embarked down a dark, unknown path with no clear idea of where it will take me.

Once more Suzanna fled to her lover's arm and her entries became more frantic as she struggled with her wifely sense of duty over the pull of her heart.

Aug 5: Robert came to my room last night. I heard his footsteps in the corridor and lay in my bed, stiff with fear and dread. I had locked the door and although he knocked softly I pretended not to hear, my heart beating as the door latch rattled. He turned away and has not mentioned the matter to me this morning. I cannot bear the thought of his touch. What happy memories we may have had of times gone by have long since been obliterated by absence and the unlovely task of heavy nursing that his injuries have required of me.

August 10: Oh, horrific day! Robert awoke querulous and ill-tempered from a bad night. He has not repeated his visit to my door but I see him looking at me with a curious expression of hurt and puzzlement and I feel that I have in some way injured him more deeply than the physical pain of his scars. I cannot meet his eye or pretend a happiness I do not feel. So what began as a minor disagreement over the dressing of his wounds, led to an explosion of anger on his part such as I have never seen before. He reared up before me, his eyes almost red with rage, and hit me with the full force of his weight, across the face. He sent me flying against the table and I fell to the floor, momentarily stunned into unconsciousness. Lady Morrow came at once to my assistance, leading me away from his presence to rest upon my bed with a compress for the bruising that already colours my face. My right eye is quite closed. Her tenderness and concern quite surprised me for I fully expected her to take her son's part. What words passed between mother and son, I regret I did not hear - all I recall are his last words to me 'You shall not lock your door against me, madam!' At the memory of these words and the fierce anger in his eyes, I can do nothing but turn to my pillow and weep for guilt and for shame.

August 11: Robert has said nothing about his actions but I saw him looking at my face. We must be the talk of the village for servants will gossip and I cannot hide my face from their view. The children sense the tension between us and have kept to their nursery. Only Lady Morrow keeps up the pretence of gaiety speaking inanely of the ball to be held at Wellmore House next month.

August 15: Robert came to my room last night and I had not dared lock the door against him. I lay supine and allowed him to do what he had to do before he departed. Neither of us spoke a word. It was a base, inhuman act of carnal need of which I was not a participant. I let tears roll silently down my cheeks as he took me and thought of S and his tender lovemaking.

Helen set the papers down and bit her lip as she contemplated the frightening picture of a violent, war-damaged man that Suzanna painted. She had seen it in her own town with men returned from the war. The bruises on the women and children described with a quick smile as 'accidents.'

Robert Morrow had become a man that war had made violent. Robert could have been quite capable of murder if he had known that his wife had taken a lover, a lover with whom she continued to tryst while her husband lay on his sick bed.

August 16: S came to me this afternoon. Even in the gloom of the crypt he could see the bruising on my face and he held me close. I could sense his anger and his impotence as he kissed my poor bruised face. 'Dearest,' he whispered. 'Something must be done.' I wept as I held him close. 'There is nothing that can be done.' 'Come away with me,' said he. 'We can make a new life for ourselves in the colonies. I have prospects in the colony of New South Wales. We will be far away from England and no one need know us.' 'But what of my children?' I cried. 'How can I leave my children? Do not ask me to make that choice!' 'Sweet Suzanna,' he said, 'That is the choice. A life with a cripple who abuses you thus or a life with me. The children will be well cared for. You need have no fear for them.'

I sank to my knees crying as if my heart would break. 'I cannot live without you,' I wept. He took me in his arms and we made love on his cloak.

The diary entries moved inexorably toward September 12 as Suzanna wrestled with her conscience and then the last entry Paul had translated, put the seal on her fate.

September 8: I fear I am with child and I know not who is the father. My shame and my ignominy are complete. If I am to go it must be now. If I tarry I shall never escape and each day is a reproach on me both as a mother and a wife. I said not a word of my fears to S when we met tonight. He held me in his arms and we made plans for our escape. He must return to London and make the necessary arrangements. He will meet me at the Church yard on the night of September 12 and we will quit this place.

The sound of running footsteps in the corridor outside alerted her and she refolded the papers and thrust them into the drawer of the bureau as Alice burst in through the door.

One look at her daughter's face told her all was not well. Alice flung herself full length on the bed, burying her head in her arms.

Helen sat down next to her and stroked her hair. 'What's the matter, darling?'

'I hate it here.' Alice's voice was muffled by the bedclothes.

'Why? It's a beautiful house. You have a lovely room and you can ride Turnip—'

'Lady Hartfield is mean to me,' Alice sniffed.

'How was she mean to you?'

'She said I was never to run in the Long Gallery and that as soon as you and Uncle Tony were married I would be sent away to boarding school and I'd learn to be a proper lady and have all my colonial bad manners knocked out of me.'

Helen stiffened with anger directed at Lady Hartfield, not her daughter.

'Were you running in the Long Gallery?'

A sniff confirmed that Alice had been committing this sin.

'I want to go home,' she wailed.

'Home? To Terrala?'

'To Holdston!' Alice rolled over, burying her face in Helen's lap. 'Home to Grandmama and Uncle Paul and Sam and Sarah and Reuben.'

'Who's Reuben?' Helen asked.

'My dog. He's a cocker spaniel. He sleeps by my bed every night.'

Dog? Helen frowned as she stared down at the fair head. 'Darling, there isn't any dog at Holdston,' she said.

'Yes there is. My dog.' Alice was in full flight now.

Helen let her daughter cry herself out and when the sobbing had subsided to hiccups, she set the girl on her feet, washed her face and gave her a big smile.

'There's the gong for breakfast,' she said, with a cheerfulness she didn't feel.

In agreeing to marry Tony, she hadn't thought about the impact on Alice, beyond the superficial thought that bringing the child up at Wellmore would be wonderful. Of course, it would be expected that Alice would go to boarding school. What was the alternative? A governess? The village school would be out of the question.

Alice took her hand and they descended the long, graceful stairs to the breakfast room.

Lady Hartfield sat at the head of the table reading the morning mail. She laid the note she had in her hand down as Helen entered.

'I see you've been for a ride, Helen,'

Helen looked down at her jodhpurs and sweater 'Do you wish me to change?'

'You're fine,' Tony said. 'Beautiful in whatever you wear.'

A footman pulled out a chair for Alice and she sat down next to her mother, hunched and miserable.

'Good morning, Sprite,' Tony said. 'You're very quiet.'

Alice cast a quick glance at Lady Hartfield who had returned to perusing her letters.

'Good morning, Uncle Tony,' she said in a low, unhappy tone.

Tony glanced at Helen who mouthed, 'Later.'

'Now,' Lady Hartfield laid a hand on the pile of correspondence beside her. 'When are we to announce your engagement, Tony?'

Helen caught Tony's eye. 'It's up to Helen,' he said.

'I suppose there will be no question of your parents attending the wedding?' Lady Hartfield enquired.

'Not unless they learn to fly,' she said.

'I suppose we shall have to find someone to give you away.'

'Do I need someone to give me away? I'm a widow. I've already been given away once. Surely I don't need to be given away again?'

Lady Hartfield looked aghast. 'Oh. That won't do at all. You will have to ask Paul. He's the head of the Morrow family. You're his responsibility.'

Helen stared at the Viscountess. 'Paul? But I...'

'I was going to ask Paul to be my best man,' Tony said. 'Which reminds me, Helen, he told me yesterday he's got another contract to go out to Mesopotamia over winter so if we want him at the wedding, it will have to be early autumn or wait until he's back in the spring.'

If he comes back, Helen thought.

Beneath the table, her fingers twisted Charlie's wedding ring, which she could not bring herself to remove just yet. Tony had shown her an engagement ring, a family piece with an emerald the size of a pigeon egg. She had closed the lid of the box and told him to give it to her when the moment was right She wondered when the moment would be.

Lady Hartfield made a moue of annoyance. 'Someone has to give Helen away and it must be Paul. You'll have to find someone else, Anthony. What about James Massey?'

'Anyone but him,' Helen exclaimed and put her hand to her mouth realising the words had come out before she had thought about them.

Lady Hartfield stared at Helen. 'What on earth do you have against James? He was a great friend of Charlie's, wasn't he Tony?'

Tony cast a quick glance at Helen and set down the papers. 'Ma, let's get one thing straight. We just want a quiet wedding in the chapel here. No fuss.'

'But darling, you're the heir. I thought a London wedding—' Lady Hartfield looked nonplussed.

'No,' Tony said. 'A quiet wedding, just family and a few close friends of our own choosing.'

'But people will think you have something to hide,' Lady Hartfield protested.

'Let people think what they want,' Tony said. 'A quiet wedding at Wellmore. That's it.'

Helen gave him a look of sheer relief. They hadn't discussed any of this, but somehow he had sensed her discomfort and guessed, correctly, what her thoughts on the subject would be. Paul was right, Tony was a good and honourable man.

Lady Hartfield sniffed. 'If you would care to start thinking about an invitation list, I shall see what can be done.'

The butler entered the room. 'Telephone for Mrs. Morrow,' he announced.

'Who is it?' Helen said.

'Holdston Hall,' the man said.

Helen bundled up her napkin and excused herself.

'Mrs. Morrow?' A woman's voice was at the end of the line. 'It's Sarah Pollard here.'

Helen heard the edge in Sarah's tone and felt her spine tingle. 'Sarah, what's happened?'

'There's been an accident,' Sarah said.

Helen felt her heart leap to her throat. 'Paul?'

'No. It's her ladyship,' Sarah said.

'What happened?'

'She fell down the library stairs. She must have lain there all night, poor lady. I found her this morning when I took her breakfast up.'

'Is she all right?'

'She's in hospital. Still unconscious. Doctors don't know whether she'll make it or not.'

'Oh Sarah, I am sorry.'

There was a long pause. 'You've got to come back, Mrs. Morrow.'

'Sarah...I can't...'

Sarah's tone became desperate. 'You've got to come. There's something happening in this house. Whatever you started, you've got to finish.'

'I can't, Sarah. I don't belong there.'

'Helen, he needs you. He can't do it without you.'

'What do you mean he needs me?'

'It will kill someone soon,' Sarah said, a note of hysteria rising in her voice. 'If it hasn't already.'

'Sarah, you're not making any sense,' Helen said firmly. 'Does Paul know you've rung me?'

'No. he's at the hospital.'

Helen bit her lip, torn by indecision.

'Please, Mrs. Morrow... Helen.'

Helen heard the desperate note of pleading in Sarah's voice. She looked at her watch.

'Very well, Sarah. I'll be there by lunchtime.'

'Pollard's taken the Major over to Birmingham with the car.'

'It's all right. I will ask Mr. Scarvell to drive us over.'

'You'll bring Miss Alice?'

'Of course I will.' She would not leave Alice alone at Wellmore with the viperous Lady Hartfield.

'I'll have beds made up for you.'

Helen set the phone back on its bench and straightened. Back in the breakfast room, she faced the Scarvells.

'Lady Morrow has had an accident,' she said. 'She's in hospital.'

Lady Hartfield set down her napkin. 'Oh dear. What sort of an accident?'

'I gather she had a fall down a flight of stairs.'

'That house is so unsafe,' the Viscountess said.

Helen looked at Tony. 'Tony, would you be able to drive us over to Holdston?'

'Of course,' Tony rose to his feet.

'Will you be back for supper?' Lady Hartfield enquired as if she thought Helen would just be making a social visit.

Helen stared at the woman. 'No, I shall be staying at Holdston, Lady Hartfield. For the time being, Lady Morrow is still my mother-in-law and I owe it to her to take some responsibility for Holdston while she is recuperating.'

'But you're engaged to Tony...'

'Not officially,' Tony put in. 'You're needed at Holdston, Helen. Just tell me when you're ready to go and I'll drive you over.'

Alice looked up with a grin. At least someone was happy.

Forty-Nine

Even as the car turned in through the gate, it seemed to Helen that the atmosphere of the house had changed. It had closed in on itself, the dark windows, brooding darkly in the sunlight.

Sarah waited at the courtyard gate and even as Helen stepped out of the car, the older woman ran across the bridge and threw her arms around her.

'I'm so glad you've come. The major's still with her ladyship at the hospital but he rang to say he'll be home this evening if there's no change.'

Helen turned to Tony. 'Thank you for the lift, Tony.'

He looked at her with concerned eyes. 'Are you sure you don't want me to stay?'

Helen shook her head. 'No. It's sweet of you but Alice and I are needed here for the moment. I'm sure you understand.'

Tony smiled. 'I understand. Not sure Ma does though.'

Helen gave a rueful smile. 'I don't think it matters what I do, Tony, your mother will never understand me.'

'Give me a ring when you've got some news, old girl.' Tony turned the car with a wave of his hand.

'Mrs. Bryant sent a note around saying for Miss Alice to come and play with Lily at the vicarage,' Sarah said as they entered the house.

'May I?' Alice asked.

'Of course,' Helen said. 'Go now. We'll be fine here.'

Sarah hustled Helen into the kitchen and sat her down while she fussed around making tea. She set the large brown teapot before her, poured two cups of tea, and joined her at the table.

'Now you've got to tell me all that you know about these spirits,' Sarah said. 'These last few months, I've been sensing them but they don't let me see. What do they want?'

'You're not saying the ghosts are behind what happened to Evelyn?'

'I don't know what to think,' Sarah stirred her tea so hard it slopped into the saucer. 'I just know there's something not right in this house and we've got to fix it.'

The tea sat untouched as Helen related the story of Suzanna Morrow and her ill-starred love affair.

Sarah sat back, her face grave. 'You say there's two of them?'

'Two that I've seen. Robert and Suzanna. I recognise them from the portraits.'

Sarah shook her head. 'That can't be right,' she said. 'There's more than two.'

'What do you mean?'

'Like I told you before, there's another one. I can't tell you anything more. Can't see it or hear it, but it's a bad one.'

'What do you mean? You said ghosts can't harm you.'

Sarah twisted her hands together. 'I just know that Lady Morrow didn't fall down those stairs by herself. There's something strange in the library.' Her face twisted. 'See for yourself.'

As it had begun to rain, rather than take the shortcut across the courtyard from the kitchen wing to the isolated corner of the house, which housed the library, Helen followed Sarah up the main stairs and through the house to the library stairs. As they descended the old, narrow staircase down which Evelyn had fallen, Helen shivered. Evelyn had been lucky not to break her neck.

Sarah flung back the door to the library and Helen gasped. The paintings of Robert and Suzanna lay face up in the middle of the floor, the canvas slashed with the accuracy of a sharp knife.

Helen picked up the ruined portrait of Suzanna and felt the temperature in the room plummet. An icy hand closed around her wrist. The same cold, cruel fingers that had tried to pull her into Evelyn's room all those weeks ago. She dropped the painting and screamed.

'Are you all right?'

At the sound of Sarah's voice, the icy grip on her wrist released, and the temperature in the room rose.

Helen turned to face Sarah. 'Did you sense it?'

Sarah nodded. 'It's the other one. It's evil. Leave the paintings, Mrs. Morrow, and we'll go back to the kitchen.'

After lunch, Alice returned from the vicarage and helped Sarah and Helen prepare supper. In an attempt at normalcy, Sarah attempted to draw Helen on the subject of her engagement and the wedding, but Helen cut her short.

As they set the kitchen table for supper, Sarah looked up. 'There's the car. I'd better get that soup on.'

The kitchen door opened and Paul entered. He stopped when he saw Helen.

'What are you doing here?'

Sarah turned around from the kitchen range. 'I sent for her, sir.'

'You had no business doing so.'

'I had every business,' Sarah declared, brandishing her wooden spoon. 'What's happened to your aunt wasn't an accident and I'm not pretending that everything in this house is fine. Ever since you got back from the war, it's been building and Mrs. Morrow coming here just got it all rolling. Whatever it is, it's up to you two to sort it out before anyone else gets hurt.'

Paul glared at Helen. 'Nothing has happened. Evelyn had an accident that's all.'

'How is she?' Helen ventured.

He ran a hand through his hair. 'A fractured collarbone, broken ribs, a broken ankle, and a bad blow to the head. She's still unconscious and the doctors have no way of knowing when she will wake.'

'I'm sorry, Paul.'

His face remained expressionless. 'Thank you for your concern and I'm sorry you had a wasted journey. Pollard can drive you back to Wellmore.'

Helen took a step toward him. 'I'm not going, Paul. This is about Suzanna and Robert. I've seen the paintings in the library. You're not telling me Evelyn did that. I'll not leave until we have solved this mystery once and for all.'

'There's no mystery.' Paul's face was white with anger. 'There are no ghosts, no mystery. Just a shell-shocked soldier and a woman with an overactive imagination.' he turned to Sarah. 'Two women with overactive imaginations. I want nothing more to do with this.'

'Paul, they are getting desperate. They've tripped Angela and now your aunt.'

'Angela? She stumbled on an uneven flag, nothing more. As for Evelyn, she fell down some stairs. It doesn't mean she was pushed or there was some other paranormal explanation.'

'Don't pretend they don't exist, Paul. You know it was them or whatever this third one is. What was Evelyn doing on the library stairs in the middle of the night?'

'Maybe she wanted to get a book to read. I don't know.' Paul glared at Helen. 'What have you told Tony? I doubt he approves of you being here?'

Helen shook her head. 'I told him what I knew. Evelyn had been involved in an accident and Alice and I were needed here. Give us twenty-four hours, Paul. I've read the diary and I think we're close, I just know we are.'

'Close to what, Helen?'

She thought she could hear a note of despair in his voice.

'Close to finding out what happened to Suzanna Morrow. I am now certain she never left this house. Someone killed her, someone hid her body and it's here somewhere. We just have to find it. There will be no peace for any of us until her disappearance is solved.'

He looked at her and drew a breath but the defiance and fight had begun to fade from him. He ran his hand through his hair and turned away. 'This is madness. I'm not solving one hundred-year-old mysteries.'

'Paul, you can't suddenly pretend this is all our imagination and nothing more. You've seen them and what they can do. You saw the state of the library this morning. Whatever we've started, it is up to us to finish.'

His lips compressed and his green eyes blazing, he turned to face her. 'Very well, Helen. Twenty-four hours but if we are no closer to solving this in that time that is it. I will never have it spoken of again.'

Helen took a deep breath and put out a hand to touch his arm. 'You're exhausted, Paul. There is nothing we can do tonight. Have some supper and go to bed and we will meet at breakfast.'

Paul shook off her hand and sat down at the kitchen table, while Sarah busied herself with warming soup and cutting bread. Helen sat down across the table for him and poured them both tea.

'What time did the accident happen?' she asked.

'She must have been on her way to bed. She was wearing her dressing gown and slippers.' He pinched the bridge of his nose. 'If she'd screamed or cried out for help, I might have heard her but it was Sarah who found her this morning while I was—' he looked at Helen, '—out riding.'

Helen flinched. He had been meeting with her in the clearing.

'Her bedroom is above the library. Perhaps she heard something? Was the light on in the library, Sarah?' she asked.

Sarah frowned and shook her head. 'No. Just the paintings on the floor like you saw 'em. You don't think her ladyship cut them up?'

Helen shook her head and looked at Paul. 'You have to finish the diary.'

'I don't have to do anything, Helen,' he muttered, his eyes on the soup bowl.

'The answer's in the diary, Paul. Would it take you long to do?'

He looked up at her and she saw the deep lines of exhaustion on his face. 'A couple of hours.'

'He's not doing anything tonight,' Sarah growled. 'If you're not careful, sir, you'll be down with a migraine.'

Paul glanced at Sarah but didn't argue. 'She's right, Helen. I'm in no state to do anything about the diary tonight.' He pushed back his chair. 'I'll see you in the morning.'

FIFTY

P aul set the telephone back in its cradle and turned to find Helen watching him from the stairs.

'How is she?' she asked.

He shrugged. 'Still unconscious but they don't seem to think she's any worse.'

'Well that's something,' Helen said. 'Paul, don't blame yourself.'

He looked away, unable to face her sympathy. Charlie and now Evelyn. He had failed them both.

'Are you ready?' she asked.

He brought his gaze back to her. 'You still think Evelyn's accident is something to do with Suzanna?'

'I'm certain of it.'

'Then for your sake. Let's get on with it.

She joined him, looking up at him with bright, eager eyes.

'If I'm right,' she said, 'And Suzanna never left the house, her body must be somewhere in these walls.'

Paul looked around at the intricately carved wainscoting of the Great Hall. 'This place is riddled with priest holes. Charlie and I spent several long summer holidays trying to find them all. I'm sure there are some we haven't discovered.'

Helen frowned. 'But we're not talking about a priest hole. We have to find the tunnel. We know from Suzanna's diary that it ran from the library to the crypt. Surely it can't be that hard to find?'

'With the help of a couple of hefty men and a few sledgehammers?' Paul suggested. 'I'm not knocking holes in the wall, Helen. I'll never sell it.'

'I am sure it is not that inaccessible or Suzanna wouldn't have been able to use it with such ease. Let's start in the library?'

The sun streamed in through the library windows and the room looked peaceful, just as it had always looked, except for the ruined paintings leaning against one wall.

'Where are the clay tablets?' Helen asked, noticing the absence of the wooden boxes.

'I've sent them back to Woolley while I sort out my affairs here. Shall we make a start?'

Helen followed Paul around the room, tapping on panels, lifting carpets, knocking on floorboards but nothing budged, nothing gave the slightest indication of being the entrance to a secret tunnel.

'What are you doing?' Alice appeared at the doorway.

'Looking for a secret tunnel,' Helen said. 'Want to help?'

'I'm not sure that it's wise to involve Alice,' Paul said.

'Oh, please,' Alice begged. 'I'm bored.'

By midmorning, Helen and Paul sat in the chairs beside the fireplace staring at the mantel having covered every square inch of the old room. They had tapped on every panel, pushed and pulled any protuberance but nothing moved.

Alice sat cross-legged on the floor flicking through a large folio of animal prints.

'I was so sure we would find it,' Helen said dispiritedly. 'Perhaps if we try the crypt?'

'Must we? I hate that place,' Paul said.

'If that's where the other entry is. It may be more obvious

Paul stood up. 'I'll find a flashlight and a crowbar and we'll pay a visit to my dead ancestors.'

They made a strange procession, armed with tools, rope, and a flash-light as they crossed the churchyard. Paul retrieved the key from the

verger and unlocked the gate. Helen entered the crypt without hesitation but Paul stopped at the entrance, his hands on the lintel as he
contemplated another dark, dead place.

'Paul?' Helen looked up at him. 'Are you all right?'

'Of course,' he said brusquely.

Helen put her arms around herself. 'What a dreadful place for a
romantic tryst.'

Alice, who had followed them, slipped under Paul's arm and stood
next to him on the top step. He caught her by the waist and planted her
back outside.

'This is no place for you.'

'Just wait for us out here,' Helen said.

Paul descended the short flight of stairs and switched on the flashlight. He held it up, scanning the shelves with the disordered coffins.
One side of the crypt was shorter than the other with what looked to be
the buttress of the church interposing into the wall. Paul crossed to it
and brought ran the beam across the stonework.

'Helen, what do you make of this?'

He pointed to a crude etching of a bird on the stonework about
four feet from the floor. Helen looked up at him and he could hear the
catch of excitement in her reply. 'It's a martlet,' she said. 'Do you
suppose it means something?'

Paul handed her the flashlight and placed his hand on the
engraving.

'It's the martlet from the coat of arms. Let's see what happens if I
push on it?'

He applied some force and jumped back at a creaking sound and the
grating of stone on stone. He took a steadying breath and pushed again.
The wall moved beneath his hand revealing a narrow entrance, only four
feet high and less than two feet wide.

Although disused for over a hundred years, the stone pivoted back
with surprising ease. The entrance to the tunnel yawned before them, a
dark, uninviting hole exuding a dusty, dank smell of long neglect.

Paul spoke first. 'So, it was true.' He sounded surprised.

'You didn't think it would be?' Helen said. 'Shall we see where it
leads?'

Paul took a step back. He could feel the band around his chest tightening. 'Helen, I can't down there.'

'Why?' Helen asked.

'I...' he paused. 'A section of trench once fell in on me and to be honest, I've never been fond of enclosed spaces since then. I can't even bring myself to go down into the trenches on the dig.'

Even as he spoke, the hand holding the flashlight began to shake. He touched his other hand to his forehead, his fingers coming away damp from the sheen of sweat that had broken out. He hated having to admit this weakness but his fear was real and he hoped she understood.

She laid a hand on his arm. The touch of her fingers, even through his shirt sleeve, heated his skin like a brand.

'It's all right, I'll go,' she said.

He looked at her and managed a smile. 'I suppose nothing I can say will dissuade you?'

She gave him an impish grin and for a moment, he saw a flash of the Helen Charlie had loved. 'I come from a family of boys. I grew up climbing trees and exploring old gold mines.'

He reached out and touched her hair. 'You never cease to surprise me, Helen.' He dropped his hand and glanced at his watch. 'It's nearly lunchtime. We'll go back to the house and come back after lunch.'

They closed the door and the gate of the crypt and stood for a moment in the churchyard, breathing in the fresh air.

The vicar's wife, seeing them from the vicarage, hurried over to invite Alice for lunch and the afternoon with Lily. Helen agreed and she and Paul walked back to the house.

FIFTY-ONE

Paul waited downstairs in the Great Hall as Helen changed into jodhpurs, riding boots and a warm jumper. He looked up as she hurried down the stairs and he felt what had now become a familiar ache at the sight of her slight figure. He wanted her arms around him and the touch of her lips on his again. The physical longing caused him to turn away, striding to the door before she had reached him.

'Paul!'

He heard her behind him and stopped to let her catch up. As she reached him, she caught his arm.

'Can you hear a dog?' she asked.

A frantic barking came from the direction of the church. They both looked toward the little gate and as they did so, a black and white cocker spaniel raced down the path. He stopped a good distance from them, barking furiously.

A familiar swooping sensation caught at him, which he recognised as fear.

'Paul?' Helen asked.

'It's Reuben,' he said through stiff lips. 'Charlie's dog. I'd know him anywhere.'

She stared up at him, her eyes huge in her pale face.

He swallowed. 'Reuben died just before Charlie left for Australia.'

Their eyes met and as one, they turned to look at the spectral dog that waited for them at the gate to the churchyard, whining frantically, his plumed tail waving in agitation.

Without exchanging another word, they both began to run to the church. As they crossed the churchyard, Lily Bryant came flying out of the church door, tears streaming down her face. Paul caught her and crouched down, bringing himself to the child's level.

'Lily, what's happened?'

Lily snuffled and wiped her nose on her sleeve.

'Alice said you'd found a secret tunnel,' she said. 'I said I'd like to see it, so after lunch we went into the crypt. She said she could hear someone crying and picked up the flashlight you left and ... and ...' Lily started to cry again.

'And?'

'I told her not to go but she went through the hole in the wall and then ... and then there was a terrible noise and I heard her scream. I called and called but she didn't answer.'

Paul looked up at Helen but Helen had already gone, running into the church and down into the crypt, calling Alice's name. Paul caught her before she hurled herself down the dark hole.

'Wait,' he said. 'If there's been a collapse, you'll only make it worse.'

He stood at the entrance to the tunnel and called the child's name. They waited, breath held but only an all-encompassing silence surrounded them.

Helen looked up at Paul, her face twisted in anguish. He couldn't let her go down the tunnel. In her distress, she could end up losing both of them. He looked into the dark cavity, the fear crawling through him with sharp claws, but it was not a time for self-indulgent phobias.

He took her by the arms and looked into her eyes. 'Stay here. I'll go.'

'But...'

'Stay here.' He made it an order and saw the answering agreement in her tear-filled eyes.

Paul turned to the yawning cavity and without another word,

ducked and stepped over the lintel, groping his way down narrow stone stairs.

At the bottom of the stairs a cramped corridor, not tall enough for him to stand, stretched blackly before him. Any residual light from the crypt would only illuminate a few yards. He crouched down, his breath coming in short gasps, fighting the growing nausea.

There is a child down here who needs you, he told himself and forced his breathing to normality.

His fingers inched along the wall feeling rough brick beneath his hand. The floor of hard packed soil beneath his knees was damp.

'Paul?' Helen's anxious voice echoed down the tunnel, muffled by the darkness.

To reply he would have had to stop and turn. He decided against it and crept forward through the suffocating blackness.

For a moment, he thought his eyes deceived him and he blinked but just ahead he could see a faint light. He quickened his pace and rounded a slight corner. The flashlight, still switched on, lay on the ground, and just beyond it the tunnel ended abruptly in a fall of earth and brick. He let out his breath with relief.

Alice lay on her stomach in the mud, quite still, as if she had turned to run when the roof caved in. Her legs were partly trapped by the fallen debris, her arms outflank and her head turned to one side.

He crawled to her.

'Alice!' he whispered, smoothing the hair away from her mud-streaked face.

When she didn't respond, he felt for the pulse in her neck and was rewarded by a steady beat. He sent a quick prayer of thanks to God and began to clear the mud and bricks away from her legs with as much care as the urgency of the situation allowed.

When he had cleared her legs, he felt for broken bones and let out a breath of relief when he was satisfied that she had not suffered any serious injury. She moaned as he gently turned her over, her eyes flickering open.

'It's all right, Alice,' he whispered. 'I'm here.'

She gave a strangled cry and wrapped her arms around his neck. Paul gathered the child in his arms, holding her slight, shaking body tightly.

He pressed her to him, overwhelmed with relief and the realisation that Charlie's daughter had become as dear to him as if she were his own. Charlie's daughter, Charlie's wife. He wanted them both in his life forever.

As he sank down against the wall, the flashlight on the ground sputtered and went out, leaving him in utter suffocating blackness. He closed his eyes and held the terrified child closer.

The damp from the floor and walls seeped through his clothes. He closed his eyes as around him, the darkness closed in, a blackness broken only by flares and exploding shells.

———

Passchendaele 18 September 1917.

Paul lay with his back against the wall of the shell hole, breathing raggedly. With the last of his strength, he had hauled Charlie up from the putrid mud into which he had tumbled. Now he could do no more except lie against the shattered earth, staring up at the darkening sky with his good arm around his cousin's shoulders.

'Paul?'

He turned his head with difficulty to look at his cousin and saw Charlie's anguished eyes turned to him.

'Don't let me go like this,' Charlie whispered.

They both knew that the terrible wounds Charlie had suffered were fatal but that death could be some way off yet.

'I'm not going to leave you,' Paul replied. 'We'll get back to our lines and...'

Charlie raised a bloody hand and gripped Paul's arm.

'It'll be too late ... please help me ... end it ...now.'

Charlie's fingers scrabbled for the cord holding Paul's service revolver.

'No,' Paul caught Charlie's hand. 'I can't.'

Charlie coughed and blood ran down his chin as his fingers tightened on the cord.

Paul closed his eyes, screwing them against the tears. When he had regained his composure, he took the cord from around his neck, lifting the revolver in his good hand. He shook so much he could scarcely hold the weapon.

Charlie's eyes met his and his cousin gave a half smile. 'Not asking you to do it,' he said. 'Just help me. Give it to me.'

Paul took his cousin's hand and closed the cold, bloodied fingers around the butt of the weapon. He shifted his weight and together they raised the revolver until the muzzle rested against Charlie's temple.

'Let go,' Charlie whispered and Paul let his hand drop.

Charlie's eyes held his as his lips moved in silent farewell.

The sound of the revolver shot reverberated around the shell hole, masked by a burst of machine gun fire across the wasteland above them. The weapon slipped from Charlie's hand, sliding away into the water with barely a ripple.

Paul buried his face in the shoulder of Charlie's tunic. With difficulty, he slid his good arm back around his cousin's shoulders holding him while a heavy, silent grief poured from him.

FIFTY-TWO

'Paul!' Helen called again, only to be met with resonating silence. Cold fear grasped at her heart. Sarah had been right—something evil had come to Holdston and now threatened all the people who meant the most to her in the world.

Sitting back on her heels, she contemplated the black hole before her that had swallowed her daughter and now Paul. She'd seen his face when the tunnel had been revealed. To have gone down there without hesitation had taken courage beyond her imagination and now she had to follow.

Rising to her feet, she found a candle from the store in the church. With shaking fingers, she lit the slender taper, pocketing a few extras and the box of matches she had found with the candles. Taking a deep breath, she recited the Lord's Prayer and descended into the hole.

Bent double, Helen made her way along the tunnel, her fingers tracing the brick lined walls. The first candle sputtered and she lit a second.

'Paul? Alice?' she called but no one answered.

A knot of fear in her throat constricted her breathing.

Ahead the tunnel appeared to turn a corner and she wondered how close the house itself would be. She must have come at least one hundred and fifty yards.

As she rounded the corner, she saw them. Paul sat with his back to the wall, Alice held tightly in his arms. His eyes were shut and the light of the candle caught a gleam of wetness on his face.

A moan of despair escaped her. Alice was dead.

'Paul?'

He didn't move but the child in his arms shifted. Helen nearly dropped the candle with relief. She lit another candle and wedged them both in the mud of the floor as she crept forward.

'Mummy,' Alice sobbed but Paul held her so tight she could do no more than turn her mud-streaked face to her mother.

Helen stroked her muddy hair and kissed the top of her head.

'Are you hurt?' she whispered.

Alice sniffed and shook her head. Helen turned to the man. He still hadn't moved, hadn't acknowledged her presence in any way.

She touched his face. His skin felt icy beneath her fingers. 'Paul, she's all right. You can let her go.'

She stroked his brow and his eyes flickered open. He stared at the opposite wall, seeming oblivious to her presence or the child in his arms. She touched his arm and felt the grip on Alice relax. Helen pried Alice from his arms and sat back on her heels holding her daughter, while tears of relief ran in scalding lines down her own face.

'Can you walk?' she whispered.

Alice nodded.

'I want you to take one of the candles and go back to the church. Wait for us. We won't be long.'

'What's wrong with Uncle Paul?' Alice asked turning her head to look at the man.

'He's all right. We'll be right behind you,' Helen said.

Alice slipped out of her mother's arms and picked up one of the candles. Helen watched until the child had rounded the corner out of sight before lighting her last candle.

She picked up Paul's hand and pressed it to her lips.

'Paul,' she whispered. 'Talk to me.'

When she got no response, Helen turned his face toward her. The unseeing eyes scared her.

'Paul, please. You can't stay here.'

She cupped his face in her hands and leaned toward him, her forehead resting against his. Her lips brushed his but she felt no answering response. Helen took both his hands and began to chafe them as she repeated his name, over and over.

Behind her the candles burned low. She had so little time.

He jerked, pulling his hands away from hers and his eyes, alive once more, met hers.

'Helen,' he whispered.

She touched his face and smiled. 'We're about to lose the light. We have to get out of here.'

She began to move away from him but he caught her arm.

'Charlie ...'

She saw the glint of tears in his eyes and felt her own eyes well. He had remembered.

'I tried to hold him but he went in the night ... the revolver ... I didn't ...'

The words, confused and ragged with grief tumbled from him. He had warned her that she may not want to hear the truth.

Helen turned back to him and took his hand in hers, pressing it to her mouth. 'Paul, don't say any more. I don't want to know.'

In the light of the last candle, Helen wrapped her arms around the man and held him to her as she had done on the battlefield. In the darkness, she sought out his mouth, and this time he responded with a desperate urgency.

Helen broke away, her fingers seeking his face. 'Are you ready? We've got to get out of here, Paul.'

He nodded and she kissed him again, lightly. 'You go first,' she said, 'I'll follow.'

The candle sputtered and went out leaving them to crawl through the thick blackness of the tunnel, heading for a thin light that marked the entrance. As they neared it, the light disappeared behind the bulk of the vicar as he extended his hand to help them out of the hole in the wall.

Paul crouched against the wall of the crypt, his face ashen, his hands hanging loosely between his knees. Helen gave him a cursory glance. He could wait. Her eyes were only for her daughter who sat on the steps down into the crypt with Lily Bryant's arms around her. Both girls were crying.

She rushed to her daughter's side taking her in her arms, while the vicar tended his own daughter. When the tears subsided into hiccups and Helen had satisfied herself that Alice's injuries were superficial, she at Alice up and tried to put on a stern face.

'Why on earth did you go down the tunnel?'

Alice's face crumpled again. 'I thought I heard someone crying.'

Over her daughter's head, Helen caught Paul's eyes. Just as she had heard a woman crying that first night? Was this the work of the Holdston spirits or just an unfortunate accident?

She smiled and smoothed Alice's mud-streaked hair. 'It's all right, I'm not cross, but we'd better get you back to the house for a bath and a rest. We've had enough adventures for one day.'

'It looks like you all need a bath,' the vicar observed. He stood and walked over to the entrance to the tunnel. 'I'd heard stories of course but these things are lost in time. Does the tunnel go through to the house?'

Paul shook his head and spoke for the first time. 'Not anymore.' He pulled himself to his feet and joined the vicar. It seemed to Helen that Paul braced every muscle in his body as he put his hand to the faint carving of the martlet. The wall creaked and groaned to a close. He leaned his forehead against the wall for a moment before turning back.

'I'll have that sealed,' he said. 'I don't want anyone ever going back down there. He crossed to Helen and as he lifted Alice from her arms, he held them both for a fleeting moment.

'Let's go home,' he said.

Alice wrapped her arms around his neck and Helen saw his eyes close as the child snuggled up against him. Alice had been brought up in a house full of men but there had never been one special man in her life and now Helen saw how important that missing relationship must have been to her daughter's life. The thought made her heart ache.

The vicar shut and locked the crypt behind them and they walked out into bright summer sunlight. Once more in control, Paul thanked the vicar for his help and they stood and watched the man take his own daughter's hand and lead her back to the vicarage.

Helen looked up at Paul. 'Paul...' she began.

A slight shake of his head warned her that now was not the time to raise what had happened in the tunnel. Instead, he shifted Alice's weight to his right arm and placed his left arm around Helen's shoulders, drawing her against him. Slowly they walked back to the house.

FIFTY-THREE

Helen stood looking down at the man on the bed. She hadn't intended to intrude into his bedroom but there had been no response when she had knocked on the door and the nagging anxiety about his state of mind, caused her to enter his room.

Paul lay sprawled across the bed cover, still in his muddy clothes as if he had reached his room and just fallen on to the bed. His face was half turned away from her and she reached out and touched his hair, gently stroking it away from his forehead. For the first time she noticed the faint line of a scar high on his temple at the hairline. Her finger traced it, wondering, not for the first time, how many scars he bore.

His hand clamped on to her wrist as he jerked awake, rolling into a sitting position with such rapidity, Helen took a step back.

He let her go.

'Sorry, I didn't mean to startle you,' she said.

He fell back on the bed. 'A soldier's reflex,' he said. He covered his face with hands. 'How's Alice?' he asked, his voice muffled.

'Bruised and a bit shaken but all right,' Helen said. 'I've put her to bed. How are you?'

He drew his hands down his face and she saw the lines of pain etched around his mouth. The pupils of his eyes were pinpricks.

'I'm sorry ... you've got a migraine, haven't you?'

His lips tightened and he gave a barely perceptible nod. 'It's been threatening for a while.'

'Is there anything I can get you?'

'No. It'll take its own time.'

'Are you sure...?'

He closed his eyes, the lines of pain etched around his mouth as he grimaced.

'Quite sure. Just leave me, Helen.'

She found a blanket and threw it over him before pulling the curtain shut and tiptoeing out of the room, closing the door behind her. Outside in the corridor she leaned against the wall and swore. Just when they were so close, Paul would be out for at least twenty-four hours, maybe longer.

She was on her own now.

FIFTY-FOUR

In the dark hours of the morning, Helen tossed and turned as her mind replayed the events of the previous day. She had so nearly lost Alice and then Paul. She blamed herself for letting him go after Alice, knowing what she did about the trench collapse.

Charlie had written to her that four men had died in the collapse and they had barely got Paul out alive but he'd been patched up and sent back to the lines as if nothing had happened.

With the ability of children to bounce back from adversity, Alice showed no ill effects from her adventure the day before, except for some bruising on her forehead and her legs.

She chattered brightly as Helen helped her dress.

Helen sent her daughter down to the kitchen for breakfast and stopped in the hall to make two phone calls; the first to the hospital to enquire after Evelyn and the second to the vicarage to see if Alice could spend a couple of nights away from Holdston.

She explained to Mrs. Bryant that Evelyn's condition had not changed and that she felt in the circumstances with their concern over her, Alice would be better off with more cheerful company. The Bryants were happy to oblige.

In the kitchen, she found Alice tucking into a bowl of porridge.

Pollard sat at the table reading the paper. He stood as Helen entered and she gestured him back. Sarah, busy at the stove, turned around. Dark circles under her eyes made Helen wonder if Sarah had also slept badly.

'How's Paul?' she asked Sarah.

'Not good. You'll not see him today.' Sarah shook her head. 'I swear the migraines are getting worse. Sooner he's back in Mesopotamia the better. It's this house that does it to him.'

'It's not the result of the war?'

Sarah shook her head. 'No. He's had migraines since he was a boy.'

When Helen told Alice that she would be going over to the vicarage after breakfast, Alice looked down at her plate and then back at her mother.

'I want to stay here,' she said.

'I think it's for the best, love,' Helen said. 'Uncle Paul and I will have to go to the hospital to see Grandmama.'

'I can stay with Sarah.'

'Sarah has better things to do than look after you, Alice. Besides Lily is looking forward to having you to stay. Just stay out of trouble this time.'

Alice gave Helen a mutinous glare as she got up from the table and stomped out of the room to pack her bag.

Helen poured herself a cup of tea and sat down at the table. As she drank, her mind went over her thoughts of the early hours of the morning.

'Sarah,' she said at last, 'I need paper and a pencil.'

Sarah found the items and Helen sketched a rough plan of the library.

'The tunnel supposedly ran from the library to the crypt. We found the crypt end of it so we know it exists. If the other entrance is in the library, there's only one place it can be...somewhere in this wall.'

She indicated the fireplace wall, dominated by the two massive bookshelves. 'If you look at the entrance to the courtyard, it's the thickest wall. It would be quite easy for something to be concealed within it—priest hole or tunnel.'

'You're not going looking for it again?' Sarah said.

Helen looked up at her. 'I have to know why this—*thing*—is so bent on us not discovering it.'

'What happened yesterday, do you think it was the—*thing*?' Sarah pulled up a chair to the table.

'Don't be stupid,' Pollard said from behind the table. 'It was just an old tunnel that gave way. Nothing funny about that.'

'Except for the crying woman,' Helen said.

'Crying woman?' Pollard laid his paper down.

'Alice heard a woman crying. That's the only reason she went down there.'

Pollard shook his head. 'Child's got a good imagination.'

'I've heard the crying woman and it was my first encounter with the third presence.' She thought it best not to mention spectral dogs.

Sarah's lips tightened. 'I said there is a third force at work here. A bad 'un.'

Helen looked back at the sketch of the library and tapped the pencil on the paper. 'Suzanna and Robert have both shown me the library. The clue must be there.'

Sarah stared at her. 'Do you mean to say, you've been seeing the house as it was back then?' Sarah said in disbelief.

Helen nodded. 'I've seen it twice.'

She closed her eyes and visualised the man lying sprawled across the desk, the pistol in his hand, the blood dripping onto the carpet. The fire burned in the grate and candles in the sconces above the fireplace flickered across the shelves of books. The slender figure of a woman standing by the fireplace also played across her memory. Suzanna had turned and disappeared through the bookcase. The bookcase held the key!

'One of the bookcases—' She opened her eyes and looked at Sarah, '—one of the bookcases was only half full when Robert died.' She stabbed a finger at the drawing, indicating the left-hand side of the fireplace. 'That one.' She pushed her chair back. 'I'm going to take Alice over to the vicarage and then can I meet both of you in the library in half an hour?'

FIFTY-FIVE

Helen, Pollard and Sarah stood in the middle of the worn carpet in the library looking at the two massive bookcases. At first glance, Helen saw nothing to distinguish them. They were identical in form, made of solid mahogany, containing similar, heavy leather bound books filled the shelves.

'I know what it is,' Helen said after flicking through samples of books from both cases. 'The books in the left hand case are all nineteenth century books. In the right hand case are the books from the purchased eighteenth century library. The left hand bookcase must be later than the other one. If Robert died in 1815 and it was only half full at that time, then it must have been more recent.'

'We can always check the household books. They're all in the estate office,' Sarah suggested.

Helen turned to Pollard. 'While we check the records, can you start emptying that bookcase?'

Pollard looked around the silent room. 'You're wanting me to stay here, alone? Place fair gives me the creeps.'

'We won't be long,' Helen said.

At least two centuries of household books were kept in the heavy oak cupboards in the estate office. Sarah threw back the doors, revealing shelves of large leather folios, the spines imprinted with the Morrow coat of arms and a date in gold lettering. Like those at Wellmore, Helen assumed that the household accounts of Holdston recorded every minutiae of life within the four walls as it had been in its heyday.

She would love to have had the time to go through them but now she was on a quest. She selected the volume that read 1809-1815 and flung it down on the desk, scanning the pages with rapidity.

'Sarah, I was right.' She pointed at an entry written in neat copperplate.

'1812, Nov 8, Payment to Jas. Hutchins, carpenter of Birmingham for bookcase for library, 25 pounds, 6 shillings and 8 pence.'

'That's only months after Suzanna disappeared. Robert must have ordered it to conceal the tunnel entrance?' Helen felt almost jubilant at having her hypothesis confirmed.

Sarah frowned. 'Do you think Robert Morrow may have had something to do with his wife's disappearance?'

'I'm sure he did. I am now certain Suzanna never left this house and her body is in that tunnel. Robert could have discovered her affair and we know from her diary he had already been violent to her in the months leading up to her disappearance. Who else could have done it?'

Sarah straightened. 'I don't know. It doesn't sound right to me. Who's the third one, the one what's causing the trouble?'

Helen touched her wrist. The physicality of the third spirit set it apart from Suzanna and Robert. It seemed to have the power to move objects and to harm people. Suzanna had a mischievous power, she could move objects and, apparently, trip people up but this third had physically hurt her and probably caused the tunnel collapse. Had Evelyn's fall been an accident? She shivered and willed herself not to think about it.

Back in the library, Pollard had emptied the lower shelves, stacking the books neatly against the far wall. He fetched a ladder and a bag of tools and, grumbling, climbed up to the higher shelves, handing the dusty books down to the women.

Emptied of books, the bookcase was still a massive piece of furniture, eight feet high and six feet wide.

'There's no way we can move it.' Pollard declared standing back to look at it.

'We are just going to have to take it apart, shelf by shelf,' Helen said.

'Are you sure?' Pollard asked.

'Don't argue, Pollard. Let's just do it.'

By lunchtime, the last piece had been unscrewed and moved away revealing the thick stone wall. Helen stepped into the cobwebby recess and ran her hands over the wall.

Her fingers found the faint indentations about four feet from the floor. Pollard passed her the flashlight and she knelt down, brushing the dust of the century away. In the beam of the light she could just see the faint etching of a martlet in the stonework, just as it had been in the crypt.

She stood up and stepped back, brushing her hands against her skirt. She knew all she had to do was to press the stone but her courage failed her. It could wait for the moment.

'Let's have some lunch,' she suggested. 'I told the hospital I would be in to see Lady Morrow for afternoon visiting hours. Any further exploration can wait till I'm back.'

FIFTY-SIX

Helen's first sight of Evelyn's heavily bandaged head shocked her. With all her other concerns Helen had assumed her indomitable mother-in-law would recover but faced with the reality of Evelyn's injuries, all she could do was to sink on to the chair beside her bed. She picked up the thin bird-like hand and curled her own around it.

'No change?' she asked a passing nurse.

The woman shook her head. 'No, poor lady. She's not moved since they brought her in.'

'Evelyn,' Helen whispered. 'I'm going to stop this thing before it hurts anyone else.'

There seemed little point in staying except to keep vigil. Finishing what she had started that morning had taken on a new urgency.

Returning to Holdston, Helen changed into her jodhpurs and an old jumper and joined Sarah and Pollard in the library. They stood in a semi-circle looking at the engraving on the wall.

'What do we do now?' Pollard said.

'Put your hand on the etching and push,' Helen instructed.

Pollard complied and just as it had in the crypt, they heard the sound of stone grating on stone. Pollard jumped back as if bitten and gave Helen a quick glance. She nodded and the man pushed again and an identical entrance to that in the crypt swung open. Pollard stepped back and the three of them stood staring at the dark hole in the wall as the trapped air rushed out smelling of damp and something else, indefinable and unpleasant.

'Pass me the flashlight, Pollard,' Helen said. 'We should have a look.'

She took a deep breath and lay down on the floor playing the beam over the dark void.

'What can you see?' Sarah asked.

'There's a straight drop of about eight feet. Wait, I can see rings and narrow stones sticking out from the brickwork like a sort of ladder. Then there's a ledge about three feet wide and then another hole so it can't be the bottom.'

'It would have to have gone down a fair way to get under the moat,' Pollard observed.

Helen stood up, brushing the dust from her trousers. 'I'm going down there.'

'Don't be ridiculous, Mrs. Morrow,' Pollard said. 'If anyone's going down, it'll be me.'

His wife looked at his imposing bulk. 'You're too big. You'll never fit in that space.'

'I'll do it,' Helen said.

Sarah straightened, shaking her head. 'No, Mrs. Morrow.' Sarah turned her eyes up to look at the ceiling. 'Wait until the Major's up and then we'll decide.'

'We can't wait,' Helen said, feeling defiant. She knew that after yesterday, Paul would have had very definite thoughts about her current activities. 'We've got to end this now.'

She lay down on her stomach and shone the flashlight down the hole again. Her breath stopped as the light picked up a gleam of a lighter-coloured object on the narrow platform.

She held her breath, playing the light across the object, immediately identifiable as bone and a human skull.

She sat up and looked at the Pollards. 'I was right. She's there. We've found Suzanna. Now all we have to do is bring her up and she can have the proper Christian burial she deserves.'

Sam Pollard and his wife, both took their turn at inspecting Suzanna's tomb.

'I still think you should wait till the Major's up,' Sarah's brow creased in concern.

'I wouldn't expect him to go down there,' Helen said. She rose to her feet, brushing her hands on her trousers. 'Now what's the best way of getting down there?'

Pollard scratched his chin. 'I wouldn't trust those handholds, lass. How about I tie a rope around you so if they give way I'll have you held fast?'

Helen nodded and turned to Sarah. 'Sarah, can you fetch a basket or something we can put the bones in and bring her up?'

'Oh, Mrs. Morrow, you shouldn't...it's not proper.'

'I'm not afraid of dead bodies, Sarah. She deserves to be properly laid to rest.'

Sarah twisted her hands in her apron. 'I don't like this,' she said, looking around the library. 'It's here. It's watching you. I have a bad feeling.'

'What can it do?' Helen said with more bravado than she felt.

'You know what it can do. It's hurt Lady Morrow and Miss Alice. It's not like the others. It's got a force to it.' As she spoke Sarah's eyes darted around the room

Sarah's unease beginning to rub off on Helen. 'We can't leave her down there. Let's just be quick,' she said with more bravado than she felt.

The Pollards left her and Helen sat down cross-legged looking at the hole in the wall.

'Who did this to you, Suzanna?' she asked aloud.

For answer, the curtains at the windows fluttered, even though the windows were shut fast. A cold shiver ran down Helen's spine. She knew they were watching.

Pollard returned with a heavy rope and Sarah, with a basket containing a folded sheet. They pulled the heavy oak table over toward the hole and Pollard looped the rope around one leg of the table to act as a cantilever, tying the other around Helen's waist.

Sarah Pollard's face creased with worry. 'I don't like this.'

'I'll be fine, Sarah.' Helen smiled. 'I spent my childhood climbing trees and rocks.'

Helen's resolve wavered as she crouched down looking into the darkness. Tentatively lowering her legs over the edge, the toe of her boot touched the first foothold and she twisted, letting herself drop over the edge, her fingers grasping the rings that served as handholds. They held fast and giving the Pollards what she hoped was a confident smile, she began to lower herself, her feet slipping on the slimy wall as she sought out each toehold. She thought of Suzanna who had made this journey many times on her way to tryst with her lover in long dresses and without the benefit of the rope securely preventing her from falling. It would have taken courage. One missed step and she would have fallen.

As her feet touched the security of the ledge, Helen looked up at Sarah's anxious face peering down at her from the opening.

'What can you see?' Sarah asked.

'Just give me a moment,' Helen unhooked the flashlight from her belt and swung its beam around the cramped space.

The brick-edged opening to the right revealed rough-hewn steps that descended into dark, murky water where the moat had flooded the tunnel. Maybe yesterday's collapse had been nothing more than an accident, the result of years of water infiltration.

Helen took a deep steadying breath as the light revealed what she had seen from above, a disordered pile of bones, probably scattered by rats over the years. A mouldy leather portmanteau lay beside the skeletal remains. Crouching down to examine the remains, Helen played the light on the skull. The breath caught in her throat. Even without touching the skull, it was obvious that the back of the head had been staved in.

She looked up at the entrance and wondered if this had been an accident and Suzanna had slipped and fallen. It would have been easy to miss a foothold and without a rope, she would have fallen hard. She looked around. Without knowing anything about injuries, it looked as if

Suzanna had hit the back of her skull on something long and thin, maybe the edge of the ledge.

Helen stood up and undid the rope around her waist, calling up to Sarah, to pull up the rope and send down the basket.

Sarah complied and the basket, secured by its handle, skittered down the wall. Helen untied it and replaced it with the portmanteau, giving a quick jerk of the rope to indicate for Sarah to pull it up. The portmanteau disappeared from the place it had lain for one hundred years.

With care, Helen unfolded the sheet and laid it in the base of the basket. She knelt down beside the skeleton again and steeled herself. Despite her bravado, she fought the natural human revulsion for dealing with the dead and it took her a moment before she could bring herself to touch the bones.

'It's all right, Suzanna,' she whispered, 'I'll be gentle.'

Fragments of light cloth that crumbled at her touch and a small, black leather slipper gave humanity to the pitiful remains as she gently laid the bones in the basket. The right femur had been broken in two. Helen frowned and looked up again at the drop. A broken leg and a smashed skull? Had it been enough to kill her or had she died slowly in agony? She shivered at the thought of the young woman possibly lying here for days.

She sat back on her heels as the questions began. If Suzanna had fallen on her way to meet her lover, would the entrance above have been open or closed? Could it be opened from the inside?

As she pondered Suzanna's fate, a door slammed in the library above her and the temperature in the musty hole plummeted. Above her, Sarah cried out in alarm. She looked up in time to see the heavy stone of the entrance slam shut with such force, that the whole wall reverberated under the force.

Helen froze, unable to move or scream, as the darkness closed in around her. Something cold touched her ankle and she flashed the light downward to see fingers of the dark, fetid water begin to creep across the narrow shelf on which she stood.

The flashlight in her hand flickered and Helen launched herself at the wall, scrabbling to find the rings and toe-holds. In her haste, the flashlight dropped and fell with a splash into the water that now swirled around her knees. In the utter blackness, sobbing in terror, she began to climb. Clinging to the topmost ring, she used one hand to push on the wall. It didn't move. Behind the immovable stone, she heard the sound of scraping on the wall and muffled voices shouting her name. Pollard would be trying his best to shift the opening with the crowbar but it held fast as if mortared in place.

'Water,' she screamed, finding her voice at last. 'The water is rising.'

FIFTY-SEVEN

Paul leaned his hands on the wash basin and scrutinised his reflection in the mirror. An ashen, unshaven face with dark, bruised stains under his eyes stared back at him. The last twenty-four hours had been hell but at least the migraine had passed. As always, it left him feeling drained.

He ran some hot water and lathered the shaving cream, drawing the razor across his chin, the familiar action steadying his hand. He dried his face and ran a comb through his hair, still damp from the bath.

As he moved to set the towel back on the rail, he froze as a woman's scream pierced the silence. The sound permeated the walls of the bathroom, a high-pitched scream of pure terror and he wondered if it was another trick by the spectres. The woman screamed again. Definitely human and coming from inside the house.

Paul bolted from his room and along the corridor, drawn instinctively to the library. At the top of the stairs, he collided with a hysterical Sarah Pollard who shrieked as he caught her by the arms.

'Sarah. Calm down. What's happened?'

She could only gesture toward the library.

'She's shut in,' she gabbled. 'It won't move.'

He released the distressed woman and took the stairs two at a time.

Inside the library, he paused long enough to take in the fact that the left-hand bookcase had been removed, the books stacked against the far wall. Pollard stood at the solid stone wall, hitting it with a hammer. Stone splinters flew at each blow but the wall remained unmoved.

The man looked around as Paul entered, desperation written in the lines of his face. 'We found an entrance and then it shut on us. I can't open it,' he said, his voice taut with terror.

'And Helen...?'

'She's in there. I can hear her.'

'Go and fetch a mallet—something heavier than that hammer. Even if we have to knock the damn wall down, we will.'

Paul seized the shaken man by the shoulder and propelled him bodily toward the door to the courtyard.

He knelt on the floor and pressed his ear to the wall. 'Helen, can you hear me?'

Even as he spoke, his breath frosted in the air with his words and he slammed his hand into the armorial carving to no avail. The wall presented as a solid, impenetrable mass, behind which he could hear Helen screaming. He thought he heard the word *water* but the wall was nearly a foot thick.

'Helen!'

A sickly sweet smell, so familiar—although he had not smelt it for many years—permeated the frosty air. The stench of death.

One of the Chinese vases that stood on the mantelpiece crashed against the wall, barely inches from his ear. The library books began to fly off the neat piles, slamming into the wall beside him and against his body, the sharp, hard corners drawing blood. Paul leaned his whole body against the entrance but it was immovable as if mortared in place.

Behind the wall, Helen's cries grew more erratic. The assault from the flying books became more concentrated, accompanied now by an unearthly howling. A heavy atlas caught him above the right eye with such force he reeled back against the wall. Paul slid down to the floor, instinct and self-preservation forcing him to present as small a target as he could. He put his hands over his head, struggling to stay conscious as blood dripped down his face and the world roared in his ears.

Through the wailing and crashing of the books around him, he heard a dog barking, loud and furious.

'Reuben?' he shouted the name out loud, and the dog responded with joyful barks.

'Charlie, save her,' he whispered as the world went black.

FIFTY-EIGHT

Paul opened his eyes to a still, quiet room littered with smashed china, broken books and torn pages. He'd only been out for a short time and he took a deep, thankful breath, wiping his bloodied face with his sleeve. He regained his feet, leaning with all his strength against the wall. It gave so easily, that it was all he could do to keep his balance and not fall over the edge.

Below him yawned inky blackness.

'Helen?'

Silence.

'Is she all right?'

He jumped at the sound of Pollard's voice. The man stood behind him clutching an armful of heavy-duty tools.

'Do you have another flashlight in that lot?' Paul asked

Pollard nodded and handed him the flashlight. Dreading what he might see, Paul shone it down the hole. On a narrow shelf below him, the beam illuminated a pale, crumpled figure. Without a second thought, he swung over the edge, finding the rings and footholds. His fingers slipped on the rings and the wall seemed to ooze water making it hard to keep his footing. He jumped the last few feet, landing with a muffled curse as the pain from his bad leg shot through him.

Helen lay face down at his feet, one hand hanging over the edge of the ledge, her fingers trailing in dark, putrid water, her head turned to the wall. He rolled her over and felt for a pulse. At first, his shaking fingers found nothing. Shifting position, he tried again, and only when he felt the firm beat beneath his fingers did he realise he had been holding his breath.

Helen was soaked, her sweater saturated and heavy with water. He cradled her in his arms, stroking the sodden hair and mud-streaked face, trying to instil some warmth back into her frozen limbs.

'Helen,' he whispered, kissing her forehead. 'Helen, come back to me.'

She stirred, coughed and her eyes opened. Her whole body shook and she clung to him, her chest convulsing with dry, retching sobs of pure relief.

'I thought I was going to die,' she whispered at last.

'What happened down here?' he asked.

'The entrance closed,' she began, 'then I dropped the flashlight and then... oh God... then the water rushed in... I thought I was going to drown. I climbed as high as I could but it kept coming.' Her voice choked on a sob.

'Let's get you out of here. Can you stand?'

Paul held her steady as she rose to her feet. He put his arm around her and she leaned her head against his shoulder, shaking like a leaf.

'I think there'll be two of us who won't like dark places after this,' she said through chattering teeth.

Hearing nothing above them, Paul called Pollard's name and the man's anxious face appeared in the entrance.

'Thank the Lord, sir! Is she all right?'

'She will be once we're out of here,' Paul replied

Paul turned to Helen. 'Are you up to climbing the wall?'

He heard a small gurgle of laughter.

'Try and stop me.'

'Up you go,' he said steadying her as she started to climb as if the hounds of hell were still behind her. He sighed with relief as her legs disappeared into the library.

'Your turn, sir,' Pollard said.

Ladders ... trench ladders. Paul closed his eyes and took a deep breath. As he opened them, the small square of light above him brightened as if the sun had suddenly come out, illuminating the library.

He put a hand to the first ring and began to climb. Hampered by the injury to his left shoulder, it took him longer to climb out than it had to climb down. Pulling himself out of the hole, he rolled over on his back and looked up at the ceiling before dragging himself up into a sitting position.

Helen, bedraggled and shivering, wrapped in a blanket, with Sarah's motherly arm around her sat on the edge of the table, dripping water onto the carpet.

Paul managed a crooked smile. 'What a pair,' he said.

He hauled himself to his feet and swung the door closed. He stood looking at it for a moment before turning to Helen.

'I have to admire your tenacity. After yesterday I had no intention of taking this any further.'

'I know,' she said. 'That's why I took shameful advantage of your incapacity. I found her, Paul. I found Suzanna.' Her eyes widened. 'I'd put her bones in a basket but I never had a chance to send it up to the Pollards. She's gone. The water must have washed her away.'

Paul glanced at the table, noticing a mildewed leather portmanteau beside Helen. 'Where did that come from?'

'That was with her.'

He ran a hand over his eyes. 'I think we've all had enough for one day. 'Bring Helen up to my room, Sarah and find some dry clothes for her.'

FIFTY-NINE

After insisting Helen had a bath, Sarah had given her a pair of Paul's old pyjamas, and with his heavy woollen dressing gown swathing her slender form, she sat curled up in the armchair holding a cup of cocoa as if it was the elixir of life. Pollard paced the room as Sarah cleaned the cuts on Paul's face, clucking and tutting when he shrank from the stinging carbolic.

'Some hero of Passchendaele you are,' she grumbled. 'There, all done.' She applied a sticking plaster to the cut above his eye. 'That should have been stitched. You're going to have a real shiner tomorrow.'

She sat down and picked up her own cocoa. 'What's to be done with the library?'

'Nothing tonight,' Paul said.

'What if,' Pollard's lips thinned at the memory. 'What if that...thing...comes back?'

'It won't,' Sarah said with certainty.

'How do you know?'

'It's gone.' When they all looked at her, Sarah added, 'I can't sense it anymore.'

'What are you talking about, woman,' Pollard growled

'I told you, old fool, that there was something evil in the house, getting stronger and stronger.' Sarah narrowed her eyes at her husband.

'And I told you, you were a fanciful old witch.' Her husband glared at her. His expression softened. 'What made it go?'

Helen shook her head. 'It was trying to prevent us from discovering its secret. Now we may have found what it was trying to hide, it's gone.' She looked up, her eyes seeking out Paul. 'But we haven't solved the mystery, not completely. We still don't know what happened. Was it murder or just an accident? Without her body, we'll never know.' She sighed. 'I wish I'd managed to get the bones out. I wanted to give her a proper burial. She deserved that.'

Sarah rose to her feet and collected the mugs on a tray. 'You two look done in.' She cast Paul a concerned look. 'Time for bed. We'll see you in the morning. Come on, Pollard.'

Help and Paul sat in a silence, broken only by the crackling fire. Once the sound of the Pollards' footsteps and bickering had died away, Helen uncurled from the chair and stood up, thrusting her hands into the pockets of the ridiculously large dressing gown.

'Paul, I don't want to be alone, not tonight.'

Paul looked up at her slight figure, backlit by the fire Pollard had lit in the grate. He didn't want to be alone either. He wanted her in his arms—in his bed.

He rose to his feet and took her in his arms. She leaned her head against his chest and he closed his eyes for a brief moment. She smelled of soap and something else, something sweet and lovely. As he held her, an image of Tony's honest, trusting face intruded into his conscience. He sighed, about to make the hardest decision in his life.

He gently disengaged her and pushed her away.

'You can take my bed. I'll sleep out here.'

She looked up at him and her brow creased. Her lips parted and he knew he only had to touch her again and she would be his for the night ... forever.

'You're engaged to Tony Scarvell, Helen,' he said, quelling the protest that rose within him. 'And you're exhausted. Go to bed and we can talk in the morning. I'll be here if you need me.'

Paul watched her stumble into the bedroom, throw back the covers of the bed and crawl under them as if the mere act of staying upright was beyond her. When he slipped past the bed to reach the bathroom, she had fallen asleep. He leaned over and tucked back a lock of fair hair, still damp from the bath, behind her ear.

It would be so easy to slip in beside her and curl himself around her. His own body, battered bruised and aching, responded to that thought and he stepped away from the bed, pausing only to grab a pillow and the bed cover. A night on the day bed would cure any desire he might feel for his best friend's fiancée.

SIXTY

Helen woke to bright sunshine, streaming in through the casement windows. She lay looking up at the unfamiliar bed hangings. It took her a moment to remember why she was in Paul Morrow's bed.

The memory of the previous day came flooding back. Not the nightmare in the library, but those few moments with Paul. She screwed up her face as she remembered, she had practically thrown herself at him and he had pushed her away.

You're engaged to Tony Scarvell, Helen.

Helen rolled over and buried her face in the pillow. She took a deep breath smelling a warm, male scent. Sighing, she sat up. The day had to be faced—Paul had to be faced.

She wandered into his sitting room, tying the belt on his dressing gown around her waist. For a moment she thought the room was empty but a shadow moved by the window and Paul turned to look at her.

She looked down at her bare feet and the enveloping dressing gown.

'I'm sorry, I must look a sight,' she said.

'I'm not exactly a ravishing beauty myself.' He gave her a rueful smile, touching the sticking plaster on his temple. As Sarah had rightly predicted he had the makings of a splendid black eye.

She flinched in sympathy. 'Where did you sleep? Not on the day bed?' She glanced at the folded coverlet and pillow on the horsehair sofa that served as a daybed.

Paul gave the day bed a wry look. 'I've slept on worse.'.

Helen ran a hand through her uncombed hair and shook her head. 'It all seems unreal now, like some awful nightmare. Terrible while I was going through it, but gone in the daylight.' She shrugged and smiled at him. 'I'll go and have a bath and get dressed and then what do we do?'

'We'll start with breakfast. Can you face the library again?'

She nodded but didn't move. Their eyes met. The library would be easy, there was so much else that needed to be said.

'Paul, we have to talk about...about—'

He visibly stiffened, interrupting her. 'If there's there anything I might have said, or done, over the last few days...? If I've upset you in anyway...? Anything I said in that damn tunnel?'

She shook her head. 'No, that's not it. Paul, I've buried Charlie, I can let him go now. My questions are answered. I know now, he died in your arms and not alone but what happened that night is between you and him. I just want the answer to one last question. If Charlie had got back to the British lines that night, would he have lived?'

Paul shook his head. 'No.'

She held up her hand. 'Thank you. That's all I need to know.'

He looked into her eyes for a moment as he said. 'And thank you for understanding that there will be some things I can never talk about. I have learned to live with those years, Helen. While I saw things no man should ever see, I'm no different from any of the thousands of men who fought in the trenches. We just have different ways of dealing with what happened and I prefer to think about what is ahead, not what has been.'

She nodded and smiled. 'I understand that. I suppose it depends on what is ahead—for both of us.'

He paused for a moment before responding and, turned back to the window as he said, 'The answer to that is quite simple. You're going to marry a good and honourable man and I'm going back to an archaeological dig in Mesopotamia.'

Helen put her hand to her throat, focusing on his broad, straight back and willing him to turn and face her but he remained quite still, staring out at the Morrow inheritance. She resisted the urge to hit him.

Sixty-One

The devastation in the library was worse than Helen remembered from the previous night. All the library books that had been taken from the new bookshelf lay scattered on the floor, pages torn, spines broken, amidst broken china and shattered paintings. Those books still in the old bookcase were untouched, as were Pollard's tools and the portmanteau.

'It looks like a battlefield. Do you suppose we won?' Helen said.

'Lucky for me whatever it was didn't touch the actual weapons.' Paul indicated Pollard's tools.

She looked up at his bruised face. Or we could both be dead, she thought.

They stood at the table looking at the portmanteau. Helen viewed the object with revulsion. Just seeing it brought back the terror of the previous day.

Paul picked up a screwdriver from where Pollard had left it and forced the locks. They gave without too much effort and he pulled the bag open.

He looked into the bag and shrugged. 'It's only what I'd expect. Clothes.'

Helen took the bag from him and began to lay the contents out on the table. The ephemera of Suzanna's life appeared to be in a good state of preservation, despite the damp tomb where the bag had lain.

'But this doesn't make sense. This bag hasn't been properly packed. Things have just been thrust in here without any order. For instance, why is her cloak in here?' Helen pulled out a sturdy blue wool cloak. 'Wouldn't she have been wearing it? And this?' She produced a squashed bonnet of matching blue velvet. 'No lady, even one running away with her lover, would pack her bonnet in a valise. From what I could tell from the skeleton, she wore only a light dress and house shoes.'

She carefully emptied the bag of its several petticoats, a couple of dresses, walking boots, stockings, hairbrushes, a purse with some gold coins in it and, chillingly, a poker wrapped in a shawl.

They both stared at the last object. Paul picked it up and looked at it closely.

'Look at this, Helen.'

Helen's eyes widened as he indicated a dark stain on the head of the poker. 'Is that what I think it is?'

'There is hair embedded in it. I am fairly certain that is blood,' Paul confirmed.

Helen took a step back from the table, her hand over her mouth.

'Helen?' Paul turned to her as she subsided into one of the chairs by the fireplace.

'Her skull had been smashed. I thought maybe she had slipped on the wall and fallen, hitting her head on the ledge, but that...thing...' she pointed at the poker, 'that is a murder weapon.' Her eyes widened. 'Paul, someone beat her to death with that poker.'

He walked over to the wall and swung the entrance open. He took one last look at the poker and threw it into the hole. Helen heard it hit the ledge and then a splash as it rolled off into the water.

'Why did you do that?'

He shook his head. 'We don't need it.'

Helen forced herself to return to the contents of the portmanteau spread across the table.

'Something puzzles me. If she were leaving, she should have been wearing boots and her cloak? It would have been cold in September.'

Helen spread her hands over the blue cloak. 'And why did she risk going by the tunnel again? She could have just walked out of the door with no one to stop her.'

Paul shrugged. 'What are you thinking, Helen?'

She looked up at him. 'I don't think she was going to leave.' Helen said, running her hands over the contents of the portmanteau. 'There's something missing but I can't think what it is.'

Paul picked up the blue velvet bonnet. 'If you're right and she was murdered, do you have any ideas about the murderer?'

'It has to be Robert,' Helen said. 'He'd hit her once and if he found out about her affair, he could have turned violent again.' She paused and looked up at Paul. 'There's only one clue left, we haven't explored. Those last entries in the diary.' She looked up at him. 'Paul, you must finish the diary.'

Paul set the bonnet down and glanced at his watch. 'The diary will have to wait, Helen. I must go and see Evelyn. I haven't been for days.'

'I went yesterday.'

He looked at her, one eyebrow lifted in surprise. 'Did you indeed?'

'Despite everything she is still my mother-in-law, and she deserves a better daughter than I have been.'

'Then we'll go together,' he said.

SIXTY-TWO

Pollard drove them to the hospital in Birmingham. Evelyn had been moved to a private room and impulsively Helen bent over to kiss the alabaster flesh of her mother-in-law's temple, appalled at how frail and old she looked.

The nurse picked up the chart at the end of the bed and flicked through it. 'There's been a big improvement, sir,' she said, addressing Paul. 'She's opened her eyes and seems more restless. I'll leave you in peace. Visiting hours finish in thirty minutes.'

Paul crossed to the bed and picked up Evelyn's hand. Helen drew up a chair and sat down.

'When I think of the hours she spent with me when I was in hospital,' Paul said more to himself than Helen. 'She came every week without fail, even when I was in no condition to acknowledge her.'

'How long were you in hospital?'

He thought for a moment. 'Hospital, rehabilitation, back to hospital again for more operations. Evelyn made sure I had the best doctors but it was nearly two years before I came back to Holdston. By then my uncle was dead, the war was over and Holdston had become my problem.'

'And she came every week?'

'Except for the month when my uncle died.'

'For someone who seemed not to care much for you, that seems strange,' Helen said.

'I always thought she saw it as her duty.' He shrugged. 'But then my relationship with Evelyn has always been complicated.'

'I suppose she is your only living relative.'

He looked up at her. 'Evelyn and I are only related by marriage. I have only one living blood relative, your daughter, Alice. But you're right. Despite everything, she is my responsibility as much as she saw me as hers and she will fight for those she loves. You know the story of my engagement?'

Helen nodded.

'Fi came to the hospital to tell me she was breaking off the engagement. It happened to be during one of Evelyn's visits and she went for Fi in a fury. I've no idea what she said but it reduced Fi to tears.'

'Did you mind?'

'About Fi? No. She did write me a letter eventually. Quite a nice letter. Truth was she didn't want to marry me, any more than I wanted to marry her. We only got engaged because it seemed the thing to do at the time. The war had just started and we were young. I was only twenty-one and she was seventeen.' He set his aunt's frail hand back on the bedcovers and looked across at Helen. 'There's nothing we can do here. Let's go home.'

On their way back to Holdston, they stopped at the vicarage. They found Alice playing cribbage with Lucy in the drawing room and seemed quite happy to remain at the vicarage. To Helen's relief, neither the vicar nor his wife asked about their battered appearances.

With a promise to collect Alice the following morning, Paul and Helen returned to the hall, where Sarah had supper ready. They all ate in the kitchen seated around the kitchen table.

'Poor soul,' Sarah said, pouring the tea. 'Do you suppose she's at peace now?' Helen asked.

Paul looked at Sarah. 'Well, Sarah?'

'Why are you looking at me?' Sarah asked, bridling. 'Do you want to know if I can still sense her?'

Helen nodded.

Sarah closed her eyes. 'I can't feel anything, but this is the wrong part of the house. I've never sensed 'em down here.'

Helen looked up at the ceiling. 'I think they're gone. Although I feel we still have to identify her murderer.'

Sarah shivered. 'Imagine that poor thing down there all those years and no one knowing and the whole world saying she'd run off with another man. That's the scandal, in my book.'

'I agree, Sarah,' Helen thought about the dreadful things that Lady Cecilia Morrow had written about her missing daughter-in-law.

'Do you want me to close off the 'ole in the library again?' Pollard asked.

'I suppose so.' Paul picked up a piece of Sarah's cherry cake. 'Mind you, all that water can't be doing the foundations any good. I should get it sealed.' He sighed. 'God knows what that will cost.'

'I'll have a good look tomorrow,' Pollard glanced at his wife. 'You don't think it will come back, do you?'

Paul shook his head. 'Whatever it was, it was trying to stop us finding Suzanna.' He rose to his feet. 'I'm going to have a look at that last diary entry. Helen?'

'Yes?'

'Do you want to join me?'

Helen nodded. 'I'd better telephone Tony first.'

'I've laid a fire in your grate, sir,' Sarah said. 'It's chilly tonight.'

Helen rang Wellmore, telling Tony that while Evelyn still remained unconscious she felt she should remain at Holdston. While not exactly a lie, she still felt guilty about misleading him.

Upstairs in his room, Paul switched on his light and indicated the grate. 'Can you manage the fire, Helen? I'll pour us both a brandy. God knows we've earned it.'

Helen set the match to the kindling and sat back on her haunches, taking the proffered glass from Paul. He wandered over to his table, picked up the small leather-bound book, and flicked through the pages to find the right spot.

Helen stared at him.

'That's it!'

He looked up in surprise. 'What is?'

'The thing that was missing from her bag. Her diary! She would never have left her diary.'

Paul looked down at the book in his hand.

'She wrote her last entry and secreted it back among her books, intending to return to it,' Helen continued. 'Even if she didn't intend to take it, she would have destroyed it, not left it in her room for anyone to find.'

'Anyone with a desire to read a commentary on one of the Saints,' Paul remarked drily. 'Maybe she just forgot it? As you say, she packed in a hurry.'

Helen walked over to the table and took the book from him. 'No, it would have been the first thing she packed.'

He took it back from her. 'If you want me to finish it, I had better get on with it.'

Helen picked up the other book that sat on his table. 'Is this your copy of Homer?' She flicked open to the first page and gasped. 'This was Robert's!'

He nodded. 'It was a birthday present from my uncle.'

Helen turned the pages. 'Where's your translation?'

He handed her a bound notebook, the leather cover stained and creased. 'Excuse its appearance. I had it with me when ... I'm afraid some of the stains may be blood. I did try and clean it.'

Helen traced the dark stains on the cover. The price Paul had paid for his life.

'This is what you worked on in the trenches?'

'War is ten percent terror and ninety percent sheer boredom. Homer filled the boredom more than adequately.' He smiled. 'I hope you can read my writing. It may be a bit shaky in bits. It's hard to write when the shells are falling around you.'

Helen poured them both another brandy and settled down in the large chair by the crackling fire, and opened Paul's notebook. He wrote in pencil, his hand firm and sure despite the conditions under which he had been working.

Taking a sip of brandy, she abandoned herself to the conversations of the gods as they decide Troy's fate. Another futile war in another time. Paul's translation moved in a gentle rhythm, capturing the grace and beauty of the prose. 'Paul, this is wonderful,' Helen said. 'Are you going to have it published?'

He looked up and shook his head. 'I'm glad you like it, Helen, but I don't suppose I'll ever finish it.'

'Why not?'

He shrugged. 'It was a means to an end and I think, maybe, I've reached the end. Like Odysseus' Penelope, it is time to put the past away and concentrate on the present. Now let me finish this.'

SIXTY-THREE

The clock on the mantelpiece showed nearly midnight before Paul straightened and pushed back his chair with a scraping noise that woke Helen, who had been dozing in the chair.

She sat up with a start. 'Finished?'

Paul stretched, easing his left shoulder with a wince. Drawing a deep breath, he gathered up the papers on his desk. 'I think we have our answer.'

She looked at him, fully awake and her eyes bright with curiosity. 'Do we?'

'You read it and tell me what you think?'

He handed her the papers and she read aloud:

September 9: Last evening Robert called me to sit with him before the fire. I took a seat and picked up a piece of needlework. 'Put it down, Anna and come sit with me,' he said. 'I have done you a great wrong and caused you great hurt.' I did as he bid and he placed his hand on my shoulder. 'Anna,' he said softly. 'I seek your forgiveness for what passed between us. I have been to hell and I hope my feet are now turned back on a path of righteousness.

'What do you mean?' asked I, seeing a new pain in his face. He

buried his head in his hands and began to weep. 'Ah Anna, such sights as no man should see...'

'You must not talk of it,' I said, remembering Lady Morrow's edict. He looked up at me. 'Please let me talk,' he said. 'I must unburden myself.' I took his hand and kissed it. 'Then talk, if you must.' And talk he did, until the small hours of the morning, of his time in Spain. Of the friends he had seen killed and of that fateful day before Badajoz. His tales were horrific and I began to understand the anger within him, the frustration of a man burdened with a terrible pain that those he loves cannot share. After a while the words ceased to have meaning, I watched just his face and his eyes, seeing for the first time since his return a certain peace and the shadow of the man I had once loved. When he was spent, he slept in his chair. I covered him with a blanket and stole away to my bed to toss sleepless with indecision.

Helen looked up at Paul and he saw the empathy in her eyes. It would have taken enormous trust on Robert's part to talk to her of his time in Spain. Helen understood that just as she understood why Paul would never talk about what had passed between himself and Charlie in no man's land.

'Go on,' he said.

September 10: Last night I went to my husband. As I slipped into the bed beside him, he took me in his arms and held me close. We did not make love, just lay together in silence. He slept fitfully. His leg bothers him again and I was most concerned not to cause him more pain or distress. As the first light of the day began to break, he awoke and kissed me. At his direction we made love and when we were done, he wept, kissing my hair and calling me his 'dearest.' When I left him, I called the maid for a bath. I lay in its steamy depths and wept as if my heart would break.

'Robert rose and dressed for breakfast and spent the day with us, laughing and teaching his son to play chess. In the evening, he insisted on taking a walk in the garden with his mother. My fear that it would overtax him has come to pass and tonight he seems tired and feverish.

'September 11: Robert is grievous ill. His exertions of the previous day have quite overdone his fragile strength. The doctor has attended

and bled him. He says the wound in his leg has reopened and must be attended to. I fear this setback will mean Robert will once more be bedridden for the next few weeks. I sat with him in the afternoon and read to him from a most amusing novel by 'A Lady' called Sense and Sensibility which I obtained while I was in London. It was quite the talk of the salons. Her observations of life in country society are unerringly accurate and quite biting in their comment. Lady Morrow would disapprove, I am sure but it was nice to see him smile though he is so weak and in such great pain. He reached out a hand across the bedclothes and encircled mine, once more beseeching my forgiveness for the cruel way he has treated me these past weeks.

Helen stared at the paper in her hand. 'Robert was bound to his bed,' she said, looking up at Paul. 'He could not have physically stopped Suzanna leaving.'

Paul nodded and she continued.

September 12: It lacks but an hour until the appointed time when I am to flee with S. He will be waiting for me at the churchyard with a coach and our passage for Port Jackson. All that is left is for me to pack a portmanteau and slip away. In doing so I leave behind my two children and a husband that I see now loves me beyond measure and needs me. If I leave it will destroy him utterly. If I stay, what passed between us cannot be undone but it can be forgiven. What appeared such a simple decision but a few days previously now presents itself entirely differently. If I do leave, my husband and my children will be disgraced and I shall spend my life looking over my shoulder wondering when we shall encounter someone who knows us, knows our past and all the hurt and anguish I will have caused will be revealed. My clock has chimed twelve. My mind is certain. My decision sure. It is time to close this book and put it safely to one side and pen a note which I will leave safely with the first baronet. When I do not appear as arranged, S will know to look there. What I will do tonight will be for the best of reasons - for love of a man and that man is my husband.

Helen looked up at Paul, her eyes misting with tears.

'You were right, Helen,' he said. 'She was not going to leave him and Robert could not have been the murderer.'

Helen frowned. 'So, what happened?'

'She left her room, in her day clothes as you observed,' Paul began.

'She reached the library, opened the secret door, and then...' Helen continued

'Go back,' Paul said. 'Retrace her steps. She slept in the green bedroom. To reach the library she had to pass this room.'

'Where Robert slept?'

'Robert, who was grievously ill and incapacitated with his bad leg. As you said, even if he had heard her, I can tell you from experience he would have been in no position to follow her, let alone do her any harm.'

'She would have had to pass Lady Morrow's bedchamber, your mother's room.' Helen looked up at him, her eyes wide. 'Cecilia. We have forgotten about Lady Morrow. Her room was above the library. Suzanna would have had to go past her door and down the stairs and then open the secret door. If Cecilia was still awake she would have heard everything.'

'But why not before?'

Helen felt the excitement rising. 'Because Suzanna's trysts were during the day or at times when Cecilia was otherwise occupied and Suzanna was thought to be ensconced in the library or on some other errand. It makes sense now. Can't you see, Paul?'

Paul frowned. 'If Cecilia heard her go past, she could have followed her down the stairs and—'

'Paul. Cecilia is our vengeful spirit who didn't want the truth revealed. She heard Suzanna go past.' Helen's hand went to her wrist. 'Did she try to stop her? In the struggle did Suzanna fall down the stairs or was she pushed?' She frowned. 'I would like to give her the benefit of the doubt, but I think the evidence points to her pushing Suzanna down the stairs.'

'Do you remember if any of her bones were broken?'

Helen frowned. 'She had a broken femur but I put that down to her falling off the ladder and then not being able to climb back up again.'

Paul's lips tightened. 'What if Suzanna fell down the stairs and broke her leg? As she lay on the floor, Cecilia picked up the poker from the fireplace and finished off her troublesome daughter-in-law with one quick blow to the head.'

Helen's brow creased. 'Oh Paul, how awful but it makes sense. Then all she had to do was dispose of the body down the hole and go to Suzanna's bed-chamber, pack her bag with what she thought an absconding wife would take with her, and throw the valise down after her. She closed the wall up and went back to bed with no one being any the wiser. Only she missed the diary.'

'Cecilia may have had her suspicions about Suzanna and Stephenson for some time,' Paul observed. 'Remember, she says in a letter that 'there have been rumours' about her daughter-in-law.'

'More than that. She'd disapproved of the marriage to Robert from the first. Suzanna's flighty behaviour only confirmed her worst fears. And Robert? Poor Robert who loved her? Did Cecilia think that by getting rid of Suzanna all would be well with her son?'

'I am sure she did,' Paul said. 'But she didn't understand what Robert had been through in Spain, the things he had seen, what he had suffered.'

Helen continued. 'She didn't understand and wouldn't even try. Robert had come back from the Spanish Peninsula every bit as shell-shocked as any soldier from the Great War.'

'And then to believe he had been abandoned by his wife, little wonder he took his own life,' Paul concluded.

'And Cecilia lost her son after all,' Helen said. 'How sad.'

Paul refilled his glass and joined Helen beside the fire, taking the seat across from her. They sat in silence staring at the dancing flames and the glowing coals. Helen's thoughts were of Paul and Charlie and how little difference there had been between their experiences and that long distant war that had sent the wounded and damaged Robert Morrow back home.

The clock on the mantelpiece chimed the hour jerking her out of her reverie. 'Look at the time. I should go to bed.'

As she stood, he rose from his chair and took a step to her, putting a hand on her arm.

'Don't go, Helen. Stay with me tonight.'

SIXTY-FOUR

Paul read the conflicting emotions in her face as she looked up at him: *Tony, propriety, respectability, reputation...*

He didn't care about any of those things any more. He knew only one thing, he loved Helen and unless he had completely misread her, she loved him too.

He gently tightened his grip on her arm and pulled her to him.

'I'm tired of doing the right thing,' he said. 'Helen, I know I'm not Charlie, but...'

'No.' Her eyes widened and she placed her hands on either side of his face, forcing him to look into her eyes. 'And I wouldn't want you to be. I love you for who you are, Paul Morrow.'

The word lay between them. Such a simple word—love—and yet responsible for so much unhappiness in this house alone.

Her grey eyes brimmed with tears as she said, 'I love you. I have loved you for a long time and I want to stay with you tonight. When I'm in your arms, I feel like I have come home to the place I belong.'

He put his arms around her and bent his head to kiss her, gentle at first, testing her resolve.

They had kissed before but always stolen, guilty, desperate gestures of unacknowledged affection. Now her body responded, melting against him as his hands rose to her shoulders, running down her arms. So slender, so delicate, and yet he could feel the strength in her that came from a life lived in the Australian bush.

He pushed back the sleeves of her cardigan, kissing the inside of her wrists. Helen threw back her head as his lips moved to her throat, finding the soft hollow at the base of her throat. He lifted her in his arms, ignoring the grumbling from his shoulder, and carried her into the bedroom.

He lay her down on the bed and turned out the light, leaving only the soft glow from the fire in the sitting room, illuminating the bed in a soft, golden light. She slipped her arms around his neck bringing his face down to hers and they kissed again.

The physical desire for her threatened to overwhelm him but he wanted so much more from this moment. He wanted this woman, body and soul. Her fingers meshed in his hair and even in the dim light he could see the wonder in her face as they came together.

They slept curled into each other until the faintest light beyond the window heralded a new day.

———

In the first grey light of dawn, Helen lay awake remembering, turning every moment of the previous night over like a precious jewel to be cherished. Nothing outside the four walls of this room mattered and for the first time in years, a happiness and contentment she thought she would never experience again, swathed her. She smiled and turned over to look at the man who slept beside her.

Sensing her movement, Paul murmured in his sleep and rolled over onto his back with a sigh. She turned on her side, watching him. Sleep robbed his face of the angles and lines of a hard life, and she could see, for a fleeting moment, the innocence and hope of youth in the gentle curve of his lips.

He had thrown back the covers, baring his chest to the chill of the morning and for the first time, she could see the damage to his left shoulder, forever marring the strong rower's chest and shoulders. There were other scars, one on his right arm and another across his ribs, but nothing like the twisted, knotted legacy of that day in 1917.

'Not pretty is it?'

She started and glanced up at his face. He watched her with hazy, amused eyes.

'No,' she admitted.

'That's what happens when four inches of shrapnel lodges in your shoulder. It's something of a miracle that I am still alive, let alone retain some use of my arm.' He flexed the fingers of his left hand. 'I was fortunate to have excellent doctors.'

She threw back the bed covers revealing the whole length of his body still strong and lean-muscled despite the damage. With tentative fingers, she reached out and touched each of the scars in turn, the legacy of war. He lay without moving beneath her and her gaze held his, willing him to trust her.

'It's who I am, Helen,' he said.

'I know and I love you for every mark on your body.'

He raised his left hand to touch her face.

'You carry scars too, Helen,' he said, 'but they are here—' his hand rested on her chest, '—in your heart. That's what the war has done to us all, a generation of permanently scarred people.'

Paul rolled over and propped himself up on an elbow and looked down at her. She reached up and touched his face and he turned his head so her fingers rested on his mouth. He held them there, kissing each one in turn.

'I should go to my own bed. Annie will notice if it's not been slept in,' she said.

'To hell with Annie and everyone else,' Paul said, his gaze not leaving Helen's face.

She closed her eyes and he saw a tear slide from beneath her lashes. 'Paul, this is all wrong. I'm betrothed to another man.'

'But you're not in love with him.'

'No,' she conceded. 'But I don't want to hurt him.'

He lay down beside her, sliding his good arm around her shoulder, cradling her head in his shoulder. 'If you marry him, Helen, you will cause him far more pain.'

'What do you mean?'

'You're not happy now and as the years go by, your unhappiness will make him unhappy and you will end up hating each other.'

'You seem very sure.'

'I am,' he said. 'I've seen it before.'

She turned her head away to hide the tears that had begun to seep from beneath her eyes.

'And if I break the engagement, what then, Paul? Will you be there?'

His lips brushed her hair. 'Always,' he whispered. 'I love you, Helen. I want you with me forever. You're my soul mate, my healer. I can't let you go now.'

She turned to look at him.

'I thought I had found my soul mate in Charlie,' she said, 'but I have been gifted another chance. I can't leave you, Paul.' She laid her hand over his, pressing it to her heart. 'I love you so much it hurts.'

His lips curved in a smile. 'And I love you, Helen ... Morrow.'

She lowered her head and kissed him gently, just a small, butterfly kiss. His eyes closed and she felt his body relax beneath her touch. Without a word, she straddled him, leaning down and kissing his face, and his neck, running her fingers through the dark hair of his chest, tracing a line from the notch at the base of his throat, down the long, lean body. He closed his eyes and groaned, pulling her toward him and the troubles that waited beyond the door could wait just a little while longer.

They slept again, a deep dreamless sleep that was only disturbed by a knock on the door of the outer room, followed by a rattling of the door handle.

Paul sat up, pushing his hair out of his eyes. 'It's Sarah.'

He swung his legs out of bed, hastily fastening a dressing gown around himself as he strode out into the sitting room.

Helen buried herself in the bedclothes. She heard Paul's voice and Sarah's response and he came back into the bedroom, bearing a tray with a teapot and two cups.

She sat up and pulled the sheet up over her naked chest. 'Oh God, Paul what are we going to do?'

He smiled down at her and handed her a cup. 'Seeing as she has gone to all the trouble to provide two cups, we're going to have a cup of tea.'

Helen began to laugh, trying hard to keep the teacup steady in her hand as Paul slid back into bed beside her, balancing his cup.

'This is absurd,' she said.

'But so terribly English,' Paul said with a smile. 'Would they do this in Australia?'

'In the right circles,' Helen said, draining the last of the tea and setting the cup down beside the bed. 'I suppose we should get up and face the world.'

'Lovely as the idea of staying in bed all day with you is, there are things to be done.' He leaned over the bed, and kissed her on the forehead. 'Up!'

'Yes, sir.'

She smiled, rolling out of the bed. Wrapping a sheet around her and stopping only to retrieve her discarded clothes, Helen ran barefoot down the corridor to her own room. She shut the door behind her and leaned on it, smiling as she saw the pristine cover on the untouched bed, looking like a reproachful virgin. She considered pulling back the sheets but remembered the two cups on the tray and decided pretence was pointless.

SIXTY-FIVE

Paul walked into the kitchen in search of breakfast. Sarah turned around from the stove and stared at him.

'You were whistling,' she said.

'Is that a crime?'

'I've not heard you whistle since I'm not sure when.'

Paul poured a cup of tea from the pot on the table. He set the cup down and laughed as he realised what tune had been going through his head. Whistling was one thing, whistling silly tunes from Gilbert and Sullivan's *Ruddigore* was quite another.

Sarah smiled and shook her head. 'Ah, lad, you've got it badly. Eggs and bacon?'

'I'm starving.'

Helen stood at the kitchen door and Paul turned to look at her. She looked radiant. Her freshly washed hair curled damply around her face and all signs of strain and exhaustion had vanished to be replaced with a soft colour and a smile curving her lips. The protective shell he had built around himself began to crack and fall to the floor like dried mud. Whatever she had done, whatever magic she had woven, it had penetrated into a part of his soul he thought could never know light and happiness. He grinned like a love-struck school boy.

She walked across to him, laying a hand on his shoulder. With a quick glance at Sarah's back, he covered it with his own hand and drew it up, kissing the inside of her wrist, their eyes locked.

Sarah turned around with two plates at that moment. He dropped his hand to the table and Helen took a step backward, pushing a curl of hair behind her ear, a faint stain of colour rising to her cheeks.

Sarah set the plates down on the table and stood looking at the two of them, with her hands on her hips.

'If you think I'm fussed, don't you worry yourselves. I don't gossip. I said to Pollard the first week you were here, Mrs. Morrow, that you were the best thing to come into this house for years. There's nothing that pleases me more than to see you both smiling. There's been enough sadness in this house.'

Paul glanced at Helen as she pulled up a chair at the table.

'Sarah Pollard, you do realise only you can talk to me like that?' Paul said. 'Even my aunt wouldn't be quite so blunt.'

Sarah poured herself a cup of tea. 'Aye and it's a privilege, sir.'

Helen's fingers crept across the scrubbed tabletop and meshed with his. He looked down and saw that she had removed her wedding band. A faint white mark and a slight indentation showed where it had not left her hand for nearly ten years. He ran his thumb over the mark and looked up at her, the question in his eyes. She smiled.

'The time was right,' she whispered. She straightened her shoulders. 'I'd better go and collect Alice after breakfast. What are you going to do this morning?'

'I've got to go into Birmingham. I've got some business with the lawyers and I want to see Evelyn.'

'I'll make a start on tidying the library.'

They didn't move, just sat staring at each other.

'Your eggs are going cold,' Sarah observed.

Sarah left the kitchen to collect the mail and Helen reached over and laid a hand on Paul's.

"Do you suppose?' Helen took a deep shuddering breath. 'Do you suppose Charlie would mind—about us?'

Paul hesitated over his next words. 'Do you believe in ghosts, Mrs. Morrow?'

Helen laughed. 'I have, as you well know, every reason to be open-minded on that subject. Why?'

'Because I think there has been a fourth spirit involved in our recent melee.' He felt foolish just saying it but if anything in this extraordinary situation made sense, the words had to be said.

Helen sat bolt upright and looked down at him. 'Who?'

'Charlie,' he said frowning. 'No, not Charlie but more his presence, watching over us ... protecting us and, bringing us together.'

'Paul, that's ridiculous,' Helen said.

'The dog, Reuben,' Paul said. 'Whenever we saw or heard Reuben, it was always in that context.' He saw the disbelief in her face and smiled. 'You forget, Helen, I'm half Irish. My mother brought me up with tales of the other worlds and a succession of ayahs in Malaya filled my head with tales of bomohs and strange spirits of the jungles.'

'No, I believe you,' she said. "Remember when Alice was in danger, I saw the dog standing on the path to the church. It seemed so real and yet had proved as much an illusion as the spectres of Suzanna and Robert and Alice kept telling me she was playing with a dog called Reuben. I thought she was just imagining it.'

She thought of Charlie's last note to her. Had Charlie kept the promise he had made to her?

I love you my darling girl, always, and whatever is in my power to keep you and the baby safe and well, I will do.

SIXTY-SIX

Paul returned from Birmingham in the late afternoon and found Helen curled up in his armchair reading his translation of Homer. She set the notebook aside and jumped to her feet as he entered his room.

'You've been ages,' she said with no reproach in her voice.

In a few strides, he had reached her, folding her in his arms, his mouth seeking hungrily for hers.

When they drew breath, he tossed his hat and coat on the daybed.

'Where's Alice?' he asked, pouring them both a drink.

'She's in the nursery playing with Lily.' Helen took the glass from him. 'Paul, I rang Tony this morning and asked him to meet me for lunch tomorrow.'

'Do you want me to come?'

She shook her head. 'No. This is best done by me alone. How is Evelyn?'

'She's drifting in and out of consciousness which the doctors think is a good sign. She seemed to be asleep when I was there.'

She frowned. 'How do we explain the library to Evelyn?'

Paul's hand tightened on his glass and he shook his head. 'I'm at a loss to explain the wholesale destruction of some of our more valuable assets but I'm sure we'll come up with some plausible excuse.'

He set the glass down and crossed over to Helen. Helen rose to her feet and slipped her arms around his neck. He circled her waist with his hands, stooping to kiss the bridge of her nose.

'You're so beautiful,' he whispered.

'And you—' she started to say, her arms winding around his neck, but didn't finish as he kissed her again.

'Helen!'

They sprang apart but too late. Tony Scarvell stood in the doorway and from the expression on his face, he had seen more than enough.

'Tony.' Helen looked up at Paul and a pang of regret shot through him as he saw the tears filling her eyes

'I came to—' Tony frowned and looked down at an envelope in his hand as if seeing it for the first time. 'This came for you. I thought—'

He dropped the envelope on the floor and turned on his heel, walking away, his heels echoing on the floorboards.

Helen stood frozen, her face chalk white. 'What have we done?' she murmured.

Without a word, Paul turned to follow Tony.

He caught up with his friend in the stable yard. Tony had ridden across from Wellmore, which explained why they had not heard the motor vehicle. Now, he leaned against his horse as if trying to gather the strength to mount.

'Tony—' Paul began. 'Wait. Let me—'

Tony turned and without any warning, a strong uppercut sent Paul sprawling to the cobblestones. As he lay there gathering his scattered wits, Tony hunched down beside him.

'Sorry,' Tony said. 'I didn't mean to hit you so hard.'

Paul pulled himself up into a sitting position, ruefully rubbing his chin. 'You did and I deserved it.'

'You're a bastard, Morrow.' Tony glared at him. 'I came to you. I asked you if there was anything between you and Helen. I would never have— If I thought for a moment—'

'I know,' Paul said. 'Believe when I say at the time I answered you with absolute honesty, Tony.'

Tony looked down at his right hand, rubbing the knuckles. 'That hurt.'

'I hope it made you feel better.' Paul rose to his feet, dusting the dirt from his trousers. He felt his jaw. Tomorrow he would have another bruise to match the bruising around his eye.

Tony stood up and leaned against the mounting block, still rubbing his knuckles. 'Is that why Helen wanted to meet me tomorrow? To tell me it was all off?'

'Yes. We intended to tell you properly. Not like this,' Paul said. 'Neither of us are cowards.'

'You always marched to the beat of your own drum, Morrow.'

Paul rounded on his friend. 'You're wrong. All my life I have done what was expected of me. Believe me, I would have stood by and let Helen marry you, even though I loved her, because I didn't think I would ever be good enough for her.'

'What changed?'

Paul's mind ran helter-skelter through the events of the previous two days. He ran a hand down the nose of Tony's horse and said, 'Don't ask me to explain it.'

'Well I think I'm damn well entitled to an explanation,' Tony fumed.

Paul turned back to face his friend. 'Tony, I love her. I have loved her from the first moment I saw her riding Minter. The last few days have been a bit rough and it threw us together. I'm sorry but for once in my life, I can't do what is expected of me. I can't let her go.'

'What about Angela? She's still in love with you,' Tony challenged

'Angela has nothing to do with this. Our moment came and went seven years ago.'

Tony looked away, his mouth tight. 'I knew Helen didn't love me but I hoped...' He looked back at Paul. 'Well, nothing I can say or do will change things now, will they?'

'No.'

'What are you going to do?'

Paul looked up at the walls of the old house. 'Do exactly what I planned to do. Sell Holdston and leave this bloody country. Even if in time you forgive me, I know damn well your mother won't. She'll make our lives a misery.'

Tony nodded. 'Yes,' he agreed, 'she will.'

'What will you tell her?'

'The truth.' Tony gathered up the reins and swung himself into the saddle. 'Helen has to go back to Australia.'

Paul put his hand on the bridle to stop the horse as Tony urged it forward. 'What do you mean?'

'The telegram. I read it. It's from her brother, I presume, asking her to come home. Her father has had some sort of seizure.'

'You read her telegram?'

'Of course I did. I learned during the war never to just give telegrams to people. Far better to know what they contain. Tell Helen I will still meet her for lunch tomorrow.'

Paul thrust his hands into his pockets and watched Tony ride away before he returned to the house. Even as he opened the door to his sitting room, he knew that Tony had been right and the news had not been good.

Helen sat perched on the edge of the daybed, the telegram dangling from her hand, her face concealed by the curtain of her hair.

She looked up as he entered and he saw that she had been crying.

He walked across to her and she stood up, falling into his arms.

'Helen?' He stroked her hair.

'It's Dad. He's had a stroke. Mum and Henry think I should come home.'

Paul felt his heart sink.

'Then you must go where you're needed,' he said.

'This is all such a mess. I wanted to tell Tony properly. I owed him that.' She sniffed and looked up at him. Her eyes widened and she touched the rapidly bruising mark on his jawline. 'He hit you!'

Paul smiled ruefully. 'A well-aimed punch, worthy of the school boxing champ, which, I hasten to add, Tony wasn't!'

'Oh, Paul...' Helen sank back onto the day bed. 'I've made such a mess of it all.'

Paul sat down beside her and put his arm around her. 'This is not your fault, Helen. It is nobody's fault. Now I'm going to tell you exactly what you are going to do. Book a passage on the next ship to Australia and go home to Terrala with Alice, leaving this whole mess behind you.'

She shook her head. 'I can't leave you.'

'You might have to for a few months while I sort out matters with Evelyn and this bloody house. I love you and I'm not going to spend the rest of my life without you. Marry me, Helen Morrow?'

She turned a tear-streaked face up to look at him and he kissed her forehead.

'Yes,' she said. 'I can't imagine life without you.'

He bent his head and kissed her, a long slow lingering kiss.

As they drew apart, Helen sighed and her eyes brimmed with more tears. 'But I have to go home and it will be months before you can get out to Australia. I don't want to just leave you, Paul, not after everything we have been through.'

'Then marry me before you go home. I can get a special license in Birmingham tomorrow.'

She stared at him. 'Is that possible? What will people say?'

He laughed. 'Helen. What are people going to say anyway? You've jilted Tony Scarvell. It's not going to get much worse than that. The least I can do is make a respectable woman of you.'

She managed a smile and hit his arm. 'I was a thoroughly respectable woman before I came here.'

'The ways of the wicked upper class have corrupted you, I am afraid.'

She shook her head. 'No. I've done nothing I'm ashamed of. I love you, Paul, and yes, yes, I will marry you.'

He took her in his arms and held her to him as if he intended never to let her go again.

SIXTY-SEVEN

Tony held back her chair and Helen sat down, removing her gloves. She hoped this hadn't been a mistake but she knew she had to see Tony and explain her side of the story to him. Although how she could explain something that in so many ways defied explanation or excuse troubled her.

'Thank you for still agreeing to meet me,' she said. 'You didn't have to—I would have understood.'

Tony indicated for the waitress to take their order and as they waited for the tea and cakes, he said. 'I wanted to hear it from you, Helen.'

'I'm not a coward, Tony. I would have told you properly, if there is such a thing as 'properly'.'

Tony's mouth tightened but he said nothing as the waitress set down the tea and plates on the table. Helen poured the tea, conscious of her shaking hands.

'Have you told your mother?'

'Not yet. Helen, I know Mother hasn't been easy...'

'It's not just your mother, Tony. She was right. I don't belong in your world. I'd have made a terrible Viscountess.' She looked straight at him, forcing him to look into her eyes as she said, 'It was a dream, a lovely dream.' The hurt in his face, made her falter. 'Tony, you knew when you asked me that I didn't love you. That's not quite right. I do love you but not in the way I should—as a wife should. It would have been wrong for us to marry. Now I just want to go home.'

'I had hoped...'

'I know. I did too, but there's something between Paul and me that I can't explain in words.'

He looked away and cleared his throat. When he turned back, he had composed his face into a shadow of his normal countenance. 'When do you leave?'

'There's a P&O ship leaving from Southampton the day after tomorrow. I'm just hoping I make it home in time to see Dad.'

'And Paul?'

She set down her cup. 'I'm marrying Paul, tomorrow morning if he can get the license.'

All trace of good humour drained from Tony's face and he ran a hand through his hair. 'The old cats are going to have fun with us, aren't they?'

'I know. I'm truly sorry.'

He looked across at her, unable to hide his emotions any longer. 'I'm sorry too. I do love you, Helen.'

She stood up, pulling her gloves on to avoid looking into his eyes. 'You'll see I've done the right thing, Tony.'

He rose to his feet. 'I suppose this is goodbye then?'

She nodded and held out her hand. He took a step toward her and kissed her lightly on the cheek. 'Despite everything, Helen, I wish you and Sprite well. I'll send over the rest of your things when I get home.'

'You're a good man, Tony Scarvell ... Too good.'

He hefted a sigh. 'Now I've got to go and talk to Mother. She already knows the engagement is broken but I won't have you vilified by her and her friends.'

'Oh, they'll do it anyway as soon as they hear that I married Paul Morrow within days of breaking my engagement with you. Tell her the truth, Tony.'

As he held the door open for her, he gave a crooked smile. 'I hope Morrow has a good bruise?'

Helen smiled. 'He does.'

———

Helen took a taxi to the hospital where she had agreed to meet Paul. He waited on the front steps, coming down to open the door for her.

'How did it go?' he asked after he had kissed her.

'As well as can be expected. Did you get the license?'

He nodded and she squeezed his hand as they walked into the hospital and up the stairs.

Their footsteps slowed at the sound of woman's voice raised in anger.

'That's Lady Hartfield,' Helen glanced up at Paul.

'Trouble,' Paul said under his breath and quickened his pace.

Lady Hartfield stood outside the door to Evelyn's private room remonstrating with two doctors and a nurse.

'I tell you the police should be called. That's him,' she shrieked as she saw Paul. 'He should be arrested.'

The whole party turned to look at Paul.

'What is it I should be arrested for, Lady Hartfield?' Paul asked removing his hat.

'Attempted murder,' she declared.

'And who have I tried to murder?' he enquired in a low, even tone.

'Poor Evelyn.' Lady Hartfield's chest puffed up like a pigeon in indignation. 'I was just visiting her and she opened her eyes and said to me as clearly as anything. 'I was pushed. Tell Paul I know I was pushed.' Before I could ask her any more she was off again. I want the police called.' She reiterated her demand of the medical staff.

'I hardly think we need to bother the constabulary,' Paul said. 'Shall we ask my aunt what she meant?'

'She's unconscious,' said Lady Hartfield.

'Then we'll wait till she's awake.'

The older of the two doctors shook his head. 'She's heavily sedated. I suggest you all go home and hopefully, in the morning she will be in a better state to explain.'

'If you won't do anything then I'm going to the police,' Lady Hartfield cast Helen a malicious glance.

Paul took Helen's arm and drew her in toward him. 'Lady Hartfield, you may do as you wish. I can't stop you and I have nothing to hide.'

He turned, bringing Helen with him.

'You'll regret crossing me, Paul Morrow. You and that hussy,' Lady Hartfield said to their backs as they walked back down the corridor.

Helen felt her heart sink. 'This isn't about Evelyn, Paul. She's punishing both of us for jilting Tony.'

'I know,' Paul said. 'But we've nothing to be afraid of. Let's forget her and go home and tell Alice our plans and enjoy the special dinner Sarah has spent all day cooking.'

SIXTY-EIGHT

Alice sat on one of Paul's armchairs, her gaze moving from her mother to Paul and back again as they broke the news to her. 'Does this mean I don't have to live at Wellmore?' she asked.

'Yes, of course, it does,' Helen said.

A broad smile had crossed Alice's face. 'I'm glad. I hated it there and I'm glad you're marrying Mummy, Uncle Paul.' She frowned. 'What do I call you? Lady Hartfield said I should call Uncle Tony 'Papa' but that didn't seem quite right.'

'Uncle Paul will do just fine.'

'Will we live here?' Alice looked around the Paul's sitting room.

'No,' Helen said. 'You and I are going back to Melbourne tomorrow after the wedding, and Paul will join us in a few months.'

'You mean we're really going home?' Alice beamed. 'And you will come, Uncle Paul? I know you'll like Terrala and Uncle Henry and ... all the uncles. Oh, Mummy, I'm so happy.' She jumped off the chair and threw her arms firstly around Helen's neck and then Paul's.

He gathered the little girl into his arms and Helen felt that sense of rightness she had experienced when Paul carried the child back to the house after the incident in the tunnel. They were a family. They belonged together.

Helen started as she heard car doors slam and a knock on the main door. Paul disengaged Alice, rose to his feet, and crossed to the window.

'I don't believe it. The old harridan kept her word. It's the police,' he said.

'Oh, Paul.'

'I'll see to it.'

Alice, sensing the sudden tension, crossed to her mother. 'Why are the police here?' she asked in a tremulous voice.

'They just have some silly questions to ask us,' Helen said. 'You go and help Sarah in the kitchen.'

Alice obeyed and Helen looked up at Paul as they heard Sarah's footsteps on the stairs.

'Police want to talk to you,' she said. 'What's it about, sir?'

'Evelyn's fall,' Paul replied. 'You go back to the kitchen, Sarah, and keep an eye on Alice.'

'I've put 'em in the parlour. Dinner's just about ready.'

'It may have to wait. Helen?'

She took his arm and they descended the stairs to face the police together.

A uniformed sergeant and a man in plain clothes who gave his rank as Inspector stood in the middle of the parlour waiting for them.

After they had introduced themselves, Paul gestured at the chair. He took one of the armchairs while the Inspector remained standing.

'It is my guess that Lady Hartfield has come to you with some story about my aunt,' Paul said.

'Not me personally, sir. She went straight to the Chief Constable,' the Inspector looked apologetic.

'I would expect nothing less of her. What do you want to know?'

The Inspector opened his notebook.

'As I understand it your aunt has been in hospital for the last five days after she fell down some stairs. Lady Hartfield says that while she was sitting with Lady Morrow, said lady woke briefly from her coma. When asked by Lady Hartfield what had happened, Lady Morrow said and these are, according to Lady Hartfield, her exact words 'I was pushed. Tell Paul I know I was pushed.' The lady then relapsed into an unconscious state. Lady Hartfield alleges that yourself and Lady Morrow had recently been involved in an argument over the selling of this property?'

'That's no secret,' Paul said. 'I wouldn't call it an argument. My aunt believed it should not be sold, whereas the reality of our situation is that it must. Lately, I believe, she had come to accept that. Let's not waste any more time, if I understand you, Inspector, the allegation is that it was I who pushed my aunt down the stairs?'

The policeman nodded. 'The accident occurred sometime during the night. Did you hear your aunt cry out?'

'No. My rooms are at the opposite end of the house to hers. I didn't hear anything. It was our housekeeper, Sarah Pollard who discovered her in the morning.'

'I would like to speak to her.'

Paul looked at Helen, 'Do you mind fetching her, Helen?'

The inspector looked at Helen as if seeing her for the first time. 'Mrs. Morrow?'

'Yes.'

'Are you the same Mrs. Morrow, lately engaged to Lady Hartfield's son?'

Helen straightened her shoulders. 'Yes.'

'Where were you on the night of Lady Morrow's accident?'

'With Lady Hartfield at Wellmore as she can testify,' Helen replied brusquely, seeing all too clearly the direction of the interrogation. Between them, she and Paul probably appeared to have not only motivation but also opportunity for dealing with the inconvenient and disapproving Lady Morrow.

'And how would you describe your relationship with Lady Morrow?'

'She is my mother-in-law. We enjoy a cordial relationship,' Helen said.

'Does she know you now plan to marry Sir Paul Morrow?'

'Not yet but as soon as she recovers consciousness we will tell her,' Paul answered.

Helen took the opportunity afforded by the Inspector making notes in his book, to beat a retreat and fetch the Pollards.

Sarah's brow furrowed when Helen told her the reason for the police visit. 'That Lady Hartfield,' she said. 'I knew she'd try and cause trouble for you.'

'There was only one person in the house when Lady Morrow fell and that was Paul. I hardly think any court of law is going to believe it was a ghost that pushed her.'

Sarah glanced at Sam. 'We could say as how he'd had one of his turns. When he gets those migraines he can't even see straight, let alone get out of bed.'

'Don't lie,' Helen said. 'It won't do any good in the end.'

Sarah could only tell the police that she had taken Lady Morrow up a cup of cocoa at ten o'clock. At that time, Lady Morrow had been sitting at her dressing table brushing her hair.

'One hundred strokes every night,' Sarah confirmed. 'I said good night to her and went to the flat. Next morning I took her up her morning cup of tea at eight o'clock and her bed hadn't been slept in. It was only pure chance I looked down the library stairs and saw her feet. Poor lady had been there all night.'

'Where was Sir Paul?'

'He'd got up early and gone for a ride. I found him in the stables and he rang for the doctor.'

'It seems to me,' Paul said, 'that the one person you need to talk to is my aunt. Lady Hartfield's statement means nothing. If she's to be believed, my aunt didn't say "Paul pushed me down the stairs," she said, "Tell Paul, I was pushed." That means something completely different.'

'We'll do just that, Sir Paul. We'll leave it till tomorrow morning,' the inspector said. 'I'll meet you at the hospital at nine o'clock?'

'I'll be there. I hope it won't take long. I have a wedding at eleven.'

After the men had gone, Paul sank back into the chair and ran a hand through his hair.

Helen perched on the arm of the chair

'Penny for your thoughts?' Helen said.

'I don't think they're worth that,' he said.

'I should be thinking about our wedding. But all I can think of is Evelyn. What if she says it was you who pushed her, Paul?'

He smiled ruefully. 'Then I am in very deep trouble, Helen, and I better be able to find a damn good lawyer.' He held out his hand. 'Come here! Let's forget about our problems for a few hours. We don't have much time left.'

He pulled her down onto his lap and kissed her.

Sixty-Nine

They sat in silence on the drive to the hospital the next morning, their fingers interlocked on the hard leather seat. In the front of the monstrous old car, Alice sat sandwiched between Sarah and Pollard, chattering about going home to Terrala and all the things she would tell her uncles.

Helen wore a simple grey, woollen suit with a black velvet collar and a matching black velvet hat trimmed with a long grey feather that draped over her shoulder. She looked wonderful, Paul thought, but not as wonderful as she had looked naked in his bed as they lay together in the small hours of the morning.

He pushed that particular recollection to one side and caught her looking at him. She gave him a small self-conscious smile that indicated her thoughts had been travelling in the same direction.

The inspector and his sergeant waited on the front steps of the hospital, stamping their feet in the crisp, early autumn air. They entered the hospital together and were greeted by a well-dressed woman who rose from a chair in the foyer.

'What are you doing here, Lady Hartfield?' Paul asked in a tone that dripped ice.

His men would have understood and ducked for cover. Lady Hartfield just stuck out her chin and said, 'I came to see if it was true. As for you...' She turned to Helen. 'I told Evelyn you were nothing more than a colonial gold digger...I warned her...'

Helen tucked her hand into Paul's arm. He felt her fingers dig in as she controlled her anger.

'Lady Hartfield,' she said, 'you may believe what you want, but if I were truly what you accuse me of, why would I throw over the chance to become the next Lady Hartfield for a penniless archaeologist?'

Lady Hartfield's lips tightened as she drew herself to her full height, her nostrils flaring with indignation.

The inspector cleared his throat. 'Shall we get on?'

As they headed for the stairs, Lady Hartfield made a move to join them.

Paul turned to her. 'Not you. This is no concern of yours. Go home, Lady Hartfield. You have caused enough trouble.'

He looked down at Helen who tightened her grip on his arm. She gave him a small, nervous smile as the Viscountess huffed, turned on her heel and strode out of the hospital in a flurry of foxtail.

Despite the protests from the ward sister, the party filed into Evelyn's room. Paul disengaged Helen's hand and crossed to his aunt. He picked up her hand, feeling the fragility of the fine bones beneath the papery skin. Her eyes flickered opened and fixed on his face.

'Paul,' she said, in a faint voice. 'How nice to see you, dear.'

Paul cast a sideways glance at the policemen. Evelyn's greeting was hardly what they would expect from someone about to accuse her nephew of attempted murder.

'Evelyn, these gentlemen want to ask you some questions about your accident,' Paul said.

For the first time, Evelyn's eyes moved around the room, settling on the Inspector who moved to the other side of the bed.

Before he could speak, Evelyn said in a clear voice. 'I was pushed,' she said firmly. 'I felt a hand on my back. I am certain of it.'

The Inspector looked taken aback by this confirmation of Lady Hartfield's allegation. 'Can you tell me who pushed you?'

Evelyn looked up at Paul. Her eyes held his, questioning, searching for answers he could not give her.

'It was a woman,' she said, turning back to the Inspector.

'A woman? Are you certain?'

'Absolutely certain. I heard her laugh.'

The inspector looked across at Paul and Paul looked down at his aunt. 'The Inspector thinks it was me who pushed you, Evelyn.'

'You? Don't be ridiculous, Paul. Of course, it wasn't you. It was a woman. Why would you want to push me down the stairs?'

The policeman's eyes turned to Helen. Paul straightened and fixed the policeman with a cold stare.

'Don't even think it,' Paul said. 'As we told you last night, Helen's whereabouts can be verified by no less a person than my accuser, Lady Hartfield.'

'What's Maude said?' Evelyn interrupted. 'She can be such a silly woman sometimes. It certainly wasn't Helen.'

Paul bent and kissed his aunt's forehead. 'Evelyn, we will just see these gentlemen out and will come straight back in.'

'Really.' The ward sister who had appeared at the door bristled. 'It's not even visiting hours.'

Paul took the woman by the arm and steered her out into the corridor. 'Thank you, sister. I appreciate your rules but we are getting married this morning and I don't have time for petty regulations. Inspector?' He turned to the two policemen. 'I trust you are satisfied.'

'Up to a point,' the man said. 'It still begs the question as to who pushed her.'

'An intruder?' the Sergeant suggested.

'I suggest that is what you put in your report,' Paul said. 'Good morning, gentlemen.'

He waited until they stomped off down the corridor, and opened the door readmitting then both into Evelyn's room.

Evelyn turned worried eyes on him. 'Did I do the right thing?'

'You gave him the perfect answer, Evelyn.'

'But who did push me? I know I was pushed.'

Paul hesitated. 'I believe you. As we told the police, it must have been an intruder. We were fortunate that you were not killed. Evelyn, I can't stay. I have a wedding to go to.'

'Whose?'

'Mine,' he said, glancing up at Helen. 'Helen and I are getting married this morning.'

Evelyn's brow furrowed in confusion. 'Helen?'

Helen crossed to the other side of the bed and Evelyn looked at her. 'You're marrying Tony.'

Helen shook her head. 'No. That would have been a terrible mistake.'

Evelyn frowned, studying her face. 'I think I was wrong about you. I can't remember what I said but it upset you.'

'It's forgiven, Evelyn,' Helen said.

'I'm sure you and Charlie loved each other.'

'We did.'

'And do you love, Paul?'

Helen looked up and Paul felt the breath leave him for a moment as he read the love in her eyes.

'I do,' she said. 'Very much.'

'Then you are fortunate to have the chance to love two men in your life, Helen,' Evelyn said. 'For me there was only Gerald.' Her faded blue eyes filled with tears and she made a feeble gesture with her hand. 'Go away, both of you. I'm tired. Make each other happy.'

'Evelyn,' Helen said, the tone of her voice had become urgent. 'This is goodbye. I am leaving for Australia tonight. My father is ill and I must get home—if I'm not already too late.'

Evelyn's lip trembled. 'But Alice? Will I see Alice again?'

'She's outside with Sarah. I'll bring her up,' Helen said.

SEVENTY

Helen leaned back against the cool leather of the car seat.

'It's over,' she said.

Paul slid his right arm around her shoulder drawing her in to him.

'It feels as if life is just beginning,' he said.

As they neared Holdston Paul leaned forward pulling down the window.

'Good lord,' he said. 'I can't believe what I'm seeing!'

As the car drew up outside the church, a mighty cheer went up. Every villager and tenant from the estate thronged the churchyard. Tears filled Helen's eyes as she looked from face to face. Her hand reached for Paul's and she saw the emotion in his face that words couldn't express. The still, silent man she had first met had vanished and she saw light and life in his face.

Sam, grinning like a Cheshire cat, held the car door open for them as Paul alighted first, holding out his hand for Helen. Lily ran forward with a posy made up of bright summer flowers. She had two smaller ones for herself and Alice.

'You knew about this.' Helen turned on the smiling Sarah Pollard.

'And did you think we'd let an occasion like this go by without properly marking it?' Sarah said. 'It'll be the last Morrow wedding in this Church so we needed to make it one to remember.'

Helen tucked her arm into Paul's and they walked slowly through the gathered crowd acknowledging the good wishes and smiles. As they neared the porch, a figure stepped out of the shadows.

Helen felt Paul stiffen and they both said in unison, 'Tony!'

Tony Scarvell smiled. 'Just in case you change your mind, Helen ... No? I thought not. In which case, I am at your service—best man or shall I give the bride away?'

'I would like you by my side,' Paul said.

'Besides,' Helen said with a smile. 'Alice is walking me down the aisle.'

Tony looked down at the child. 'Are you, Sprite? Well, I think that is quite right too. I'm yours, Morrow. Do you have the ring? I think the vicar is waiting for us. Ladies and gentlemen,' he addressed the throng. 'I think it is time to take your seats.'

Inside, the church had been filled with flowers and greenery and candles burned in every sconce, illuminating the faces of the congregation. Helen, holding Alice's hand and clutching her little bouquet tightly, looked down into her daughter's face. Alice smiled and squeezed Helen's hand.

'She'll be right, Mummy,' she said, lapsing into her uncles' Australian idiom.

Helen laughed and bent and kissed her daughter.

She cast a quick glance at the brass war memorial and her lips moved in silent prayer for her beloved Charlie but it was not Charlie who stood at the altar or turned to watch her as she walked down the aisle of the old church. Paul Morrow, tall and straight, a lock of his dark hair falling across his forehead, waited for her, his gaze never leaving her face as she came to stand beside him.

She handed the little posy to Alice and slipped her gloved hand into his. His fingers tightened around hers and his shoulders straightened as he drew himself up. The familiar words of the wedding service blurred and the Reverend Bryant declared them man and wife. As Paul bent to kiss her, a cheer went up from the congregation. Paul hesitated, smiling down at his new wife.

They had been through so much and now they faced long, uncertain months of separation, but they had this moment in time and a future which would be theirs to build together. They had something that they had both thought lost to them forever, hope and a promise of happiness.

'I love you, Paul Morrow,' she whispered as his arms circled her, drawing her into an embrace.

'And I you, Lady Morrow,' he replied before his lips met hers in a kiss that defied the normal propriety of a wedding service.

EPILOGUE

Paul jumped down from the truck at the gate to Terrala. A warm, northerly wind rustled the dry grasses and caught at the back of his throat. When he had left Melbourne that morning, it had been cold and raining but it didn't look like it had rained in this part of the country for months. He looked up at the blue tinged mountains hemming the valley in and took a deep breath of the warm air, the soft scent of grass and eucalyptus made him smile. He could not have been further from England and, in a way, it felt like he was coming home.

He threw his jacket over his shoulder, hefted his suitcase and walked up the dusty, rutted track that led to the solid red brick house, surrounded by a wide verandah. As he neared the house, he set his suitcase down and turned to look back at the road. From its position on a small hillock, the house commanded a view up and down the valley. The track turned into what had once been a neat, gravelled driveway lined with large conifers, leading up to the front of the house. It circled around a dry fountain sitting forlornly in a circle of brown grass and cracked earth.

'Who are you?'

The child's voice came from above him and Paul looked up into the dark shadows of the nearest conifer, where a small, rather dirty face peered down at him.

'Who are you?' Paul retorted.

'I'm James,' the child announced. 'Wait there.' The boy's face disappeared, and cracking twigs marked the child's descent.

A boy of about six emerged at ground level from the conifer hedge. He looked up at Paul, his head cocked to one side.

'I know who you are.'

'Do you?'

'You're the man in the picture.'

'What picture?'

'The one in Auntie Helen's room.'

'Is your Auntie Helen here?' Paul asked.

Before James could answer a woman called out. 'Get inside, Jamie and make sure you wash those hands! Can I help you?'

Paul turned to the house. A grey-haired woman stood at the top of the steps to the verandah, wiping her hands on an apron. Paul smiled. He could see where Helen got her beauty. Age could not take away the perfect oval face, the fine high cheek bones and wide, grey eyes of her mother – his mother in law, he reminded himself.

'Mrs. Mitchell?'

'Yes?' She eyed him suspiciously.

He removed his hat. 'I'm Paul Morrow.'

She gasped, her hand going to her throat. 'Good heavens, of course you are,' she said. 'I should have recognised you from the picture.'

Paul wondered what picture she and her grandson could be talking about. There had been no photographer at their hurried wedding and to the best of his knowledge, Helen had no recent photograph of him. In fact he couldn't recall the last time anyone had taken his likeness.

Helen's mother hurried down the stone steps and Paul held out his hand but no formal handshake for Kate Mitchell. She threw her arms around him and hugged him.

'Welcome to Terrala, Paul,' she said as she released him. 'I'm afraid Helen's not here. Henry sent her down to Mulligan's Flat. They're bringing the cattle down for the winter. Come inside and join us for some lunch.'

Piles of dried leaves heaped around the front door and a spider's web across the glass panel indicated that the door was rarely used. Kate led him around the side of the house where another door stood open admitting him to the kitchen. Inside a pregnant woman was laying the scrubbed kitchen table for lunch and the room smelled of baked bread and cakes that sat cooling by the window.

The other woman looked up as Kate ushered Paul inside, her eyes widening in recognition.

'It can't be,' she said, but got no further.

'He's here at last,' Kate said tucking her hand into the crook of Paul's elbow. 'Paul, this is Henry's wife, Violet, our Jamie's mum.'

Paul found himself again encompassed in another warm hug, Violet released him and gave him a scrutinising look. 'You look just like the picture,' she said.

'What picture are you all talking about?' Paul asked.

'You show him, Jamie,' Violet said to her son who had trailed them into the kitchen, 'and then scrub those hands for lunch.'

James marched through the kitchen and into a wide, dark, wood panelled hallway. He stopped outside a door and threw it open, revealing a small, pleasant bedroom. Paul recognised the silver backed hair brush and mirror on the dressing table as Helen's. The photographs of Charlie that had been the feature of her room at Holdston were not in evidence. Only a single photograph of Alice graced her bedside table.

'There!' James pointed.

Paul took a breath. On the wall behind the door, hung the second painting in Angela's triptych. He stared at it for a long moment. If this one was here where were the other two? And how had Helen come by it?

'You're very dirty,' James observed, scrutinising the picture with a furrowed brow.

'It was very wet and muddy,' Paul said.

'Lunch!' Kate Mitchell called from the kitchen and Jamie bolted for the door.

'Hands, Jamie,' Violet stood in the kitchen door barring entry to her son.

A man stood at the kitchen trough washing his hands. He looked around as Paul entered the room and Paul saw the resemblance to Helen and this man's mother in the wide smile that greeted him.

He held out his hand. 'Paul Morrow.'

The other man, wiped his hands dry and took Paul's hand in a firm grip, his clear gaze, so like his sister's scanning Paul's face with interest.

'Henry,' he said. 'Nell's brother. I can't tell you how pleased we are to see you at last. We were beginning to think you were a figment of Nell's imagination.' He glanced out the window. 'You should have sent word you were coming up today. I've sent Nell down to the Flat to set up for the muster. We graze the cattle up in the High Country over summer and bring them down before winter, all fat and ready for the market. Tell you what, have some lunch and then we'll ride down to the Flat. I want to see the mob they're bringing in.'

'I'm not exactly dressed for riding,' Paul looked down at his linen suit. 'And most of my luggage is still at the railway station.'

'We'll find something to fit you,' Kate put in. 'You're about my late husband's height and build. Now, sit down, Paul, and tuck in.'

Henry dipped a chunk of bread into his stew and chewed on it as he studied Paul. 'That's a good painting of you,' he said.

Paul felt the heat rise to his cheeks. 'A friend painted it,' he muttered.

'Yeah, Nell said. Mum thought Nell should put the first one up, but she said she liked the second one better. Said it was more like how she knew you.'

Paul laughed, 'I assure you I never looked like that when I first met your sister.'

'Or like the third painting,' Kate remarked casually passing him the bread.

Paul's heart sank. Helen had the whole triptych.

'I reckon they're bloody good,' Henry said.

'Henry, don't swear in front of James!' his wife chided.

'Well they are,' Henry said defensively. 'Shows it like it really was. I was there.'

The two men exchanged a glance that said more in the silence than a thousand words.

'Your friend knew what was what,' Henry added.

'She did,' Paul said.

Everyone's gaze turned to him.

'She?' Kate said.

'Angela Lambton. She drove a VAD ambulance on the Western front.'

'A woman artist!' Violet said. 'Who'd have thought.'

'She never used her real name to show her war paintings,' Paul said, 'but there are some hanging in the National Gallery in London.'

Henry glanced at Violet and she nodded in answer to his unspoken question.

'Vi was a nurse. We both reckon those paintings say it all,' he said

'Mummy saved Daddy's life,' James put in.

His fond parents looked at him and Henry rumpled his son's hair.

'I was wounded at Gallipoli... Lone Pine.' He paused and took a breath. 'They evacuated us from Gallipoli to Lemnos and that's where Vi was nursing, my bad-tempered Florence Nightingale.' He reached across the table and his hand circled his wife's.

'I was only bad tempered because of the flies and the lack of water,' Violet said.

Henry's fork clattered on his plate and he pushed the empty plate away. 'I was sorry about Charlie. He was a good mate. We had plans ...' He shrugged. 'We had plans for after the war.'

'I'd be pleased to hear those plans,' Paul said. 'I'm not going back to England. I've married an Australian and Australia will be our home.'

Kate smiled. 'I'm pleased to hear that, Paul.'

Henry nodded. 'That land Charlie was interested in down in the King Valley is still for sale. Half the price now.' He pushed his chair back. 'Let's get moving. I want to be back before dark. You can ride?'

———

Helen's horse picked its way carefully through the cool water of the Howqua River. At this time of the year, the water level ran low, but it still provided a welcome relief from the warmth of the autumn day. Alice followed behind her on her reliable, stock pony.

Mulligan's Hut, a stockman's hut built of solid slabs of river gum, stood about fifty yards from the river, the empty stockyards behind it, one of the many flat areas on the banks of the river used by the locals as a base when they brought the cattle down from the High Country in autumn or before sending them up in early summer.

Helen dismounted, unloaded the supplies into the hut, unsaddled her horse and let it into the horse yard. She inspected the wood pile, split some of the massive logs and lit a fire in the hut, putting the billy on to boil while she began chopping the vegetables for the men's stew. Alice had wandered down to the river where she was soon lost in a world of her own imagination.

With the fragrant stew, cooking slowly in a camp oven, Helen took her pannikin of tea and sat down in the shadow of the verandah to wait for the drovers.

She heard them long before she saw them. The hallooing of the men, the thunder of hooves, lowing of cattle and the barking of dogs presaged the arrival of the muster. Helen set down her empty mug and called Alice up from the river.

They stood in the shadow of the hut as the cattle came along the river bank at a brisk pace. The young cattle, anxious from the long drive, the whites of their eyes rolling in fear at the strange creatures that harried them at every corner, ran at a breakneck speed. The men and dogs expertly turned their frightened charges towards the stock yards. A couple of young heifers broke away but the bulk of the cattle were inside, brought up short by the solid posts and rails while the men chivvied the breakaways inside among their fellows. Helen and Alice shot the rails home as the exhausted cattle, their heads drooping, cast her reproachful, frightened glances.

Helen wiped her hands on her trousers and walked over to the foreman.

Pat slid off his horse and patted her on the shoulder. 'Good job, Helen. That's the last of 'em. The boss should get a good price for this lot. Speaking of the boss, here he comes.'

Helen shaded her eyes and squinted up the track that led up to the house. Henry's familiar bay gelding picked its way down the stony road. Beside him, her father's chestnut stallion ridden with a sure and a familiar hand. Paul.

Paul had come home to her.

She gave a shriek as her husband put his heels to the horse, urging it into a canter.

He was off the animal, sweeping her into his arms almost before she drew breath.

'You found me,' she said at last. 'You found me,' she repeated her words muffled by his shirt, hardly daring to believe that he was real. Here - so very, very far from Holdston Hall.

She drew back and gave him a mock thump on the arm. 'Took your time about it!'

Paul laughed and put his arm across her shoulder. They walked along the river, away from the amused stares of the men.

'It took a hell of a long time to sort out Holdston,' he said when they were out of earshot. 'It's leased to some fat industrialist from Birmingham who fancies himself as Lord of the Manor. I gave the tenants the option to purchase their properties. Most of them took it up.'

'What about Evelyn?'

'She's comfortable enough in the Gatehouse. Sam and Sarah have a good apartment there as well.'

He placed his hands on her shoulders, turning her to face him. She melted against him, cupping his face in her hands.

'I can't believe you're real. Tell me you are not one of the Holdston ghosts.'

'I'm real, Helen and I'm here to stay. I never want to see England again. Tell me you still want me. Tell me nothing has changed.'

She looked up into his face, scanning every familiar feature. Freed of the burdens that Charlie's death had imposed on him, with the rest of his life ahead of him, he looked younger, the deep lines engraved by those long years of war, softening and blurring. Paul Morrow had come to life and she knew she would never let him go again.

'Nothing has changed,' she whispered, and they kissed, oblivious to the rousing cheer and cat calls from the cattlemen.

ACKNOWLEDGMENTS

I would like to thank my husband, DJB, for his unswerving love and support (and for taking me to visit the battlefields of World War One), my mother in law, PJB, for her eagle eye and my writing group, the Saturday Ladies Bridge Club, for their encouragement.

About the Author

Alison Stuart writes historical romances and short stories set in England and Australia and across different periods of history. She is best known for her English Civil War stories and also THE POSTMISTRESS, THE GOLDMINER'S SISTER and THE HOMECOMING - stories set in the Victorian goldfields in the 1870s.

She also writes historical mysteries as A.M. Stuart and her popular Harriet Gordon mystery series is set in Singapore in 1910.

She lives in Melbourne, Australia with her husband and a geriatric cat. In a past life Alison worked as a lawyer across a variety of disciplines including the military and emergency services. She has lived in Africa and Singapore and, when circumstances permit, travels extensively - all for research of course!

To discover more about Alison Stuart visit her website or follow her on any of the social media accounts below.

BOOKS by Alison Stuart

Australian Historical Romance

THE POSTMISTRESS (also in audio)

THE GOLDMINER'S SISTER (also in audio)

THE HOMECOMING (also in audio)

The Guardians of the Crown Series

BY THE SWORD

THE KING'S MAN

EXILE'S RETURN

GUARDIANS OF THE CROWN (BOX SET)

The Feathers in the Wind Collection

AND THEN MINE ENEMY

HER REBEL HEART

SECRETS IN TIME (also in audio)

FEATHERS IN THE WIND (BOX SET)

Regency/World War One

GATHER THE BONES (also in audio)

LORD SOMERTON'S HEIR

A CHRISTMAS LOVE REDEEMED (Novella)

(Writing as A.M. Stuart)

The Harriet Gordon Mysteries

SINGAPORE SAPPHIRE (Book 1)

REVENGE IN RUBIES (Book 2)

EVIL IN EMERALD (Book 3)

TERROR IN TOPAZ (Book 4)

Printed in the USA
CPSIA information can be obtained
at www.ICGtesting.com
CBHW020521220124
3647CB00007B/514